INESCAPABLE DESIRE

"Why did you run away?" Joshua asked, his dark eyes gleaming.

"I didn't," she insisted.

"You can't fool me, Maddie. What were you afraid of?"

"The storm," she answered, unable to meet his gaze.

"Ah, Maddie, I think not."

"Then . . . what?" The moment the breathless words were out of her mouth, Madeline knew they were a mistake.

"This."

She felt the word more than heard it as his mouth brushed hers. With a slow, sensual rhythm, his lips gathered raindrops from the corner of her mouth— tasting, testing. Rainwater had never been sweeter. He wanted more.

She returned his kiss, hesitantly at first, then with an ardor that made him moan. The sound rumbled up from his broad chest. She could hear it, this noise more eloquent than words; could feel it vibrating through her body. Madeline molded closer to him, unwilling to miss even his tiniest tremor . . . eager to experience every glorious sensation. . . .

THE CAPTAIN'S CONQUEST

CHRISTINE ELLIOTT

ZEBRA BOOKS
KENSINGTON PUBLISHING CORP.

ZEBRA BOOKS

are published by

Kensington Publishing Corp.
475 Park Avenue South
New York, NY 10016

First printing: April, 1989

Printed in the United States of America

To Judith French and her daughter Colleen Culver for making it possible.

To Chip, Ben, Chris, Elizabeth, Steve, Rachel, Stephen and Andrew with love and gratitude.

The author wishes to express appreciation to the Virginia Romance Writer's Chesterfield Critique Group. Thank you for your unselfish assistance.

For who are so free as the sons of the waves?
                    —David Garrick, "Heart of Oak"

Chapter 1

March 1759

"Fire!"

Captain Joshua Whitlock's battle cry erupted from his massive body more as a raspy croak, but its intensity pierced the heavy layer of acrid smoke enveloping the *Chesapeake*'s sand-strewn decks. With a dogged efficiency belied by their sweaty, grease-stained appearance, the gunners ignited the two four-pound cannons on the larboard side, hurling a second deadly salvo across an expanse of gray Atlantic. The thunderous roar of guns gave way to echoes of heavy oak splintering as the foremast of the French warship *Dolphin* crashed to her deck. A wild, undisciplined cheer rang through the privateers, and the *Chesapeake*, cleanly tacking to starboard, swept out of range of the French guns.

Captain Whitlock, standing tall and erect on the quarterdeck, lifted a heavily muscled arm, silencing his men. "She's not ours yet, lads," he yelled. "Shall we make another try?"

Again the crew voiced their enthusiasm for harassing the French warship.

"Well then, men, prepare for another run by!"

The strong westerly wind sang in her canvas as the Bermuda sloop veered to larboard, smoothly maneuvering into the turn that would take her back toward the huge enemy vessel still riding the broad swells.

"She'll be expectin' us this time, Cap'n," Oliver Chappel prophesied, rubbing the only hair on his head, a shaggy, grizzled beard, as he moved beside the younger man.

"That she will, Oliver, that she will," Joshua Whitlock replied, giving his first mate a friendly slap on the back. He then wiped his once-white linen sleeve across his damp visage. His was a strong, handsome face, with slashing-straight brows of the same raven hue as his hair, a narrow, finely chiseled nose, and a wide sensual mouth that seemed to hold its present serious bent with some difficulty. Grime and sweat served only to emphasize the sun-darkened glow of his skin, and to accent the tiny lines radiating from eyes as black as the midnight sky, as bottomless as the sea.

Joshua took a deep breath of the salt air. Relieved that most of the noxious fumes of saltpeter and brimstone had dissipated, he relaxed and his mouth extended in a broad grin. "We have the advantage of the wind, though, and she's still not under full sail." There was a hint of contempt in his voice. Not that he wasn't pleased with the lack of quickness in the response of the French. From the moment the *Chesapeake* and the *Dolphin* had emerged, almost simultaneously, from the heavy blanket of fog off Long Island Sound, each noticing the other with shock, he had counted on complacency in the French. Of course the *Dolphin,* seemingly invincible, would never have expected an attack by an arrogant, outgunned sloop. But that was just what she had gotten.

Hardly allowing his surprise time to register, Joshua had ordered all practical sails hoisted and extra shot and bags of powder positioned by the cannon. It wasn't often he could pit the *Chesapeake,* and himself, against anything other than pigeon-plump merchantmen bound for Quebec, so he silently thanked whatever fates had drawn this prize across his bow. Somewhere beyond the

8

murky veil of fog, the rest of the French convoy floundered blindly, just as the *Chesapeake* had done for the past day and night, till that moment, not thirty minutes past, when the strong westerly wind had rolled back the blinding mist just enough to reveal some of its secrets.

"Ya think we can ram another volley into that French bitch?" Oliver asked, motioning toward the square rigger.

"We're sure as hell going to try!" Joshua answered, not surprised by Oliver's enthusiasm. Joshua had grown up disliking the French, due to the hostility they had frequently shown the colonies. And for the past three years, since the declaration of war between France and England, he had done his best to harass French shipping, partly out of a sense of patriotism, partly because doing so made him rich, and just a little—well, maybe more than a little—because he enjoyed it.

But to Oliver Chappel, France was more than the country which claimed all the territory drained by the Ohio River. It had been Frenchmen, allies of the Algonquins, who had encouraged the Indians to raid the frontier homes of English settlers. Settlers like Jeremiah and Elizabeth Chappel. It had been near half a century since a frightened five-year-old boy had hidden in the bushes and listened to the agonized screams of his family, but Joshua knew those screams still lingered in Oliver's head.

"Check all for readiness. We are going to have to make this count," Joshua commanded, casting a calculating glance at the French vessel before following the wiry first mate to the main deck.

"God's blood, Cap'n," Oliver exclaimed as the younger man descended behind him, "I never thought we'd be goin' up against a damn man-of-war. Excitin', ain't it?"

Joshua grinned. "Aye, it's exciting, but let's just hope and pray that she doesn't blow us out of the sea."

9

Oliver gave him a look, clearly showing how unlikely he thought that possibility. Then he strode over to where those of the crew not busy with other chores stood checking their muskets.

His mate's eagerness notwithstanding, Joshua was, indeed, cognizant of the risks involved. The first run at the unprepared ship had been daring; he hoped this second and final sweep was not foolhardy. If he were a cautious man, he would steer clear of the *Dolphin* and hightail it for New York harbor. After all, the *Chesapeake*'s hold was full to bursting with French cargo they'd seized. But no one had ever accused him of prudence—or of timidity.

The thunderous guns of the *Dolphin* split the silence of the early spring afternoon, the *Chesapeake* racing toward her. Firepower, ominous and deadly, the French craft had; maneuverability was what she lacked.

"Fire!" Joshua's command rang out. The sudden lurch caused by recoil was felt by all aboard as the *Chesapeake* unloaded a sally prior to dancing away on the waves.

Before the smoke had cleared enough to ascertain the damage inflicted on the *Dolphin*, the lookout's excited yell made Joshua look to the west, where the turgid bank of mist formed an eerie backdrop for five French men-of-war.

Let's get the hell out of here, he thought. Not even he liked these odds.

"We're headin' straight for 'em!" Oliver wailed as Joshua grabbed the helm, setting the *Chesapeake*'s sharp lines on a course due west.

"They've yet to surmise what we're about." The calmness of Joshua's statement masked the wild beating of his heart. But a quick perusal of the hulking ships revealed the leisurely manner with which their tars worked the ropes.

Still, Oliver's voice was shrill with anxiety at his captain's madness. "Their guns!"

"Will be useless against us," Joshua finished. "We'll

10

slip between the ships, and they won't dare fire for fear of blowing each other from the water. Then all we need do is hide in the fog."

"And what if we run into more of the convoy in the mist?" Oliver asked. For all his pessimism, relief was now evident on his face.

"I didn't say it was foolproof." Joshua laughed as he concentrated on steering the sloop through the narrow channel between two of the ships.

The plan proved to be foolproof indeed, and this time when the crew cheered its success, the *Chesapeake*'s captain deemed it unnecessary to quell their enthusiasm. Indeed, his deep baritone could be heard above his men's voices.

Within the week, the *Chesapeake* was unloading ornate porcelain, gold-embroidered cloth, and French lace onto the wagons and carts of New York's merchants, while Joshua delivered his letters of marque to Lieutenant Governor DeLancey.

Once he'd been assured that all was in order, he succumbed to the lure of the common room of the waterfront inn where he was staying while in port. Some of his men were already in the cramped, smoke-filled room, their raucous laughter testimony to the copious amounts of rum they had consumed.

"Guvnor happy with our haul?" Oliver called across the room before leaving his seat by the brightly blazing hearth to join his captain.

With an exaggerated flourish, Joshua straightened the lace spilling from the sleeve of his blue, lozenge silk waistcoat. "Have you ever known Lieutenant Governor DeLancey to be anything but pleased with a hefty profit?"

Oliver laughed deep in his throat. "Ya sure got it right

11

there, Cap'n." He pointed toward the narrow wooden stairs leading toward the second floor. "Your sea chest is in your room, 'long with a hot bath. Oh, and there was a packet o' letters for ya. I stashed 'em in the table by your bed."

"Thanks, Oliver. Hear anything about the war?" Joshua inclined his head toward the few occupants of the room not in his employ.

"Nah," Oliver growled. "Thought ya might have heard somethin' from DeLancey."

"He's still singing the praises of William Pitt for sending British troops to New York," Joshua explained as he headed for the stairs. It had been a long time since he had enjoyed a hot bath in fresh water. "But apparently there hasn't been much action since Bradstreet captured Fort Frontenac last summer."

"Hey, Cap'n!" the voice belonged to Jamieson, the tall, blond boatswain. "Hope ya don't mind. We started celebratin' without ya!"

Joshua's hearty laugh rang out as Jamieson raised his tankard in mock salute and then pulled a passing barmaid onto his lap. "Now, Jamieson, I'd have been right disappointed in you if you hadn't."

"And when do you plan on getting started, Captain?" The voice was as sensual as the amber eyes that glided seductively over his virile, broad-shouldered frame.

"Molly, girl." Joshua's eyes twinkled as he recalled long nights spent exploring the lush body she so provocatively displayed.

"One and the same, Captain," the dark-haired beauty purred. "Did you miss me on all those long, lonely nights at sea?" As if to influence his answer, she sidled nearer and pressed full, ripe breasts against his hard-muscled chest.

With one efficient motion Joshua pulled the sultry woman hard against him and, amid the towdy cheers of his crew, gave her a hearty kiss. "Give me just a minute, Molly pet, and I'll be only too happy to show you how much I missed you," he countered, letting one large hand slide intimately down to her rump, and giving her an affectionate pat before bounding up the stairs to his room.

But it was nearly an hour later when Oliver pounded on his door. "Ya all right, Cap'n? Wouldn't do for ya to drown in that little bitty tub o' water, ya bein' the terror o' the seas an' all." Oliver chuckled at his own joke, but when no answer was forthcoming, he opened the door, filling the tiny room with the bawdy clamor of the crew below.

"Cap'n?"

"What?" Abruptly drawn from his musings, Joshua tensed, and as his head swung around, years of living by his instincts sent his hand to the sword resting peacefully on a nearby table. "Oh, it's you, Oliver." Joshua slumped back into the chair he had occupied moments earlier.

"Everyone's waitin' for ya. Is somethin' wrong?" Oliver scanned the room, taking in the captain's disheveled appearance, his discarded waistcoat and rumpled hair, before fixing on the open packet of letters beside the sword. "Bad news, Cap'n?"

Joshua raised eyes that seemed bright despite the gathering dusk. "They're from Nat," he said, gesturing toward the letters and ignoring Oliver's reference to bad news.

"Nat, huh?" Oliver picked the satin waistcoat off the floor and folded it across his arm. "And how is young Nathaniel? Still playin' the peacemaker?"

"I suppose you could say that." Joshua straightened into a more conventional sitting position. "He wants me to come home."

"How long's it been, Cap'n?"

Taking a deep breath, Joshua reached over to pick up the letters. He smoothed their edges and systematically refolded the parchments before answering. "Nearly four years now—three years when the first of these letters was written."

13

"We was out to sea a long time, Cap'n," the first mate offered by way of explanation.

"Aye, a long time," Joshua parroted, but it was not of the sea voyage he spoke. "Nathaniel says they're having problems."

"What kinda problems?"

Joshua rose to light the candles by the bed, suddenly aware of the deep shadows penetrating the room. "Lost cargo mostly, but Nat says they lost one of their ships, too."

"Those damn French!" Oliver spat out the words.

Shaking his head, Joshua slumped back into the chair. "Nat doesn't think so. He says they stay well clear of any French holdings. He's inclined to think it's the work of pirates. Even thinks it might be the same group every time."

"What da ya think?" Oliver threw the words over his shoulder as he knelt to light the wood already laid in the fireplace.

"Seems unlikely to me. I can't imagine that many unlucky coincidences."

"Aye. Hey, Cap'n," Oliver straightened and turned, placing his fists on his hips, "ya ain't thinkin' like any o' this is your fault, is ya? 'Cause ya know, ya didn't exactly walk out on that pa o' yours."

A weak imitation of his usual grin flickered across Joshua's face. "If you're trying subtly to remind me of the night my father ordered me from his house, you needn't worry. I haven't forgotten." Of course, it had been much more complicated than his words indicated. To Joshua, that winter night four years ago had seen the culmination of a long, emotionally taxing war—a war that had been raging for as long as he could remember. It had been based on differences in ideas and beliefs and actions, but the undercurrent, the common thread of all the disagreements, had been the clash of two strong, divergent personalities.

"Good. Well, see that ya don't," Oliver's words

brought him back to the present. "What's he want? Money? Your pa hear tell o' your exploits and wish he'd backed ya 'stead o' tryin' to wrastle that sloop from ya?"

"Nay, these letters aren't from Father, and you know Nat wouldn't ask for anything. Hell, Father wouldn't either, for that matter!"

Oliver grunted in agreement as Joshua slowly unfolded himself from the chair and walked to the window. "He's dying." Joshua rested his forehead against the pane, and his breath made lacy patterns of moisture on the cold glass.

"Your pa?" Oliver's tone was incredulous.

"Yes. That's why Nat wants me home—to make my peace with him." Joshua straightened, turning his back on the gathering twilight outside. "I know I promised the men some time, but . . ."

"I reckon they'd be just as happy in Baltimore as here. That is where we're headin', ain't it?"

May 1759

The Caribbean

Madeline O'Neil gripped the sea-slicked hemp of the ladder that led from the deck of the *Primrose* to the small boat below. At least she assumed the boat was below, for the night was black as pitch, too dark for seeing. But then, though it frightened her to have to feel her way down the side of the hull, this moonless night was part of the plan. "It will be too dark for the pirates to see a small boat full of women leaving the schooner," Captain Evans of the *Primrose* had assured her. It was his idea that she leave the vessel that was taking her home to her father's sugar plantation in Jamaica. Earlier that day sails had been sighted, and try as she might the *Primrose* had been unable to pull away from the ship that was following them.

"Pirates," Captain Evans had told her after advising

15

Madeline to retire to her cabin. "We could surrender and take our chances with them except . . ."

"Except for what," she'd asked, fearing she knew the answer.

His reply had been succinct. "You."

Actually, it had been more than just her. Madeline had found out there were several other women aboard—women of questionable character.

The lapping of the swells against the hull was louder now, and when Jake Rogers's hands grabbed her about the waist, Madeline knew she was almost to the boat.

Her eyes became more accustomed to the darkness, and she could make out the shadowy shapes of other women and of Jake, the seaman assigned to row them to a nearby island.

"You can make it easily in a day," Captain Evans had said. "And, as soon as the pirates are finished with us, we'll set sail and come for you."

The small boat wobbled as Jake guided Madeline toward the bow. Her ankle struck something hard, but she didn't need Jake's hand over her lips to stifle her cry of pain. Blatant proof of sound's ability to carry over water came from the crude voices drifting to them from the not-too-distant pirate ship. With very little imagination, Madeline could fill in the few phrases lost on the trade winds or covered by the pirate's lusty laughter. Her father's language had often been colorful, but this . . . Madeline shuddered at picturing the vile men whose bawdy carousing now assaulted her ears.

Jake pushed the muffled oars against the *Primrose*, setting them adrift on an adventure that even Madeline did not relish.

Bright sunshine sent her hands searching for the comforter to cover her eyes. With a start, Madeline realized there were no soft, fluffy blankets, and remembered where she was. "The pirates." She sat up

16

quickly, brushed errant tawny curls from her face, and looked out over the water.

"Well, Lordy me, her ladyship's finally decided to rise. Probably wants her tea and biscuits, too," squawked a woman whose unnaturally red hair hung over her ample shoulders.

Jake Rogers pulled in the oars for a well-deserved rest and glared at the whore. "Hush your mouth. More'n likely, Lettie, she ain't use to staying up all night like you."

Madeline purposely ignored the exchange and the scowl tossed her way by the sarcastic woman. Instead, she gazed toward the horizon. "Are they gone? The pirates, I mean." This was addressed to Jake, who had moved gingerly to the back of the boat so he might get a drink from the barrel of fresh water.

"Well now, little lady," he said, leveling dark eyes on her, "I'd say, more'n likely it's us that's gone. Imagine them pirates are still pretty much where we left 'em." He replaced the dipper and tested the barrel's lid for tightness.

"Do you think they took the *Primrose?*"

"Aye, they took her," Jake answered as Madeline looked about till she found her hat, crushed and flattened from having been unwittingly used as a pillow. She stuck it on her head anyway, glad for the shade it offered from the already searing tropical sun.

"Do you suppose anyone was hurt?"

"Naw, they weren't gonna put up no fight." His calm, matter-of-fact manner was meant to be reassuring.

"You have encountered pirates before, haven't you, Mr. Rogers?" Madeline asked.

Jake Rogers smiled, took off his flat-brimmed hat, waterproofed with tar, and wiped the back of a sunburned hand across his sweating brow before answering. "Aye, little lady, that I have."

Lettie cackled. "You ain't never fought no pirates, ya bloody little liar!"

17

Jake's face reddened. "I told ya once ta keep that mouth o' yours shut. Didn't say I fought no pirates." He turned toward Madeline. "But I've been on a ship that was taken by 'em."

"Are they as awful as I've heard?" Madeline asked, her eyes shining despite the shade provided by her hat.

Jake leaned over the oars, thoughtful for a minute. "Well now, little lady, there be pirates and then there be pirates. And you don't rightly know which kind you got till they's got you."

Madeline swallowed, the hot sun forgotten as he continued.

"Ya take a pirate like Blackbeard. Now there was a blackguard for ya. Carried six pistols across his chest, he did, and stuck burning fuses under his hat when he attacked. Mean! They say he once shot his best friend in the knee for no other reason than to show him who was boss."

"You don't suppose it could be he . . . ?"

"Blackbeard?"

At the affirmative nod of her head, Jake laughed. "Naw, he's long gone. Nailed his head to a bowsprit, they did. Lawd, can you imagine the sight that musta made?"

"Yes. That would have been something to see, all right," Madeline agreed, fighting a wave of nausea.

"I'm starvin'," whined Missy, the youngest of the group on the small boat. Her hair was limp and greasy, but Madeline imagined it would be pale blond if clean. As she handed her a sea biscuit, Madeline was struck by the girl's youth. Missy couldn't be a day over fifteen. Madeline was not totally naïve. She knew there were women who sold themselves to men, but that this girl, hardly more than a child, did so seemed beyond belief.

The rest of the afternoon passed in a monotonous blur. Jake Rogers no longer seemed inclined to share his tales, real or imagined. His silence and that of the other women—they cackled and smirked among themselves, but never spoke directly to Madeline—left her plenty of

18

time to think. And the thoughts that filled her mind, as she pulled the cloying fabric of her gown away from her skin, were of her father.

She should never have left him. It did not help to remind herself that she had had no choice; her Aunt Libby had come from Williamsburg for the express purpose of taking her back. And Patrick O'Neil, after many arguments with his sister, had agreed that living alone with him had left Madeline's education sadly lacking in certain important matters, like sipping tea or tatting edges on linens or flirting so that she might catch a husband.

She had gone with her aunt, but she should have known her father would be lost without her; and it didn't make her feel less guilty to admit that she had enjoyed the trip. Papa lived comfortably in a world of ideas, a world he shared with his only child; but the other world, the outside world, he had sought to blot out since the death of his wife. Had the real world proven too much for him? Was that what had caused the melancholy in the last letter she had received, or was he sick and trying to hide his illness? Whichever, she wished this nightmare were over and she was safely back at Hopewell.

But her wish was not to be granted that day, or even the next. As the long hours passed under the baking sun and the fresh water in the barrel diminished alarmingly, Madeline began to doubt that they would reach the island in time.

By nightfall of the third day she fell into an exhausted sleep, wondering if she would ever awake.

"Are any of 'em alive?" The words drifted through to her consciousness an instant before she felt a huge callused hand gently touch her neck.

"Aye, this one is. Looks like the others are, too." The voice was strong and nearly as comforting as the thumb tracing the pulse under her chin.

19

"What do you reckon they was doing floatin' 'round out here?" This voice was more distant.

"I'll tell you what we was doin'." Madeline thought it was Lettie's voice she heard, but she was so tired, too tired to open her eyes or listen, and when strong arms scooped her up, she felt safe, secure. With a contented sigh she nestled against a hard, clean-smelling chest and let oblivion overtake her.

Chapter 2

"Drinkin' alone, Cap'n?"

"I was." Joshua Whitlock cryptically replied as he motioned Oliver further into his cabin. It was small but neat and tidy, the swaying cabin lantern alternately casting light and shadow across the wooden bunk and chart-strewn desk.

"Ain't good for a man, ya know, drinkin' alone."

"And I suppose you have a cure for this dilemma of mine?" Joshua grinned, then motioned to the low-back chair on the other side of his desk.

"Well now, I just might. That French brandy ya got there, Cap'n?" the first mate asked, eying the pewter mug Joshua held in his large hands.

"Afraid not, Oliver." Joshua swirled the amber brew around once before draining his cup. "This is good old Jamaican rum."

Oliver sputtered. "But we've a whole store of brandy in the forward hold. Should I . . ."

He started to stand, but Joshua reached across and pulled him down. "Not in the mood for brandy."

Oliver sat down and slid his mug across the polished surface of the desk. "Never knowed you to pass up good French brandy for rum," he mumbled.

Extracting the jug from under the desk and filling

21

Oliver's mug and then his own, Joshua explained. "Brandy's for savoring; rum's for getting drunk."

"That's what you're about, getting drunk?"

Long legs, clothed in buff-colored breeches and high black boots, found their way to the desk top. There, crossed at the ankles, they rested, forming a V through which Joshua regarded his friend. "Objections?"

"I'm worried about ya, Cap'n," Oliver said, rubbing his hand through his beard and putting his drink down, untouched.

Joshua's laugh was sharp and abrupt. "Is that supposed to surprise me? You've been worrying about me since I was seven years old, whether I needed it or not. Why would I expect you to cease your mother-hen act now?"

"Laugh if ya want, but ya ain't been yourself, and ya know it as well as I do. Ya ain't sleepin', for starters."

"How in the hell do you know that?" Joshua slapped his mug down on the desk, sloshing some of the liquid over the sides onto the log board. Damn that Oliver; there was no keeping secrets from him.

"Seen ya on deck lotsa nights, and I ain't the only one either. Crew says you're becomin' a regular addition to the night watch."

"Crew's becoming like a gaggle of old biddies, gossiping. And you," Joshua pointed a long slender finger at the older man, "are their ring leader."

"It ain't your fault, ya know." Oliver ignored Joshua's jibes and offered encouragement.

Joshua didn't have to ask what he meant. They both knew what was causing his sleepless nights, the sudden desire to drown his memories in drink. He steepled his fingers under his chin and studied Oliver before shaking his head. "I should have been there."

"Of course ya shoulda, but you weren't, and it weren't your fault you weren't. You've gotta stop blamin' yourself, thinkin' you coulda done somethin' different."

Joshua stared at his first mate, but his mind was traveling back to that night almost a month ago when he had arrived in Baltimore. He had rushed to the large Georgian house in which he'd spent his childhood, only to stand hesitantly in the shadow of the large oak near the entrance, not wanting to approach the doorway and sound the knocker. He had tried to think of his father as Nathaniel had described him in the last letter he'd received—tired, mellow, ready to face death and to arrive at a truce with his elder son. It wasn't easy. Memories of his father's stern, unyielding voice kept interfering. *You were a feckless lad, Joshua Whitlock, always courting mischief, and mark my words, you'll never amount to much of a man.*

Finally Joshua had gathered his courage and entered the house, his home, only to discover his father gone, dead for more than a fortnight. Much to his chagrin, his younger brother, Nathaniel, was gone also, off on some wild-goose chase. Pursuing pirates who, he was convinced, were waging a personal vendetta against Whitlock & Co. Joshua, however, did have to admit the decline of Whitlock & Co. was not imagined. Out of the two schooners and three snows it had boasted on the eve of his departure, there was naught left. The vessels had all been captured or destroyed—if the letter Nathaniel had left for him was to be believed—by the same group of cutthroats.

The house and grounds, too, showed signs of neglect. The few servants who remained did so more out of loyalty than any hope of monetary gain. Of course, Mrs. Jenkins had stayed, and it was from her that Joshua had learned about his father's last days. She had also told him as best she could about Nathaniel's departure. Whereas the details of his father's death made him sad, the thought of his brother's foolhardy leave-taking made Joshua mad—roaring mad. "Why did he go? Didn't he think I would come?" he had demanded of no one in particular. "What in hell does he think he can do, alone, against pirates? That is, if there are any pirates," he was quick to add. Of course, his questions went unanswered. Not even the letter his brother had left for him told him much.

Joshua pressed his palm against the crinkled parchment inside his shirt, reassuring himself of its presence. After all, that letter had sent him sailing out of Chesapeake Bay and down the coast to the warm waters of the Caribbean.

"Ya know, Cap'n, I think yer right about this rum—it could make a body drunk. I'm about ready to snooze this one off," Oliver said, emptying the last of the liquor from the jug into his cup.

Joshua kicked back his chair and stood, more than a little unsteadily. "Well, I feel more restless now than I did before. I can't stand this blasted inactivity. I'll feel like a good sleep after I find Nat."

"Ya worry too much, Cap'n. Young Nat can take care of himself."

"You don't say!" Joshua's words were slurred. "You just tell me one time Nat was able to take care of himself. In all the scrapes we ever got into, who was it that got us out?" Joshua queried rhetorically, pointing his thumb toward his chest.

"Mr. Benville's cow."

Joshua stopped his pacing and stared blur-eyed at Oliver. "What?"

"Mr. Benville's cow," Oliver repeated. "That's a time Nat took care o' hisself. You too, as I recall."

Joshua roared with laughter, flopped onto his bunk, and struck his head against the wall. He remembered well the time he and his brother, while playing at being Indians, had deployed their trusty bows and shot their neighbor's cow with arrows.

"Doesn't count," Joshua shook his head, his laughter subsiding. "He talked us out of that one. You know damn well I meant fighting his way out of trouble. If there really are pirates, they're not going to want to listen to Nathaniel's silver tongue."

Walking back to the desk, Joshua slumped into his chair and dropped his head into his hands. "God, I'm tired. But tomorrow morning can't come too early for me. The sooner we reach Jamaica, the sooner I can find that brother of mine."

"Ya know what ya need?"

Joshua stared. "What?"

"A woman."

"A woman? You're crazy."

"Crazy like a fox, maybe. Nothin' like a good roll in the hay to make me sleep like a new babe." Oliver rolled his eyes and seemed to doze off.

"Like a babe, huh?"

Oliver nodded.

"Well, that's you. I've never been one to end a good tumble by falling asleep."

Oliver shrugged, "Worth a try."

Joshua grinned at his friend. He should have known Oliver would have an answer for everything—even restless nights. "And where do you suggest I procure this woman who will send me speeding toward dreamland?"

"Got some women in steerage right now who'd be more than happy to oblige you, Cap'n."

"You mean those prostitutes we fished from the sea this morning? Good God, man, you think I'd chance getting the pox for a night's sleep?"

"One of them ain't so bad. Matter o' fact, she's been askin' to see ya. Looks pretty clean, too."

Joshua scowled, searching his memory. "Which one is that?"

"The one ya carried up the side."

"You mean the one with the sunburned face and freckles?" At Oliver's affirmative nod, Joshua burst out laughing. "She was the poorest excuse for a whore I've ever seen!"

25

"She looks a mite better up and about, but hey, 'twas just an idea. Ain't forcin' ya." Oliver got up and headed for the door. "Beggin' your leave, Cap'n, I'm goin' to bed."

"Wait a minute." Joshua's scowl deepened as he sighed. He really did need some sleep, and it had been a long time since he'd had a woman. It was unlikely that one would help, maybe . . . "Do you think she'd be willing?"

Shock registered on Oliver's bearded face. "Hell, she's a whore, ain't she? Besides, I told ya she's been askin' to see ya. Probably had in mind to thank ya for savin' her hide."

"Send her up. I guess it can't hurt."

The point of the wrought-iron candle holder was stuck into the slimy beam. It held the taper that offered Madeline her meager allotment of light. From the tiny bunk on which she lay she could barely make out the reclining forms of the women who had been her companions on the small boat, but she felt certain they all slept. If only she could . . . She had slept most of the day, barely waking in time for the evening meal of pork and pease. Madeline ran her hand down the front of her torn gown and let it rest on her stomach, wondering if perhaps she wouldn't have been better off missing the repast altogether. The greasy concoction seemed to have turned to lead in her belly, and that discomfort combined with the noxious fumes of pitch and bilge water below decks left her feeling less than rescued.

She noticed with alarm that the damp, mildewed canvas—she assumed it had been hung to afford herself and the other women some privacy—was being slightly pulled aside. Madeline recognized the man she had talked to earlier in the day when she had first awakened and had started to wander up on deck.

26

She rose shakily to her feet.

"You're awake. Good," he stated without preamble.

Madeline smiled. She wondered vaguely why it should matter to him, but repressed the desire to ask. He seemed harmless enough. She would guess his age to be at least sixty, though his movements seemed those of a younger man.

"I'm feeling better," Madeline offered, the ensuing silence stretching out as the fellow peered at her through the dim light. He finally grunted and continued his perusal.

"Why are you staring at me?" she demanded, knowing her words were rude, but not nearly so rude as this ill-mannered sailor's behavior. She could only guess what she looked like. Her skin felt dry and tight and not altogether clean. The bucket of cold sea water she'd managed to find that evening had hardly made a dent in the layers of accumulated dirt and grime. And her hair—she saw his dark eyes travel upward—well, four days without a brush had left what there was of the braid matted and what had come loose was wildly tangled. Still, her appearance was hardly her fault, and she was just about to chastise the man again when he spoke.

"Cap'n wants to see ya."

"Now?" Her voice left little doubt that she considered the timing ill-advised.

"Aye, now." He narrowed his eyes and glared at her suspiciously, "I thought ya said ya wanted to see him."

"Well, I did; I mean, I do." Madeline looked frantically about the area, as if one of the women might awake and explain to this insensitive man the lateness of the hour. But the others slept peacefully, oblivious of her.

"Well, ya comin' or no?" he asked impatiently, holding back the canvas for her.

Madeline sighed. "I suppose the time makes little difference. There are some concerns I have." Not the

27

least of which is the disrespectful treatment I have received from the crew, primarily you, you vile little man, Madeline said to herself. Well, late or not the captain could give her some answers. Where was she? Were they headed for Jamaica, and if so, when would they arrive? If not . . . She tried not to think of what that would mean as she followed the man from the port side of the berth deck aft, to the captain's cabin.

She didn't hear any response to her guide's knock, but apparently he did, for without ceremony—and so quickly she was dumbfounded—the door opened and shut, and she found herself within the cabin, the man who had brought her without.

Before she could begin to ponder the fact that he had deserted her without having made an introduction, Madeline saw a form rise from the chair behind the desk. Up, up, up. After staring straight into the eyes of her impolite guide, she found her chin tilting to a decided angle as she tried to make out the features of the man she presumed to be the captain. Not that she could discern much of his countenance; the only light in the cabin was positioned behind him, making that next to impossible.

He came around the desk and slowly advanced on her, his broad-shouldered body soon filling her entire line of vision.

Much as his man had done, the captain stared at her appraisingly. But this scrutiny, unlike the previous one, did not provoke Madeline. Instead, she felt a strange tingling radiate from each spot the captain's dark eyes touched. His intimate gaze wandered over her, pausing now and then as if to assess her charms. Her face and hair, he passed over quickly, and Madeline felt her chin rising defiantly at this apparent dismissal. How dare he treat her thus? The man hadn't even offered her a chair, and dizzy as she was, she could certainly use one. But he'd said nothing since she'd walked into the cabin. Well, she would simply have to teach this boor some manners.

Madeline began to speak, then noticed where his glance had strayed. Impulsively she folded her arms across her breasts, unknowingly pushing more of those soft mounds into view. Since her ordeal with the elements, her stomacher was in shreds. The area it had covered was now concealed by only the thin ruffled linen of her shift. Obviously a man of coarse breeding, the captain, instead of ignoring this unfortunate circumstance, seemed intent upon taking advantage of it. On the small boat Madeline had been glad she had chosen to forgo the confinement of her stays; now she longed for the camouflage they supplied. Why did she feel as though a suit of armor would be an insufficient bulwark against this man's gaze?

He lifted it now, till his amused black eyes met hers. "You do look a mite better, though you're still redder than anyone I've ever seen." His voice was mocking, even though his words were slurred.

Red was she? Well, what would he look like if he had sat unprotected in the sun for three days? Reluctantly Madeline decided he probably wouldn't appear much different, for he had the look of a man used to the out-of-doors. Skin darkened by wind and sun stretched across his straight nose, high cheekbones, and square chin. It gave his face, handsome by any standards, a rugged appearance that, against her will, she found rather appealing. Even the expanse of hairy chest exposed by his billowing white shirt was darkened to a deep bronze. Suddenly conscious of where her eyes had wandered, Madeline stiffened. What gentleman would entertain a lady in such a state of undress? Never mind her own appearance—she had her reasons—he looked as disheveled as an unmade bed. Heavens, why would she compare him to a bed, of all things!

Astonished by the meanderings of her own mind, Madeline forced herself to recall his last remark. He had criticized her appearance—hers. "Your opinion of me

29

has absolutely no bearing here," she chastised in her haughtiest voice, trying to ignore the nausea that again threatened to relieve her of her last meal.

"Well"—he smiled, a most disarming grin Madeline had to admit—"that is a very businesslike approach. I'm too much the romantic, I suppose." He shrugged, seeming to dismiss her statement.

Madeline's stomach was in such turmoil she didn't consider anything amiss when he inched closer, thinking perhaps he only meant to help her to a seat. After all, this was the longest she had stood in nearly four days, and her body was rebelling. However, when two consoling arms encircled her she was taken aback!

"What do you think you are doing?" She pushed against his chest, surprised by the warmth of his bare skin, and at the same time, noticing the noxious odor of rum on his breath.

"I was going to kiss you." At the look of shock and disapproval on her face, he continued, "What? Am I to be allowed no amenities? Unfortunately, my appetite doesn't respond well to this all-business method. Well, perhaps sometimes it does, but"—he let his appraising gaze travel over her matted hair, her reddened complexion, and salt-encrusted clothing—"I'm afraid this is not one of those times."

"You're drunk!" She shot the words at him, trying to distance herself from the sickening smell of alcohol. Madeline was having an extremely difficult time understanding—even listening—to his words. Her skin felt clammy, and she could only guess how very upset this man would be if she were to be sick all over him. But he seemed blissfully unaware of her dilemma, for he threw back his head and laughed. "Drunk, huh? You have a sassy mouth as well as sassy looks." His expression sobered. "I do apologize for my inebriation; however, I would think you'd consider it an acceptable hazard."

The room, suddenly suffocatingly hot, whirled about

Madeline. "Please, may I lie down?"

She didn't even wait for an answer, though by the confounded grin on his face as she left his arms, she doubted one would be forthcoming, but collapsed onto the thin ticking of the bunk. The prone position relieved her dizziness very little, but at least her wobbly legs no longer had to support her. The room seemed to begin spinning in earnest when she closed her eyes. Determinedly she opened them and stared at the ceiling. Then she remembered where she was. How could she have lain down on a man's bed? Sick she might be, but she wasn't dying and that was the only way she'd allow herself to be in such a situation. Madeline sat up quickly—too quickly. She could almost feel the blood rush from her head, leaving her weak and imagining silly things. Her conscious grasp of her surroundings was slipping away, and as she swooned back onto the pillow she even thought she saw the captain removing his breeches! So silly.

Without a doubt, the strangest lightskirt he had ever been around, Joshua decided as he danced about on one foot trying to divest himself of his breeches. He had been around his share, but this one really took the prize. Not that she didn't have some redeeming qualities. Maybe she was red and peeling, but that only meant her complexion was normally fair, and those freckles across her nose were really rather appealing. Her hair, now that was another story—too wild; and her body was too thin and slight for his taste. But hell, he was only after a quick tumble. It wasn't as if he were seeking a wife—heaven forbid! And that was a good thing, because this woman was strange! First refusing his kiss, then climbing uninvited into his bed.

He climbed in after her now, totally nude. God, the softness of the bunk felt good. Joshua leaned over and kissed the girl's generous mouth, glad that she no longer protested. Protested, hell, she did nothing! This wasn't

31

turning out well at all. In his present state, he would appreciate someone pleasantly responsive, even aggressive. "It wouldn't hurt if you kissed me back," he complained. She ignored him. Even caressing her satin-smooth thigh brought forth no reaction. He let his head fall to the pillow for a minute, to think. It was so comfortable. His last thought before sleep overtook him was that for a common whore she was an uncommonly cold witch.

Madeline's eyes flew open, but saw nothing. The darkness of the room surrounded her like soft, black velvet.

Hesitantly she raised her right hand, one of the few parts of her body she was able to move freely, and tentatively touched the constricting weight that held her upper torso immobile. She gasped and jerked her hand back as if it had been burned. Her tiny movement seemed to cause a counterreaction in the warm, muscle-hardened arm she had felt, for it shifted till a large hand found and gently cupped her scantily clad breast. Aghast, Madeline tried to squirm away from the warmth of the captain's hand, but this only created more problems. In trying to escape from his dream-induced fondling, her leg, vulnerable and exposed where her skirt had ridden up, inadvertently rubbed against a naked, muscular, hair-roughened thigh.

As if this contact were not dreadful enough, what followed would have sent her flying from the bunk if his trunklike leg and arm had not imprisoned her. The feel of her leg and breast, coupled with what Madeline could only surmise were quite randy dreams, caused the growth and stiffening of his most private part, and that now pressed blatantly, hot and rock hard, against her thigh.

He nuzzled closer. She froze. He mumbled something indiscernible, his breath sending aflutter the curly tendrils about her ear. She held her breath. Time stood still as she waited, hoping a lack of response would cool his ardor, and to her great relief, his movements became less sensual as she felt his body relax in deepening sleep.

Madeline lay in the blackness of night, willing herself not to move. When finally she knew she must start to breathe or pass out, rendering herself helpless before this monster who was her bedfellow, she took slow, deep, even breaths, matching her cadence to his, hiding even the faintest sound in the deep resonance of his soft snores. If she could have matched the rhythm of her heart, which vibrated like a drum, to the thumping deep inside his broad chest, she would have. No noise or movement from her would incite him again.

She could only be thankful the mind sent abroad no proof of its activity, for hers raged. Indeed, she was near hysteria. This man, nay this animal, had used her, had forced her to commit an act she could only imagine, and had done it while she was unconscious, unable to defend herself or even try. If she had been awake, she would have kicked, screamed, bitten, scratched, and fought. He might have had her in the end, but it would not have been a pleasant experience for him and he would not be lying peacefully beside her now; he would be nursing his wounds. But she had not been allowed even that tiny revenge for the atrocity he had committed and was obviously quite capable of repeating.

Her thoughts became more patterned. Planning, that was what was needed now. Somehow she had to get away from him, off this boat and to Hopewell. Tears drifted down her temples to dampen her hair. Papa needed her, and she had endured so much to get to him, leaving Aunt Libby's on her own, surviving the endless days on that tiny boat, and now this.

Madeline set about finding an answer to her plight. One step at a time, she told herself. First, she must get away from this man, then work on steps two and three.

But try as she might, no way to accomplish her first goal came to her, and long after she'd heard the faint bells that marked the end of midwatch, she lay awake and unmoving. Not until the first pale streaks of dawn defined the line separating the sea from the sky, did she fall into an exhausted slumber.

Chapter 3

Joshua leaned against the polished rail of the sloop, surveying his surroundings from the commanding elevation of the quarterdeck. For the moment he was pleasurably lost in observing the beauty of the area. Not Kingston harbor, of course. Its water was clogged with vessels of every description. Not even the city itself, though it teemed with life and vitality. It was the region beyond that captured his eye. Verdant tropical forests, as yet untamed by man, rose gently to meet the majestic Blue Mountains. It was a sight that always left him in awe. When he had worked on and later captained vessels for his father, he had visited this port often.

Those had been years when he had followed the order of things according to Justin Whitlock. Joshua had started as a cabin boy and had worked his way up to ordinary seaman when he knew every spar, every shiv through which the tackle wove, when he could climb the ratlines blindfolded, though he never would, then, and only then, had he earned a position of authority.

The first time he had sailed as an officer he'd feared that he might love the mind of the great lady of the waves less than her body, that the intricacies of commanding the ship would be less of an adventure than working her, but that thought had lasted less time than it took the wind

35

to catch a sail. He had become a sailing master, fixing his position by Hadley's quadrant if the days and nights were clear or by deduced reckoning if they were not. By the time he captained his first schooner, filled with flour ground at Jones Falls to be traded for sugar in Jamaica, he could make decisions with authority and lead men effectively and with compassion. He was everything his father could ask for in a son.

That short time of being his father's pride had lasted till he was twenty-seven. That was the year the last phase of Justin Whitlock's master plan for his son was to go into effect, the year Joshua was to give up life at sea and settle down so he might take his father's place at Whitlock & Co. It was then his father had to remember why he had sent the rebellious, independent boy to sea in the first place.

"You're lookin' better this mornin', Cap'n." Oliver's words interrupted Joshua's musings.

Joshua gave his first mate a wry look but said nothing.

Undaunted, Oliver continued, "Knew my plan would work."

Again Joshua said nothing, choosing instead to look back over the water and to hope that, if he ignored him, Oliver would change the turn of his conversation. He should have known better.

"Can't say as your little tumble did much for your disposition. It's about as sour as that lightskirt in your cabin."

"What do you mean?"

"I thought there was still a tongue in that mouth o' yours, though I wouldn't o' been surprised none if she'd bitten it off. I never saw no woman more full of vinegar."

"What's she upset about?" Joshua's words did little to reduce Oliver's delight in his own jest.

"Damned if I know. You spent the night with 'er."

* * *

36

Actually, Madeline had awakened stiff and uncomfortable and in a black mood, but it had improved at once. Almost immediately she'd realized she was alone in the cabin. The captain was gone! Step one had been accomplished with no difficulty. Then, when she arose, the lack of movement became obvious. Was it too much to hope that they were at anchor?

With all haste she darted for the door, opened it, peered out, then jumped back inside and leaned against the door as it slammed shut. She hadn't expected to see sailors in the companionway. They hadn't seemed to notice her, but heaven only knew what kind of ship she was on. She had even pondered whether it was some sort of pirate vessel; surely no honest captain would have treated her as that man had last night.

Her eyes frantically searched the room. A weapon was what she needed, but nothing caught her eye. Before she could move away from the door to begin looking for one, she heard a soft tapping sound, and then the door opened. Caught unawares, Madeline could only back away from the grizzled sailor who entered. With a start, she recognized the man who had brought her to this cabin on the preceding night.

"What do you want?" She hurled the words at him, hoping to take the offensive.

His dark eyes popped open, but he gave no other sign that her manner of speech surprised him. "I brought ya some breakfast," he said, brushing aside some papers with his forearm and lowering the heavy pewter tray to the desk.

"I don't want it!"

Again he ignored her outburst. "Well now, the cap'n left word ya was to be served some, so I thought I'd do it, seein' ya know me and all."

Madeline bristled at the mention of that hated man. "Where is he?"

"On deck, I s'pose. We came into port this mornin', so

37

he's been pretty busy. He hardly had time to see to his own victuals, yet he thought o' yours."

"He's a saint among men," Madeline countered sarcastically. But she tried to moderate her tone as she asked, "What port did we come into this morning?"

"Why, Kingston, o' course."

Kingston! She could hardly contain her joy. Kingston! She was almost home. All she had to do now was find some sort of weapon, in case she needed it, and then get off this ship.

She glanced up to see him staring at her, a strange expression in his eyes.

"Did your noble captain leave instructions for you to stand there staring at me?"

"Nay, I was just—"

"Then don't. Go away and let me"—she hesitated till her eyes landed on the bowl of mush—"eat my breakfast."

Once he was gone, she wasted no time in searching through the sea chest at the foot of the bunk. "You'd think a pirate captain would have a pistol or cutlass or something," she mumbled, then gasped at her own words. When had she started thinking of the captain as a pirate? Madeline wasn't certain but it probably had been during her long sleepless night. No self-respecting sea captain would have abused her as this man had. He must be a pirate.

Madeline renewed her search with more vigor. Yanking the contents from his sea chest, she found only clothing and books. Jake's description of the pirate Blackbeard came to her mind. "Of course, there are no weapons in this room because they're all strapped to his person," she said aloud.

The small commode by the bunk caught her attention, and in it she found his ditty bag. She opened the small canvas sack and dumped the contents on the bunk. Scissors, a wooden shaving dish and brush, and assorted sewing gear spilled out, but it was the razor that Madeline noticed. Opened, it appeared to provide a satisfactory knife of sorts.

Sudden footsteps in the companionway, just moments before the door opened, allowed her no time to plan this weapon's use.

"What the hell!" The mug had crashed against the wall only inches from Joshua's head, splattering hot tea over the snowy whiteness of his shirt as he'd entered his cabin.

"Don't you touch me!"

He looked in amazement from the weeping scar on the wall where the mug had hit to the woman who had thrown it. If possible, the wench he had bedded last night looked even more disreputable in the unkind light of day. Her hair was hardly more than a tangled mass of wild frizzy curls; she blew a strand of it out of her face as she eyed him warily. Her clothes were more wrinkled and disheveled than ever, and the dirt—my God! didn't the woman ever bathe! Still, something about those green eyes intrigued Joshua. Maybe it was just because they looked greener because of the redness of her face. Nonetheless, they might have captivated him had she not held the razor belligerently in her right hand.

He stepped forward cautiously, crunching broken shards of pottery into powder beneath his boots.

"Don't touch me, or I'll use this," Madeline threatened, lifting the razor.

"Listen, lady," Joshua raised his hand in what he hoped was a placating motion, "I don't know what you think you have, but last night was hardly memorable. I would not go up against that to touch you." He pointed to the razor.

Madeline had lowered it slightly, but she quickly lifted it when she realized her slip in concentration. "Let me off this ship at once!" she demanded, riled anew by his reference to the past night.

39

"Sure, lady, whatever you say. But first do you want to tell me what the problem is?"

Madeline was aghast. Her eyes blazed and her whole body stiffened. "You know very well what the problem is. Now step out of my way!"

Joshua walked slowly in the direction she indicated. "Does this have anything to do with last night?"

She tightened her grip on the blade and said nothing.

"Did I hurt you?" Concern softened his voice and shadowed the sparkle of his eye. He had never knowingly hurt a woman, but he realized last night could have been a first because, try as he might, he could not remember what had transpired. Somewhere in the cloudy recesses of his mind was the memory of her climbing into his bed, and he after her, but what had happened between that moment and this morning, when he'd awakened draped over her, was lost. He did recall thinking her quite strange, and her behavior today certainly seemed to bear that out. However, if he had harmed her . . . Joshua wished he could remember.

Madeline was startled by his tone as well as his words. She had not expected any show of concern from him, of all people, yet there was no mistaking his solicitous manner. But she wanted no sympathy, no discussion of their dreadful liaison. She didn't even want to think about what had happened. "No, you didn't hurt me," she hissed, and suddenly realized it was true. Stiff and uncomfortable though she was, there was no physical pain to remind her of what he had done.

Relief washed over his face, to be replaced by bewilderment. "Then what is the matter?"

Madeline ignored his question and inched toward the door. Sweat ran in rivulets down her back, and the ivory handle she grasped was slippery. She watched his every move, knowing in her heart he was not standing there so complacently because he feared a ragtag girl who barely reached to his shoulders, though she brandished a

40

makeshift knife. She saw his eyes leave hers and survey the room, to rest briefly on his ransacked belongings before returning to meet her glare, a knowing twinkle in their black depths.

"Ah," he said, a mocking grin playing at the corners of his mouth, "you must think me terribly dense. I would think you'd consider saving your life payment enough but . . . Now don't give me that bewildered look. You didn't have to go to such extreme measures, you know." He casually glanced around the room. "All you needed to do was ask. I would have been happy to pay you for last night."

Madeline blanched beneath her burn. The tiny fissure his concern had created in her armor of hatred closed up. "Pay me! Why, you insufferable bastard!" she shrieked as she launched herself at him.

Deftly sidestepping her violent but unpracticed slash with his razor, Joshua caught her flailing arms and twisted her wrists behind her back. Shame and anger flaring, Madeline struggled desperately, impotently grasping her weapon. She kicked out at him, mindless of the pain his boots caused her barely protected toes, and she squirmed and writhed till, with an abrupt movement, he crushed her against his muscular chest. Yet even then she did not yeild. Tears of frustration stung her eyes as she tilted back her head to allow the venom to spill forth. "You filthy pig, whoreson, defiler of—" Before Madeline could begin to hurl all the swear words she had ever heard at him, his mouth descended on hers with brutal force, effectively silencing any further outburst.

He had had enough. This wretched hoyden had caused him more trouble than she would ever be worth. More trouble than he needed now. He wanted to punish her, and he knew she hated what he was doing to her. Joshua could feel it in the slight quiver of her bottom lip beneath his bruising attack, in the tension of her small body. She should have been defeated, and yet with every ounce of her fragile strength she fought on. Guilt over what he was doing overcame him. Without realizing it his kiss altered, slightly at first, then, as he allowed himself to notice the pleasure of her body pressed against his, more radically. No longer was he the aggressor seeking to punish; he became the partner seeking to please.

And please he did. What had happened, Madeline did not know, but at one moment his mouth had been hard and ugly—hurtful—and in the next, his lips were warm and soft. His imprisoning arms ceased to confine and now only comforted, soothing her rage, quelling her assault. She could not explain what had happened, nor did she try. Her heartbeat raced, but her muscles relaxed and her breath caught in her throat, only to be released in a soft moan. When his tongue, brash and bold, sought entrance to her mouth, she opened to him, welcoming this invasion as if it were a habit of long standing. She pressed closer, lost in the aura of him. He smelled of sea and fresh air and freedom, and she loved it—loved the wild free way she felt. His large, work-roughened hands left her wrists and moved up the soft curve of her arms, freeing her hands and the razor. But her body no longer had any need other than to be closer to his. She now had no desire to hurt or maim this man who, by the touch of his lips, had forced all reason from her mind.

Neither seemed to notice the clatter of ivory and steel upon the wooden planking of the deck as her hands snaked about his slender waist. The cotton of his shirt was smooth and soft, but the corded strength beneath it rippled, hard and taut, as he enfolded her deeper in his embrace. She went willingly, pressing her sensitive breasts against his chest, eliciting a deep, guttural moan from him as her hips pressed wantonly against his.

Slowly Joshua raised his head, forcing himself to stop while he still could. She nestled comfortably in his arms, her eyes still closed, their long dark lashes forming a lacy web across her cheeks. He brushed his lips across the

42

freckles on her nose and grinned when emerald green eyes slowly opened to him. "Well, you are full of surprises," he chided softly.

Surprises aren't the half of it, Madeline thought, as reason started to filter through the sensual longings that held her in their grasp. Somehow, she must try to figure out what had happened, what he had done to make her react that way—to make her still reluctant to leave the shelter of his arms.

"I have to go back on deck," he told her as he gently brushed a tangled curl off her forehead, "but I'll be back." He released her, and to Madeline's amazement she did not melt into a puddle at his feet. He patted her rump intimately before starting toward the door. "If you can come anywhere close to delivering what you promised in that kiss, you most certainly will not need to ask for payment."

Reality, which had receded from Madeline's mind, now burst forth upon it, instantly rekindling her fury. "Get out!" she screamed at his departing figure.

Shock turned him around to her. "If you aren't the most changeable wench I've ever seen," he muttered. Then he opened the door and stalked out, as flying cutlery hit the wall.

Startled, Madeline stood arms akimbo as he stuck his head back through the doorway. "I'd like this room cleaned up by the time I return, and"—he grinned—"it really wouldn't hurt if you took some soap and water to yourself." She heard his laughter echo as he walked down the companionway.

Despicable swine! The words were on the tip of her tongue, ready to be hurled at him, but Madeline held them back. He was gone. There was nothing to be gained from letting her temper take control. On the contrary, if he were to return to answer her insults, there was no telling what he might do. And, she thought with disgust, what I might let him do. That forceful kiss had been bad

43

enough! She wiped the back of her hand across her mouth, effectively erasing for the time being the memory of his lips on hers. Spotting the razor, Madeline pocketed it and left the cabin without a backward glance. She made her way forward till she reached the main hatch, bypassing the aft hatch that would have brought her onto the main deck too close to the quarterdeck. She had no desire to encounter her tormentor again.

Chapter 4

"Did ya find 'im?"

Joshua strode across the gently swaying deck of the *Chesapeake*, ignoring Oliver's question.

"Cap'n?"

"Hell, no, I didn't find him." Joshua stopped and faced his first mate. The grim set of his jaw and the pain in the onyx depths of his eyes spoke more eloquently than his words.

"What did Smythe say?" Oliver had followed the captain below to his cabin, damn near trotting to keep up with the younger man's long strides. He watched Joshua begin to remove his jacket.

Joshua's elbow stuck in the tight-fitting sleeve, and in frustration he jerked at the blue silk, freeing it, only to wad the expensive fabric and throw it to the floor. "He hadn't seen him."

"But the letter . . ."

"Dammit, Oliver, you think I don't know what the letter says?" Joshua dropped onto the sturdy wooden chair beside his desk. "'I'll contact Henry Smythe upon my arrival in Kingston and apprise him of my plans.' I think those were his exact words, but"—Joshua pointed a long, slender finger into the air for emphasis—"he didn't do it."

Oliver rubbed his beard, a slow hiss of air escaping

through the space between his front teeth. "It ain't like Nathaniel not to do what he says."

The bark of laughter from Joshua was as sudden as it was mirthless. "None of this is like Nathaniel."

Oliver sank onto the chair opposite the desk and nodded his head. "You've got the right of it there, Cap'n." An instant later he leveled his eyes at the younger man. "I guess ya considered that the *Sailfish* ain't arrived yet?"

Joshua met his gaze, held it, and the hard planes of his face softened. "I can grasp at straws as well as you, old friend. After I left Henry I spent the rest of the day at the Admiralty." Joshua paused. "The *Sailfish* arrived April 12."

Oliver sank further into the chair. "Nearly a month ago."

"Aye." Nearly a month. There it was. For twenty-seven—no, today was nearly spent—twenty-eight days, Nathaniel had been in Kingston, and he hadn't contacted Henry Smythe. Joshua thought again of his visit that morning with Whitlock Trading Company's solicitor. It had been nearly four years since he had seen the man, but very little about him had changed. His office still looked as if it belonged on an English country estate rather than in tropical Kingston. For that matter, so did the man himself. Wide of girth, florid of complexion, Smythe's ever-constant wig and country-squire clothing seemed to trap the heat of the day and repel the breezes proffered by the trade winds. But that was Henry Smythe, Esq., transplanted English solicitor.

It hadn't taken Joshua long to realize that, though Henry knew about some of the problems Whitlock Trading Company was having (Nathaniel had written asking for his assistance), he did not know about Justin Whitlock's death nor had he seen Nathaniel.

"What ya gonna do now?" Oliver's voice brought Joshua back to the present.

Joshua answered his first mate's query with one of his

own. "Do you recall the name Patrick O'Neil?"

"No." Oliver shook his head once and then stopped. "Wait a minute. Ya took his sugar to Baltimore."

"You've a good memory, Oliver." Joshua rose and opened the sea chest at the foot of his bunk, noticing for the first time that someone had put his cabin to rights. It certainly hadn't been the one responsible for creating the havoc in the first place, for when he had returned to his cabin yesterday morning she'd been gone, but the mess had remained. Well, that was of no consequence now. Oliver was staring at him, no doubt wondering why he had brought up O'Neil. "He owns a sugar plantation on the Hope River. Henry Smythe said his estate manager is selling wheat flour, and rather a lot of it, too."

"Patrick O'Neil's manager?"

"Yes."

"But why would he be sellin' flour?" Oliver asked, rubbing his chin again.

Straightening from attempting to fold a white linen shirt, Joshua responded, "That's exactly what I'd like to know." Flour was one of the commodities from the Colonies that the sugar planters traded for, but he could think of no logical, or should he say legal, reason for a planter to have so much flour that he would need to sell it. Yet Henry Smythe had been quite certain that was what was happening. He also had suggested that Nathaniel might have uncovered this same information and gone to investigate it. After all, he was trying to discover who was stealing the cargo—the flour—from his ships.

"Goin' somewhere, Cap'n?" Oliver eyed the growing pile of clothes Joshua was haphazardly stacking on the bunk.

"Patrick O'Neil was a friend of my father's. I visited his plantation years ago on one of my first voyages here, but he was not at home at the time so we've never met. I think it's about time I remedy that situation."

"Ya think he might have somethin' to do with that

47

lost cargo?"

"I don't know, but I intend to find out and I hope to find that brother of mine in the process." Satisfied with his packing of the small traveling chest, Joshua returned to his chair and studied his first mate through narrowed eyes. "You could help me if you would."

"Anythin', Cap'n. Ya know that."

Joshua smiled at seeing the earnest expression on the weather-ravaged face of his first mate. He felt some of his anger fade away. There were some things in this world you could count on, and Oliver Chappel's friendship and help were among them. "What I ask shouldn't be too hard."

"Ya want me to come with ya?"

"No." Joshua chuckled in spite of himself. "I should be able to handle this little visit by myself. All I ask is that you keep a sharp eye out when you visit the local bawdy houses and grog shops. A sharp ear out, too. Think you can do that?"

Oliver leaned forward, his elbows on the desk, his eyes bright with amusement. "Well, now, Cap'n, I always tries to keep me wits about me. What exactly am I supposed ta be watchin' for? Ya think young Nat is drinkin' and whorin' round?"

"Good Lord, no!" Joshua laughed aloud as he tried to imagine his staid younger brother with a tankard of rum in one hand and a buxom partially clad woman in the other. "But you might run into someone who saw him. Maybe a crew member of the *Sailfish* who decided to stay on for a while after the brig sailed back to Maryland— anything."

"Ya can count on me, Cap'n."

Rising and circling the desk, Joshua laid his hand on his first mate's shoulder. "I know I can, Oliver." He walked to the small commode by his bunk, picked up the tinder box, and proceeded to light the lantern suspended above his desk. There was a hiss, then the tiny spark bloomed, enveloping the cabin in its soft glow. "There is one other thing I would ask of you. I'd do it myself, of course, but I won't be here." Joshua opened a desk drawer and took several coins from a leather pouch. He glanced at Oliver and saw the older man waiting expectantly for his orders. He almost stuffed the money back into the pouch and bid Oliver good night rather than risk seeing the amusement in his first mate's eyes when he made his request. But he took a deep breath and plunged on. "If you should happen to run into the young lady that was here the other night . . ."

"Ya mean the whore?" Oliver asked with obvious enjoyment.

"Yes." Joshua gritted his teeth and went on. "Would you please give her these coins?" That said, he tossed the gold coins across the desk.

Oliver picked up the money and shook his head. "Mighty high-priced little piece, if ya ask me. I heard ya askin' them others 'bout her this mornin'." He shook his head. "She musta' had mosta' her charms hidden, so to speak."

Hidden? Buried is more like it, Joshua thought. Then he remembered the kiss and, just for an instant, those green eyes. "Hell, just give her the money if you see her. And don't make her work for it." The last words were out before he'd known they were coming. "I owe her the money" was all he could think of adding. He turned away. "I'll only be gone a couple days, a sennight at most," Joshua was deliberately changing the subject.

Oliver was not to be diverted. "I'd think she'd be owin' the money, the way she wrecked your cabin."

"Perhaps she had reason." Joshua smiled at the shocked expression on Oliver's face, then wished he could remember if she had. More quietly he continued. "Just give her the money, please. She seemed somewhat"—he searched for a word—"desperate."

Desperate was exactly how Madeline felt as she slid her

49

body lower into the brass tub, letting the warm water soak away some of her aches. At Hopewell less than twenty-four hours, she was beginning to realize that, difficult as her journey had been, her homecoming was not going to be as placid as she had hoped. She already foresaw problems.

The fields she'd passed on her way to the great house had been weed-clogged, and even the stately white manse with its abundance of sparkling windows and its wrap-around veranda had shown signs of neglect.

"Oh, Hattie, I don't ever want to leave this tub," Madeline groaned. Then she smiled up at the black woman who had taken care of her for most of her twenty-one years. Hattie's dark face was comforting. Looking at her, Madeline could have sworn it was only yesterday when she had boarded the *Deliverance* bound for the Virginia colony. The slave's wildly colored skirt and head cloth had not changed, nor had her wide smile that showed more gums than teeth.

"Take it ya didn't enjoy da ride."

Madeline rose slowly, conscious of the muscles in her legs as they rebelled against her abuse of them that afternoon. She had ridden for hours, not the least bit concerned that it was the first time in months she had sat a horse. Madeline stepped gingerly from the tub into the linen towel Hattie held. "Of course I didn't enjoy my ride. You know very well I went with Eli Creely." Madeline paused a moment, trying to fight down the anger that swept over her whenever she thought of the estate manager. "I made him show me everything. Oh, he was madder than a hornet, I can tell you, though he tried not to let me know." Finished drying herself, Madeline held up her arms and let the soft linen shift slide down her body. "He had an excuse for everything, of course. Too much rain, slaves running away."

Hattie grunted as she pulled the cords through the eyelets of Madeline's stays. "I ain't surprised he has his excuses."

50

"Have there been problems with the slaves?"

"Some." That was all the black woman would say, though Madeline asked her again.

"I don't want any hoops," Madeline said as Hattie lifted the whalebone and linen garment from the bed. "All I'm going to do this evening is sit with Papa. Has he wakened from his nap yet?"

"Yes'm, Miz Madeline. Your papa, he's downstairs in da library."

"Downstairs!" Madeline swung around, sending her underpetticoats swaying about her ankles. "What is he doing downstairs? He promised me he'd stay abed today."

"He has a visitor."

"Well, he's much too weak to be receiving visitors." Madeline sat in front of her vanity and let Hattie brush the tangles from her long, golden brown curls. Her father's appearance, of course, had been a most unpleasant shock to her. Maybe not a complete shock. Wasn't that why she had left Williamsburg in such haste? Hadn't she suspected he might be ill? But she had hardly thought to see her robust father shrunk to a mere shadow of his former self. Why wasn't he eating? He had always enjoyed a healthy appetite, but last evening when she had insisted on bringing a tray to his room he had hardly eaten a thing. Oh, he had pretended to eat, but Madeline hadn't been fooled.

"You're sure a doctor has been to see him?" She turned to face Hattie, clenching her teeth to hold back an unladylike oath as her head was tugged back.

"If ya don't keep your head still I ain't gonna be able to fix your hair," Hattie grumbled as she pulled the brush through Madeline's curls.

"Hattie."

The single word seemed to draw the old woman's attention away from her charge's burnished head. "I told ya yesterday, same as I'll tell ya today. Dr. Holt from Kingston done come up here and looked at da massa."

51

Unable to keep her shoulders from slumping forward, Madeline sighed. "Papa said the doctor told him it was only sour stomach, but even so the tonic he was given doesn't seem to be working."

Hattie nodded, "Well, maybe now 'at your home, Miz Madeline, da massa will feel more like hisself."

Madeline winced, startled that her old mammy's words so closely paralleled her own thought. She shouldn't have gone to visit her aunt in Virginia. She had known at the time that her father hadn't been interested in running the sugar plantation on his own, let alone in supervising things at the mill. She had known that since she'd been old enough to ride around by herself. At first, she had just offered suggestions to her father now and again, whenever she'd noticed things were running less than smoothly. Gradually, however, she had taken over most of the decisions. It hadn't been that difficult. Zeb Turner was an efficient manager, and despite an initial reluctance on his part she and that crusty old gentleman had developed quite a good working relationship. She had even thought he'd liked and admired her, grudgingly, of course. But that was before he'd left—just disappeared one day over a year past, with nary a word. Papa had said the wanderlust must have gotten him, but Madeline had never believed it, though after her own experiences at sea she was closer to understanding what her father meant.

Eli Creely had shown up as if by Providence, not long after that, and he'd seemed to have a real flair for managing Hopewell. If he hadn't, of course, Madeline would have put her foot down and refused to go to Williamsburg. Which is exactly what she should have done, since it was obvious her father's worrying and fretting over the running of the sugar plantation had affected his health.

She sighed and nodded absently as Hattie picked a length of rose-colored ribbon from her dresser. "I never should have left."

Hattie's hands found their way to her ample hips. "Da massa, he wanted you to have a good time, maybe find a husband," she admonished, as if Madeline was highly ungrateful.

Madeline laughed in spite of herself. "I know exactly what Papa had in mind for my little visit, but you see it didn't work."

"Well now, Miz Madeline, and whose fault does ya think that is?"

"Why, Hattie," Madeline asked, her eyes dancing in amusement, "are you implying it is my fault I did not find a husband?"

"Humph" was the black woman's only response.

"I did have someone ask for my hand, you know." Madeline bit her tongue because she hadn't meant to tell anyone, but it was too late.

The whites of Hattie's eyes showed sharp contrast to her dark skin as she gaped at Madeline. "Then why didn't ya bring a strong husband back here?"

That was a good question, one she hadn't seriously considered before. She had liked Philip Spencer well enough. He was handsome, charming, and was obviously enthralled with her, but then she had gotten her father's last post and had left. She hadn't departed without a word, of course. She had sent a note for him, explaining her sudden departure.

Madeline simply replied, "I left."

"Ya left a man who wanted to marry ya?"

The young woman wondered if Hattie's eyes could stretch any wider. Agitated by her old mammy's response, Madeline suddenly stood. Why, Hattie almost acted as though she had left the only man in the world who would ever want to marry her!

"Yes, I left," she said with conviction. "I received Papa's letter, and I left. And I'm glad I did. I didn't really want to marry him anyway. Hand me my dress. I'm going downstairs to get rid of that visitor. Who is he anyway?"

53

Hattie helped Madeline smooth the overskirt of her pale rose silk lustringed taffeta. "He's a friend of da massa and"—Hattie rolled her eyes—"one beautiful man."

"Beautiful?" Madeline laughed. "A friend of my father's?" She could think of several acquaintances who might have come to call but not one who could be described as beautiful. As a matter of fact, she decided she had never seen a man she would call beautiful except maybe . . . No. He was too tall and virile to be called beautiful—handsome certainly, but not beautiful. Recalling the captain of the rescue ship gave her a twinge of pain. She'd thought she had succeeded in pushing him from her mind. "Men aren't beautiful, Hattie," Madeline stated with as much conviction as her twenty-one years would allow. "They are handsome at best."

"Yes'm, Miz Madeline," Hattie agreed, but her wicked grin was made all the more lascivious by her missing teeth.

Silly old woman, Madeline thought somewhat unkindly as the heels of her brocaded silk slippers drummed determinedly against the steps. I care not if he is handsome or beautiful or ugly as sin; he shall find his visit cut as short as courtesy allows.

Madeline swept through the wide central hallway, thankful for the cooling breezes that traversed the area. The dark mahogany door of the library was closed, but when she rapped her father bid her to enter. His voice, if nothing else, remained staunch and firm.

The interior of the room was cool and dim, smelling mildly of pipe tobacco, just the haven she'd remembered from the heat of a tropical day. Her eyes searched for her father and found him sitting, as was to be expected, in the depths of his favorite leather chair. Madeline thought at first Hattie had been mistaken, had imagined this veritable god of a visitor. Except for Papa and herself, the room seemed quite empty. Then she heard it. A slight movement behind her, near the rows of leather-bound volumes she and her father often read and discussed. Patrick O'Neil's visitor must enjoy literature, she thought idly as she turned, a smile of welcome beginning to curve her lips. But then she froze, the half-formed smile still teasing the corners of her mouth, her eyes large with shock. "You," she breathed, and could say no more.

Chapter 5

Joshua hardly noticed the girl who entered. As his callused thumb idly traced the spine on the volume of Voltaire he held, his gaze rested on the older man seated across the room. The tall mahogany clock in the corner had moments earlier tolled the passing of an hour since he'd first met Patrick O'Neil, yet Joshua already felt more comfortable with this man than with many people he had known all his life.

Hell, it wasn't people in general of whom he was thinking. It was his father. These two men had been friends. His father had mentioned it, and Patrick O'Neil had confirmed it. Yet it was still hard to believe. Where Justin Whitlock had been stern and inflexible, always certain his own beliefs were right, Patrick O'Neil appeared to have the open mind of a philosopher. He was not judgmental. Joshua had realized this while they were discussing England's Acts of Trade and Navigation. Patrick O'Neil could see both sides of the issue and, more importantly, respect another's right to a point of view. How very different he is from Father, he mused.

"That will be Madeline now," Patrick had said in response to the light tapping at the door. "Stay clear of her temper, boy. She'll be mad as hell because I'm down here. I promised her I'd stay in bed today," he added with a chuckle as he drew his frail form to a more upright position.

Joshua looked from father to daughter. His mind registering a rustle of silk and the pleasing tilt of a chin just visible behind cascades of golden-brown curls before she faced him. Then her jaw dropped, and her wide-eyed expression made the hair on the back of his neck prickle. That she thought she knew him was evident by that whispered "You," that she hated him was even more obvious as the shock in the green depths of her eyes was replaced by bitter scorn.

What made this encounter all the more disconcerting was that Joshua could not place her. If he had met her in Kingston on his last voyage she would have been a mere child, and he had never done anything to one so young that could warrant such hostility. His eyes quickly tracked over her slight frame as his mind raced feverishly. Her body was small but nicely rounded, not at all unpleasant. Certainly he would remember her if they had met before. Obviously she was the one whose memory was failing. His gaze sought hers and the instant deepest onyx met piercing emerald, he knew who she was. It had not been the sun-reddened skin that had made her eyes appear so green when he had last encountered her in his cabin. For, with the exception of the twin dots of angry color that adorned her cheeks, her face was a ghostly white. As he felt the hot blush of guilt pulse upward beyond his stock, he thought they must appear quite a pair.

How? Why? The questions that flooded his mind would have to wait. Patrick O'Neil was saying their names, rising slowly from his chair to make the introductions.

Madeline wanted to scream. Fearing that she would, she clamped her teeth together till her jaws ached. How dare he come here! How dare he!

"Madeline?"

"What?" she snapped at her father, then colored to match the deep rose of her gown upon realizing what she

57

had done.

But Patrick only laughed. "See, Joshua, I told you she'd be angry because I'm not in bed. Stop fussing so, Madeline. I feel quite well."

Pasting a poor imitation of her usual smile on lips suddenly gone dry, Madeline watched her father exchange a knowing glance with the man he called Joshua. "I am not angry, Papa."

"I see." Her father's tone was disbelieving. "Then perhaps you could give Captain Whitlock a proper greeting."

Madeline noticed the thickening of her father's Irish brogue. It was a subtle change, this return to the inflection of his ancestors. It occurred when he was amused. He's enjoying this, Madeline realized. He realizes this man has me flustered. She wished she could tell him the reason for her state. Then he might not find the situation so amusing. But, of course, she never would. "Sorry, Papa." Madeline made a slight curtsy. "Captain Whitlock," she murmured without even looking his way.

"That's my girl. What did I tell you, Joshua? She never stays in a temper for long."

Captain Whitlock stayed for dinner, and it was during that unpleasant meal that Madeline learned her father and his father had been friends and business partners. Papa had never mentioned owning a share in the ship he had captained, the *Providence*.

Madeline sat at the polished mahogany dining-room table. The rich, spicy tang of pepper pot soup tickled her tongue as her father and this man discussed sea travel. She toyed absently with fried conch as they debated the effects of Pitt's war plan. And she blurted out "Three days!" when she heard her father extend the hospitality of Hopewell to the captain.

"Madeline, are you all right?" Her father's gaunt face was a mask of concern.

"Yes! No!" She was acting like a complete fool and she knew it. Three days was on the short side for a visitor's stay at the plantation, yet she could not imagine surviving a longer one. "I'm tired. Riding over the cane fields again is going to take some getting used to," she offered by way of explanation for her outburst. "If you will excuse me, I am in need of some fresh air, and then I'll retire."

"Of course, my dear." Her father's hot, dry hand covered hers. "I understand. Madeline has been in Williamsburg visiting her aunt. She only preceded your arrival here, by one day, Captain." Her father explained as she made good her escape.

The cool smooth surface of the pillar that partially supported the sweeping veranda relieved some of the heat in her cheek as Madeline pressed herself against it. The night was soft, tender. A gentle breeze laced with the heady fragrance of jasmine curled its way up from the bay. She stretched out her arms and slowly lifted the heavy fall of curls from her neck. Her movements were innocent in intent, but to the man who watched from the shadows, the silvery glow of moonlight gilded her silhouette in a shockingly sensual way.

"I convinced your father I needed fresh air, too."

The shining halo of hair tumbled down her back as Madeline whirled toward the deep voice she remembered too well.

"Well, find it elsewhere!"

Joshua chuckled. "You're a hard woman, Madeline O'Neil." The puddle of moonlight beckoned him even if the woman standing in it did not. "At least now I know 'tis really you. The meek little lady I met earlier this evening hardly seemed capable of throwing cutlery about my cabin."

Madeline glared up at him. She was in the mood for neither banter nor his company. She turned toward the French doors.

"Wait." Joshua grabbed a satin-covered arm, effectively halting her retreat. "What the hell is going on here?"

Madeline looked at the hand, large and brown, that

59

contrasted with the shimmering rose of her dress, then up at the man who towered over her. "You are quite the bully, aren't you?"

Her words were spoken with a quiet dignity that shamed him. He dropped his hand. "I apologize. I won't touch you again." Joshua stepped back as if to prove his good intentions.

It was the perfect time to leave. She wanted to, but for some unknown reason Madeline could only stand on the veranda and stare. He looked as handsome as she remembered, even in the dim light afforded by the full moon. His eyes were blacker than black, their obsidian sparkle the only indication they watched her. He started to speak, then stopped, his lips moving soundlessly. Had they moved thus against her own?

He advanced slightly, and Madeline flinched. My God, had he read her mind?

"That night in my cabin . . ."

"Good night, Captain." She turned quietly on her heel and withdrew into the shadows, unwilling to think about, much less speak of, what had happened.

"I need to tell you." His voice held such urgency Madeline stopped, but she did not face him. "I thought you were like the others."

Others? What was he talking about? The only other women aboard were Lettie and her friends, and they were . . .

Indignation seized her. She turned on him, her tawny curls spilling across her shoulder. "You thought I was a whore!"

Joshua's eyes flew open in shock, and he glanced toward the house. "Lord, will you watch your language?"

"You"—she stabbed at his waistcoat with the tip of her finger—"take an innocent young woman and treat her like a— Oh, you know what you did to me, and then you have the audacity to complain about my language!" Her words had been well punctuated, but her voice had been lower.

60

"Well, you could have told me."

"Told you!"

"Aye, it would have staved off quite a few problems if you had simply let me know."

Of all the nerve! He was trying to lay his dastardly deed at her feet. "Captain Whitlock, it has never been my practice to start a conversation with the phrase, 'I am not a whore.'"

"For heaven's sake, would you stop using that word?" Joshua took her arm to pull her away from the door, but dropped it abruptly when he saw her expression.

"Does it strain your sensibilities to hear it?" she hissed.

"When you speak it, yes."

"I see. In your opinion it is acceptable for me to be treated as a whore, yet unacceptable for me to voice the word."

Joshua's jaw tensed, then fell slack. God, she was even worse than he remembered. Full of vinegar, wasn't that what Oliver had said? Well, the arguing was getting them nowhere. It was time for a cooler head to prevail—his. "It would be desirable if we discussed this situation in a more civilized manner."

"Is that the way you usually discuss matters such as this?"

"Dammit, Maddie, I do not make a habit of conducting this type of conversation!" Now she had him yelling. Joshua's fingers further mussed his wayward black locks. He needed to think, but was finding it almost impossible to do so. How had he gotten into this mess, anyway? Oliver, damn his crusty hide. Nothin' like a good roll in the hay to make me sleep . . . Well, Joshua had had his tussle, though the experience had not even been gratifying enough to remember, and now he was paying the price.

And what price did one pay for stripping a lady of her virtue? Joshua sighed—a sound barely audible in the tropical night, yet one that Madeline did not miss. "I will

61

marry you."

"What did you say?"

"You heard me, dammit. I said I'd marry you. That is what you expect, isn't it?" God, he couldn't believe he was saying it, sacrificing himself like this. But it must have been what she was waiting for because her demeanor certainly changed. Her hickory-straight backbone became more pliant, and her entire body seemed to flow toward him, though he could have sworn she hadn't taken a step. And a smile sweetly curved her lips—too sweetly.

"Why, Captain Whitlock," she crooned, "you would do that for me?"

Black eyes narrowed suspiciously.

She closed the gap between them with a rustle of silk. "You are too kind, too gallant for words."

With her nearness the fragrance of roses, newly washed by a June shower, wafted around him. He watched her lips, remembering how soft and inviting they could be.

"There is just one little problem."

She was so tiny, but if he lowered his head and held her close . . .

"I would not marry you if the alternative were to be boiled in oil, you arrogant bastard!"

Joshua came back to reality with a start. To think he had almost considered kissing the shrew. "Does your father know of the language you use?"

Madeline was halfway across the tile floor when she turned and shot back, "There are other things my father doesn't know, and somehow I cannot believe my language would be so disturbing, were he to find out all!"

Joshua ignored her jibe. "And what if you are with child?"

"How dare you speak to me of such things. I am going inside."

"It's not unheard of that a child be conceived when two people do what we did." He was purposely making her angry now, and thoroughly enjoying it. The boiled-in-oil remark had riled him.

"*WE* did not do anything, Captain. You alone are the guilty party."

"Me, we—that matters not, my dear Maddie. The point is the possibility of conception remains."

"Well, you needn't worry."

"Are you certain?" A raven brow cocked questioningly.

Madeline wasn't certain of anything at that moment, least of all whether or not she was enceinte, but she refused to stand there and discuss such a personal matter with this vile man. "Of course I'm certain."

His relief was evident.

"How much longer are we to endure your odious company?" Madeline gripped the brass knob of the French door.

Joshua presented a leg and bowed stiffly to her back. "I shall remove myself by tomorrow afternoon."

She tipped her chin, glancing at him over her shoulder. "The morning would be preferable."

"I am most unhappy to disappoint you, but I have come to Hopewell for a purpose, and I will not leave until it is realized."

"See that your business is accomplished as far from my presence as possible!" Madeline opened the door.

"It will be my pleasure, Mistress O'Neil."

His acerbic voice followed her as she crossed the polished floor of the center hall.

Chapter 6

When Madeline opened her eyes the next morning only the slightest hint of pearly gray brushed the heavens. With as much haste as the grainy darkness of predawn allowed, she shed her nightrail in favor of a linen chemise. Tying the corset laces was a struggle, but she could not call for Hattie's help. Papa had asked her to show Captain Whitlock around Hopewell, and the only way she could get out of that dreadful chore was to leave the house before their guest awoke. The riding habit she chose was well worn but sturdy. Its hue of washed-out indigo hardly had the appeal of the more colorful outfits she had brought back from Williamsburg, but this one had always been her favorite. And it was easy to don.

When the last button was fastened, Madeline cast a worried eye toward the window. The dull pewter sky obscured the night's sparkle of stars. More anxious than ever to be out of the great house, she ran a brush through her curls, jammed a floppy island-woven bonnet on her head, and grabbed her riding boots. Time enough to put those on when she reached the front veranda.

She tiptoed down the hall, interrupting her departure only long enough to notice whether any light shone beneath their guest's door. Total darkness. He must still be sound asleep. The thought so elated her, she gave a small hop, stubbing her unshod toe on the banister's newel in the process.

"Ouch!" Madeline clutched her wounded appendage, all the while watching the captain's doorway. Counting the moments by heartbeats she watched for a pale thread of light under his door. When none appeared—he was a deep sleeper or her outcry had sounded louder to her own ears than it actually was—she descended the stairs. Only cool gray shadows awaited her in the wide central hall. She turned the brass knob of the heavy paneled door, thankful for its well-oiled hinges, and quickly slipped through the narrow opening she had allowed herself. The veranda's gray and white tiles, brought to Jamaica long ago as ballast on some voyage, chilled her stockinged feet so she wriggled into her boots with dispatch.

The wispy white gauze of mist did little to muffle the crunching of her boots on the shelled drive, but by now Madeline didn't care. The guest bedrooms, like her own, faced the bay. The entire house would block any sounds she might make.

Madeline was sorely tempted by the fragrance of fresh-baked bread as she crossed the dewy grass by the kitchen. Even this early the cooks were busy preparing all the food needed to fill the bellies of Hopewell's people. Her growling stomach almost convinced her to make a side trip into the whitewashed log building. Almost. But not even for a hunk of bread, Bessie's bread, did she want to explain to her father why she was up and about so early. Let Papa and Captain Whitlock think she had missed them by mere minutes.

Just the thought of the captain sent her tramping through the grass with a vengeance. That insincere proposal of marriage he had offered was the most embarrassing thing she'd ever experienced. Madeline paused and kicked at a clump of weeds. No. His reference to the possibility of her being with child was the most embarrassing. The thought that she might be carrying his child led her to ponder the act that would have produced such a consequence. Could anything ever have been as

65

disconcerting as awakening with the captain's large muscular frame draped over her? The memory was so vivid Madeline could almost feel his hard, hair-roughened body against her tender skin. A prickle of gooseflesh—not entirely an unpleasant sensation—swept over her.

Annoyed by her reaction, Madeline jammed her hands into the riding gloves she had brought. Thank heavens he would be gone by the time she returned to the house, and she'd never have to see him again. The thought lightened her step as she entered the ripe, hazy world of the stables.

"Looking for me?" The words pierced the muffled, expected sounds of hooves stomping and horses' snorting, shattering the early morning peace. Madeline, who was about to lift the latch to Medusa's stall, could only turn and gape at the man casually leaning against a supporting beam. He was dressed in snug-fitting buff breeches that were thrust into gleaming black boots. As he pushed off from the beam, his snowy white shirt was stretched taut over the muscles of his broad chest and shoulders. "I expected you earlier." Joshua advanced on Madeline, pausing only long enough to shut her dropped jaw with the upward motion of a single finger before proceeding to lead Medusa from her stall.

This brief touch galvanized Madeline into action. "Why aren't you in bed?" she hissed, her fists pressed tightly against her hips.

Joshua shrugged. "Too lonesome."

Madeline could sense the silent laughter in his voice, though none of it registered on the chiseled planes of his handsome face.

"One would think you'd be used to that." The words were out before she considered their implication. The midnight twinkle in his eyes made her vow to forgo further impetuous speech.

"Give me that." Madeline grabbed the bridle from Joshua's hands as he began to put it on her mare. "I will saddle my own horse, and then"—she gave him an

66

imperious glance—"I am riding out of here—alone."

"Tsk, tsk," Joshua shook his head, his smile very near the surface now. "Such a disobedient wench. Don't tell me you have forgotten your father's request that you show me around Hopewell."

Madeline fitted the bit into Medusa's mouth. "I haven't forgotten. I'm simply choosing to ignore it."

"Does Patrick O'Neil know what a rebellious daughter he has, I wonder?"

Rebellious daughter indeed! Madeline could barely control her temper as she lugged the saddle over to Medusa. She had always done exactly as her father had asked. The very fact that she'd come to know this horrid man who rested his forearms on the uneven boards of Medusa's stall was testimony to that. Papa was the one who had wanted her to go to Williamsburg, and her return from that visit had set her up for Captain Whitlock's "rescue."

Madeline slanted a glance toward the captain. A piece of straw had found its way between his straight white teeth. He lounged lazily against the rough boards, seemingly unaware of the effort she was exerting to perform the unaccustomed task of saddling her own horse. He looked indolent and supine and more virile than any man had a right to look.

It wasn't until Madeline had tightened the cinch that Joshua eased his body to its full height and walked toward the door.

"Move out of my way." Madeline led Medusa toward his imposing figure, but he stood his ground.

"I think not, little Maddie. Your father promised me a guide, and you, I gather, are the best available."

"I will not shepherd you about." Madeline's chest heaved in impotent anger as he continued to stand between her and the stable door.

"Oh, I think you will." Joshua smiled down at the young woman glaring at him from beneath a ridiculous straw hat. "Because if you don't, I may be forced to explain the reason for your reluctance to your father."

"You wouldn't!"

"Wouldn't I?" Joshua cocked his head to one side.
"But he's old and ill. Surely even you can see that. The
shock might, might . . ."

"It's your choice, Maddie."

Madeline nearly shook with rage. "You bastard, you
rotten, no good, low-down—"

"Ah, Maddie," Joshua interrupted. "You have such a
colorful vocabulary, but this little recitation is only
wasting time, and I thought your greatest desire was to
see me gone as quickly as possible."

"It is," she gritted out through clenched teeth.

"How nice, Maddie. We finally agree upon something,
for I am just as anxious to quit this plantation as you are
to bid me good riddance. So you see," Joshua explained,
"the sooner I assuage my curiosity, the sooner we can
both be happy."

Madeline was silent for a moment. She didn't really
think he would go to her father, though she was in no way
certain that showing him around would make him leave.
Still, it was probably her best course of action. "All
right," she finally agreed. "I'll play the guide, but I want
to make one thing perfectly clear."

"And that is?"

Madeline sighed. "I do not like you, nor do I wish to be
in your company, so there are to be no pleasantries between us."

Joshua grinned, "Hardly an amiable attitude."

Green eyes flashed. "I don't feel amiable; besides, I
thought you were in a hurry." With a gentle command
and a not-so-gentle tug of the reins, Madeline maneuvered Medusa and herself outside into the fast-ap-
proaching day.

"Oh, I am, Maddie," Joshua assured her, and he
followed close on her heels despite the time it took him to
retrieve the dun-colored stallion he had chosen and
saddled earlier.

"One more thing." She stopped abruptly. "Do not call me 'Maddie'!"

"What am I to call you then?"

"Nothing. You need call me absolutely nothing. Don't even talk to me."

"That's quite all right with me except . . ." The last word was fertile with meaning as it hung in the space that separated them.

Try as she might Madeline was not totally immune to his charm. "Except what?"

"Except, if I can't speak to you I won't be able to ask you."

"Oh, for heaven's sake, ask me what?"

Joshua reached into his saddlebag and pulled out a package wrapped in a linen napkin. With the slow pace of a born tease, he exposed the contents. "Ask if you would like this." He extended his arm to Madeline two chunks of fragrant bread lathered with butter and jam. "A woman called Bessie said this was a favorite of yours."

Madeline's stomach growled. She swallowed compulsively to counteract the effect the sight and smell of the bread was having on her, suddenly wishing she could throw it in his face or toss it to the ground and stomp on it. But she didn't. In the end, hunger prevailed over pride and she accepted his gift, favoring him with an icy glare and a mumbled thank you.

Joshua watched her bite into the bread as if she suspected it might be poisoned. Silly chit, he thought. He hadn't had to bring her the food. He didn't even know why he'd bothered. When he'd stopped in the kitchen before dawn, the cook had been only too eager to fix him a hearty breakfast. It hadn't been till he was leaving the cozy building that he'd thought about Madeline. He'd figured she'd try to get out of acting as guide. Even their short acquaintance had given him some insight into the workings of her rather clever mind. She wouldn't directly disobey. That would provoke too many questions. No. He had guessed right. She had planned to be up and gone before he awakened. Well, he had foiled her little scheme.

So, why had he brought her breakfast? Joshua watched her hungrily eat the bread. She was apparently convinced that he meant her no harm. He studied the tiny figure clothed in faded blue. She was too thin by half. Could she still be feeling the effects of her ordeal on the open sea? Worry over her father's health had probably done nothing to improve her state either. Well, whatever the reason, he was sorry to be adding to her troubles, sorrier still that he'd threatened her earlier. But he had already wasted too much time searching for Nathaniel, and if there was a clue to his whereabouts on Hopewell, he could use some assistance, albeit reluctant, in finding it. Still he hoped Madeline didn't truly believe he would have gone to her father with an account of their first meeting. Hell, sick as he was, Patrick O'Neil would probably tear him limb from limb if he did find out.

"Are you ready?"

Madeline's words put a stop to his musings.

"Ready." Joshua leaned down to give her a leg up onto the black mare. The movement put him on eye level with her waist. Had he thought her too thin? Joshua's gaze lingered on the part of her that separated gently rounded hips from the soft rise of her breasts. He revised his assessment. Fragile. Yes, he would have to say her waist was more fragile than thin. Fragile and very feminine.

As Madeline placed her foot into the cupped hands held out for her, Joshua forced himself to look down at what he was doing. Her feet were tiny, even shod in riding boots. He straightened as she settled her bottom into the sidesaddle. Maybe she wasn't too thin.

Shaking his head to clear his errant thoughts, Joshua mounted the impatiently stomping stallion and led the way toward the manor's drive.

"Would you answer a question for me, Captain?" The sun had exploded full-blown and tropic-bright over the horizon.

"Does this mean we're speaking now?" Joshua glanced over at the woman whose mount kept pace with his own. He caught her baleful look.

"What is your interest in Hopewell?"

"Maybe I have a burning desire to learn all I can about sugar cane." This comment earned him another look—one of disbelief.

They had reached the end of the drive lined with coconut palms, and Madeline reined in Medusa. She shaded her eyes so she might gaze over the swaying stalks of sugar cane. "Does this burning desire call you toward the fields or the mill?"

Joshua leaned on the pummel of his saddle and cocked his head. For the moment he appeared intent on the tropical morning sounds. "I think I hear the wharf calling."

"The wharf?"

"Hopewell does have a wharf, doesn't it?"

"Of course, we have a wharf. I just can't understand why you'd want to see it. Nothing is going on there at this time of year."

"Are you refusing to show me the wharf?" Joshua's dark eyes glittered mischievously as he positioned his stallion close to Madeline's horse. Due to the maneuver, his leg brushed against the blue material of Madeline's riding habit. The nearness was disturbing to her. It washed her in warmth and stole the air from her lungs.

"No." The word was little more than a breathy whisper. Madeline swallowed and forced herself to look down at her gloved hands. "We can go to the wharf if you like." Relieved that her words sounded almost normal, Madeline turned her horse down the road toward the bay.

Joshua chuckled, then galloped after her retreating figure. He was having too much fun teasing her, and even, he admitted, hearing her sharp little retorts. But now it was time to get down to the business at hand. Maybe he could find some clue at the wharf. If Henry Smythe had been correct about the large amounts of

71

flour being sold from Hopewell, then it had to be coming from someplace, and the sea was the most likely source.

It took Joshua a moment to catch up with Madeline. She hadn't slowed her pace when she'd headed for the wharf, so he gave the stallion free rein and galloped along the road beside her. She was an admirable horsewoman. Her seat rivaled any Joshua had seen in Maryland.

"If we're racing, don't you think you should have told me?" he yelled over the rhythmic pounding of the horse's hooves.

"We're not racing." The wind whipped tawny curls across Madeline's face as she turned her head to offer her riposte. The captain flashed her a broad grin and, regardless of his words, appeared to be enjoying the run. His muscular legs hugged the dun's flanks, and the two powerful animals seemed to move as one. It was obvious to Madeline that Joshua could have left her behind at any time, but he was content to temper his horse's speed to keep their undeclared race competitive.

The turnoff to the wharf was just before the mill, and it was there that Madeline slowed Medusa to a walk. It took a few moments for Joshua to realize his mount had galloped on, but as soon as he did, he turned and cantered back to where Madeline sat. Her hair was in disarray, windblown curls flying about beneath the loose lattice-work of her hat, flowing across her narrow shoulders, down her back, and over her small rounded breasts. It was at these that Joshua stared. The exertion of the ride had obviously winded her, for with each breath her chest expanded to accommodate the needed air. Joshua found the process fascinating, and would have watched it much longer if he hadn't sensed Madeline's glare. He looked up into green eyes in time to see her watching him as he watched her.

He smiled; she didn't.

"Race over?"

"We were never racing." Madeline's reply was curt. The nerve of the man, to stare at her like that. He hadn't

72

even feigned innocence when she'd caught him, only given her that stupid grin, as if that made it all right. Well, it didn't, especially when his was the kind of smile that made her wonder if he could see what the hot touch of his black eyes did to her. Of their own volition her breasts had swollen and their tips had hardened, as if making themselves ready for more than just his eyes to feast upon. Shocked by her thoughts, Madeline pulled sharply on Medusa's reins. "The wharf is this way."

They rode the remaining distance in silence. The tangy fragrance of sea air heralded their arrival at the bay before they left the shaded coolness of the road.

Joshua dismounted and reached up for Madeline. She hesitated a moment, sure that he would let his hands linger on her waist and uncertain of her own reaction. But she needn't have worried, for the captain acted as if he couldn't let her go fast enough.

"So, this is Hopewell's wharf." He sounded incredulous as he viewed the area.

Madeline was appalled at seeing the structure she had not viewed in over nine months. "Damn you, Eli Creely." The words slipped out without her noticing as she walked along the wharf. She proceeded cautiously, careful not to step on one of the many rotting boards. Because she had been in Williamsburg, Madeline had missed last season's storms, but there was no doubt in her mind as she surveyed the damage that they had been bad. Still, why hadn't the wharf been repaired? In another three months the small droguers that picked up sugar from coastal plantations would start arriving. By the looks of several of the pilings the wharf was lucky to support Madeline's slight frame, let alone the weight of burly slaves with cones of sugar and hogsheads of rum.

Well, she would get to the bottom of this and quickly. Madeline turned and marched back toward the beach, heedless of the man who knelt at the edge of the wharf assessing the structural damage.

"Where are you going?" Joshua jumped up as she

73

swept past him.

"The storage sheds." Madeline didn't break stride.

Joshua caught up to her as she pried open the door. The interior smelled of rum and dampness. It reminded him of the *Chesapeake*'s hold.

"Just look at that!" Madeline was washed by a beam of sunlight as she pointed toward the roof.

"You've got yourself a pretty big hole there."

Her eyes snapped toward him. "I know what I have. What I want to know is why."

Joshua accompanied Madeline on her tour of other equally dilapidated sheds, all the while scouring the area for anything that seemed out of place.

Nothing did. If contraband cargo was coming into Hopewell it wasn't being unloaded here, at least not recently.

"Is this Hopewell's only wharf?" Joshua had followed her back to the horses.

"Yes, the only large one."

"There isn't any other natural harbor deep enough for seagoing vessels on the plantation?"

Madeline shaded her eyes from the sun as she stared up at him. "Not that we use. Why do you ask?"

"Just curious," Joshua shrugged. "Do you think we could take a look at it?"

"No."

"Why not?" He helped her up onto the saddle.

"Because the tour is over. I have work to do. And"— Madeline held up her hand as if to stave off an attack— "Don't bother threatening me. I have no more time for your silly games."

Joshua assumed an expression of shocked indignation. "I'm hurt by your implication that I would threaten a defenseless woman."

She gave him a wry look. "Just follow this road and you'll find your way back to the great house. As a matter of fact, you can follow it the entire way to Kingston."

He ignored her directions and turned the dun to follow

her mare off the main road. "Where are you going?"

Madeline stopped Medusa and circled back toward the man following her. She had fervently hoped she'd seen the last of him, but she should have known better.

"I am going to find Eli Creely." At this quizzical look, she added, "My plantation manager."

"May I come?"

"No."

"Why not?"

"Because I must see him on plantation business," she explained none too patiently.

"But you told me you were going to teach me to run a sugar plantation."

Madeline bristled. "I never said anything of the sort." She would have continued with her denials, but she noticed the laughter lurking in his dark eyes. She took a deep breath, trying to control her anger. It wasn't enough that her plantation manager was letting the place crumble around them; now she had to deal with this . . . this . . . Words failed her. "Captain Whitlock," she began, with as much authority as she could muster.

"Yes, Mistress O'Neil." All respectful innocence.

Madeline ignored that. "I have no idea why you have chosen to bedevil my life, but let me assure you I do not believe for one minute that you are here because you wish to master the workings of a sugar plantation."

"And why is it so difficult to believe that I may want to settle on a plantation?"

"Because, Captain, you would be forced to give up the sea, and that is something you would not want to do."

"Ah, Maddie, you do know me well."

Madeline's cheeks reddened. She was shocked by the familiarity the words implied—familiarity not of the physical sort, though she could not deny there had been that, but emotional intimacy. She knew the way he felt about things. And she had no idea how she knew.

He seemed to be reading her thoughts as he watched her with those bottomless, ebony eyes. It was unsettling.

"Oh, come along if you must." Her manner was brusque. "I don't care why you're here. Just do whatever it is you came to do and then be on your way."

"I wish I could, Maddie, I wish I could," Joshua whispered, but the trade winds caught his words and bore them away unheard.

The sugar works was situated by a fast-moving tributary of the Hope River, well downwind of the great house. As Joshua and Madeline rode past the boiling house, several dark-skinned workers emerged from within. Their sweat-slick bodies attested to the heat produced by the fires burning under the nine giant cauldrons.

"Do you know where I might find Mr. Creely?" Madeline bent forward to pat Medusa's neck.

Her question was met by mumblings and motions Madeline took to mean no.

At the mill she had more success. "He be out in da east cane piece, Miz Madeline." A slave carrying a bundle of trash, the pithy remains of the sugar stalk, had responded to her query.

"This should have been the last crop from the season's stubble," Madeline explained as she rode between the tall grassy plants that reached near as high as Medusa's withers.

"And it isn't?" Joshua knew little more about sugar than how to pack it in his sloop's hull and how much he liked it in his tea, but he sensed there was more wrong here than a pier in disrepair.

"No." Madeline removed her hat and dabbed at her perspiring forehead with a handkerchief. "On my way home from Kingston I passed fields that had been cut and allowed to sprout." At his puzzled look, she continued. "Once a year, especially for the prime growing time, we plant new stem cuttings. In between plantings we just allow the cut-off stems to sprout, but if you do that too often, the yield becomes poor.

"There he is." Madeline directed her mare down a

dusty trail not much wider than the wheel marks of the cart that sat awaiting the cut sugar cane. "Mr. Creely, a word with you, please," she called out to a man Joshua assumed to be the manager.

Eli Creely was leaning against the cart, toying absently with the splayed ends of the whip looped through his belt. He took his time in ambling forward, though it had been obvious from the jerk of his head that he had seen the approaching riders long before Madeline had called out.

"Well now, Miz Madeline, didn't expect to see you about today, it bein' so hot and all." He removed his sweat-stained tricorn and wiped a grimy sleeve across his face, as if to emphasize the fact.

"I thought I made it clear to you yesterday, Mr. Creely, that I intend to be about every day." Madeline straightened her shoulders and glared down at the man standing beside Medusa.

"Did ya?" Creely stuffed the hat back onto his head. "I don't rightly recall."

Madeline slid from the saddle onto the road before Joshua knew what she was up to. Dust motes swirled around the hem of her blue riding skirt as she approached Creely. Though having little to recommend him in way of size, he dwarfed the woman before him, but she appeared not to notice.

"And do you recall my asking if all was in readiness at the wharf?"

Creely's narrow eyes shifted toward Joshua sitting atop the gray stallion, then back to Madeline. "Come to think of it, the wharf was mentioned."

Several slaves, naked to the waist, their bodies glistening in the relentless sun, lingered near the cart. They made a show of stacking the deleaved sugar stalks, but the job was finished, and Madeline knew they remained only to listen.

Purposely, she lowered her voice. "I've just come from the wharf. Both it and the storage sheds are sorely in need of repair."

"Ain't got the men."

"Well, you will simply have to find the men, for without the wharf we have no way of exporting the sugar."

"We ain't had no problems so far."

Joshua watched the confrontation with no less interest than the field hands. He had taken an immediate dislike to the plantation manager, and ached to leap down and grab him by the scruff of his neck. But he didn't. He sensed Madeline would welcome no such interference on his part. So, with his leg hooked over the pummel, he watched—and waited.

Madeline was aghast. "Mr. Creely, you don't seem to understand—"

"No, Miz Madeline, it's you that don't understand. We been doing jest fine while you was off on your little trip, and we don't need no help now's you decided to come back. So, why don't you just go on up to the house and do whatever it is you fancy ladies does with your time, and leave the running of these here cane pieces to me." This speech ended as a stream of spittal was propelled from Creely's mouth to land in the black dirt inches in front of Madeline.

She sensed movement behind her an instant before she saw it, barely in time to stop it. The captain, with a fire in his eye that didn't bode well for Creely, had leaped from his horse and crossed to the overseer in the span of a heartbeat. He seemed not to hear her first admonishment. Madeline even thought for a moment that he would bodily remove her as an obstacle to his reaching Creely.

"Captain Whitlock, will you stop!" Something in her tone must have caught his attention because he abruptly desisted. She observed the tic in his clenched jaw as he glowered at the cowering manager. "Joshua." His given name had slipped through her lips. He looked down at her, and his expression softened. She stood very close to him, her hands pressed against his broad chest. His

78

heartbeat vibrated through her body, his smell surrounded her. "I don't need you to fight my battle." She spoke the words quietly, yet there was no denying she meant them.

The distant sound of thunder echoing off mountains erupted suddenly then faded as she waited to see what Joshua would do. Just when Madeline thought she could bear the tension no longer, he nodded once, then stepped back. Her hands, bereft of their resting place, dropped heavily to her sides as she turned to face Creely. He had regained some of his composure and was even uncoiling the braided whip that had hung from his belt. Madeline thought it almost laughable that the little man seemed to think his whip would make a difference if the captain had chosen to ignore her plea.

Madeline approached Creely with more assurance than she felt. None of the slaves made any pretense of working; instead their dark eyes watched her. She could hardly blame them. The scene the three of them had created was, no doubt, more entertaining than bending their backs over the cane. Creely would have his hands full getting them back to work. His authority had suffered crippling blows, the first inflicted by her, the second by the captain. It had been an impetuous act, coming here and confronting the overseer. She shouldn't have done it, but she had just been so angry.

"I want to see you at the great house after dinner." Her words were for Creely's ears alone.

The filthy hat was removed, an awkward bow of the head was attempted, and he mumbled, "Yes, m'lady." But none of these civilities could disguise the contempt that emanated from Creely's pale eyes.

Madeline was angry. Joshua didn't know why it should bother him, but it did. He slanted a glance her way as they rode through a clump of cotton trees. Her back was stiff, her profile sharp and unmoving. Dapples of sunlight filtered through her hat, providing the only animation on her face. Joshua eased the dun slightly forward, trying to catch her eye, but Madeline continued to stare straight ahead. No doubt about it, she was mad as hell.

Joshua purposely turned his head away. She could ignore him until she turned to stone. He'd survey the Blue Mountains. Immense, they were covered with thick tropical forests.

Maybe, he admitted to himself as he watched the thunderclouds roll off their peaks, just maybe he shouldn't have gone after the overseer like that. It had been stupid, and if he'd thought about it, he wouldn't have done it. Well, he might have, but he hadn't thought. He'd only reacted. He'd seen the bastard spit toward her, and the next thing he knew her hands had been on his chest and she'd been imploring him to stop. He had. And it wasn't as if he'd started the quarrel. No, she should have known better than to confront Creely in front of the field hands. So, it really was her fault.

"All right, I'm sorry. Is that what you want to hear?" His words surprised even him.

Madeline cocked her head to one side. "And what, pray tell, are you apologizing for now?"

Joshua watched her through narrowed eyes. "You know damn well what I'm referring to."

"The scene with Creely?" He made no reply so Madeline continued. "I hold myself entirely responsible for what happened."

"You do?" He couldn't keep the amazement from his voice.

"Of course. Knowing the mercurial quality of your character I still let you accompany me."

"My character!" The dun started and jerked his head at the sharp tone of Joshua's words. "That man spit at you!"

"He was angry. I should never have compromised his position like that." Madeline flicked a stray lock of hair behind her shoulder.

"Well, at least you recognize that." Joshua followed Madeline onto a path that twisted through lush foliage. "But what are you going to do about his lackadaisical way of taking care of the plantation?"

"I shall handle it." Her words chilled the heavy, humid air.

"By yourself?"

Eyes as green as the backdrop of vegetation glared at him. "You doubt I can?"

"Hell, Maddie, I'm the man you ordered about at knife point."

"Razor," Madeline corrected.

"Sorry, razor point." He continued, "I don't doubt you can do anything you set your mind to. I'm just saying it won't be easy. You could use some help."

"This isn't another proposal of marriage, is it?"

"Hell, no." Joshua threw back his head with laughter. "One unfavorable comparison to boiling oil is enough for me."

Madeline smiled. "Good." She slipped from her saddle. "Let me take care of Mr. Creely."

Joshua dismounted, noticing his surroundings for the first time. "Where are we?"

"You asked earlier if Hopewell had any other natural harbors. This is the only other one I know about."

Chapter 7

"This was the location of Hopewell's first wharf, when my grandfather was alive." Madeline led the black mare to the edge of the beach and looped the reins around a bamboo plant. "Papa moved the wharf to its present location when the new mill was built."

"Was your grandfather the first O'Neil to live here?"

Madeline laughed. "You're fortunate he's buried in the family plot behind the great house. If he ever heard you call him an O'Neil you'd probably find yourself called out as a matter of honor. He was a Bartlett, and Hopewell had belonged to his family since the Treaty of Madrid."

"I certainly meant no disrespect." The corners of Joshua's mouth twitched merrily. "I gather old grandpa wasn't too pleased with the O'Neil name.

Madeline shrugged as she walked toward the shoreline. "The name, the man, there was no difference as far as Grandfather Bartlett was concerned. He disliked both equally. Till his dying day he never considered an upstart Irish sea captain worthy of his daughter or Hopewell."

Joshua fell in step beside her. "Your father doesn't seem to be the type of man to stay where he isn't wanted."

She stopped suddenly, putting an end to the procession of footprints her boots made in the damp sand.

"Did I say he wasn't wanted?" Madeline eyes glittered in the shadow of her straw hat. "My mother wanted him very much, and his love for her more than compensated for any hardships he endured."

"A case of love conquers all?" The captain sounded cynical.

"Something like that." Madeline began walking again, but her mind was on his words. She wondered what could have happened to give him such a jaded concept of love. Perhaps there had been a woman who'd cast him off. Madeline glanced at him surreptitiously. No, that didn't seen likely. Who would do that to him?

The rumbling of thunder made her look at the sky. "I hope you've gained whatever knowledge you sought, for I fear we are in for quite a storm."

Joshua's gaze followed hers toward the angry black clouds that approached from the north.

Damn, with all their chatting about grandfathers and love he had completely forgotten his purpose for coming here. His mind returned instantly to his mission, and Joshua realized that this was a perfect place for unloading contraband. The inlet was deep enough for seagoing vessels, and the beach was secluded and private.

"Aren't you coming?" Madeline had untied her mare and was standing beside it, waiting for Joshua to give her a leg up into the saddle.

The wind, which had picked up considerably, was carrying the hot, sultry air out to a now-choppy sea. It whipped at Madeline's skirts and forced her to jam the straw hat down even further on her head.

Joshua started walking toward her when something unusual about the rocks caught his eye. Some of them, those to the west, appeared to be hollowed out.

"Are these caves?" He moved toward one.

"Yes," Madeline hissed. Her irritation at his lack of haste was evident.

"What are they used for?" Joshua paid no heed to her impatience.

83

Madeline trudged over to him. Evidently more direct methods were needed to get him to leave. "Playing."

He stopped exploring the entrance to the first cave to look up at her questioningly.

"I played in them. That's the only use I know they've ever had. Now will you come on? You may not be familiar with thunderstorms in the tropics but—"

"Recently?"

"What?" Madeline had to yell the word to be heard over the rasping of the wind through the bamboo reeds.

"Have you played in them recently?" Joshua stuck his head out of the opening.

"Of course not! What do you think I am, a child? I don't play anymore." As if his obvious disregard of the weather wasn't enough, now he was insinuating she was some babe in arms who wasted her time cavorting in caves.

Madeline followed him into the opening. After the raucous wind outside, the cavern seemed oddly calm—and very dark. She couldn't even find him.

"Too bad."

The voice emanating from a point above Madeline's right shoulder startled her. "Don't sneak up on me," she snapped. Then, after a slight pause, she asked, "Too bad?"

"Sorry." Joshua took her elbow and guided her back toward the cave entrance. "I meant it's too bad you don't play anymore."

Madeline thought it a bit suggestive for him to be talking about games—at least games that children play. She decided to ignore the remark. Besides, one look outside showed they'd have to hurry to get back to the big house before the storm broke. The heavens, a dark, tempestuous gray, were brightened only by an occasional zigzag of lightning.

"Oh, now look what you've done. We've spent so much time in this stupid cave we'll never make it to the house before it starts raining.

Joshua had to admit she was right. It was going to rain, hard and soon. "I don't suppose you'd want to stay here till the storm blows over?"

Madeline glared at him over her shoulder. "In this cave—with you?"

Joshua nodded, a hint of a smile tugging at the corners of his sensual mouth.

"I think not."

There was no mistaking the grin now. "What's the matter, Maddie? Don't you trust yourself with me?"

Not even the dim light afforded by the cave could mask the green fire in Madeline's eyes. "Why, you conceited oaf! I . . ." The rest of her words were drowned out by Joshua's laughter and the approaching storm which met her head on as she rushed from the shelter.

Though she rode as fast as she could, it had started raining by the time she reached the stables. The captain had changed his mind about staying in the cave, for by the time she'd handed Medusa over to a groom, he appeared and was as wet as she.

Madeline pointedly ignored him, but as soon as she left the stables he caught her by the arm, drawing her toward him.

"Why did you run away?"

"I didn't."

"Like hell you didn't. You lit out of that cave like the devil himself was on your tail."

Madeline stopped and turned on him, oblivious of the rain streaming down her face. His talk of the devil mirrored her own thoughts as she'd run away—for run away she had. "I didn't want to get wet." Her words sounded ludicrous, standing as they were, their clothes soaked and molded to their bodies, water dripping from their chins, eyelashes, and the tips of their noses; Madeline expected to be greeted by one of his hearty laughs.

She wasn't. Instead, he merely stared, if a gaze that intense could be called a stare. It warmed her, and she

85

thought the film of water on her body would begin to sizzle.

"You hadn't a chance of beating the storm."

Madeline swallowed. "I had to try."

"What were you afraid of, Maddie?"

"I told you, the storm." She shifted uncomfortably under his gaze.

"Ah, Maddie, to use your phrase, I think not."

"Then of what?" The moment the breathless words were out of her mouth Madeline knew she'd made a mistake.

He smiled. It was the same smile she'd seen in his cabin and then in her mind's eye.

"This."

Madeline felt the word rather than heard it for his lips were brushing hers.

With a slow, sensual rhythm, his tongue gathered raindrops from the corners of her mouth—tasting, testing. Rainwater had never been so sweet. He wanted more. His tongue delved farther, suddenly driven by a thirst water could not quench.

His neck was slick, warm and wet, as Madeline's arms slipped around that column of sinew and muscle. He straightened, his arms lifting her, pressing her firmly against him. Now her body, like her mind, floated in space.

Their kiss deepened. Her tongue joined in the moist love play, hesitantly at first, then with an ardor that made him moan. The sound rumbled up from his broad chest, more eloquent than words. She could feel it vibrating through her, and molded herself to him, unwilling to miss even the tiniest tremor. The moisture from his clothes seeped through her gown, her shift. It was hot—like him.

Joshua slid her down his long length, seeking some relief from his aching tumescence in the softness of her body. There was none. Rain-soaked clothing was not what he sought. What he wanted—needed—was Madeline, clothed in nothing but him, while he was sheathed in nothing but her.

The thought shocked him enough to bring to a halt his nibbling exploration of her neck. Reluctantly he set her down and away.

Madeline's boots hit the ground with a squish. For whatever reason, the dreamlike world she'd enjoyed only moments ago had been shattered. Her world was still wet, but the falling droplets were no longer a filmy curtain separating her from reality, they were just . . . rain.

It seemed to hit them at the same time, how foolish they must appear standing as they were, unprotected from the elements, for they both ran for the veranda as if their lives depended on reaching it quickly.

Captain Whitlock was the first person Madeline saw when she entered the library that evening. At least she didn't gape this time. Had she learned to expect the unexpected from him, or had she known all the while that he would be there?

"Ah, Captain." She walked across the room and leaned over the back of the leather chair to plant a kiss on her father's cheek. "I thought your plans were to absent yourself from Hopewell by now."

When she straightened, the captain was so close his breath riffled the tiny spirals of tawny hair that had already escaped the lappet cap.

"And deprive myself of such charming company. Do you take me for a fool?" he retorted.

"I don't take you for anything at all, Captain." Madeline moved toward the front of the chair. The brocaded flowers of her pink, ribbed-silk gown fluttered gracefully to the floor as she sank onto the stool by her father's feet.

"Joshua tells me you made an excellent guide today, lass." Her father's voice was more animated this evening, but Madeline had noticed that his cheek had been cold and dry against her lips.

"I did my duty."

She had meant the words to be no more than a jab at the captain, who now leaned against the breakfront bookcase to her right, apparently enthralled by the array of titles therein. But they seemed to go unnoticed. Joshua's head never turned as he looked at the tomes. If anything, he appeared to grow even more intent on studying the leather-bound volumes.

But her father had caught the remark. When Madeline's gaze finally left the captain's white wool broadcloth coat, which was stretched taut to accommodate his muscular shoulders, she noticed Patrick's face revealed his undisguised concern.

"My poor little Madeline," he said. He looked as if all life had been drained from him.

"Papa?" Madeline dropped to her knees and grasped his hand.

"I have put so much responsibility on you these past years, and I've just begun to realize how unfair I've been."

"No, Papa." She squeezed the cold hand wrapped in the warmth of her own, but he didn't seem to notice. When he looked up at her, Madeline blinked to hide the moisture in her eyes.

"You're very attractive, Madeline. Do you know that?" The lace of her lappet cat fluttered as she nodded, but when she met her father's eyes they were no longer focused on her. "Your mother was small like you. Those green eyes are hers, too. Do you know that, Madeline?"

"Yes, Papa." Something was terribly wrong. He seemed to be retreating into the past. "Would you like some wine? I can get you a glass of Madeira." Madeline attempted to force him back to the present.

She thought at first he hadn't heard, for he didn't answer. But when she began to pull away, his hands, all but lifeless moments ago, clamped hers in a death grip.

"Your freckles . . . Elizabeth always hated her freckles. Sun spots, she called them. Tried every cure and potion Hattie came up with. But they never worked. I was glad. I loved those freckles."

"Papa." Madeline couldn't hide the sob as she choked out the word. He hadn't been like this since she was a little girl, since the years right after her mother's death. He had been inconsolable at first. Even the seven-year-old Madeline had seen that, but he had overcome his sorrow. Though he'd still grieved, in time he had become, once again, the loving, slightly boisterous man he'd been before losing his wife.

Till now.

"Madeline, lass, why are you crying?"

She raised wet lashes. His eyes were clear now, though they held a puzzled expression. He wanted a reason for her tears, yet she could give him none.

"My hands." It was a feeble excuse, but the best she could do. "You are hurting my hands."

"Oh, my dear, I'm sorry." His surprisingly strong grip relaxed. Madeline meant to pull her hands away. She wanted to secure the handkerchief in her pocket, but her father still held them. He raised one, then the other. "Such tiny hands, Madeline." He examined them with a father's loving eye. "How unfair for me to have put so much responsibility in them."

Madeline yanked her hands away. "You've never asked me to do anything I didn't want to do."

She couldn't help glancing toward the captain. He had given up any pretense of perusing the collection of classics in the book cases and was now viewing the scene being enacted before him with frank interest. Madeline quickly looked away. His expression of sympathy and understanding was too unsettling to deal with.

Her father was shaking his head. "It took my own sister to show me how selfish I'd been, keeping you here with me all the time."

89

He seemed to be sinking further into melancholy, and obviously her weepy denials weren't helping. "Nonsense." Madeline ignored the tightness around her heart and spoke brusquely. "This is exactly where I've always wanted to be. Now I think you need some rest. Come with me. I'll have a tray sent up later, Papa."

He ignored her.

"You did enjoy Williamsburg, didn't you?"

Madeline cast another cursory glance toward the captain. "Of course I did. Aunt Libby is wonderful. But I was quite ready to come home."

Patrick smiled. He seemed more like himself. "I'm glad you're home, too, lass, but it's just too much for you to handle by yourself."

"What is?" Madeline heard the delicate chair creak as the captain sat down.

"Hopewell. The plantation is too much for you to deal with by yourself."

Madeline crossed her arms. "I'm not by myself. I have you . . . and the manager."

"Oh, Madeline, I've been precious little help to you for years. Elizabeth's father was right. I was never meant to be a sugar planter. And as for the manager, it was different years ago when Zeb Turner was here, but this Creely, he's no good."

Madeline walked to the window and peered out. Fireflies dotted the darkness. She couldn't imagine why they were having this conversation. Her father had always been perfectly content to leave the running of Hopewell to others. Why now, when he could least afford to worry, was he so concerned?

Two days ago he'd been pleased with the job Creely had done in her absence. Now he considered the man useless. Even though she shared that opinion, Madeline didn't want her father to be worrying.

"Don't fret over it, Papa."

"But I do."

"I can take care of him."

"You shouldn't have to. It makes me sick when I think of the disrespectful treatment you receive at Creely's hands." Agitated, Patrick started to rise, then slumped back into the chair.

Madeline rushed to her father, but her icy green stare was for Joshua alone. "My God, what did you tell him?"

Chapter 8

"Dammit, Maddie, I didn't tell him a thing that someone with half a mind couldn't figure out for himself." Joshua loosened Patrick's neckcloth and pressed a hand against the older man's chest. A sigh of relief escaped him as he felt a heartbeat. "He's alive."

Madeline pushed her way between the two men and knelt beside her father. "His hands are so cold." She rubbed the icy flesh, willing her own warmth into Patrick's body.

"He must have fainted when he tried to stand up so fast. I know he was rather upset earlier."

When Madeline met his gaze, her expression clearly indicated she thought him to be the cause of Patrick's condition as well as every other woe known to man.

"As much as I'd love to confirm your opinion of my character, I'm going to have to decline to do so this time. Your friend Eli Creely came by this afternoon demanding to see Patrick, and apparently he spilled his guts. Of course, in his version he sounded more like Saint Eli pitted against the Dragon Lady and her heathen giant." Joshua held a cup of brandy under Patrick's nose, then touched some of the amber liquid to his colorless lips.

"Why that miserable . . ." A word foul enough to convey her dislike for the overseer did not come to Madeline. "Why didn't someone tell me he was here?"

"I have no idea. The first I knew of it was when I came down for dinner and found your father wringing his hands over the matter."

"But you did tell him what happened today?" Madeline demanded, squeezing her father's fingers in her own.

"He asked me, dammit. I wasn't going to lie."

Patrick swallowed, then his eyes sprang open as he coughed. He grabbed for the silver cup.

"Easy, Patrick, just a sip."

"Papa, are you all right?" Madeline stepped in front of the captain.

Her bewildered father wiped at his eyes with a bony hand. "What happened?"

"You fainted, Papa."

"Little too much excitement. Your daughter's right," Joshua agreed. "A good rest is what you need. Here, let me help you to your room." Joshua passed the brandy to Madeline, then took the older man's arm. Patrick looked thin, but he felt cadaverous. Joshua started to lift him from the chair.

"No!" Patrick's unexpected command caused his hands to slip, and Madeline spilled a drop or two of the brandy she was carrying back to the sideboard.

"Patrick, bed really is the best place for you. I don't think you realize—"

"I realize this: I am not going to allow Madeline to face Creely alone."

"Don't worry about Mr. Creely, Papa. I can take care of him. He's—"

"No, I won't have it." His face grew redder by degrees as his voice grew louder.

"But Papa—"

"I'll stay with her."

The reactions of father and daughter were precisely what Joshua had expected. Patrick calmed immediately, and his face took on a healthier hue. The bright flush he'd exhibited moments earlier seemed to have been

93

miraculously transferred to his daughter's face. She hissed, "Oh, no you won't!" But her words were drowned out by Patrick's eager acceptance of Joshua's offer.

Madeline stared aghast at her father. How could he so readily accept the help of this stranger? Hadn't she always taken care of the plantation? Why did he now doubt her ability to do so? She started to protest yet again, but a glance at her father's weary countenance prompted her to remain silent. She'd take care of the captain later.

After her father fell asleep, Madeline found Joshua in the dining room eating their forgotten dinner. He fixed her a plate and for a while they ate in almost companionable silence. "I'm curious about something."

"And that is?" Madeline glanced over at the captain. He looked relaxed, his sun-darkened hands laced across his flat stomach. The pose was reminiscent of her father, and yet not. This man made even the act of lounging seem sensual.

Madeline let her gaze travel slowly up from wide shoulders to his strong neck and then to his face. It was a study in serious contemplation, as if he didn't really know how to ask the question that would assuage his curiosity. This in itself was curious. Madeline had learned many things about this sea captain in their short acquaintance, but she most certainly had never before noticed hesitancy.

He swallowed, and Madeline's eyes followed the tiny ripple of musculature till it disappeared into the milky whiteness of his neckcloth. "What were you doing floating around in the middle of the ocean in that longboat?"

At any other time she would have taken offense at his bringing up their first encounter. Hadn't she made it clear the topic was taboo?

Maybe it was the gentle touch of the soft tropical night that permeated the room, or the way the candlelight danced merrily upon the silver epergne, or the gooey-sweet taste of raisin cake on her tongue. Whatever the reason, the inquiry seemed almost benign, and she answered it.

"I was escaping pirates."

"What?"

With regret, Madeline bid farewell to his relaxed attitude. He bent forward, elbows on the table, every thread of his being expectant. "You mean pirates set you adrift like that?"

Without realizing she was doing so, Madeline shrank back from his intensity. "No, pirates didn't do it. I was trying to get away from the pirates. Captain Evans did it."

His black eyes narrowed, but at least he leaned back in his chair. The mahogany creaked under his weight. Madeline sighed and sat up.

"This Evans, is he the captain of the vessel you sailed on from the Colonies?" His voice seemed calm, deceptively so.

"Yes, the *Primrose*."

"And he put a defenseless young woman off his ship— alone and in the middle of the ocean." There was nothing calm about his voice now. "The man should be horsewhipped. As a matter of fact, if I ever see the bastard I shall be only too happy to do the honors myself."

Madeline sprang to her feet. "Would you please settle down?" Her hands gripped the edge of the table as she leaned toward him. "Don't you dare touch Captain Evans." Madeline had no idea why she was defending the man, but Joshua's reference to her as defenseless had piqued her. "His judgment may have been less than sound"—she ignored the captain's loud "Humph"— "but his intentions were sincere. He prevented my ravishment by pirates."

"Aye, *that* dubious honor he saved for me."

Madeline recoiled as if he had struck her. In truth, his words hurt nearly as much as a blow. "How dare you!"

"Oh, I dare, Maddie. I dare quite a lot. I have always

95

found that preferable to hiding my head in the sand."

"I don't do that."

"The hell you don't." Then, because he saw the pain his words had caused and he really didn't want to hurt her, his voice softened. "Listen." He rose and stepped toward her, but she backed away. "No one is saying you aren't brave—hell, I've never known a more courageous woman—or that you don't try. It's just that things have happened, are happening, that you have to face."

Joshua sank back into his chair, dropping his gaze from her face, yet he could still feel her stare, that wide-eyed green stare. "What happened on the *Chesapeake* was my fault, but it happened to you; and pretending it didn't isn't going to make it go away."

He paused, and her silence made him bolder. "And this"—his arm swept about the room—"I don't know much about sugar plantations, but *I* can see it's not running smoothly. Without a decent profit, this land will eat you alive."

Slowly Madeline sat on the hard surface of her chair. Too much of what he'd said was true, and he hadn't even mentioned her father. Of course, there was no need. She already knew his assessment of that matter.

Madeline clasped her hands together and rested them on her pink- and blue-flowered skirt. "What do you propose I do? Give up?" She arched one delicate brow questioningly.

"You!" The single syllable shot from him with all the force of a musketball. "Good God, Maddie, give me credit for knowing you a little better than that."

The compliment, for that was how Madeline took his response, lightened her spirit.

"No, don't give up, but do get some help."

"From you?"

Those emerald eyes were searing into him again. Why wouldn't she consider him a likely candidate? Hadn't he done nothing but meddle in her affairs since he had arrived? But he wasn't going to stay and help—he couldn't stay and help—and it was cruel to let her believe aid would come from him. "For tonight, yes. But I'm leaving tomorrow."

"If only all my woes were so easily eliminated." Her glib words didn't conceal the uncertain expression on her gaminelike face.

"Henry Smythe!"

"What?"

Joshua couldn't control his excitement. Perhaps because when the inspiration had flashed into his mind, it had done much to wipe away the guilt he'd felt at leaving her alone. "Not what, who. Henry Smythe, Esquire, of Kingston. He's a solicitor—worked for my family for years." Joshua didn't mention that Smythe was the reason for his being at Hopewell in the first place. "Henry will be able to find you a manager, a good one. I'll talk to him as soon as I get to Kingston."

Madeline looked skeptical. "We already have a solicitor."

"It doesn't matter, Henry will do this as a favor for me." Joshua silently hoped this was true. "A decent manager is just what Hopewell needs. You would still be in charge, but it would free up your time for more important matters."

Again he didn't mention her father; again she was grateful. "All right, I would appreciate it if you would talk to this Mr. Smythe on my behalf."

"Good. Now," he said, "all you have to do is take care of Creely. By the way, he's in the library."

"What? Why didn't you tell me?"

Joshua chewed his cake with agonizing thoroughness. "I just did."

"I mean earlier." She ground out the words. "How long has he been here?"

"A while." The captain was a study in indifference. "You needed time to finish your dinner. And besides, it won't hurt Creely one bit to cool his heels." He winked at her knowingly. "Lets him know who's boss."

97

Madeline sighed, "I suppose what's done is done." After her little display of temper, she hated to admit this delaying tactic had some merit, but she did, grudgingly. "You may be right. Mr. Creely could probably use some time to contemplate his actions."

"Was that so hard to say?" He whispered the words into her hair as he pulled out her chair.

As soon as she entered the tobacco-scented confines of the library, Madeline realized two things. A pacing Eli Creely was furious, and she had forgotten to warn the captain that he was to keep quiet unless she needed him. Luckily, for her own peace of mind, neither really mattered. If the wait hadn't made Creely angry, their conversation would have, and as for the captain, she had yet to see him follow a dictate from her.

"'Bout time ya got here, Miz Madeline. I've got pressin' plantation business to take care of. You know how long I been sittin' in here waitin' for you?"

"Approximately." Madeline's smile was cool and distant. "Please have a seat, Mr. Creely." She indicated an armless side chair. Though she felt certain he had spent his waiting time lounging in the soft leather of the wing chair, she chose that seat for herself. Her presumption had been right. The rich leather was still disgustingly hot from the overseer's body. She perched near the edge. There were two chairs left in the small grouping. They were less commanding than hers, yet easily superior to the one she had assigned Creely. Madeline paused a moment for the captain to choose one. He sat in neither but instead positioned himself behind and slightly to the right of her, like a guard—like a giant heathen guard.

"Well, Mr. Creely," Madeline stared boldly into the pale eyes of her manager, "I have asked you here this evening to discuss some observations I have made at Hopewell in the past days. Frankly, I'm quite displeased with the conditions I have found."

"Your pa ain't had no complaints."

98

This rude outburst was followed by the creaking of leather as Joshua adjusted his hand on the high back of the chair. But he said nothing.

"Possibly so. And it is unfortunate if you took my father's silence as a sign that he condoned your . . . er, management of our plantation. You see"—Madeline reminded Joshua of a mother explaining one of life's truths to a recalcitrant child—"my father is not a person to worry over such details as the number of hogsheads of sugar produced per acre or the condition of the wharf's pilings. I am. And I, Mr. Creely, am the person who will be receiving your report from now on."

Creely's attempt at an amiable smile faded. He squirmed on his hard wooden chair. The creaking of leather sounded behind Madeline's right ear.

"Well now, Miz Madeline, if what you say is true and I'm supposed to be reportin' to some woman, I'm thinkin' maybe I better hear this from the boss."

"You just did." The firm baritone voice sounded without so much as a warning crinkle of leather.

Creely swallowed. Madeline could hear the sound echo in the silence the captain's words had created.

Madeline watched the overseer, but he seemed to have forgotten she was in the room. His near-colorless eyes stared at a spot over her right shoulder.

"Well, Mr. Creely, I hope you understand my position now." Madeline's attempt to regain control of the situation worked. Creely redirected his gaze to her.

"Yes'm, Miz Madeline." He made a gushing sound in his throat, and for a moment she feared he just might spit on the black and red designs of the carpet. The captain noticed it, too. This time when he moved she could feel it as well as hear the protesting leather. It was almost as if he was waiting—hoping—for Creely to do something low enough to give him an excuse to . . . to what? Madeline wasn't sure she knew, but she didn't want to find out. It was past time to bring the conversation to a close.

"First thing tomorrow morning I want to meet with

99

you at the mill. I'll have a list of improvements I'd like implemented."

Creely squirmed in his seat, and his eyes shot up to her right. "He gonna be there?"

Creak.

"I don't think that will be necessary." Madeline leaned against the back of the chair and felt the pressure of the captain doing the same.

"I thought you handled that quite well, Maddie." These words were the first Joshua had spoken since they'd both watched the dismissed Creely find his own way out.

Madeline looked around toward the man whose presence she had felt but not seen since they had entered the room. He was, as she had imagined, leaning lazily against the high back of her chair.

"Do you think Mr. Creely will mend his ways?"

"He could." The captain uncrossed ankles shod in gleaming black boots and walked toward the window.

"But you don't think so?"

Joshua turned away from the view of the moon-gilded garden. "Let's just say I will still be glad to talk to Henry Smythe for you, if that's what you want."

"I think it would be best." The window, or was it the man, beckoned her as the shore does the tides. "At least this interview is over. I felt as if I was the only thing keeping the two of you from tearing each other apart."

Joshua watched her approach. "Now, Maddie," he teased, "each other?"

"You're right." Madeline laughed as she sank into the deep-cushioned seat built into the casement of the window. "I felt as if I was the only thing keeping *you* from tearing *him* apart."

Joshua leaned against the casement. "I told you I'd be good."

Madeline looked up. Why had she come over to him?

This nearness wasn't good. "Maybe I didn't trust you."

"You should have." She was too close. He could now smell the roses, count the freckles. He had to leave before he did something else he'd live to regret. "I think I'll go for a walk."

"In the moonlight?"

Joshua peered out the window. "Yes. I'd say any walk out-of-doors at this time of night would include moonlight."

Of course it would, especially when the tropical moon was shining like a giant, luminous ball.

Joshua cocked his head. "Care to join me?"

Madeline felt all the air leave her lungs. "Oh, no, I couldn't."

"Still don't trust me?" His black eyes glittered like agates.

"It's not that." They both knew it was. "Papa is, no doubt, awake now and worried about my talk with Creely. I'd better go upstairs and check on him."

Joshua pushed away from the casement. "You're probably right." He walked toward the door, then turned for one final look. She sat amid the crewel pillows of the window seat. Behind her the night boasted a profusion of twinkling lights. Fireflies and stars, near and far, mingled and shone and somehow paled in comparison to the woman who watched him.

"I'll be leaving in the morning."

"I know."

"Say good-bye to your father for me."

Madeline nodded.

"Good luck with Creely, and I'll be sure to talk to Henry Smythe, if not tomorrow, then the next day for sure." He was rambling, sounding like a complete fool. Just say good-bye and then leave, he told himself. "Good-bye."

"Captain Whitlock?"

"Aye." He had almost been out the door when her words stopped him.

"I'll see that the dock is in good shape by the time your vessel comes to pick up the sugar crop." Madeline was amazed that it was so hard to say good-bye to a man she disliked.

What was she talking about? "The *Chesapeake?*"

"Yes, isn't that why you wanted to see Hopewell and the wharf, because you plan to carry our sugar to the Colonies?"

"No, the *Chesapeake* isn't a merchant ship." He sounded indignant.

"Well, what is it?" She was on her feet now.

"She's a privateer."

Her green eyes sprang open. "You *are* a pirate!"

"I'm no bloody pirate! Didn't you hear what I said?"

"I heard."

"Don't you know the difference between a privateer and a pirate?" His tone was patronizing.

"Enough to know there's damned little difference between them." The calm beauty Joshua had admired earlier was gone. Hands on hips, Madeline looked as if she would start spitting fire at any second. It was how he remembered her from his ship.

"Aw hell, Maddie."

"What are you doing? No . . ."

It was quiet out in the garden and lonely. The fragrance of jasmine mingled with the potent peaty smell of the earth. Joshua leaned against a coco palm. He would miss this place: its tropical beauty, the old man who treated him as an equal, and, hell, he might as well admit it, the woman who had just slapped him across the face.

Joshua chuckled at the memory. She had been so angry, ranting on and on about how she'd thought from the very beginning that he was a pirate, that he'd figured what the hell, how much madder could she get if he grabbed her and gave her one final kiss?

A lot! Not that she hadn't liked it. She had. Maybe that

102

was what had made her so angry. When he had finally, reluctantly, let her go, she had hit him. For a small woman Mistress Madeline O'Neil could throw quite a punch. But the kiss had been worth it.

Tomorrow morning, early, Joshua planned to go back to that cave he'd noticed before the storm, and look around. Then he would leave. He hoped Oliver had found some sign of Nathaniel in Kingston. There was probably a better chance of finding him there. If only he knew where his brother was . . .

With a sigh, Joshua pushed off from the tree trunk. The glow from the windows of the house seemed warm and inviting. He glanced toward the second story, wondering which windows belonged to Madeline's room.

That was when he first noticed it. He stopped to listen, heard nothing, then continued again toward the great house. There. It was louder this time and unmistakable. Joshua started running, faster, racing toward the pitiful screeches, the anguished cries of a woman begging for help.

Chapter 9

As Joshua ran blindly toward the sound, his boots ravaged the lush foliage he had only moments ago admired. He tore around the side of the house, toward a copse of cotton trees, and just before he broke into a clearing he heard Creely's voice. "This'll teach ya who's boss round here."

"Creely!" Joshua's voice rang out on the moist tropical night. In the flickering torchlight before the overseer's cabin, he made out the overseer. The man's foot was halfway through the kick he was about to inflict on the quivering, rumples mass at his feet. Relief washed through Joshua at the realization that the victim wasn't Madeline.

He knelt, found an arm, and helped the young black woman to her feet. She recoiled from his touch.

"What the hell are you doin' here?" Creely had obviously recovered from his initial shock.

Joshua fumbled in his pocket, found a handkerchief, and handed it to the woman who was bleeding from a cut lip. All the while he ignored the enraged overseer.

Creely foolishly moved closer. "I asked what you was doin' here?"

Joshua acknowledged the man's presence with a scathing look. "I'm helping a lady in distress."

"Well, that," Creely cocked a thumb toward the black

woman, "ain't no lady, and she ain't in no distress."

"It would appear otherwise."

"This ain't none of your concern." The overseer stomped about in impotent anger.

Joshua glanced back at the woman. He recognized her now as one of the house slaves, one of the girls he had seen straightening the beds and cleaning upstairs.

"You hear me, I'z talkin' to ya." Creely stepped between Joshua and the girl.

Joshua grabbed the front of the shorter man's shirt and pulled him up to eye level. "No, I'm talking to you. And what I'm saying you'd better heed. I don't like to see men kicking helpless women, and I'm sure Miss Madeline doesn't want her people beaten up by her overseer. Do you understand?"

Creely's only response was a hate-filled stare.

Joshua shook him like a terrier shakes a rat. "Do you?"

"Yeah."

"Good." Joshua set him down with a thud. "Now, you ought to be glad I'm such a gentleman because if I weren't, you'd find your ass plastered to that ground so fast you wouldn't have time to beg for help."

That was what he wanted to do. Ever since he'd seen this scum spit at Madeline, he had had an almost uncontrollable urge to beat the man to a bloody pulp. Reluctantly, he turned away.

"Let's go." He motioned for the girl to follow and headed out of the clearing.

Apparently emboldened by what he saw as the captain's retreat, Creely yelled after them. "She won't give it to you any faster'n she would me. What's a matter, that tight-assed O'Neil woman turn ya out so ya hafta settle for my leavin's?"

Joshua stopped. He turned in time to see naked fear appear in Creely's eyes as the overseer realized his mistake. In two giant steps Joshua reached him. Why not? Madeline wouldn't like it, but she didn't consider

105

him any better than a damned pirate anyway.

His large fist shot out and connected with Creely's face to the satisfying accompaniment of crunching bones and teeth.

Creely lay where he landed. Joshua stared down at him for a moment, flexing his bruised hand. "Hell, I never was much of a gentleman," he said.

Then he walked over to the girl, who looked with round-eyed terror from him to Creely's inert form. "Come on, I'll take you back to the house." He reached for her arm.

"No, I ain't goin'."

Joshua ran long fingers through his hair, but stopped when a tangled curl caught on some loose skin. "Damn," he mumbled, as he examined his right hand. Creely's bony jaw had skinned his knuckle. Well, it had been worth it.

The girl still stood shaking her head, her fear evident. Joshua moved toward her, but she cowered behind an acacia trunk. He was having one heck of a time with women lately.

"Look . . . what he said"—Joshua gestured toward the man sprawled out on the spongy ground—"it's not true. I'm not going to hurt you. I just think you should have someone look at your cuts."

"Not at de great house."

"All right, where?"

"My cabin."

"Fine, I'll take you there." Joshua was beginning to lose his patience.

The woman, who had begun walking, turned on him. "I got me a man."

This time Joshua combed his fingers through his mussed hair despite the pain. "Wonderful. I'm glad. You've got a man; I've got a woman," he lied. "We're both happy."

She eyed him suspiciously, but at least she began picking her way through the dense undergrowth. She

106

found a path, and Joshua followed.

"This man of yours, why wasn't he back there?"

She plodded forward. "Ya mean fightin' Massa Creely?"

"Yes."

"Ya wants 'im dead?"

"Who, Creely?"

"Both of 'em. My man, Sau, he finds out what Massa Creely been doin', he kills 'im; then Massa O'Neil he kills Sau."

Joshua couldn't argue with that. There was no way any plantation owner could condone a slave killing a white man.

"Ya ain't gonna tell him, is ya?" The girl's face, with its swollen lip, looked grotesque in the moonlight.

"Your man? No." Joshua looked down at the woman. "But I think Patrick O'Neil should know. This isn't the first time Creely's done this to you, is it?"

"First time?" The woman laughed, then touched her lip gingerly. "Massa Creely under my skirts any chance he git. He's mean, but he ain't usually hittin' and kickin' like dat."

"Did you fight him this time?"

The woman glared up at Joshua. "I always fight 'im. Wants no parts o' him. Told ya, I got me a man." She walked a few more paces. "I don't know what got into Massa Creely tonight, but I do know tellin' Massa Patrick ain't gonna help. He be old and sick."

"There's Miss Madeline." Even as he said the words Joshua wanted to recall them. Madeline might be able to help, but she didn't need any more trouble.

The girl shook her head. "Miz Madeline, she try but she ain't nothin' 'gainst Massa Creely and dem others."

"What others?"

"Nothin', I'z just shootin' off da mouth, ain't no others. Ya can't go no further. This here's the slave place."

Joshua nodded. "What are you going to tell your man?

107

Your face is cut up pretty bad."

"Don' know, but I sure gonna tell him how ya flattened Massa Creely. He be real happy 'bout dat."

Joshua peeled off his frock coat as he walked back through the humid air toward the great house. So, the girl thought her man would be glad he had socked Creely. Well, that was good because he sure didn't think Madeline was going to be too happy about it. It would just give her one more reason to hate him when he was gone.

He paused in the large circular drive to look at the house. It was late, and most of the windows were black. As he had earlier, Joshua caught himself scanning them, wondering behind which the lady of the sharp tongue, the wicked right punch, and the adorable freckles slept.

He loosened his neckcloth and unbuttoned the top of his shirt. The linen material clung to his body. God, it was hot. If he weren't so tired, he'd go down to the bay and cool off. Yes, he thought, as his boots rang against the tiles of the veranda, a swim in the sea would feel real good right now.

"Been visiting the slave quarters, Captain Whitlock?"

Joshua turned toward the voice, and noticed what he had completely missed before. There, sitting in the shadows, prim and proper and straight backed as you please, was the little lady herself. He couldn't see her expression, but he could well imagine it.

"Taken to spying on me now, have you, Mistress O'Neil?"

"I was not spying," she snapped with the same authority with which she closed her fan.

"I see." Joshua ambled to the pillar nearest her wicker chair and leaned against its cool surface. "And I suppose you always sit out here in the moonlight, watching people walk up the drive?"

"I wasn't watching you walk up the drive."

"Then how did you know I was coming from the quarters?"

Madeline opened her fan and waved it angrily. The

108

movement of hot humid air did little to cool her burning face. This odious man had no sense of shame, sauntering up in the middle of the night, half-dressed.

"I was taking some air and couldn't help noticing your approach. As to where you were, I'm sure it is no concern of mine."

"But you assume it was the slave quarters?"

Oh, for heaven's sake, why didn't he just let the matter drop, and why had she started on this in the first place? "I can't imagine why you would go there in the middle of the night."

"Can't you?"

She knew his brow was cocked, even though the light was too dim for her to see it.

She should just ignore that, ignore him. But for some reason she couldn't suppress an image of the captain's long, bronzed body entwined with the chocolate-colored form of one of the slave girls. And that picture was causing a painful tightening around her heart. Madeline rose from the high-backed wicker chair and started toward the door. "It's as hot out here as it is inside, so I'll say good night."

"Maddie." The word spread over her like warm honey.

"Yes." She turned.

He pushed off from the column and advanced toward her. "If you wanted to know whether I went seeking a slave wench, why didn't you just ask?"

"Oh!" Madeline shuddered at his uncouth remark. "I assure you that never entered my mind."

He was beside her now, his hot, musky scent surrounding her. "Ah, Maddie, you are such a lousy little liar."

Madeline met his amused black gaze. How dare he accuse her of lying when he was the one who . . . "Your disgusting appetites are of no interest to me, I am merely curious as to how long it will be till we can expect the birth of another mulatto baby."

He grinned, his teeth flashing white in the darkness.

"It normally takes nine months."

Madeline turned from him in disgust. He was right. She had been waiting for him, wondering why a walk was taking so long—that is, until she'd seen the direction from which he'd come, his disheveled appearance. Then she knew, and the knowledge brought her more pain than she cared to admit.

She moved again toward the door.

"Cheer up, Maddie." She kept walking.

"A man's seed doesn't always bear fruit."

Keep going. Just go inside, he'll be gone tomorrow.

"After all, mine didn't with you."

Madeline stopped. If only she had made it inside the door before he'd said that, before he'd made her think about it again. This worry that she might carry his child was something she didn't need.

Her skirts swayed as Madeline again moved toward the door.

"It didn't, did it, Maddie?" The teasing tone was missing from his voice now.

"No." she whispered, but there had been a hesitation, and he had not missed it.

Joshua caught her and, cradling her shoulders in his large hands, turned her to him.

"You don't know if you are with child or not, do you?" The words were ground out through his teeth, and Madeline could do naught but stare into the black depths of his eyes.

"Do you?" His hands tightened.

"No!" She spat out the word while twisting from the confines of his powerful hands. "No, I don't. There hasn't been time to find out."

"But you told me—"

"I told you what you wanted to hear."

Joshua looked up from his contemplation of the patterned tiles. "Why should you care what I wanted to hear?"

"Because it was what I wanted to hear, too." Her

110

hands lifted imploringly. "What I wanted to believe." Her hands dropped to her sides. "It makes no difference, you know."

"The hell it doesn't."

"Oh, for heaven's sake." Madeline folded her arms across her chest and glared from under brows lowered in a scowl. What did he want her to do, to say? Was she supposed to believe he was really concerned that she might be carrying his child? He was a pirate, a ravisher of young maidens. Oh, he might call himself a privateer, but what was that, really, except a pirate sailing on the very fringes of the law?

And if he were so concerned about where his damned seed might sprout, why had he been so quick to sow more of it tonight?

He was glaring at her now, with an intensity she could only guess matched her own.

"This is ridiculous. It's not as if I am with child. I told you, it's too soon to know." His black stare never wavered. "Besides, if there is a baby, perhaps I can bring the other child into the house so they can grow up together."

"What the hell are you talking about?"

Madeline moved closer, her chin set at a defiant angle. "I'm talking, Captain Whitlock, about that poor slave wench you forced your attentions on tonight—about her baby. If our brief acquaintance is any example, you must have bastard offspring throughout the islands . . . or wherever you do your pirating."

"Dammit, Maddie, I did not force myself on any poor woman tonight."

"Her willingness is beside the point." Madeline remembered the way he could make her feel with just the touch of his lips and decided the woman had, no doubt, been eager to bestow her favors.

Joshua raked his fingers through his perspiration-dampened hair. "I was with no woman tonight—willing or otherwise." He enunciated the words so that even she could understand.

Her eyes widened. "But you said—"

"No, Maddie, *you* said. All I did was walk up the drive. 'Twas you and that suspicious little mind of yours that had me and my 'disgusting appetite' bedding everything that wiggles beneath a skirt."

Madeline wanted to believe him, ached to. "Why didn't you tell me right away?"

"And spoil your fun?"

Fun! Did he believe she enjoyed thinking about him bedding another woman?

"You, Maddie, appear to gain a perverse joy from thinking the worst of me. Who am I to spoil your pleasure?" Somehow, voicing what he had suspected since his arrival made him feel desolate. He peered down at her through the gray veil of night. Her shoulders, usually so straight and firm, sagged. Her bottom lip, ordinarily so poutingly luscious, was gnarled between her teeth, and the sheen of her green eyes made him wonder if tears were miminent. Her sadness only served to deepen his own melancholy.

"Go to bed, Maddie. I'm tired. You're tired. It's been one hell of a long day." He reached out and turned her gently toward the entrance of the great house. She felt warm and pliant in his hands. There was no fight left in her now. Joshua wished there were.

"You still have to see Creely in the morning. He'll be trouble, but try not to let him bother you. I'll ask Henry Smythe to ride out and talk to you about procuring a new overseer. He'll be here in a few days."

Madeline looked up at the man offering her encouragement as if she were a child. "Do you think he will come that quickly?"

She looked so damned young and vulnerable. "Aye, he'll come." He'll come if I have to threaten his generous girth with the tip of my cutlass. "And Maddie . . ."

"Yes."

God, he wished she wouldn't look at him like that.

112

"Henry knows how to get in touch with me. It would probably take a long time, maybe more than a year." Joshua thought of Nathaniel's letters which had lain waiting for months while he was at sea. "But if you ever need me . . ." He didn't say why she might, yet they both knew the possibility that a child could have been conceived was never far from the thoughts of either of them.

"Thank you, I'll remember that." But she knew she'd never contact him. He was leaving, and she was glad—or should be.

He lifted the huge brass latch, and together they entered the dim interior of the great house. The candles in the wall sconces had burned down into tallow, and were giving off more smoldering odor than light.

"I'd stay, if I could . . . till Henry gets your new manager." Joshua's words echoed through the sleepy predawn quiet of the hall.

Madeline smiled and nodded before beginning the long ascent of the spiral mahogany staircase. Five steps into her climb she realized the treads held only her. She turned and found him still at the bottom, leaning against the carved newel, watching her.

"Aren't you coming to bed?"

Joshua smiled. She didn't even realize how inviting and tempting her words were. "No, there is one more thing I must do before I leave. Since it's almost dawn, I might as well take care of it now."

"I see." But of course, she didn't. At this moment she could understand nothing except that he was leaving. Her eyes drank in the sight of him till she feared he would turn away in embarrassment. He didn't. She did. "Well, good night then." Madeline took one more step, then another.

"Good-bye, Maddie." She nodded, unwilling to trust her voice with a similar reply, and climbed to the second floor.

Joshua watched her disappear, with a feeling too close

to regret for his comfort. Blaming the slowness of his steps on fatigue, he retreated into the steamy darkness of the night.

Tired though he was, Joshua knew there would be no sleep for him that night. Something was happening to him here. Something in this house drew him in and tangled about him. Whatever it was, he seemed unable to defend himself against it—there were even times he didn't want to try.

Leaving was the only way to stop the spiral in which he found himself, but first he'd promised himself a more thorough inspection of that secluded cove. He followed the garden to the bay, planning to trace the coastline to the inlet. He didn't really think Nathaniel had been at Hopewell. Patrick hadn't seen him. At their first meeting, Joshua had asked Madeline's father about his brother. He had casually inquired as to whether or not Nathaniel had visited O'Neil on his last trip to the island, but Patrick's surprise that Joshua had a brother had been too genuine to be feigned. Besides, Joshua didn't believe Madeline's father was working with pirates.

And Creely? He might be selling some stolen flour in Kingston, but he simply wasn't smart enough to be masterminding anything of the scope that Nathaniel had described in his letter. No, there was only one person around here with the intelligence and the ability to do that.

The thought remained suspended in his mind as Joshua picked his way over the long shadowy roots of an ebony tree.

Madeline might be clever enough to oversee the plundering of ships and the sale of stolen goods, but he didn't think she had the temperament for that. Besides, she had been off the island for months. Joshua himself could vouch for the timing of her recent arrival in Jamaica.

He might as well face it. Regardless of what Henry Smythe had said about Hopewell selling flour, coming here had been a desperate stab in the dark that had come to naught. The sooner he returned to Kingston, the sooner he could resume his search for Nathaniel—and free himself of the bewildering sentiments that shrouded his mind.

The shoreline was no longer flat and sandy. As sharp rocks knocked against his shins and thick underbrush tore at his breeches, Joshua cursed his impetuous decision to seek out the secluded cove in the predawn darkness. He had stopped at the kitchen and put a candle in his pocket, but he didn't think its meager light would be much help. He tried to gauge how long it would be before first light would aid his passage. He wasn't sure, and the thick foliage of coconut palms made it impossible for him to read the stars.

Resolutely, he continued. The cadence of pounding surf was his only sure guide. The terrain no longer allowed him the option of thought. His every resource must be called upon to traverse it. Joshua considered stopping, sitting upon a flat rock or leaning against one of the smooth thigh-thick tree trunks to wait for the pink fingers of dawn to top the horizon, but he didn't.

It had become a challenge, getting to that cave—a struggle that pitted him against the night-blanketed secrets of this land. At the moment, Joshua needed a victory, however small and insignificant, to assure him that though he still had not succeeded in learning Nathaniel's whereabouts, there were things he could master.

Thump!

Joshua had just emerged from a thick grove of ceibas and was looking out over the Caribbean to the southeast, his gaze drawn to the first definable brushstrokes of morn, when he bumped into something. Instantly, he knew the resiliency his body had met could only come from a living creature.

"What the? . . ." He reached out and grabbed the arms of a man whose skin, even in the faint flush of day, shone

115

like polished ebony. They were thick and strong, the naked arms he held, and as Joshua looked straight into eyes black as his own, he recognized a man whose brawn and power very nearly matched his.

Their accidental meeting had obviously startled the black man, too, and by the wild look in his eyes, it was more than the physical jolt that concerned him. He was, no doubt, a slave or a runaway. In either case he had no business stealing about in the darkness.

"What are you doing here?" Joshua released the man and took a quick look around. No one else seemed to be about, but in the shadowy dawn he couldn't tell for sure. Joshua only wished he had brought his pistol, or at least a cutlass.

"I'z sorry, massa. I got lost and can't find my way. I won't cause no trouble, jus' be on my way." During this short speech the man kept his eyes fixed on the rose-tinted sand at Joshua's feet. That said, he began backing away, slowly, meekly.

"Wait just a damn minute." Joshua's hand snapped out and grabbed the man's beefy biceps. The subservient-slave performance was convincing. It might even have fooled Joshua, if he hadn't, for that brief, unguarded moment, looked into this man's eyes. No, this was no meek servant who had lost his way. This man had a reason for being here, something important enough to risk punishment for if he were discovered, and Joshua wanted to know what it was.

"Please, massa, don't hurt Sau. He ain't doin' nothin'." The big man tried to cringe away from Joshua's grip.

"Sau? Your name's Sau?"

"Yes, massa, I'z one of Massa Patrick's field hands, and I ain't done nothin'."

So, this was Sau. Joshua remembered the black woman's fear that her man might kill Creely, and now that he'd seen him, Joshua had to admit that possibility. With his size, the man could crush Creely. Of course, his

116

meek act was intended to give the impression that he wouldn't hurt his worst enemy. Joshua thought he knew better.

"Dammit, Sau. I've listened to all the mealy-mouthed crap I intend to. Now, are you going to tell me what the hell you're doing here, or am I going to have to knock you flat on your ass?"

"You'z welcome to try."

"I'm welcome to . . ." Joshua's laugh billowed out into the mauve-tinged dawn, scaring a sea plover that was seeking to break its night-long fast. "Why, you son of a bitch, if I wanted to, I'd do a lot more than try."

"Maybe." White teeth gleamed in the broad, black face. "You that white man Dora tell me 'bout, ain't ya?"

Joshua's eyes narrowed. "Who's Dora?"

"She tell me how ya sent 'im sprawlin'. Wished I coulda seen it. Course, I almost did. Saw ya go after Creely in da cane piece."

"Yeah, well, none of that answers my question, now does it?" So, the man had been one of the slaves who'd witnessed his loss of temper. Now that Joshua knew who Dora was, he wondered idly what she had told Sau about her battered face.

"I watchin' for da fires."

His answer was as curious as it was unexpected.

"What fires?" By the look on Sau's face before his lips clamped shut, Joshua imagined he had spoken without thinking. He didn't look as though he planned to elaborate.

"Dammit, Sau, I said what fires?" Joshua wasn't certain the fear he saw in the depths of Sau's eyes was contrived this time.

"Massa Creely's fires." The black man looked about, as if he now feared there were others nearby. "He lights 'em, signals men in boats."

Joshua could hardly believe what he was hearing. "Where?" He stepped closer to Sau. "Where does he light these fires?"

"Back dere." Sau motioned behind him with his calloused thumb.

Joshua stalked off in the direction the slave had indicated and squinted into the rising sun. "That inlet over there, is that where these fires are, near some caves? He looked back at Sau.

The man was nodding his great, gnarled head. "Yeah, there's caves. Dey uses 'em to keeps the stuff in."

"Anything in them now?" Joshua looked toward the east. He was, more than ever, curious to see those caves.

"Nah, we moves the stuff out."

"We?"

"Massa Creely makes the field hands do it."

"I see." But there was much that Joshua didn't understand. Could Creely actually be leading a group of smugglers or even pirates? Joshua doubted it. But if he wasn't, then who was? And unlikely as it seemed, could Nathaniel have stumbled upon this place, and if he had . . .

Joshua turned back to the black man, who appeared to grow more nervous as the brilliant sun rose in the sky. "Have there been any other white men here asking questions? Someone about my height but not as big with . . ." Joshua's voice trailed off as he watched Sau shake his head in denial.

"Ain't been no one here 'cept dem men from de boats." He paused. "I gotta gets back. Massa Creely find me gone past first light there be trouble sure."

"Oh, of course." Joshua walked back toward him. "But first I need—"

"Massa, please." There was no mistaking the slave's fear.

"Go." Joshua watched as the man turned and sprinted into the woods. He seemed to find a path of sorts, for Joshua could hear his steady footfalls long after the tangle of underbrush should have slowed his pace.

A refreshing breeze swept off the bay, cooling Joshua and rearranging his raven locks as he gazed out upon the

118

azure beauty of the Caribbean. He longed to rest, yet feared if he gave in to the fatigue that had suddenly sapped his strength he would be unable to rise for hours.

And there were still the caves to explore. That might lead to nothing, but Joshua couldn't shake the feeling that there was some link between what was happening here at Hopewell and Nathaniel's disappearance.

He shook his head to clear it, then rubbed his weary eyes with the backs of his hands. He'd take a good look at those caves, and then he'd put some more questions to Sau and a few other people.

Chapter 10

Madeline left the stable's musty shadows and stomped into the dazzling light of late morning, thankful that the cooling trade winds had carried away the past night's stifling heat. She jerked her woven coco-leaf hat off to allow the breezes to soothe her aching head.

Oh, if only she now had the hours she's wasted tossing and turning on her bed, she would put them to good use. Her lids slipped over gritty eyes. Yes, she would be asleep the moment her head touched the pillow. No more wriggling and squirming, tangling the linens into knots, staring wide-eyed into the darkness, blaming the heat, yet knowing it innocent.

Well, she wasn't going to think of him anymore. He was gone, for good this time; and besides, she had plenty of other things to think about—Eli Creely, for one. Madeline stomped her boot at the thought of her disobedient overseer.

The nerve of the man! He'd ignored the order to meet with her this morning. Tired as she was, Madeline had been at the sugar works, seated behind the heavy walnut desk, the list of changes she wanted implemented written in her neat, precise hand. She'd waited—and waited.

The thump-thump and grinding of the water-powered roller that squeezed the dark brown juice from the third crop of ratoon cane had reverberated inside her head.

She had stood, smoothing the skirts of her scarlet riding habit, and called for Micah. The old slave had long since lost his ability to handle the heavy ladles used by the boilers, but his expertise was still needed to help determine when the bubbling syrup was tempered. When he wasn't so occupied, the spry older man made an eager and reliable messenger.

With that in mind, Madeline had sent him after her recalcitrant overseer. After what had seemed like hours, Micah had returned—alone. "Massa Creely, he sick, can't come," he declared, his crinkly white hair contrasting with his wizened black face.

"Sick?" Madeline had jumped from her chair, bumping her knee against the desk. "What do you mean sick?"

The old man had simply shrugged his narrow shoulders and started to turn away.

"Wait a minute." She'd grabbed a handful of homespun shirt. "Does he look sick?" It had immediately occurred to her that Creely might be faking illness to put off their meeting.

"Don't look sick."

Aha, she had thought not.

"Looks plenty beat up though."

"Beat up?" But who, why? She hadn't had to ask.

Micah had chuckled, and an amused sparkle had lit his tiny eyes. "Heard the big white man done laid 'im out good." Joshua? she'd thought and had quickly corrected herself: the captain. Oh, even gone the man caused her trouble!

Now she stomped up the tile steps to the veranda, angrier than ever. Her walk from the stables to the great house had allowed her time to ponder the morn's events.

Madeline lifted the latch and entered the hall. Maybe she'd take a nap. Her head throbbed so that she could barely think straight. Yes. She'd check on Papa, then lie down for a while. She could almost feel the cool, down-filled pillow against her cheek as she started up the stairs.

121

Somewhere off the hall a door opened, closed; but Madeline paid little heed. Actually, she noticed nothing until she heard the voice.

"Madeline, dear, there you are."

Madeline didn't recognize it at first. It wasn't the captain's; she knew that for certain. This voice was more dandified and not as deep. She should know to whom it belonged but couldn't quite— Madeline turned, and her mouth formed a perfect O.

"Philip?" Her eyes matched her lips. "Philip, is that you?"

The handsome man stepped to the foot of the stairs and held out his hand. "Of course it is I. Who else would you expect?" He smiled, and Madeline placed her hand in the smooth confines of his before descending the stairs.

"Well, certainly not you." Madeline allowed her gaze to roam over him. He was as neat and immaculately turned out as he'd been in Williamsburg. His lightly powdered, smooth blond hair was caught in a ribbon that matched the bright salmon shade of his voided-silk velvet coat. Worn over a ribbed silk vest, the coat should have made him appear uncomfortable in this clime, but it didn't. He seemed as cool as the hand that drew Madeline toward him.

She hesitated. "Why are you here, Philip?" Not that she wasn't glad to see him. She had enjoyed his company in Williamsburg, had even encouraged his attentions, if the truth be known. But this wasn't the fantasy world of her aunt's Francis Street home. There her major concerns had been what fan to take with her new gown, whether she should wear white silk stockings with clocks, or without, under her green silk damask dress. But here, now—

"I've come for you, Madeline. Did you suppose I would allow you to leave me without a word?"

His cool, smooth, lace-edged hands crept about her waist, drawing her closer. He had held her like this once in Williamsburg, the day he had asked her to marry him.

She had liked it then, or thought she had. But now it made her uneasy. Madeline shifted, raising her hands to his chest, keeping space between them.

"I left a note. . . ."

"Yes, and your aunt was most prompt in her delivery of it. But, Madeline dear, it told me naught except that you had left Virginia to return home."

She sighed with impatience as his arms tightened.

"Was it I, my dear? Was I your reason for leaving?"

"No." He hadn't been the cause for her departure, but he hadn't been a strong enough reason for her to consider remaining in Williamsburg either.

"Excellent!" His thin lips, soft and cool, touched her forehead. Had he always smelled so . . . sweet? "I have missed you, Madeline, more than you can imagine." His mouth descended on hers. The kiss was not unpleasant, at first. It was almost placid, and Madeline tolerated his physical nearness, maintaining a somewhat detached attitude. But then he deepened the contact, demonstrating a passion she just did not feel.

In vain, she tried to push his marauding tongue from her mouth. Philip seemed to take this maneuver as sensual play on her part, for his lips and tongue became bolder. Her fists were caught between their bodies, useless.

When his lips went on a nibbling quest down the tense stem of her neck, the best she could do was turn her face away from him.

Her sharp intake of breath didn't stop Philip's ardent caresses, but Madeline no longer cared what was happening. Her gaze was locked with a pair of smoldering black eyes she'd never thought to see again.

The captain leaned against the door frame, looking even more disreputable than he had that first night she had seen him in his cabin. His once-white shirt, stained and torn, billowed open nearly to his waist, exposing a broad chest covered with curling black hair. And the white wool breeches she remembered as appearing stylish

123

last evening were in similar condition, though they did not gape open.

He was watching her wordlessly, but that did not imply there was no message conveyed. His bloodshot eyes spoke volumes, and not pleasantly. Madeline watched his beard-shadowed jaw clench and relax, and her mouth went dry.

"Philip." The feel of his too-smooth cheek against her neck had reminded her that she still stood wrapped in his amorous arms and that his mouth was meandering over her neck and shoulders.

"Yes, Madeline dear."

The slight abatement of his ardor allowed her to push him away. The absence of Philip's supporting arms betrayed the weakness in her knees, caused by the captain's stare, and she was forced to grab for the newel post.

"Are you all right, Madeline?" As Philip reached out to her, it was obvious he considered her disorientation a direct result of his sexual prowess.

"I'm fine," Madeline replied, but her eyes were drawn back to the man whose scowling stare had never left her.

As if those twin burning orbs could draw more than just her, Philip turned toward the captain. His sudden intake of breath was doubtless caused by a different emotion than Madeline's had been.

Her right hand fluttered to her throat, and she hoped it wasn't as red as it felt. "Wh-what are you doing here?" The question felt vaguely familiar on her tongue.

The captain bared his teeth in what could have been called a smile though it bore more resemblance to a snarl.

"Here, Maddie?" Joshua pushed away from the doorjamb and advanced on her. "You want to know what I'm doing *here,* in the hall?"

Madeline swallowed and nodded till her curls bobbed.

"I'd say"—the captain's voice was curt—"that question is more like, what the hell do you think *you're* doing here?"

"Sir," Philip stepped forward as the captain slipped into profanity.

Madeline watched Joshua give the other man a quick perusal, taking in his appearance from his silver-buckled shoes to the tip of his powdered head, and then summarily dismiss him.

But he didn't dismiss Madeline.

The captain appeared unconcerned about the disheveled condition of his clothing or the inappropriateness of his scowl as he stood waiting for an answer. Well, she would have to show him the error of his ways.

"Any actions I may take in my own house are none of your concern."

"Well, they need to be someone's concern. Anyone could have walked in and seen what you were doing." His bristly jaw jutted toward her accusingly.

Of all the nerve. Not more than twenty-four hours ago this very same man who was now lecturing her on propriety had kissed her himself. And the place he had chosen had been a lot more public than her front hall. Granted, it had been raining and the chances of someone happening onto the front drive had been slim, but that had been more than offset by the kiss itself, which had been a hundredfold more passionate and soul-wrenching than Philip's. Still, that was hardly something she wished to point out to him now, especially with Philip Spencer looking as if he were about to demand satisfaction from this scruffily dressed intruder.

"Philip." Madeline's hand found the velvet of his sleeve just as he started toward the captain. He stopped, turning questioning hazel eyes to her. Thank heavens one of these men was reasonable, and a gentleman.

"Captain Whitlock," Madeline began by way of explanation, "is an *old* friend of my father's and, I'm afraid, in the absence of that gentleman, has decided he needs to assume the duties of guardian." She felt the muscles in Philip's arm contract when the captain's name was mentioned. But Madeline decided that reaction

125

had been caused by the absurdity of her explanation. Of the two men, Madeline would guess Philip to be the elder by some half-dozen years, and of course, the captain's actions were more reminiscent of the behavior of a jealous lover than of a guardian.

That realization caused a funny sensation in the pit of Madeline's stomach and brought a bloom to her cheeks as she turned to address the captain. "I do apologize for insulting your sensibilities," she said, but he'd have had to be blind not to notice the insincerity in her eyes. "You are, of course, correct concerning the impropriety of our public display of affection. But you see, Philip— Oh!" Madeline paused, as if realizing for the first time that she had failed to introduce the two men. "Philip Spencer, Captain Joshua Whitlock." Each man eyed the other warily, and then, with a formal bow of his head, acknowledged the introduction.

Madeline released her pent-up breath and continued. "As I was saying, Philip is a very dear friend of mine from the Colonies, and I was just so thrilled and surprised to see him, I let my emotions cloud my judgment."

How she was able to recite this asinine little speech Madeline didn't know, but it did seem to have the desired effect. A placated Philip took her hand, and a fuming, but chastised captain backed off. She really had to admire his control when he smiled.

"Of course, Madeline dear." Was he mimicking Philip or playing the role of indulgent uncle? "I do understand your exuberance over seeing your friend again. Please excuse my display of temper. I can only assume my lack of sleep and physical discomfort"—he let his hand sweep over his attire—"contributed to my rudeness."

"We quite understand, Captain." Her smile would have lured a worm from its apple. "Please do not let us keep you from your bath and bed."

The captain's bow was elegant. "Thank you, Madeline . . . dear."

Her green eyes blazed. Damn him! He was making fun

of Philip. Under her glare, the captain merely grinned and marched up the steps with the dignity of one in full military regalia.

"Your friend, the captain, appears a bit odd," Philip observed when the other man had disappeared above stairs.

"He is, but he's not my friend."

Philip patted her hand. "I know; he's your father's friend. By the way, when am I to meet that illustrious gentleman?"

Madeline tore her gaze away from the staircase. "At dinner, I suppose, though I can't be sure. He's been very ill and—"

"Is that the reason for your abrupt leave-taking from the Colonies?" At Madeline's nod, he continued, "Libby hinted as much. All the more reason for my hastening to your side, Madeline dear."

Madeline couldn't help herself. She flinched when he called her "Madeline dear." Philip had made a lovely speech about helping her in her time of need. Yet all she could think about was the smirk that would be on the captain's handsome face if he had heard those words.

What had she done to deserve this? The captain was still here, and now Philip Spencer had appeared. Not that it hadn't been thoughtful of him to come so far, but the truth was, Madeline just wasn't sure she appreciated the gesture. He had been very solicitous when she had shown him to his room, inquiring about her own health, showing concern for her obvious fatigue, even kissing her hand, though mercifully nothing else. Still, she just couldn't help but think of him as an extra burden. Perhaps she'd feel differently after she'd rested.

And that was exactly what Madeline intended to do. She had assured herself that Papa was resting comfortably so there was nothing to stop her from doing the same.

She smelled the fresh flowers that Hattie had placed on her dressing table. Her room seemed an oasis of calm and peace in her hectic life. Crossing to the clothespress she began to loosen the buttons of her riding dress.

"Just how dear a friend is he?"

Her fingers grasping the third carved-bone button of her bodice, Madeline swung toward the man who lounged on the mauve and blue flowered damask chaise. He had yet to touch comb to hair or razor to chin. The one concession he had made toward improving his bedraggled appearance was the removal of his dust- and sand-splattered boots. Large, white-stockinged feet, crossed at the ankle, caught Madeline's eye. His toes were long and narrow, their shape well defined through the cloth, and the sight of them, so male and out of place in her very feminine room, took her back. She raked her gaze up his long, sprawling form until she reached those mischievous eyes.

"What are you doing in my room?"

He placed his hands behind his head. "I was waiting for you."

"That's obvious." Madeline's hands dropped to her hips. "I'd like to know why."

"There are a few things I'd like to discuss with you—alone." He stretched, hands clasped, elbows extended at right angles to his head.

Madeline tried not to notice the smooth, rippling motion of his chest and stomach muscles, but it was difficult. With his shirt gaping open, there was just too much bronzed, hairy flesh to ignore.

Forcing herself to turn away, she showed him her back and began arranging the already neatly organized bottles on her dressing table.

"Is that the stuff that smells like roses?"

"What?" Madeline caught his reflection in the mirror and saw him point a long, lazy finger toward the cut-glass bottle of amber liquid with which she toyed.

"I noticed you smell like roses . . . most of the time." He grinned.

Her hand tightened, the bottle tipped slightly, rose-laced drops wet her fingers. She took a fortifying breath. "I have no intentions of discussing my fragrances or anything else with you while you're in my room."

"Fine." He wriggled down further into the cushions of the chaise. "We'll just rest. I feel like hell, and truthfully, Maddie, I've seen you looking better. Did you get any sleep last night?"

Madeline stole a surreptitious glance in the mirror before turning back toward him. "You can't stay in here." Had he lost his mind?

"Why not?" He looked for all the world as if he planned to hibernate where he lay. "You may have the bed. I'll just stay here on this—what do you call this thing, Maddie?"

That was it. He *had* lost his mind—or maybe she had. After all, he was lying there calm and serene, while she— Weren't the insane prone to ranting and raving? She needed to calm down.

"I cannot rest with you in the room."

For a moment she thought he had actually fallen asleep, for he seemed not to hear her. Then those wicked black eyes slid open, and his strong sensual mouth spread into a suggestive smile. "But, Maddie honey, I'm too tired to do anything else."

"Oh!" Madeline clenched her fists involuntarily, wishing they were squeezing his strong, tanned neck. "If you don't get out of here, I'll . . . I'll have you thrown out."

"By whom, Maddie? Your 'dear friend Philip.'" The words sounded blasphemous when he said them.

She glared at him.

"What's the matter? Are you afraid to call him?" He looked less languid now.

"Of course not, and if you don't leave this instant, I shall." *Oh, please leave.*

"Watch it, Maddie, you'll have me quaking in my stockings."

Again, her eyes were drawn to the long, narrow feet

129

resting intimately on her chaise.

"Well, you should be nervous. Philip is an excellent swordsman . . . and horseman." How this last observation was going to help him move this uncooperative man from her room she had no idea.

"So, old Philip is a fencer, is he?"

"Yes, he's quite renowned actually." This was a fabrication, although she did seem to remember her cousin Thomas mentioning that Philip had bested him in a bout. Of course, Thomas tended to be flabby, and he was slow. . . .

"That's peculiar. And here I thought your 'dear friend Philip' nothing more than a dandified fop."

A fop? Maybe his dress was a little flamboyant, especially compared to—she gave the supine captain's apparel a quick perusal and dismissed it as not even comparable—but a fop? An idea sprang into her mind. The same thought had come unbidden when the captain had confronted Philip belowstairs. It sounded ridiculous but . . .

"Do you know what I think?" she purred.

"No, what do you think, Maddie?" he asked, his voice relaxed and lazy.

"I think you're jealous."

"Jealous!" He sat up on the chaise with such force Madeline took a step backward. "That's ridiculous."

"Is it?"

"What would I possibly be jealous of?" He demanded, as if daring her to come up with one thing.

"Well"—Madeline raised her hand and touched each finger as she enumerated—"there's his wardrobe for one thing, his manners, his wealth. He is very rich, you know, and good-looking. Philip is quite attractive." She pretended to ignore the captain's snort. "And, of course, there is my obvious affection for him."

"Hah! You think I'm jealous over you? That is absurd."

"Well, you were certainly angry enough when you saw

130

me kissing him." Philip had actually been kissing her, but Madeline wasn't about to correct herself.

"Angry? You thought I was angry?" He watched her brows raise. "I was embarrassed for you, that's what. Such public displays of affection are most unbecoming to a lady such as yourself."

He sounded so sincere. Now Madeline was embarrassed. Not for what had happened earlier, but for accusing him of jealousy. She quickly looked him over. Even in his present untidy state, with two days' growth of black, bristly beard, dirt-streaked and with his hair mussed, he was beyond a doubt the most handsome man she had ever seen. It *was* absurd. The very thought that he could be jealous because of her was ridiculous. Yet she had accused him of it.

Madeline sank onto the vanity bench, all the fight gone from her. "Are you going to leave or not?"

"Not. Unless you want to answer a few questions about Hopewell for me first."

Madeline sighed. "All right."

"What is your relationship with Spencer?" He hadn't meant to ask that. Hell, he had just convinced her, if not himself, that he cared not a fig about their feelings for each other. Then he'd turned right around and asked about the man as if he were some moonstruck lad just out of leading strings.

She looked up at him with those damned green eyes. "Why do you want to know that?"

"I don't." *Then why did you ask?*

Madeline's eyes narrowed, and for a moment Joshua thought she was going to ask that very question, but she seemed to think better of it.

"Good. Because I have no intention of discussing Philip with you, Captain." Ah, she called that man Philip, but did she ever use his Christian name? Hardly ever. It was "Captain" this and "Captain" that.

"Are you going to marry him?"

"I thought you had questions about Hopewell?"

131

"I do."

She gave him a look that clearly said, Well then.

"What about Spencer?"

"What about him?" She dropped her hands onto the vivid crimson of her skirt, and then stood. "Excuse me, Captain, but I fail to see what this has to do with Hopewell."

Joshua turned and dropped his feet onto the soft Turkish carpet. "But it does. We discussed the fact that you need help to run this place." At her nod he continued, "If you married him, it would be Spencer you'd rely on, and I just don't think he's the right person to help you."

"Captain!"

"All right." He held up his hands in defeat. "But don't say I didn't warn you." By the look in her eye he knew he'd pushed her too far.

"Is that all?" How dare he try to dictate to her who she should or should not marry.

"No, it's not all. Does Hopewell import flour?" This was what he had meant to ask her in the first place.

Madeline was taken aback by the sudden change in topic. "Yes, we import flour. We have some fields planted in corn, but wheat doesn't grow well here."

"How much?"

"Flour?" At his nod, she replied, "I don't know for certain. My ledgers are—"

"Enough to sell?"

"No. If I had any extra, I'd ration it out to the slaves. Why? What's going on?"

Joshua studied her. She had been surprised by his question. Of course, with her tumbling golden curls, wide green eyes, and freckled nose, could she look anything but innocent? How had he ever taken her for a whore? He must have been drunk indeed. She was watching him, waiting for an answer, an answer he couldn't give because he didn't know what it was.

He stood up, sorry to leave the soft comfort of the

chaise. It really would have been pleasant to lie back and get some sleep. Of course the bed would have been nicer. It was all frilly and ruffled, with white lacy things hanging from the canopy and stitched around the pillows; yet it looked comfortable and cozy, and if she were in it, too, that would have suited him even better. But he had a strong feeling she wouldn't consider the arrangement acceptable.

He started toward the door.

"Wait." Madeline reached for his sleeve; touched bare arm instead, strong hair-roughened arm. "You didn't answer me."

She let go of him, but not before he had felt the effects of her touch. With her standing as close as she was, smelling of roses, her obviously forgotten bodice open almost to her small, rounded breasts, Joshua knew he had two choices. The first, and the one he'd rather opt for, was to finish unbuttoning her gown and then roll her onto the fluffy white bed. The latter, and the one sanity forced him to choose, was to leave the room altogether.

"I'd really love to stay, Maddie dear." Her eyes flared, and he knew she realized why he'd called her that. "But I really am very tired, and your incessant chatter is keeping me awake."

"My chatter, why you—" But before she could get out exactly what she thought he was, Madeline was addressing empty space. He was gone, and despite her earlier protestations, she was sorry.

133

Chapter 11

"Whitlock?"

The single word broke the tense mealtime silence. Madeline looked beside her, at the person who had spoken it. Philip Spencer toyed with the stem of his wine glass, swirling the dark red liquid, and watched, with a speculative eye, the captain who sat opposite him.

"Whitlock," Philip repeated, as if saying the name aloud would jar open some long-forgotten door in his mind. "The name sounds familiar. Are you perchance in the business of trade?"

"No." The monosyllable made no pretense toward civility, and Madeline wished for longer legs so that she might kick that jackass, the captain, under the table. She tried to catch his eye, but he had already resumed eating the enormous portion of food he had piled on his plate.

"How long are you planning on visiting our fair island?" Madeline turned her brightest smile on Philip, hoping to lessen the sting of Joshua's deplorable manners.

"That, my dear Madeline, depends upon you."

Patrick O'Neil was the recipient of Madeline's first embarrassed glance. He seemed not to have noticed Philip's use of an endearment or its implied meaning. Madeline then stole a look across the table, at the captain. The expression on his face left no doubt that he had missed nothing.

Well, it was simply too bad if he didn't like Philip talking to her in that manner. She found Philip's attentions very— She really wasn't sure how she found them.

Flattering? Of course. Exciting? Maybe. Though she had to admit the comments the captain made to her— most of them—were more so. But his were rarely complimentary. Why would she prefer negative remarks—and from a man she found offensive? The thought was shocking. Obviously she needed to hear more from Philip.

But though she daintily touched the linen napkin to her lips for his benefit, when she turned her gaze on Philip, she again found him studying Captain Whitlock.

"Strange." Philip steepled his fingers over the jerked pork he had barely touched. "I find it difficult to expunge the connection from my mind." He paused, and Madeline wondered briefly if he was attempting to bait the captain. But that was silly. Philip wasn't stupid, and he wasn't blind. The captain hardly had the look of a man one trifled with. Still, as Philip continued, Madeline wasn't sure.

"Whitlock and shipping, shipping, and Whitlock."

"He's a privateer." She had blurted out the words without thinking, and now that she had, she thought better of it. But it was too late. They hung suspended in the air like candle smoke.

Her father's laughter, weak but sounding stronger than it had the day before, relieved the tension. "An honorable profession during times such as these, eh, Captain? Without privateers where would our fine French brandy be? Not warming our bellies, I'd warrant." Patrick took a sip of his wine. "But, Joshua, lad, you are being too modest. Spencer has obviously heard of your family's trading company."

"Ah, so I was right."

"The trading company belonged to my late father and

135

now is my brother's."

"Not yours?"

"I chose a different path."

"The true adventurer."

During this intercourse the two men had seemed oblivious of the others at the table.

Patrick O'Neil reminded them of their oversight. "Gentlemen, I'm afraid we may be boring the lady with our discussion. Perhaps it should best be postponed to a later time."

Madeline certainly wasn't bored, though she was perplexed by the obvious dislike the two men had for one another. But her father was right. It was past time to end the conversation. "If we have all finished our meal"—a quick inventory revealed that the captain had been the only one to do it justice—"perhaps we would be more comfortable in the parlor."

"You young people go along. It was a great pleasure to meet you, Mr. Spencer, and I look forward to talking with you again, but I think I shall retire for the night."

"Are you feeling ill?" Madeline reached across the corner of the table to clasp her father's hand.

"No, no, sweetling, just fatigued. I really am much improved from yesterday." Madeline squeezed his hand. At least he was following her advice about getting more rest.

Of course with her father gone, she would be the only buffer between the two men, who'd faced off like two roosters in a henhouse. Before she could even wonder at her analogy, a deep voice drew Madeline's attention.

"I fear I also must beg permission to decline your kind invitation, Mistress O'Neil, as I have other matters that demand my attention."

Was that the captain speaking? Madeline had to turn toward him to be certain, though his voice ws unmistakable. She knew him to be capable of refined speech, though he'd rarely graced her with displays of it. Still, she was surprised. "Sorry, Maddie, but I have more important things to do" was all she might have expected.

His departure obviated her role as peacemaker, but it also left her alone to entertain Philip. Hardly a disagreeable task, she told herself; yet she wondered what the captain could possibly have to do at this time of evening.

"You seem preoccupied."

Madeline looked over the harpsichord to where Philip leaned, holding open the pages of her music. "Why do you say that?"

Philip smiled, and Madeline thought again what a very attractive man he was. He folded the music and pulled a Chippendale chair over close to her. "You finished playing the Minuet in D Minor several minutes ago, and your fingers have yet to leave the keys."

She looked down to where her hands rested upon the ivory. "I'm sorry, I didn't realize."

"Oh, don't apologize, Madeline dear. Actually you are very lovely with that faraway look in your eye. Tell me, of what were you thinking, or . . . of whom?" He inched his chair closer.

Madeline felt a guilty blush creep up from the satin-stitched ruffles of her stomacher. She hoped he mistook its cause. As her mind searched for an excuse to offer for her woolgathering, something other than the truth, she noticed the music. "Maybe it's Bach. I always find his pieces thought provoking, don't you?"

"Perhaps, though I had hoped it was another man who was invading your mind—one a bit closer."

Oh, if Philip only knew the truth. Her thoughts had been with another man, but not the one who took her hands in his.

"Thank you for bringing the music, Philip. It was so thoughtful." He had surprised her with the collection of Bach's works when they had entered the parlor.

"I know how much you love to play and how ac-

137

complished you are. Your Aunt Libby told me, in the strictest of confidence, of course, that Abigail and Betsy don't play nearly as well as you."

"Oh, she didn't say that."

"You would doubt my word, dear Madeline?"

Madeline tilted her head to the side, and her smile brought forth dimples. Now she remembered why she had enjoyed his company so much in Williamsburg. "Only when I know your lies to be a matter of fact. Abigail and Betsy are far more accomplished than I. Compared to them, I do naught but play around with the notes."

"Ah, but the way you play around." Philip lifted her fingers one by one with his right hand, letting them drop slowly into the open palm of his left. The lazy motions were hypnotic, calming to her senses. "You have yet to answer my question. What were you thinking about?"

The tranquillity deserted her.

Gently she retrieved her hands, wiping their now-damp palms on the apple green, ribbed silk of her gown.

"Philip, I . . ." She stopped speaking. I what? she thought. She looked into his hazel eyes. They were watching—hopeful.

Then why did she hesitate? Wasn't a husband exactly what she needed and, if she were to be honest with herself, even wanted? She loved Hopewell and had always prided herself on its management. But there were times—like now—that it could be a burden, a burden it would be pleasant to share. And contrary to what the captain had said, Philip could help her.

Thinking of the captain brought another consideration to mind. She still did not know if there was to be a child born of their misbegotten union. But, much as her mind rebelled against the idea of foisting another man's child on Philip, she imagined it could be done and did not doubt that countless others had accompanied similar deceptions.

Besides, Philip wanted her. The proposal he'd made in

138

Williamsburg had been heartfelt, genuine. And hadn't he sailed to Jamaica in pursuit of her? How very different his offer of marriage was from the one conscience had wrenched from the captain. . . .

"Madeline?"

Her eyes focused on Philip's concerned face.

"You were lost in thought again, dearest. Is it worry for your father that intrudes upon your mind?"

"Yes." She seized on that excuse, then, just as quickly, experienced pangs of guilt. Her thoughts should have been on her father. Since Madeline left him at the table she had felt uneasy.

"He seemed quite energetic tonight, a trifle thin perhaps."

"He was always so robust, I barely recognized him when I arrived." Madeline swallowed the lump in her throat.

"Poor dear." Philip's thumb traced the fine bones of her hand. "But he appeared to be, while admittedly not in the best of health, certainly in good spirits."

"He was." Madeline smiled, then worried her bottom lip with her teeth. "Yet it's not like him to go off to bed so early." She chuckled. "At least not willingly."

"Perhaps he was simply tired."

"Maybe . . ." She turned worried eyes on him. "Philip, would you mind too terribly if I went to check on him?"

He pulled her gently to her feet.

Hadn't he been taller in Williamsburg?

"Of course not, dearest. Do whatever it takes to ease your mind." He smiled, and Madeline ceased gauging his height and the breadth of his shoulders. He wasn't quite as manly as the captain, but certainly kindness accounted for much more in a person than physical attributes.

Damn, she had been so busy musing about that obnoxious Joshua that she had missed what Philip had said. "Excuse me, I'm sorry, I didn't—"

"My dear, you are in a state. Please, by all means, go to

139

your father. I simply said that I plan to retire also. The road from Kingston is tedious."

"To say the least."

"Madeline." He stepped closer, and her body tensed. "It would probably behoove you to seek your bed soon, too." The tip of his finger traced a curve high on her cheek. "While I'm sure lavender is a color that quite becomes you, it does not belong under these lovely eyes."

Madeline nodded and hated herself for hoping he would not try to kiss her again. He didn't, but his next words reminded her that it was of small consequence.

"Remember, I am most anxious to make you my wife."

The words echoed through her mind as she crept into her father's room. A glance under the door had revealed that no candles glowed within. He was, no doubt, asleep. He must really have been tired.

The room was wrapped in shadows, a ribbon of silvery moonbeams its only light. Thru the open window, the trade winds, as if in atonement for the stifling heat of the previous night, fanned off the bay, setting the seersucker window curtains adance.

Moonlight and the refreshing breeze gave the room such a pleasant aura that Madeline felt like a spoiler as she stole across it, tiptoeing in her green, silk damask shoes, to close the window. But cool night air was not what her father, whose reclining frame she could vaguely discern upon the high tester bed, needed.

By the window she paused. The breeze caught first at a few loosened tendrils of her hair, then at the lace of her lappet cap, and finally it set the linen ruffles at her neck and arms to dancing. Reluctantly she touched her fingers to the cool smooth glass.

"Don't close the window, sweetling."

Madeline turned at the sound of the voice she loved so well. "Papa, I thought you asleep." She stepped toward the bed. "You should be, you know."

"You're probably right, but I was resting." From his

tone, she knew he was smiling.

Madeline giggled. "Resting, indeed. Why didn't you tell me you were awake when I came in?"

"I was watching you, lass. Come." He patted the linens, indicating a spot on the bed. "Sit by me for a while."

Madeline hesitated. "Are you sure this is not too much cool air for you?"

"It's fine. I've weathered enough stiff breezes in my day, a little trade wind isn't going to hurt me."

"Maybe so, but you were much younger then," Madeline retorted cheekily.

"My, but you are a saucy little lass. I had hoped your Aunt Libby would have cured you of that." Patrick laughed as Madeline stacked another pillow under his head.

"Oh, she tried, but you, of all people, know how stubborn I can be." Madeline climbed the steps of the platform, and sat on the edge of the bed.

"A family trait I fear."

"Does that mean I'm stuck with it for life?"

"I'm afraid so, lass."

"Fine, then I shan't try to change in that respect."

Patrick laughed till he shook, then spasms of coughing racked him. Trying to seem composed, Madeline tugged him to a more upright position. "I'm all right," he said when he was able to speak.

"Are you sure?"

"Aye." He coughed again, though without the previous intensity.

This time Madeline held a firm rein on her panic and waited for the seizure to pass. When it did, her father appeared spent, though his eyes shone merrily in the silvery light. He reached out a hand to her.

"Ah, Madeline lass, you do make me laugh."

"Maybe so, but laughing hardly seems the best thing for you right now." The thread of worry in her words was wound round her heart.

"Nay, lass. Laughter is always best." He paused, and when he spoke again, his tone was humorless. "Forgive a selfish old man, girl, but I did sorely miss you while you were away."

"I missed you too, Papa." She touched his hair, once so vibrantly red, now bleached white by age.

For a moment neither spoke, for they were lost to memories. Then Patrick's voice came to her above the night sounds of crickets and frogs, and the faint but eternal song of the sea.

"It seems like yesterday that I was sitting on the edge of your bed—"

"Telling me stories—"

"About the sea."

Madeline's smile was spontaneous. "I used to lie with my eyes wide open after Hattie snuffed my candle, waiting for you to come."

"I always did."

She nodded, remembering. "And most of the time I had managed to stay awake."

"You'd say, 'Tell me a story, Papa, about when you were a captain.'"

"They were always so exciting."

Patrick chuckled and patted her hand. "Well, lass, I suppose I can tell you now, there were times when I may have garnished the tales just a wee bit."

"No!" Madeline feigned shock. "You mean you didn't fight off a horde of pirates with naught but a cutlass and your wits?"

"'Tis poking fun at your old dad, you are now, lass."

Madeline held her breath as her father's laughter, feeble but true, rang out. There was no coughing this time.

"Papa?"

A question had been gnawing at Madeline for the past two days; now she hesitated to ask it.

"What is it, lass?"

She released her pent-up breath. "Why didn't you

142

ever tell me you were a partner in the *Providence?*" He had often talked of the vessel, but had never mentioned owning a share in her, nor had he spoken of Justin Whitlock.

Her father was quiet for so long Madeline thought he had not heard her or that perhaps fatigue had overtaken him. She had about decided it was time to leave when he began to speak.

"There were some parts of that involvement I wanted to forget."

"To forget?" Madeline suddenly wished for a shawl to combat the chill his words had caused.

"Aye, the tales I told, the ones you liked as a child, all had a happy ending. This one did not."

Madeline saw that he was examining her face as if trying to decide whether or not to proceed. She could only answer his gaze with a look of wide-eyed curiosity.

"There were three partners in the *Providence.* We had met by chance aboard the schooner in Boston harbor. I was there to inquire about a vessel to take our tobacco to England."

Madeline nodded. She knew that her father and Aunt Libby had been born and raised on a small plantation on the James River, not far from Williamsburg.

Patrick continued. "Justin Whitlock lived in Boston. His was a prosperous ship-building family. And Matthew Burke . . . I never really knew why he was there. But anyway, we became friends, then partners. I had been sailing most of my then-young life. My brother, John, was due to inherit our plantation, and anyway, sailing was in my blood."

"We made a good profit on our first voyage; more on the next. The three of us were doing very well until . . . ."

"Until what, Papa? What happened?" Madeline leaned forward, expectant.

"Justin had a sister. She was young and very pretty, and if the truth be known, I suppose I was a wee bit in love with her."

143

"You, Papa!"

"'Twas before I met your mother, lass. I was young and I did say 'a wee bit.'"

"What happened to her?" Madeline urged, wanting him to get back to the story. Her exclamation had been involuntary, and she now wished she hadn't interrupted his tale.

"What happened to her?" He repeated her question, almost to himself. "It seems Matthew Burke was neither the gentleman Justin and I had supposed, nor the friend."

"Did he do something to her?"

"Aye, lass, he did."

"What?"

"That, lass, is something I cannot discuss with a sweet young thing like yourself."

"Papa." Madeline was exasperated. She almost considered revealing the fact that she was no longer an innocent maid, but decided against that bit of impetuousness.

"No, Madeline. Let me just say this. There was a terrible fight—"

"Between you and Matthew Burke?"

"Oh, I got my licks in, though it was mostly between Matthew and Justin; it was his sister after all."

"What happened after the fight?"

"Justin called him out."

"And he killed him?"

"Nay."

"Then what happened?" Obviously Matthew Burke hadn't killed Justin Whitlock, for during his first night at Hopewell, the captain had mentioned that his father had just passed away.

"Just settle yourself, lass, and I'll tell you."

Obediently, Madeline assumed a more relaxed pose, but her interest remained acute.

"I was to be Justin's second. The following morning

144

was chilly, for it was late October and frost covered the fallen leaves. I remember thinking how cold I was, then feeling guilty as hell. The two men I had considered my closest friends would soon be trying to kill each other, and I was worried about my own discomfort. Not that Matthew didn't deserve to die, mind you. Still, Justin had beaten him pretty severely the night before, and Burke had been my friend."

Patrick paused, and Madeline suppressed the impulse to spur him on.

"He didn't die, though." He snorted. "The coward never showed up. While we were stomping our feet on frost-gilded maple leaves trying to keep warm, he was sailing the *Providence* out of Boston harbor."

"He stole her?" Madeline was aghast.

"Aye, he stole her all right, from underneath our noses."

"But you must have found the ship—him. I mean, a schooner doesn't just disappear."

"This one did. Never saw her again. We did hear from Matthew Burke though. At least, Justin thought we had. I was in Jamaica by that time, but he wrote and told me about . . . I never could quite believe even Burke would do that." His voice drifted off as if he were reliving some awful event.

"Do what?" Madeline urged.

Patrick's head snapped around, and he seemed to notice his daughter anew. "'Tis nothing, lass. Story over. You wanted to know what happened to the *Providence*, and now you do. She disappeared."

Madeline's hands found her hips. "There's more to this story than you're telling."

Patrick chuckled, and the last of his unpleasant memories seemed to disappear. "Now, Madeline, don't pester your old dad. 'Tis all the storytelling I intend to do for one night. Besides, I have a question for you."

"But—"

"Now don't be giving me buts. I said that was all, and I meant it. 'Tis too pleasant a night to be dredging up old memories."

He had been right. Stubbornness was a family trait, and her father had it aplenty. Madeline resigned herself to not hearing the rest of the story—that night. But she, too, had this family trait, and one day she knew she would find out what had happened.

At that late hour, however, her father looked tired. "I think I'd better let you sleep, Papa," she said, and started to rise. But a surprisingly strong hand on her arm stopped her.

"No you don't, lass. I answered your question. Now it's your turn to answer mine."

Frustration over not hearing what had happened to Justin Whitlock's sister had caused Madeline to forget her father's question. "All right." She settled back onto the bed, and her father's grip on her relaxed. "What did you ask me?"

"Who is this Philip Spencer?" The query was so unexpected that it took Madeline a moment to realize it had not been couched in the most pleasant tone.

"I told you at dinner; we met in Williamsburg. He's an acquaintance of Thomas, Aunt Libby's eldest son."

"You needn't be telling me who Thomas is; I'm aware of my nephew's names. What I'm waiting to know is what this man is to you."

"Well, he's—"

"Now remember, lass, I'm always able to tell when you're not being entirely truthful."

Damn! Why had he said that? She hadn't been going to tell him about Philip. At least not now. Of course, that had been before Philip had shown up on her doorstep.

Resignedly Madeline confessed the truth. "He asked me to marry him in Williamsburg."

"And followed you here?"

"Yes."

146

Patrick wriggled up higher on his pillows, stopping Madeline with a shake of his head when she tried to help. After he was settled more comfortably, he asked, "Why didn't you tell me before?"

Madeline shrugged. "I don't know. Perhaps I was afraid it would upset you."

"Upset me?" Her father appeared genuinely confused. "Do you think I don't wish for you to marry, to find the happiness your mother and I had?"

"No." Madeline barely whispered her answer. She herself now wondered why she hadn't told him. But he had looked so weak.

"Good, because I do. I don't like the idea of your being alone here."

"But I'm not alone; you're—"

Madeline's father interrupted her. "Did you accept him?"

"Not yet."

"Do you intend to?"

"I don't know." Madeline studied her fingers, now tightly entwined and resting on her lap.

"What about Joshua?"

Her head shot up. "The captain?"

"Aye, what about *him?*" Her father seemed to have warmed to the subject.

"Well, what about him?" Madeline's tone sparked with fire but not warmth.

"He'd make a fine husband for you."

"He would not!"

"And just why not, lass?" Patrick asked, his Irish brogue more evident.

"For one thing he's a privateer." Madeline had almost said pirate, but she'd decided her argument would hold more weight if she stuck to the truth. She could have spared herself the effort. Her father dismissed that objection with a flip of his hand. All right, she'd have to tell him what she thought of the captain. "He's rude and overbearing and . . . and stubborn."

Patrick O'Neil positively beamed at that last comment.

Madeline scowled. Stubbornness was hardly a common trait on which to build a marriage. "Well, Papa," she began smugly, "it may have escaped your notice, but the captain and I do not get on well together."

The smile hadn't vanished. "Come to think of it, lass, I have noticed a few sparks flying between the two of you."

"It wasn't sparks you saw. It was hatred." Madeline jumped off the bed and stood facing her father, hands on her hips.

"So you hate old Joshua, do you?"

"Yes." The word was a hiss.

"H'm." Her father appeared to seriously consider this last admission, though he remained more amused than contemplative. "Mighty strong emotion, hate. 'Tis hard to fathom you could feel it for someone you've known such a short time."

"Well, I do."

"And Joshua, does he . . . hate you, lass, with the same intensity?"

"I have no idea." How did this silly conversation ever start, and more importantly, how could she stop it? "Papa"—Madeline moved closer to the bed—"I really do not wish to discuss the captain. It does nothing but agitate you."

"'Tis not I who is agitated."

Madeline ignored his remark. "If I marry anyone, it shall be Philip." She put her fingers to his lips to hush any further comments. "Right now, however, I am going to marry no one. I'm going to bed." After gently pulling the extra pillow from beneath her father's head, she helped him to snuggle beneath the covers, kissed him fondly on the cheek, rearranged the mosquito netting, and then tip-toed across the room. He had settled in so quietly she thought him already asleep.

"Madeline." His voice reached her just as her hand

148

touched the window sash. "I love you, lass."

"And I love you, Papa." She closed the window, then thought better of it and reopened it a few inches. Let him enjoy the breeze, she thought as she left her father's room.

A melody, hauntingly sweet, drifted through Joshua's mind as he shrugged out of his blue, lozenge silk coat. His bedroom was dark, except for the pale moonlight that shone through the open window. Sinking into a chair to remove his boots, he began to hum a tune, and then he remembered where he'd heard it. Madeline had been playing it for Philip Spencer earlier that evening.

Joshua jerked open his waistcoat buttons and took the garment off. It felt good to get out of his clothes; they were too hot for the clime. But this was the best suit he had, and he'd have roasted in hell before he'd have gone down to dinner dressed in anything but his best. Still he should have changed before traipsing off to the stables to meet Sau.

The black man was a mystery, and Joshua wasn't sure he trusted him completely. But Sau had come when he'd sent a message through Dora. And he had answered Joshua's questions, though his answers had brought forth more questions.

Joshua grabbed the tail of his shirt and pulled the bleached linen over his head. Why was someone using Hopewell to unload cargo, secretly—and at night? And why was so much of that cargo flour? Joshua had found old, rotting bags of flour in the third cave he'd explored that morning.

Flour was a much-needed commodity in the islands, and transporting it there had helped to make his father wealthy, but it was hardly a cargo most pirates would chose to steal. Nonetheless, Sau had claimed that he and the other slaves unloaded flour most of the time.

Joshua poured some water into the washbasin and splashed the tepid liquid over his face and chest, then grabbed a towel off the mahogany stand to dab at the rivulets as they trickled down his flat belly toward his pants.

He loosened the fall front and undid the buttons behind the flap of his breeches. Tomorrow he would leave, Joshua told himself as he stepped out of his cotton underdrawers. Nathaniel wasn't at Hopewell, and finding him had to be his first concern.

The sheets were cool and smooth against his nude body as Joshua climbed into the bed. Tonight he would sleep. Tomorrow he would leave. His mind repeated the thought like a litany until he slipped into slumber.

Chapter 12

At least he's still alive, Madeline mused as she walked along the shore. The setting sun sprinkled diamond dust upon the waters of the bay, but she barely noticed. Since before dawn, when her father had suffered the agonizing attacks of pain, she'd been running on nervous energy, and it was almost sapped. Except for the short time that Papa had spent with Captain Whitlock, she'd sat by his bed, watching for any sign of a worsening in her father's condition. Moments ago, Patrick O'Neil had fallen into a restful slumber, and Madeline had been unable to stem her tears of gratitude.

When a sound caught her attention, she looked around to see the captain striding through the trees toward her. He appeared quite different than he had this morning when they had rushed together into her father's room. His shirt had not been pristine white then, nor had it been topped with a frock coat and a smartly tied stock. It had been rumpled, stained by wear, and it had smelled of him. The deep slit down its open front had revealed the thick, curling black hair on Joshua's chest, hair that had matched the dark strands on his stockingless lower legs.

Heavens, Madeline would have sworn she had not noticed such details during the frantic happenings in her father's room. The realization that she had, and had remembered them, made her angry.

"What do you want?" she snapped.

Joshua was taken aback by her tone. He had seen her walking toward the bay and had decided that this was as good a time as any to ask her. He shook his head. He still couldn't believe he'd let Patrick O'Neil talk him into this, but there was no way out now. Joshua had not been with his own father when he'd died, and he wondered if that was why he'd been unable to resist granting Patrick his dying wish.

"Marry Madeline," Patrick had said, his voice weak from fighting the pain. When Joshua had just stood there, stunned, Patrick had offered Hopewell as further incentive. In the end, Joshua had agreed, but it hadn't been the plantation that had swayed him. Admittedly, he carried some guilt about their first time together, but mostly it was the woman standing in front of him that had made Joshua concede. He wanted her. He just wasn't sure she wanted him.

He had never offered marriage to another, though with Madeline, the tender was taking on the earmarks of a habit. With some measure of conceit Joshua remembered a goodly number of ladies who'd wished he would propose. Anything other than a positive response to his advances had been unheard of—unthought of—till . . .

"Well?" Madeline glared up at him.

Joshua swallowed, then smiled. "I thought we might share the calm of the evening."

"Actually, I was enjoying the solitude as much as the evening." Madeline knew she was being rude, but didn't care. She'd just been through too much to feign politeness.

The saucy wench isn't making this easy. Joshua sidled closer. "Ah, but if you were alone you wouldn't be able to hear my question, Maddie."

Madeline cocked her head to one side. "You have a question to ask me?" He was acting strange, almost nervous, but it was inconceivable that the bold Captain Whitlock would be skittish.

152

"Yes, I do." His words were gruff and too loud.

Madeline retreated a step in the soft sand. Whatever his problem was, he had no right to yell at her. She was tired, and she wanted to be away from this man who played havoc with her senses and her mind. "Well, ask me the damned question so I can go to bed."

"Suppose we go to bed; then I'll ask you the damn question?"

"What?" the word left Madeline's throat as a squeak.

"You heard me, and don't act as if you misunderstood my meaning."

Joshua advanced on her retreating form until she was flattened against the rough bark of a palm tree. The feel of the solid trunk against her back strengthened her anger.

"Oh, I understand the meaning of your vile words all right. I'd just like to know why you think you can talk to me like that?"

Joshua wished he knew. Obviously he hadn't thought before speaking because he'd been taught better than to make such a proposition to a lady—at least an unwilling lady.

She had made him mad—again—with her uncooperative attitude. And he'd been sick and tired of fluttering around like some silly old spinster. Besides, the idea of bedding Madeline did have some merit; at least he thought so. And he wasn't convinced that she didn't think so, too.

In the next instant, he compounded his blunder by saying as much.

Madeline gasped. The implication that she desired him made her angry, yes, but more to the point, it embarrassed her. Had he noticed the way her gaze lingered on the handsome planes of his face, or caressed the breadth of his back and chest, or dallied while observing the cut of his breeches?

She looked shocked and turned almost as red as she'd been the first time he'd seen her. And why not?

Whatever devil had taken control of his tongue had done a fine job—no chance of a wedding now.

"Damn it, Maddie," Joshua whispered as he stepped toward her.

She raised stricken eyes to him, and he noticed the shimmering teardrops caught in the thick fringe of her lower lashes. With the pad of his thumb, he wiped them away, then traced the soft contours of her cheekbones, the sensual curve of her bottom lip.

She told herself she should leave. Just standing here was making a farce of any denials she might make regarding her feelings. But it felt so wonderful, the way he touched her. It made her tingle to the tips of her toes. If just his thumb, one lazy thumb, could do that, what could all of him do? Of its own volition her body moved to find out.

When Joshua felt the full length of her soft, uncorseted body mold to his, he lost all the control he had striven to gain.

His hands twined in her golden hair, angling her face toward his. Until the very moment lips touched lips he feared she would pull away.

She didn't. Madeline could no more have turned away than she could have stopped the tides from hugging the shore. The closer she sank into the shelter of his arms—his body—the more greedily she clutched at him.

Her lips parted, allowing his tongue—hot, wet and boldly delicious—to seek hers. Like a magnet it drew her. This initial mating of tongues was delightful. Hers, retiring and demure; his plunging audaciously. Soon she, now as bold as he, directed a counterthrust into the sensual haven of his mouth.

His deep moan of primeval pleasure began in the depths of his chest. The vibrations still reverberated through Madeline's body as his lips left hers to caress the blush of her cheek, the tip of her ear.

Her neck lost the rigidity needed to stay erect as the flame that was his tongue burned a path down its slender

154

column. Like a flower stem it bent for him, exposing its sweet secrets.

He sighed her name once, then more demandingly, as his large hand molded the curve of her breast.

"Maddie, Maddie."

His voice was a husky song of desire. Its rhythm matched the kneading motion of his palm, the beating of his heart. It hypnotized her with its earthy need.

"Maddie, Maddie."

"No, please don't." She wasn't certain she'd actually voiced the words before his lips again found hers. But it didn't matter. She didn't mean them.

She pressed closer to him, contact making her giddy. And she throbbed with desire. His body was strong and hard, while hers was melting, dissolving into a hot molten liquid that seemed to pool in that part of her that ached for him.

And then he was touching her.

Madeline's leg quivered when his work-callused fingers touched the smooth, soft skin of her thigh. Then she felt herself slowly sinking toward the silvery sand. The sensation was too wonderful to resist; he gently was lowering her to the beach.

But his hand was not gentle, nor was his mouth. As the captain lay beside her, he pressed hungry, passionate kisses to her eyes, her hair, the underside of her chin. And all the while his fingers reached higher, through the tangle of petticoats toward the core of her yearning.

"Oooh!" Madeline's dreamlike moan mingled with the sighing of the wind through the palm fronds, then drifted out to sea. She arched, crushing herself against the hand that stroked back and forth, stoking fires that had lain dormant till now.

Had it been like this before? Had her body known this wild surge of pleasure while her mind slept? Madeline didn't know, and in the next moment she didn't care. Something was happening that she couldn't control, couldn't stop, even if she wanted to.

Her eyes fluttered open, only to meet the dark, intense stare of Joshua. He was watching her with an odd mixture of pleasure and arrogance, as if he knew what she was feeling. But how could he? How could he?

Wild stormy waves of pleasure rippled through her, tightening her breasts, pumping her hips against his hand. Her breath came in ragged gasps, and she dug her fingers into the warm, moist sand to keep the joyous scream lodged in her throat from escaping into the sultry air.

The buttons of his breeches had never proven such a barrier. Joshua fumbled in the twilight, opening one, then another. He hadn't meant for this to happen, but happen it would. There was no denying the main reason he'd agreed to the marriage. He wanted her—had wanted her since that morning he'd kissed her on board the *Chesapeake*. And it wasn't as if they hadn't made love before. He just couldn't understand, given the force of his desire, why he couldn't remember the other time.

And then he knew.

Joshua paused but a moment against the moist heat of Madeline's undulating body before thrusting forward. At first he thought he imagined the delicate shield that impeded his passage into her fiery sheath. It couldn't be—he'd rent her maidenhead himself. But his second, more cautious plunge proved his earlier impression correct. She was a virgin!

Reluctantly, his mind bid his body stop. He needed time to think, to decide why she'd lied to him about that night at sea. But his traitorous flesh was buried deep inside her essence and knew no logic. The rotation of his hips was involuntary. Though he told himself he wanted to break away from her, the touch of her lips, the pressure of breasts burning through the fabric of their clothing, the engulfing heat that surrounded him were too sensual to resist. His movements built to a crescendo of maddening pleasure, and his seed exploded inside her.

"Miz Madeline."

She tried to ignore the words she'd barely heard over the beating surf, the rasping of the captain's breathing in her ear, the blood pounding through her head. How could she have done this? The other time had been one thing, she'd had no choice, but this . . . She'd not only known exactly what was happening, she'd been willing to let it happen again. Nay, "willing" wasn't the word. She'd been eager. Even when he'd hurt her, when his large swollen manhood had entered her, she'd writhed beneath him, begging for more.

"Miz Madeline!"

The voice was closer now, and Madeline suddenly realized it wasn't a sound to be ignored. "My God! Get off me." Madeline pushed against the captain's strong shoulder as she struggled to rise.

Without a word, he levered himself up and began buttoning his breeches. Madeline self-consciously yanked down her skirts and sat up. She was covered with sand, and tried desperately to brush the granules from her gown.

When she lifted her arm to finger-comb a riot of tangled curls she noticed that the captain was looking at her. Even the gathering darkness could not disguise the anger in his eyes, anger directed at her. She was about to ask why, what had she done? But then the voice came to her again.

"Miz Madeline. It's the master. He's real bad."

Madeline forgot all else as she pulled up her skirts and raced toward the great house.

Chapter 13

He was gone.

It had been three hours since her father had died, and still Madeline could not accept it. She sat, chin resting on drawn-up knees, huddled against the headboard of her bed, staring without seeing. She had failed to remove her silk damask shoes, and their soles left tiny patches of dirt on the white ruffled counterpane whenever she moved.

A footfall echoed in the hall beyond the mahogany door, and abruptly Madeline's gaze fixed on the portal. She clutched the rumpled flower-strewn skirt tighter about her legs and waited.

I stayed awake. When Papa comes he'll tell me a story, and will laugh over the shared jokes and then he'll . . .

No. Madeline's breath caught on a sob as she remembered the events of that night. Idly she watched as a lone tear dropped onto her cotton-covered knee. The tiny droplet shimmered momentarily in the glow from the candle placed beside her bed; then it disappeared as the fabric of her skirt embraced it, drawing it into a slowly widening circle of dampness.

No more would Papa come to her room. No more would he tell her his wonderful stories. No more would they share laughter and tears. He was lying in the parlor, awaiting the morrow when he would fulfill the prophecy—ashes to ashes, dust to dust.

The end had come so quickly Madeline had barely had time to absorb what was happening. She had left her father sleeping more soundly than he had all day and had returned, tearing through the open door of his room, to find him in the throes of those deadly pains.

Anticipating another tear, Madeline wiped at her face with the lacy sleeve of her gown. As she did so, she heard someone tapping on her door, lightly at first, then with more vigor. Resting her forehead on her knees, she tried to ignore the sound. But it became more persistent.

"Who is it?" She flung the words at the mahogany panel, annoyed that any of the servants would bother her now.

"'Tis Joshua. May I come in?"

"No."

He had been there, too, when the end had come. He had followed her up from the bay.

Madeline winced as she remembered what she had been doing on the beach. While her father lay dying she had been in the captain's arms succumbing to the lust he inspired in her.

The tapping sounded again.

"Go away."

"Dammit, Maddie. I need to talk to you."

Madeline could almost picture him, braced against the door frame with his large hands, his face close to the panel so his words could more easily carry through the stout wood.

"We've nothing to discuss." Oh, how she wished those words were true.

"The hell we don't." Even without seeing him, Madeline knew he was losing patience. Her silence was met by another sharp rap on the door, this one so hard her gaze whipped up to make certain he hadn't splintered the wood. He hadn't, but his next words justified her suspicion that he soon would.

"Dammit, Maddie, open this door or so help me I'll break the bloody thing down!"

If his pounding hadn't alerted the rest of the household—since Madeline heard no one challenging him, she could only assume it hadn't—shattering timber certainly would. Reluctantly she left her perch on the bed and stepped to the door. Drawing a deep, fortifying breath she released the lock and swung the door open.

Obviously he hadn't expected his threat to work, for as she caught sight of him, his fist was raised ready to pound on the wooden barrier again.

He had enough decency to look contrite, but not enough to leave.

"For God's sake, Maddie, why do you always have to be so stubborn," he said as he pushed past her slight frame and entered the room.

"Me?" She slammed the door and turned to confront him, but he had strode to the French doors that opened onto her balcony and was staring out at the star-sprinkled night. Determinedly she marched toward him. "You call me stubborn? Who stood pounding on my door at this late hour, refusing to leave?" Her voice rose to a fevered pitch, and she somehow hoped he would take up the gauntlet and yell back at her. A screaming, scratching fight with him held some appeal for her at that moment. But he didn't oblige.

"I sent Hattie with a message that I wanted to see you," he stated.

"Well, I didn't want to see you." Again she baited him; again he ignored her taunt. Now that he had gained entry into her room, he appeared the calmest of men. One would never guess him to be the madman who had moments ago threatened to splinter her door.

"I knew you were still awake when I saw the light beneath your door." His explanation was unnerving. She turned from him and sank onto the bench in front of her dressing table. Resting her elbows on smooth polished wood, she tried to ignore his presence.

Impossible.

In the next heartbeat, he was behind her. "I'm so very

160

sorry about your father."

"Are you?" Her tone implied that she strongly questioned his sincerity, and the mirror's reflection of his shocked countenance revealed that he'd caught her meaning.

"You doubt my grief?" His gaze caught hers in the looking glass, and she was forced to glance away. Joshua was trying to ignore his anger at her because of what she'd been through. But it boiled beneath the surface, and her attitude was doing nothing to keep it there.

"Perhaps that is going too far," she granted. "But you must admit my father's death does much to improve your circumstances."

"I never asked for that, Maddie."

"Didn't you?" She whirled to face him, tired of trying to read his expression secondhand in the reflection.

"No, I didn't." He faced her defiantly. "And if the truth be known, I was hardly in favor of the idea."

"Fine." She almost believed he had not gone to her father coveting Hopewell, but the idea that he had been coerced into agreeing to marry her angered Madeline nearly as much.

She glared at him, daring him to challenge her next words. "Then we can forget the whole insane idea."

"No."

Madeline had started toward the French doors when she heard the monosyllabic rebuttal. Her soft, cotton skirts swirled around her slender body as she turned on him.

"What do you mean, no? You yourself said—"

"I said"—his voice had regained the angry timbre it had possessed when the door had blocked him from her—"the idea was not mine, nor was it desirous. I never said I did not agree to it."

Oh, the man was insufferable. To stand there and admit he found the idea of marriage to her undesirable was an insult of the highest order. She twisted her hands into the fabric of her skirt. "How could you agree to a plan you found so repugnant?"

He laughed, but the sound had naught to do with mirth. "You forget, my little Maddie, I heard you agree to abide by the very same promise. Of course, maybe the implication is that you"—his emphasis on the word was impossible to miss—"do not find the arrangement distasteful."

Madeline heard the rending of delicate stitches as she tore at the wads of balled-up skirt material in her hands. "Oh, I find the idea of marriage to you distasteful, all right, distasteful and vile and totally—totally—unacceptable!"

"Then you shouldn't have granted his wish." His voice had regained some semblance of control, but the throbbing tic in his clenched jaw showed the depth of his anger.

"I had no choice." He had been there, in the room. Certainly he knew.

"We all have choices, Maddie."

Damn him! Tears threatened to spring to life, but she swallowed hard, concentrating on the hateful man before her, and fought them back.

How could he stand there and imply she had been given a choice? He had seen her father clutching his chest, fighting for every raspy breath, begging her. "Accept him," papa had said, and at first Madeline had thought she had misunderstood the strangled words. Accept whom? she'd wondered. What could he mean? Though firmly in the grip of pain, he must have recognized her confusion, for in his next labored breath he had clarified himself.

"Marry him; marry Joshua," he'd said, clutching at the front of her dress. When she had only stared at him in disbelief, he had uttered his final plea. "Promise me . . ." The words had drifted off, and she had felt his hand relax, then fall to the bed.

Frantically, she had reached for him. "I will; I will. Papa, I promise." *I promise.* Were the words to haunt

162

her forever?

"He was dying," Madeline protested. "I would have promised him anything."

"Precisely. Few of us can deny a deathbed wish."

Madeline studied the handsome face before her. So he wished her to believe his reason for agreeing to their joining as man and wife was the same? Perhaps. Though no one could deny he had more to gain from their union than she. The very thought made her wish to deny him that advantage.

"Since we appear to agree that we want no part of this marriage, I propose we jointly pledge to forget the words we spoke in the throes of emotion. Such a pact would be easy enough to keep. No one else knows of it."

"Tsk, tsk." He shook his head solemnly. "Forget a promise freely given, a vow to a father you professed to love? It hardly seems like you."

"I did love him, damn you!" Madeline cried. "But he couldn't have wanted me to bind myself to you if he had known how I feel."

"Oh, he knew how you felt. I told him not only of your dislike of me but of your, shall we say, opposite feelings for Spencer; still he insisted."

"Spencer?" Madeline was truly amazed that Philip's name had entered the conversation. "What does he have to do with any of this?"

"I wonder"—Joshua let his fingers trail along the tiny crocheted balls that fringed the edge of her canopied bed—"if your reluctance to marry, to accede to your father's request, would be quite so vehement if it were Spencer your father had suggested you wed."

"That is preposterous. I wish to marry no one." She didn't point out that Philip at least desired to wed her.

"Unfortunately, you shall wed. Unlike you, I consider a promise made to a dying man very binding."

"You bastard." Madeline advanced on him, her green eyes flaring.

"Such endearments are touching, Maddie, on the eve

163

of our wedding day."

She halted. "Eve? You can't possibly mean you plan to see this vile deed through tomorrow. I'm in mourning."

Joshua ran his hand down the column of the bedpost. "I admit it is a bit irregular, but it's what your father planned. He had already sent for a minister, and the man arrived no more than an hour ago. It's what I came to tell you. That, and to offer my condolences."

Madeline watched as he walked to the door, apparently deciding their interview was over. His arrogance astounded her. He had walked into her room, into her life, and had done nothing but try to take charge. The desire to let him know that control was not his became overwhelming.

"I won't marry you tomorrow."

He paused, his hand swallowing the brass doorknob in its tanned depths, and turned toward her. "Oh, I think we both know you will."

The cavalier manner in which he said the words infuriated her.

"It will never be a marriage in the true sense," she lashed out.

"Meaning?" His black eyes narrowed.

"Must I spell it out for you?" Madeline asked as she watched his ominous scowl. "I may be forced to marry you, but I will not tolerate any more disgusting advances such as you forced on me tonight."

For a moment Madeline feared she had gone too far. They both knew he hadn't forced her, this time. He strode toward her, ceasing to advance only when any more forward motion would have knocked her over.

He ground these words through tightly clenched teeth. "Tomorrow I take a wife, not a sharp-tongued asp, to my breast. If, and please note my use of the word if, I wished to make advances to said wife, I would expect them to be more than tolerated. They had damned well better be welcomed!" His eyes narrowed. "As welcomed as they were tonight."

Madeline was saved from making a rebuttal to his crude pronouncement by the abruptness of his departure.

She stood for several minutes, the echo of the slamming door ringing in her ears. With very little imagination, she could fancy the mellowed wood vibrating in response to its rough treatment at the captain's hands. It was then she noticed the quivering of her own body.

His treatment of her had been no less brutal. Oh, there had been no banging or slamming about, but he had threatened and bullied. The very idea that she would marry him on the day her father was buried was unthinkable—but not to the captain. He not only thought it; he expected it.

Madeline wrapped her arms about herself; then, finding that but slight relief from the chill that permeated her, she opened her clothespress and found a shawl.

The house seemed asleep when she crept out into the hallway. Gently, she closed her door. Madeline had no wish for company on her nocturnal pilgrimage to the parlor. The candle she carried flickered as she hurried along the corridor, then down the great winding staircase.

At first, as she entered the open doors of the parlor, she didn't notice the man in the shadows. Her attention was focused on the body of her father. Someone, she assumed it was Hattie, had dressed him in his best suit of clothes. Madeline hadn't seen his lavender, ribbed silk jacket since they had gone to the McCain's plantation three years ago. She remembered thinking at the time how handsome it made him look. Now, it simply emphasized the gauntness of his body. Madeline's fingers traced the raised texture of the silk. The full skirt of the jacket dated the garment. Idly she thought, If only there were more time, I could cut the jacket down, make it more stylish, make it fit better.

"Madeline dear, are you all right?"

165

The unexpected voice caused her to tilt the brass candleholder she still held, spilling hot wax on her hand.

"Ouch." She quickly placed the taper on the table by her father's body and grabbed her burned hand.

"I didn't mean to startle you." Instantly Philip was by her side, examining the sprinkling of red welts on her hand. "I thought you saw me when you came in."

"I didn't." Madeline tried not to let the annoyance she felt seep into her expression. Gently, she retrieved her hand, but not before he had placed a kiss upon the abused flesh, a gesture that Madeline realized did nothing to soothe the pain.

"Why are you down here, Philip?" She had hoped for some time alone with her father. Soon she would never see him again.

If he was shocked by the bluntness of her question, Philip didn't allow that to register on his handsome face.

"I was concerned about you, Madeline. You have been through so much, and you've been such a brave little darling. I just wish you'd let me help you."

While he talked, he led her into the small family parlor off the more formal room. Gratefully, Madeline sank onto the cushions of a love seat. She looked at Philip, who was sitting beside her, and felt guilty for her earlier annoyance. Then she smiled at him. Philip, unlike another she could name, had never been anything but kind and courteous toward her. His stating that he wanted to help her proved that. She had let her anger at Joshua affect her treatment of Philip.

"That's very kind of you, but you are helping me. Your presence during these last trying days has given me a great deal of comfort."

He took her hand again, and she tried not to mind.

"If only I thought that was enough, Madeline dear."

"But it is. Your friendship—"

"Is that what I am to you, Madeline, a friend?" He hushed her reply by touching a finger to her lips. "For if it is, I shall try to be grateful for that, but dearest, my desire is to be much, much more." His hazel eyes pleaded with her. "You must know how I feel about you. I made my intentions toward you clear even before you left Williamsburg."

"Philip," Madeline began; then she turned away. Tears clouded her vision. She wished things were different. His sweet declaration should determine that he was the one to win her, not a demand issued in the inappropriate confines of her room.

"I realize you are in mourning and my words may seem poorly timed, but I hate to see you forced to face the hardships of administering this plantation alone when I am so willing to help you."

"I won't be alone." Madeline saw the spark of hope in his eyes, and knew he had misunderstood her softly spoken words.

"May I hope that you will allow my—"

"I'm marrying the captain tomorrow."

"Whitlock? You're marrying Whitlock?" He was incredulous and angry. And though Madeline realized he had every right to be provoked, she was surprised by his outburst. She had never seen him vexed.

Before she could wonder at this new facet of his character, Philip shocked her further by grabbing her shoulders less than gently and turning her towards him.

"Why, Madeline?" It was a reasonable question, one to which he certainly deserved an answer.

"I promised my father." The words barely made it out of a throat suddenly grown tight. If Madeline had ever doubted that Philip loved her, his reaction to the news of her impending marriage would have convinced her otherwise. With obvious effort he eased the irate set of his features and loosened his biting grip on her shoulders.

"Philip, please understand. It has nothing to do with my"—Madeline could not speak the word "love"—"feelings for you. Papa didn't want me to be alone, he—"

"You didn't tell him about us?"

167

His use of the term "us" annoyed her as much as his demanding tone, but she tried to remember he was a spurned suitor and his reaction was to be expected.

"He knew of your proposal."

"And?"

"And apparently he chose to ignore it." Madeline was tired of his anger, tired of the conversation, just tired.

Philip apparently realized this, for his next words bore no hint of his earlier ire. "Do you love him, Madeline dear?"

A sudden vision of herself, joined intimately to Joshua, flashed across her mind before she could stop it. But surely that hadn't been love. "No!" Now it was her voice that was raised.

"Then forget this plan." His hazel eyes pleaded with her. "Your father was ill. He may not even have realized what he asked of you." He ignored the negative shake of her head. "You needn't be alone. I'll marry you whenever you like. Madeline dearest, I can make you happy."

Madeline ignored the fact that less than an hour before she had tried to renege on her promise. Now the very thought that she might fail to grant her father's dying wish was repugnant. She opened her mouth to tell Philip that, but before she realized his intent, he had drawn her to him and his lips were covering hers.

"Well, well, how very touching. Saying our farewells are we, my precious bride?" At the sound of the sarcastic voice she knew only too well, Madeline recovered some of the strength that had failed her moments before and she pushed Philip away.

Joshua watched her with barely controlled anger. Theirs was hardly a love match. Still he had not expected to find her, on the eve of their wedding, in her lover's arms. No, not her lover. If there was one thing he was certain of, it was that Madeline had had no lover except himself. Still, seeing them together had made him feel like a cuckolded husband—and he didn't like the feeling one bit.

At least he wasn't the only one experiencing unease. Judging from the high color of her cheeks and the surprised gape of her mouth, Madeline also found the situation disconcerting.

Not so Spencer. Unlike his amorous partner of moments ago, he still sat on the brocaded pillows of the love seat, a smug smile curving his lips. His total lack of surprise at the groom's appearance made Joshua wonder if Spencer hadn't heard him approach.

"Captain, I can explain." Madeline nervously smoothed the wrinkles of her flower-sprigged skirt.

"Can you?" Joshua's brow rose cynically.

"Yes, I can." She resented his scorn-laced words, and stood before him, now defiant, all suggestion of guilt wiped from her expression. "I was simply explaining to Philip—"

"Spare me your rationales, Maddie. They interest me very little."

"Now see here, Whitlock, you can't speak to Madeline like that."

Joshua glared at the man he was beginning to dislike intensely. "On the contrary, Spencer. I can talk to my betrothed any damn way I please."

"You arrogant ba—"

"Speaking of which, my sweet little bride"—Joshua turned toward the woman whose less than complimentary description of him he had just interrupted—"I wish to see you in the library, alone."

"Well, I do not wish to see you!"

Joshua shrugged. "Fine, I shall simply take care of the matter myself." He strode toward the open doorway.

"What matter?" Madeline hated herself for asking.

The vexing captain never broke stride. "The library, Maddie," he ordered. At the entryway he paused. Turning, he allowed his gaze to wander intimately over her. "Do keep your farewells brief."

"Perhaps he will refuse to marry you now that he

knows about us." Philip's statement interrupted Madeline's contemplation of the empty doorway. Again she found the term "us" annoying.

She glanced over her shoulder. "Oh, I don't think so."

"Then *you* shall simply have to do it. Where are you going?"

"To the library, of course." Madeline didn't stop or look around as she left the parlor. The sharp intake of breath she heard was the only further evidence of Philip's displeasure she wished to experience that night.

It wasn't as if Madeline didn't know better than to blindly follow where the captain led, but she needed to know what to expect. And she was quickly learning that, most likely, it was the unexpected.

Somehow, in three short days, he had managed to beat up her overseer and to ingratiate himself with her father to such an extent that the dying man had offered him Hopewell and his only daughter in one neat package. And he'd so unnerved her that she hadn't given him the dressing down he'd deserved when he'd deemed it necessary to touch her.

"What took you so long?"

She had paused in the corridor just outside the open door of the library to try to gain control of her emotions. To her knowledge, she had made no sound. The captain had not turned from his perusal of the night sky through the far window; yet somehow he had known she was there.

He turned to face her now, his hands clasped behind his back, his stance one she was beginning to think of as uniquely his. "Well?"

He expected her to answer his question. Madeline's spine stiffened. "Farewells, you know, can be lengthy." she answered waspishly.

"Ah." He rested his hips against the edge of the window seat and folded his strong arms across his chest. His black eyes studied her intently. "I trust they are all accomplished."

170

Madeline advanced into the room. It was obvious he was angry and was trying to keep his feelings under control. Suddenly she wanted to see exactly how far his control extended.

"And if they are not?" She let her query trail off in the tension-filled air.

"'Tis no matter."

No matter? Madeline stared at him, her baiting words of moments ago now forgotten. He didn't care if she indulged in amorous affairs with other men? Well, what had she expected? A fit of jealousy, perhaps. She was so shocked to realize that some form of possessive behavior was exactly what she had expected, had hoped for, that she almost missed his next words.

"After tomorrow you will no longer be tempted by the fair Mr. Spencer."

Perhaps he was a tad jealous. "Why? Are you forcing him to leave Hopewell?" He might consider Philip a rival, but she wouldn't have him ordering her guest out of her home, even if it would soon be his home, too.

"On the contrary, Maddie. Your Mr. Spencer may stay as long as he likes. It is you and I who are leaving."

"Leaving? Hopewell?" Madeline searched his face for an answer, but saw none. His countenance appeared devoid of emotion, as expressionless as the rocks by the cove. She wondered if he planned to take her on a wedding trip, but it seemed unlikely, considering the circumstances of the marriage.

Madeline opened her mouth to ask, but he saved her the trouble.

"Aye, Maddie, leaving Hopewell."

"But—"

He quieted her interruption by raising his hand.

"I told you I had a reason for coming here, and whether you believe it or not, my motive has nought to do with acquiring Hopewell or you for myself." Joshua watched her expression change from concern to anger.

"Why are you here then?"

Joshua leaned back further into the cushion of the window seat. "I'm looking for my brother."

"I don't think he's here," she responded with a shrug.

"Nor do I. That's why we must search elsewhere."

"We?" Her hands had clenched into fists at his use of the term. "I don't even know your brother. Find him if you must. I shall remain here." Her tone was haughty; her small chin was raised.

"Ah, but Maddie, what you suggest means that we would be apart, you and I. A separation holds very little appeal to me, especially so soon after our wedding." The obsidian twinkle in the depths of his eyes was aggravating. His remarks indicated he was about to ruin her life even more, Madeline reflected bitterly, yet he made light of it.

"I won't go." She voiced the words with all the determination she could muster, yet before the echoes drifted away, Madeline knew the battle was lost.

He stood and strode past her toward the door. "Tell Hattie to pack your belongings. We'll leave for Kingston as soon as"—he hesitated—"things are settled here." He was sure her father's funeral was never far from Madeline's mind.

"Let me stay." She had been drained of her earlier anger, and now her green eyes pleaded with him. "Hopewell is my home."

Joshua's lids slid down over his tired eyes, and he drew a deep breath. Seeing her beg was not his wish, especially when there was nothing he could do to grant her request.

"You'll have to come with me. I can't leave you here."

"Can't, or won't?" Her tone was no longer beseeching.

"In this instance, Maddie, they are one and the same."

Madeline tried to understand why he was so intent upon taking her away. It almost seemed as if he were more worried about her remaining at Hopewell than actually desirous of her company on his little quest. But why? There was Creely, of course. But yesterday the captain had been perfectly willing to leave her to her own devices with the overseer. And there was his solicitor friend, who was willing to help her find a new plantation manager. She didn't think Creely was the reason. Then what?

An idea fell into her mind, was rejected, then found fertile soil in which to sprout.

Joshua watched the glimmer of inspiration shine in her eyes with something akin to apprehension.

"It's Philip, isn't it? You won't let me stay here because you're afraid he'll stay too, and you won't be around to bully us."

Had she doubted her presumption, the tight clench of the captain's jaw would have convinced her of its validity. But not so his words. "If it pleases you to think that Spencer's the reason, then, by all means, indulge in your fantasies."

That isn't the reason, of course, Joshua told himself. Still, her conclusion that he was jealous, that there was anything to be jealous about, made him furious. What could she possibly see in that fop of a man? Well, that was her business, he supposed. But whether he liked his situation or not, once they were married, keeping little Madeline O'Neil safe *was* his business.

And Joshua's conversation with Sau had convinced him that leaving Madeline at Hopewell, alone, was not the way to keep her from harm.

Of course, taking her with him on his quest for Nathaniel was not without peril, but at least he'd be there to protect her. Maybe, if his search took him close to the Colonies, he could drop her off in Baltimore. Certainly, closeted there with Mrs. Jenkins, she'd be out of harm's way.

For now, all he had to do was make certain they were married and she came with him—two difficult feats, knowing the independent mind of the woman involved. And two things he preferred to handle after he'd had some rest.

Joshua again turned toward the door. "I'm planning to

seek my bed. I suggest you do the same. Tomorrow will be here only too soon."

Madeline couldn't resist a parting stab aimed at his wide, erect back. "What, no lewd suggestion about sharing a bed?"

He stopped, and the look he shot her over his shoulder made the breath leave her body in a silent explosion of air. "There'll be time enough for that, Maddie."

Chapter 14

"This is highly irregular."

And you don't know the half of it, Joshua thought, but he deemed this an inappropriate response to offer the minister seated across from him, so he remained silent. The Reverend George Elgin, a wiry, middle-aged man with a nose large enough to seek out sin, had arrived from Kingston Parish Church late the past night, but it hadn't been till moments ago that Joshua had revealed to him the extent of his expected duties.

"Patrick's message wasn't clear concerning the reason I was needed . . ."

"It was the wedding," Joshua offered by way of explanation.

"I didn't suppose Patrick foresaw he'd need me at his own funeral."

"He knew he was dying. I think that's why he wanted certain matters executed expeditiously."

The rector drew a bony finger down the length of his nose. "You refer, of course, to your marriage to Madeline."

"Exactly."

"And is there some reason for this haste to unite the two of you in God's eyes?" The minister leaned forward in the high-backed leather chair.

The implication that there had already been a union of the more physical sort was clear in his words. Joshua, for

Madeline's part, started to take offense, then realized that any argument against the minister's insinuation was not only irrelevant, but detrimental to his goal of having the man marry them. Besides, the sanctimonious gleam in Elgin's eyes told him the minister probably wouldn't believe him anyway.

"Let's just say," Joshua began, "it would be beneficial to all concerned to see this marriage accomplished with a modicum of wasted time."

"I see." Reverend Elgin's body relaxed back into the chair. He was apparently content now that he had ferreted out at least one of the younger man's mortal flaws.

Joshua couldn't keep back a smile. "Then I assume there will be no problem with the arrangements I outlined earlier?" His tiny surge of triumph was a bit premature. He hadn't counted on the Reverend Elgin having any concern other than to eradicate sin.

"How does Madeline feel about this?" It was obvious from the minister's tone that, though he might readily assign Joshua to the ranks of the damned, his feelings toward Madeline were quite different. It occurred to Joshua that his intended bride had her share of admirers.

Joshua looked the most recently discovered one straight in the eye, and answered with more assurance than he felt. "She'll do what's expected of her." That didn't really answer the curate's query, but to do so would have assured the cessation of any wedding plans.

Joshua's response seemed sufficient, though; for the Reverend Elgin simply sighed and said, "Yes, she always does, doesn't she?"

Though the words had been spoken softly they did not lack conviction, and Joshua hoped the minister did know Madeline had a penchant for doing her duty. He himself wasn't certain she would go through with it—especially after the announcement he'd made last night. He probably shouldn't have told her they were leaving Hopewell. But he had been angry. Upon realizing that she'd lied to him about their first encounter on the *Chesapeake* and upon seeing her with Spencer.

Before he'd made love to her and discovered her lie, he had even considered staying on at Hopewell for a few days. He had planned to send word to both Henry Smythe and Oliver, asking them to meet him here. Though it would have delayed his search for Nathaniel, he would have left Hopewell with a clearer conscience knowing its management was in his solicitor's capable hands.

And it hadn't only been his own peace of mind about which Joshua had been concerned. He knew how Madeline felt about the plantation. Indeed, he had been willing to indulge those feelings as far as he was able. But not after what she had put him through—making him think he'd raped an innocent when all the time she knew he hadn't. Why she hadn't even acknowledged her lie after what had occurred between them last night. Granted, circumstances had not warranted a discussion, but she could have said something. What did she take him for, a just-whelped lad who didn't know when he'd bedded a virgin? A sudden thought blazed through his mind. What if she did think that? Perhaps this marriage had been her idea all along and she thought he'd been so driven by desire on the beach that he hadn't noticed.

"Where is Madeline now?"

It took a moment for Joshua to realize the minister was addressing a question to him. "She's still abed. Last night was difficult for her. I've sent one of the women to awaken her." Actually, he had ordered a curious Hattie to begin packing her mistress's trunks for an extended voyage. Joshua really hoped his betrothed was still abed and would stay there until time for the wedding ceremony.

He should have known better.

"What do you think you're doing?" Madeline had

177

fought hard against the fingers of consciousness that had tugged at her sleepy mind, but in the end she'd yielded to the inevitable and awakened to face the dreadful day. The moment she had pried open her gritty eyes, she had seen what Hattie was doing, but that hadn't stopped her demanding inquiry.

Hattie returned from the clothespress, dropping a neatly folded petticoat into the yawning aperture of the open trunk as she did. "Child, I didn't know you was awake."

Madeline surveyed the near-empty confines of the tall, mahogany clothespress before turning her attention back to Hattie. "Who told you to pack my clothes?"

Again she had asked a useless question, a question to which she knew the answer. There was only one person with the arrogance to order such a thing.

"Where is he?" Madeline threw her legs over the side of the bed, her angry query effectively silencing Hattie's response.

"He in de library with dat church man, but Miss Madeline, you can't see him now."

"And just why not?" Madeline stopped in her wild rush for the door and turned to confront a Hattie who looked more flustered than Madeline had ever seen her.

"You ain't dressed."

"Oh." The small breath of a sound escaped Madeline as she glanced down at the wrinkled nightrail she had come close to wearing to the library. What was it about the man that made her act before she thought?

"There, there, child." Madeline felt herself being enveloped in Hattie's motherly arms. "You ain't yourself today, and it sure ain't no wonder."

Madeline settled down onto the daybed, trying not to succumb to tears. "Has anyone arrived yet?" she asked as Hattie put a cool, damp cloth over her forehead. The one rational thing Madeline had done after her father died was to send messages to the surrounding plantations.

"The Silers come early dis mornin', and Miss Amanda, she here, too."

Madeline nodded, never opening her eyes. "What about the Addisons?"

"Got word dis mornin' they's in Kingston."

"All right. Well, I suppose I should go downstairs and see to my guests." As she sat up Madeline gave Hattie a weak smile. "But don't worry, I'll dress first."

Hattie's touch was gentle but firm as she guided her mistress back down onto the chaise. "No need for you to worry none 'bout dem folks. Your captain done already seen to it."

"He's not my captain." Madeline opened her eyes and stared fixedly at the black woman to add emphasis to her words.

The gesture appeared to have little effect. Hattie just smiled her wide, gap-toothed grin and answered in a voice thick with innuendo. "Maybe not yet, but if'n I know dat man, he will be 'fore dis day is done."

"Well, you don't know him." Madeline snapped, and this time even Hattie's strong hands couldn't keep her prone on the daybed. The more pressing thoughts of her father's funeral had momentarily blocked from her mind the other reason she dreaded this day, but Hattie's words had reminded her of it. If she chose Hattie's way of thinking, the captain was hers, twice over! Madeline rubbed her temples.

"How do you know about the . . . wedding?"

Hattie had called for bathwater and had returned to her packing when Madeline finally asked the question. She hadn't told anyone but Philip about her father's dying wish.

The large woman's efficient hands never ceased their shaking out, folding, and storing of Madeline's clothes as she answered. "He done told me, your captain."

Madeline let Hattie's use of the possessive word "your" pass. "Did he tell you he was forcing me to marry him?"

That stopped Hattie. The woman who had mothered Madeline looked up with questioning eyes. "Forcing? He done said you both promised da dead massa. Ain't dat true?"

Damn the man. Did he always have to be so right? "Yes, it's true."

"Humph." Hattie set back to work.

Madeline found Hattie's casual acceptance of what she considered the ruination of her life aggravating. She searched her mind for more ammunition to use against the formidable captain and quickly found it.

"Did he tell you he's taking me away from Hopewell?" She waited for the turbaned head to rise in shock. It didn't.

"Yeah. Wanted to take ol' Hattie, too. But I done heard tales o' them boats, and I say 'No sir, you ain't gettin' me on one o' dem, not even to take care of my baby.'"

Madeline's eyes narrowed. "What did he say to that?"

"Just laughed mostly. Den he say not to worry, he'd take care o' my baby for me."

"He didn't say that!"

Hattie chuckled, "Sure 'nough did."

"Well, I can take care of myself."

Hattie's chuckle had changed to laughter that shook her massive body.

"I can!" Madeline insisted as she marched over to Hattie. "Besides, doesn't it bother you that he's taking me away from Hopewell?"

"Now, child"—Hattie stopped her packing long enough to give her mistress a hug—"'course it do. But you ain't gonna be gone long."

Madeline raised her face from the warm musky shoulder. "How do you know that?"

"Your captain done told me."

Madeline threw up her hands and walked back to the dressing table. Things were very simple for Hattie. The captain said something; she believed it. Well, she herself was not so easily convinced. Not that there was much she could do about it, but she'd certainly let the captain know that she did not take everything he said at face value.

"Miss Madeline, I'z leavin' out your dark blue ribbed silk for the massa's burial . . . and dat purty pink thing for your marryin'."

"Pack the rose silk. I'll wear the dark blue for both." Madeline was just stepping into the tub of warm rose-scented water that had been brought to her room.

"But child, dat dark blue just ain't purty enough for no marryin'."

Madeline settled back into the soothing water. "I have absolutely no desire to look pretty today."

When she descended the great staircase an hour later, Madeline knew she had done her best, despite Hattie's objections, to achieve her goal. Her tawny curls, tightly braided about her head, had been hidden by her plainest lappet cap. The severe lines of her midnight blue gown were unbroken by contrasting petticoat or stomacher, and white ruffles flowing from her bodice and elbows were, like her cap, the most unelaborate she could find.

It was how she felt like dressing. On a good day, Madeline had little use for lace and finery, and today, the day she buried her father, even less. But it also wouldn't hurt to show the captain exactly how she viewed this so-called marriage of theirs.

She went first to the parlor, to spend a last quiet moment alone with her father. The cabinetmaker had been busy during the night, and now Patrick O'Neil lay in a simple mahogany coffin. Madeline checked the black silk gloves she had brought down with her. There were a dozen pair each of men's and women's, enough for the small group of mourners who had arrived. When she was sure all was in order, that staying any longer would only bring on a new flood of tears, she left the parlor to face her adversary in the library.

"Ah, there's our sweet Madeline." The Reverend Elgin was the first to notice her standing in the doorway.

It had been almost a year since Madeline had seen the minister from Kingston Parish, but before her trip to the Colonies he had been a frequent visitor to Hopewell. He hadn't changed much, and she found his presence comforting.

Not comforting was the look Madeline received from the captain as she greeted her old friend with a kiss.

"It was so good of you to come."

"When Patrick sent word that I was needed, I had no idea this is what I'd find. Of course, I knew he hadn't been well but . . ."

"It was a shock for all of us." Madeline agreed. "But at least you're here."

Though she had been unable to ignore the sensations the captain's presence had elicited in her since she'd entered the room, Madeline had pointedly avoided acknowledging him. Now Mr. Elgin's words made that impossible.

"Captain Whitlock and I have been discussing what's to be done."

"I see." Madeline glared at the captain. "And what have the two of you decided?"

For a large man, the captain was extremely quick. Madeline had thought so before, and she was convinced of it now. She had been staring right at him, but the move he'd made had been so abrupt and agile she had not known what he'd been about until he was beside her, his muscular arm about her shoulders. His embrace wasn't painful, but it was firm and possessive, and there was no way she could leave it without creating a scene.

"Mr. Elgin and I agree," Joshua began, "that a small, quiet wedding would be best, under the circumstances." He paused, knowing he should not give her a chance to protest, yet unable to stop himself.

Joshua was surprised when she said nothing. He was

182

even more amazed to feel her small hand insinuate itself at his side between his waistcoat and shirt. Was she offering him a caress? He glanced down into her sweetly smiling face and knew a twinge of apprehension before he continued. "We thought before the funeral would be the most appropriate . . . time."

Madeline heard the captain's sharp intake of breath as she gave fabric and skin a vicious pinch and twisted her fingers. It had been difficult to get a good grip on him, his body was amazingly hard. But when she'd gotten one Madeline had not been about to let go.

She knew she was hurting him, but he gave no outward sign of it as he looked down at her. "What do you think of that plan, sweetheart?" A fool could tell the endearment was really no such thing.

Madeline merely smiled as the arm around her tightened. "I think we need a moment alone to discuss this matter, dearest."

She knew she'd seemed rude, but the minister didn't seem to mind. "Please excuse me," he was saying. "You have much to discuss. I'll be in the garden. Let me know what you decide."

Madeline thanked Elgin as he closed the door behind him, but it wasn't until she felt the captain's arm leave her shoulder that she released her hold.

"My God, Maddie," Joshua yanked back his coat and tugged the long tail of his shirt from his breeches. "What in the hell were you trying to do to me?"

She ignored his bellowing. "What do you think you're doing, planning the wedding with Mr. Elgin?"

"That's what he was asked to do, come here to marry us." Joshua answered, but it was obvious he was more concerned about his wounded skin. "Will you look at this?" He twisted around to view the section of midriff he had bared. "It's all red. By tonight it will no doubt be black and blue."

Disgustedly, Madeline followed his urging and glanced

183

toward her handiwork, promptly wishing she hadn't. Not that she could detect a mar on his body—quite the contrary, it was perfect, too perfect for her peace of mind. While he seemed intent upon pointing out her crime against his flesh, Madeline could only gaze in wonder at the naked expanse he had bared. She noticed no red, only bronze, a hue made more apparent by the contrasting strip of lighter skin visible where his breeches had ridden down on his slim hips. Her mouth felt dry as she realized how lucky she'd been to find anything to pinch. Sun-kissed skin was stretched taut over the rack of his ribs.

"Well?" The captain dropped his bunched-up shirt and stared at her. He seemed intent on making her feel guilty for her abuse of him.

That was a response Madeline could not conjure up. She glared at him. "You're lucky I didn't have a knife."

"A knife?"

He appeared genuinely shocked. Provoking this reaction from him was surprisingly gratifying. Madeline's smile was smug. "Yes, a knife. The next time you manhandle me, you'd best be sure I haven't one readily available."

"You call a simple hug for my betrothed manhandling?"

"When it's meant to intimidate, yes."

The captain's black eyes twinkled. "Well, maybe I was, shall we say, anxious for a positive response. Still, I'm a little concerned about this violent streak in your character."

"Me, violent? I'm not the one who beat up Creely." A few wisps of tawny curls had escaped her braid, and she swiped angrily at them.

Joshua smiled, and his expression was too fun-loving for Madeline to take offense. "You found out about that, huh?"

"Did you think I wouldn't?"

The shrug of his broad shoulders convinced her he hadn't really been concerned one way or the other. "I just gave him a small lesson in manners."

"Because of the incident in the cane field?"

"In part."

Madeline waited a moment, but if there had been some other reason for the captain's behavior toward Creely, he didn't seem inclined to share it. Besides, Creely wasn't her main concern at the moment. Her future was.

"Hattie said you told her you would bring me back to Hopewell soon." Madeline watched his face intently.

"I did."

"Were those words only spoken to soothe an old woman or did you mean them?"

Joshua busied himself with tucking the tail of his shirt back into his blue silk breeches, a process Madeline couldn't seem to stop herself from watching.

"I have no desire to keep you separated from your home one moment longer than necessary." He had finished rearranging his clothing, and the steely conviction in the obsidian depths of his eyes was difficult to doubt.

But Madeline was—she had to be—concerned about more than her own future. After today, it would be irrevocably linked with his. "What about you?"

The captain apparently understood the meaning behind her question, for he threw back his head and laughed. "Are you afraid that I intend to hang around and wrest control from you? 'Tis not my plan, Maddie. I'm a man of the sea. You know that. Oh, I'll help you, and be here when I'm needed, but I think we both know that won't be often."

He was saying what she wanted to hear, wasn't he? Apparently Creely was the reason he'd refused to leave her behind at this time, because he certainly sounded as if he planned to do it in the future. Well, that was just fine. She'd have Hopewell and occasionally some help to run it. And it was obvious from what he'd said last night that he had no desire to press for his husbandly rights. Oh, she'd probably have to hand over some of the sugar profits to help finance his privateering or whatever it was he did, but she didn't really mind doing that. All things considered, perhaps she should be pleased with the arrangement her father had forced on her.

Then why wasn't she?

Madeline hazarded a covert glance at the captain. He stood tall and straight, his powerful arms folded across his broad chest, waiting patiently for her response. He was patient, all right, because he was confident. He knew she would agree. Despite her protestations, she had promised her father.

And he was happy with the arrangement; Madeline realized that was the reason she wasn't. Maybe she would feel happier if he'd wanted to take charge of Hopewell and she wouldn't let him, or if he'd wanted—no, not just wanted, coveted—her with an unrequited lust that left him breathless. Yes, that would be nice, to have him beg for her favors again, and to refuse him. . . .

"Well, Maddie, shall I retrieve the Reverend Elgin from his wanderings in the garden?"

Brought up short from her ridiculous musings, Madeline was thankful the captain couldn't read her thoughts. "I suppose since there's no help for it, we may as well get on with this wedding."

"Ah, Maddie, you really are the romantic."

His mocking retort made her turn toward the hall door he had paused in front of. "This marriage has naught to do with romance, does it?"

Their eyes met, locked. Madeline watched as the humorous glint in those black depths faded and was replaced by a steely cynicism.

"Damn little."

*   *   *

186

His sardonic words still echoed in her head an hour later as Madeline stood in the library by his side. He was holding her hand, had been through most of the ceremony, and she had become almost used to the sensation his touch evoked.

The droning resonance of George Elgin's voice ceased momentarily, and some sixth sense warned Madeline that it was she he waited on. Mindlessly, she spoke a few affirmative words, then sighed with relief as the droning continued. She forced herself to pay closer attention, and this time when the minister stopped, it was the captain who answered in his strong, deep voice.

More blurred words, a prayer, and it was over. Still, the captain held her hand. He held it until Amanda Watkins, a widow from a neighboring plantation, hugged Madeline and gave her a kiss. It was then Madeline realized the captain, her husband, hadn't kissed her. She tried to remember if Mr. Elgin had told him to, but she couldn't. Madeline was glad, of course, that the captain hadn't tried to kiss her. It would have been embarrassing to have suffered his attentions, especially in front of the few people the minister had gathered as witnesses. Still, she wondered if Mr. Elgin had suggested a kiss.

"My dear," Amanda was saying as she alternately dabbed at her eyes with a tatted-edge handkerchief and hugged Madeline, "it was lovely, I just wish Patrick could have lived to see it."

"Yes," Madeline mumbled before she was led to the open writing desk. She sat down, and whether it was the contact of the hard wood with her softer body, or the feel of the feather quill between her fingers, or the sight of the captain's bold signature on the marriage lines, her mind focused and reality set in.

She had married the captain. Joshua Logan Whitlock, she read, knowing for the first time his middle name. And for the first time she wrote her new name, Madeline O'Neil Whitlock. When it was done, she replaced the quill in its silver holder and sprinkled the document with sand. Only when this ritual was complete did she rise to face her future.

"Madeline dear, it's time."

"Yes, of course." She took George Elgin's arm, and together they led the small congregation from the library to the parlor. The rest of the mourners were already there. Madeline smiled a sad greeting to the Silers and the Addisons, who appeared to have made it in time for the funeral after all. When her gaze met the cool, hazel stare of Philip Spencer she merely nodded. She wondered if he knew what she had just done.

Though she clutched a black silk handkerchief, Madeline remained dry-eyed. Sometime during the eulogy, she noticed that the captain was seated beside her. It seemed only natural when he reached for her hand as they walked toward the family burial plot behind the great house.

They buried Patrick O'Neil deep in the land that had been his home, beside the woman whose love had brought him there. The sacrament of burial had been very refined and civilized, so unlike the slave funerals Madeline had surreptitiously witnessed in the past. She wondered if tonight the slaves would hold their own observances of the master's passing. Would there be wild dancing and sacrifices to the duppies, the spirits of the dead? If so, she would not be here to see it.

"When are we leaving?" Madeline asked her new husband the question that had gnawed at her since the small party of mourners had reentered the great house. She knew her trunks were packed in the coach and that there was no way the captain would change his plan. Still, he appeared to be in no great hurry to depart. He stood, a silver goblet in one hand, conversing with George Elgin. His smile, when he turned toward her, was warm and gentle.

"I had thought to wait until our guests were finished

188

eating." He motioned with his cup toward the small knot of people who still lingered by the buffet table laden with jerked pork, shellfish, and sweetbreads.

"You're leaving Hopewell?" The minister took a sip of Madeira and looked first at Madeline, then her husband.

"For a short while." It was the latter who answered. "I've a sloop in Kingston harbor to see to."

"Kingston harbor's not the safest place to be right now."

"Oh?" Joshua studied the minister with narrowed eyes. "And why is that?"

"Bompar."

"The French admiral?" Madeline watched her husband's brow wrinkle questioningly.

Elgin nodded. "Rumor has it that he commands a large squadron off the coast."

"I've learned not to deal in rumors."

The minister shrugged. "I would take this one seriously. The admiralty has. They've delayed sending the sugar convoy out because of it. Most of Kingston is in a panic due to fear of an invasion."

"By the French?" Madeline tried to still the worry in her own voice. "We can't leave if there's to be an invasion."

Joshua dropped his free hand on to his wife's shoulder. "Now, Maddie, calm yourself."

She found his patronizing tone infuriating, and shrugged off his hand. "I am calm, perfectly calm," she hissed. "I simply refuse to leave Hopewell to the French."

Joshua glanced about the room at the faces now turned toward them. It appeared that all were eager to witness the first official spat of the newlyweds. He looked down at his wife, who seemed anxious to accommodate their guests. "You haven't a choice." He delivered the words quietly, but he knew she heard them when green fire flashed into her eyes. Obviously, his plan to nip her

189

disobedience in the bud had failed.

"I will not leave this plantation undefended."

"And what do you propose to do, Madeline? Fight off the French single-handedly."

His response had obviously taken her aback. "Well no, I thought you—"

"Me?" In his anger, Joshua forgot that there were people watching. "Now you consider me of some use. Well, forgive me if I seem reluctant to spring to your assistance this time. I have no intention of sacrificing myself for the cause."

"But Hopewell—"

"Will be perfectly safe. Besides the British admiralty is not about to allow the French to keep Jamaica. Its sugar exports generate too much revenue."

His argument had substance; still, Madeline hesitated to accede to his wishes. He sensed her reluctance, and deposited his goblet on a nearby table, then turned toward her. Taking her shoulders firmly in his large hands, he forced her to meet his gaze, using only the irresistible intensity of his midnight-black eyes. "I can't stay, and I will not leave you here alone, Maddie, especially now."

This was not what she wanted to hear, yet Madeline could not deny that feelings vibrated through the flesh that connected them, the air that didn't; and she was thoroughly shaken. She had questioned why he hadn't kissed her after the wedding, wondered if he had shied away from displaying a familiarity in front of strangers, but the touch of his eyes, the possessive splaying of his fingers, the language of his powerful body were much more intimate than any postnuptial kiss Madeline had ever witnessed.

The moment hadn't lasted long, Madeline realized later as she bounced along inside the coach on her way to Kingston. Surely her heart had skipped no more than a beat or two before George Elgin had coughed self-consciously, and the captain had glanced away. But the length of time, or lack thereof, hadn't dimmed the moment's intensity.

Had he felt it? Madeline poked her head through the window and squinted against the glare of the late afternoon sun. She caught sight of the captain riding, straight-backed, slightly ahead of the coach horses. Sinking back onto the leather seat of the coach, she was hard-pressed to believe he had. His words, when he'd hurriedly released her shoulders, had been a gruff reminder to ready herself for the trip. And she had. Madeline had been as anxious to escape his presence as he'd seemed to be to have her gone.

There hadn't been much to do. Hattie had done a thorough job of packing the gowns, whose wrinkles had barely had time to relax from their previous enclosure in her sea chest.

She had kept her good-byes to a minimum. Philip had not been in evidence. Hattie had seemed convinced that their separation was to be so short-lived as not to warrant any lengthy farewells. And when Amanda had begun her gentle warnings about the horrors of wedding nights, Madeline had cut her farewell short.

"We're almost to Kingston," the captain said as he entered the coach. Madeline had been so deep in thought that she had hardly noticed the coach stopping. He must have tied his horse to the back of it she surmised, for he settled himself into the seat across from her as if he planned to stay and then rapped sharply on the roof with his fist. The coach sprang forward, the motion knocking Madeline's silk-skirted knees against her husband's long legs.

He smiled apologetically. "I thought it might be a little safer for you if I were inside."

Dusk was falling rapidly, Madeline noticed, as she glanced out the window at the outskirts of Kingston. "You fear the French have landed?"

191

The captain laughed, and the sound was deep and rumbling. "Hardly."

"You didn't believe what Mr. Elgin said about Admiral Bompar?" Madeline watched her husband in the gathering glow.

"Oh, I believed him. Bompar's out there all right." He motioned idly toward the sea. "But he hasn't invaded Kingston."

"How can you be so certain?"

"Do you suppose the city would be this quiet if he had?"

They were headed down Duke Street now, and though Madeline would hardly call the scene outside her window peaceful, it didn't suggest anything as violent as an invasion. She grudgingly admitted the truth of his statement, then sat back to take in the view from the coach's side window. Gradually the large spacious townhouses of sugar barons gave way to the seedier commercial buildings situated near the quay.

"Are we headed for the docks?" It hit Madeline again, just how little she knew about her immediate future.

"Aye, for the *Chesapeake*."

"Why are we going to your boat?" She wasn't sure what she expected, but she was tired and at the very least wished for a room at an ordinary.

"The *Chesapeake* is a sloop, Maddie. Kindly don't refer to her as a boat. She's one of the fastest Bermuda sloops ever built."

"Sorry." The sarcasm in her voice belied the word. "That still doesn't answer my question. Why are we going there?"

"I need to check in with Oliver. You remember my first mate?"

Madeline nodded, hoping the thin light disguised the color she knew had risen to her cheeks. The last time she had seen the old sailor her clothes had been in shreds, and she had just spent the night in the captain's cabin.

"Do you think he found your brother?"

The captain shrugged. "I don't know."

"But you doubt it."

"Let's just say, I'm anxious to find out."

Madeline was leaning back against the cushion when an idea impelled her to lean forward. "Did you ask George Elgin about your brother? He knows virtually everyone on the island."

"I asked."

"And?"

"He's never seen him, never heard of him."

"Oh." There seemed nothing more she could say. Since the captain seemed uninclined to continue the conversation, the rest of the ride took place in silence.

The tang of salt air and the cloying smell of tar heralded the end of their journey.

The captain gave orders concerning the disposition of the trunks fastened atop the coach, and then escorted Madeline up the gangplank onto the main deck of the *Chesapeake*. They were immediately accosted by the grizzled old seaman Madeline remembered from her first, ill-fated time on board. Embarrassment reddened her cheeks as she remembered where the man had last encountered her, but she needn't have worried. He didn't even give her a cursory glance.

"That you, Cap'n?" He moved nimbly around a barrel and clasped the younger man's arms. "We expected ya yesterday. Didn't have no trouble, did ya?"

The captain laughed. "No, no trouble. Things just took longer than I expected."

"Well now, I know for a fact ya didn't find young Nat."

"Do you now?"

"Hell, yes." The words forced the first mate's rather beady eyes to glance toward Madeline, but in the oscillating light of the ship's lantern she could detect no sign of recognition, only a mild annoyance. "'Cause I found him."

"Nathaniel's here?"

Madeline couldn't suppress the spark of happiness that shot through her at her husband's obvious delight, nor the disappointment that followed at Oliver's denial.

"Ain't here, Cap'n. But I was askin' 'round like ya said, and I run into a tar who knew 'im. Sailed with 'im from Baltimore Town on the *Sailfish*. Said he sailed back on the same ship."

"You're certain?"

"He seemed sure. Ben Hurly was his name. Knowed a lot about Nat. I reckon he was tellin' it straight. Ain't got no reason to lie that I can see."

"Well, that would explain finding no trace of him. Maybe he finally saw the foolishness of his scheme to capture pirates and decided to head for home."

"What pirates?" During most of the conversation, Madeline had been content to stand silent and be overlooked as if she were one of the belaying pins in the rails. But when the talk had turned to pirates, she could stand it no longer.

By the look of him when he turned toward her, the captain had entirely forgotten her presence. "Madeline, I'm sorry," he declared. "You remember Oliver Chappel. Oliver, this is Mistress Madeline Whitlock, my wife."

"Your w-wife!"

It was all Madeline could do not to laugh at the startled expression on the first mate's face.

"B-but Cap'n . . ."

"Yes, I know it comes as a surprise, Oliver, but these things happen." The captain looked down and gave Madeline a bold wink that she thought implied much more than it should have.

The first mate was still stammering when the captain excused himself and his wife to go below.

"I'll be back to hear more about this Ben Hurly once I get my wife settled in," Madeline heard him say as she started down the gangway toward his cabin.

"You remember the way." Joshua had come up behind her and bent over until his warm breath fanned the lappets on her cap.

Madeline looked over her shoulder as she reached the portal to his cabin. "Did you think I'd forget?"

The captain paused before reaching across in front of her and opening the door. "I don't know. You were only here once."

Madeline forced herself to enter his quarters. They were exactly as she remembered, neat, efficient, masculine. The lantern still hung over the desk, and she watched as the captain used the flame of the candle he had brought down with him to light the wick.

As light seeped into the tiny corners of the cabin, Madeline waited for the pain and fear she had known in this place to wash over her. It didn't.

She looked at her husband and suspected he was thinking of that same night. "Are you going to be all right here?"

"Yes."

"You're sure?"

"Of course. I'm just tired." Madeline looked for a place to sit down. She rejected the bunk and chose the chair.

"It's been a long day."

"Yes."

"Well," he began, "I better go see what Oliver has to say. I'll send someone down with something to eat. And your trunk, I'll have that sent down, too."

"Thank you."

"Certainly." Joshua backed toward the door. "I'll probably be very late. So just go to bed, and get some rest." Madeline nodded just before he turned to make good his exit.

"Captain?" He stopped and turned toward her. "I'm glad you've had word about your brother."

195

His spontaneous grin was mirrored on her face. "I am, too, Maddie. I am, too."

He reached around and lifted the latch. "Well, good night."

"Good night."

Madeline breathed a sigh of relief as the heavy oak panel shut behind him.

Chapter 15

"Hush your mouth, you black bitch."

Eli Creely levered himself off his cot and yanked up his breeches. The whimpering stopped.

"Did ya hear that sound?" Creely asked the slave wench, who was frantically trying to cover her nakedness.

"I ain't heard nothin', massa." On the cot, she cowered against the rough boards of the wall.

"Well, I sure as hell did." He buttoned his breeches, then felt under a pile of smelly clothing for his pistol. "There's somethin' out there."

Creely raised his fist threateningly as his remarks set off another bout of whining. "I told ya to shut your mouth."

He found the gun beside a half-empty bottle of rum. His fingers shook as he rammed the shot home, and he cursed when some of the powder spilled. Brushing it away, he wiped his damp hands down the front of his breeches. The sound came again.

"Stay there." Creely swung the loaded pistol toward the girl, then headed for the door. The leather hinges creaked as he opened it. Cautiously he slipped into the moonlit clearing in front of his cabin.

The noise came again—louder—and Creely whirled, searching the shadows with frantic eyes.

197

"The gun won't be necessary."

Creely jerked around at the sound of the cultured voice, and noticed a shadowy movement in the darkness. The pistol dropped to his side, and he rubbed his grimy shirtsleeve across his forehead. "Damn, you scared me."

"Did I? I'd have thought you'd have been expecting me." The cool voice came from the shadows.

"Oh, I was, Cap'n. I—"

"Haven't I told you not to call me that." The frosty tone barely concealed the fire beneath.

"I-I'm sorry. I forgot. It won't happen again."

"See that it doesn't." The shadowy man's tone became friendlier. "How are things going here, Creely?"

The overseer started to shrug, appeared to think better of it. "Things've kinda been at a standstill since that O'Neil bitch came back."

"Yes, her return was unfortunate," the voice agreed. "Madeline has proven more difficult than I anticipated. She is taken care of, though, at least temporarily."

Creely watched as the tall, slender man emerged from the shadows.

"What happened to your face?" he asked the overseer.

Creely's hand gingerly touched his nose as he spat out. "Had a run-in with that bastard visiting up at the great house."

"A run-in, huh?" The other man sounded amused.

"Yeah, he was nosin' 'round where he ain't got no business."

"So he broke your nose? No, don't bother explaining." He raised a slender hand. "Did you have any idea who it was who hit you?"

"Some friend of that O'Neil bitch."

"Perhaps, though I doubt it. It was Captain Joshua Whitlock."

"Whitlock! You mean—"

"Exactly. The brother."

Creely lifted his pistol. "Let's go kill the son of a bitch

198

before he gets away."

"Oh, he already has."

"What—"

"Today while you were doing whatever it is you do around here, the mighty captain took as his bride the fair Madeline. They're on their way to Kingston right now in search of his brother. As a matter of fact, they may already have received the good news that Nathaniel has sailed for the Maryland colony."

"But he's on the *Sea Witch*, and she ain't headed for Maryland."

"No, she isn't, is she? What a shame the captain and his bride will have to make that long voyage for naught."

Creely rubbed his whiskered chin. "Why you lettin' him get away?"

Slender, aristocratic brows lifted over hazel eyes. "It amuses me to build hope only to dash it. Besides, this little game we play may keep him occupied for a while, but in the end the captain will return. We do have his brother."

"Yeah," Creely chortled.

"In the meantime, I see no reason why we cannot resume our rather innovative use of this plantation."

"When's the next shipment due?"

"They'll be watching for our signal tomorrow night."

"I'll have the slaves ready."

"I knew I could count on you, Creely." With these words Philip Spencer melted back into the shadows.

"I'm going to arrange for Henry Smythe to look after Hopewell. Do you want to come along?"

The words awakened Madeline. She slowly opened her eyes, trying to remember where she was. The rough walls of the cabin brought everything back to her in a flash. Last night she had sat up for hours, waiting for her husband to return and discuss their sleeping arrangements. Finally, when she could no longer stay awake, she

199

had changed into her nightrail and had fallen asleep on his bed.

Now she did her best to pull the rumpled covers up over her body as she turned her head toward the captain. "What are you doing here?" It was a most unpleasant question, but Madeline didn't care. During the night, she had kicked off most of the blankets, and it annoyed her to realize that the captain had been staring at her barely covered body while she slept.

He seemed to take no offense, however. "I came to ask if you wished to go with me to see Henry Smythe," he repeated.

"Of course I want to go," Madeline snapped. "But don't you think you should have knocked before you came in?"

"On my own cabin door? Tsk, tsk, Maddie, you are getting uppity, aren't you?"

Madeline clutched the blanket under her chin. "But I'm not dressed."

The captain's smile was slow and suggestive. "No, you're not."

Madeline felt the blush all the way to her naked toes. "Why you sneaky, gawking oaf—you were looking at me!" The smile never faltered. "A husband's prerogative, I believe. Now hustle and get your charming little body clothed. I have more important things to do than wait for you." With that, he was out the door.

Madeline wasted no time in jumping from the bed and dressing. There didn't appear to be any way she could lock the door, and she didn't want the captain wandering below again while she struggled with her stays. Not that she couldn't have used his help. His hands were large and callused, but she had no doubt that his long slender fingers could make quick work of lacing the eyelets. But would they? In her imaginings they didn't. Instead, his fingers were slow and thorough, and he was removing her stays rather than fastening them.

Annoyed with herself and the wicked thoughts she

200

seemed unable to control, Madeline yanked at the stay cords before tying them around her slender waist.

Last night she had been so tired and so upset about her father that she had failed to unbraid and brush her hair. She now quickly went about the process. Not that she was worried that the captain would return to find her indisposed; she was already decently covered in the same dark blue silk she had worn the day before. But she wanted to give him no excuse to take care of Hopewell business without her.

Within minutes she had rebraided her tawny curls and wrapped the long rope of hair around her head in a chaste coronet. Atop this she plopped a wide-brimmed sun hat, tied its pink satin ribbons, and rushed from the cabin.

She found the captain on the quarterdeck, staring out over the harbor, hands clasped behind his back, in that stance she had come to recognize as uniquely his. He was wearing tall, black boots, snug-fitting buff breeches, and an unadorned broadcloth frockcoat of nearly the same hue as her dress.

His concentration was so complete that he didn't notice her standing by him even though she had done nothing to muffle the sound of her approach.

"I'm ready." Madeline touched his arm lightly as she spoke.

Joshua started, more from her touch than her words. He turned quickly and saw his wife take an involuntary step away from him.

"I'm sorry." Joshua reached out to draw her back, thought better of it, and let his hand drop to his side.

"No, no. It was my fault." The intensity of his gaze when he had turned had her flustered. "I shouldn't have come upon you as I did."

"Aye," he agreed, a sensuous smile tugging at his lips. "I might have mistaken you for a Frenchie and tossed you overboard."

Madeline couldn't help responding with a grin, but as the meaning of his words took hold, her brow furrowed in

201

a worried frown. "Is that what you were thinking about, the French?"

Joshua's deep laughter rang through the morning air. "No, little Maddie, I was not thinking of the French." He touched the crease on her forehead and watched it melt away as she stared at him with her wide, green eyes. Slowly, he let his finger drift down the curves of her face: the delicate arch of brow, the sweep of rosy cheek, the soft but defiant little chin, the full, tempting lower lip.

Tempted, he was. Madeline was his wife, dammit. He had every right to do exactly what he wanted. and what he wanted was to take her back to his cabin, his bed—the bed he had given up last night—and make love to her.

The pad of his thumb replaced his finger. He watched it skim across the silken flesh of her mouth, slowly, sensually. But he wanted to do more than caress her dewy lips with his thumb.

"He weren't there, Cap'n." Madeline recognized Oliver's voice. Gratefully, she turned toward the sound. The first mate was clomping up the steps, obviously heading toward them, and Madeline stepped back from the captain with a sigh of relief. Another moment and she would, no doubt, have done something she'd have regretted. Even now her legs seemed boneless as she leaned against the polished rail of the quarterdeck. Whatever it was that happened to her when the captain touched her didn't seem to affect him. Obviously unhampered by rubbery knees, he strode purposefully toward his first mate

"Did you ask around about him?" Joshua thanked fate that Oliver had shown up when he did. It was inconceivable to him that just gazing into his wife's eyes could make him forget her scheming lies.

"Aye, ain't no one seen 'im."

"Who?" Madeline's voice sounded timid and wavering, and neither man seemed to hear her. At least they made no sign that they intended to answer. But the next time she asked the question, she had their attention.

202

They both stared at her in surprise; however, it was the captain who spoke. "What did you say?"

"I said"—Madeline moved toward him until she had to angle her head to look him in the face—"who?" The word was a challenge. Madeline was not used to being ignored, and it was time the captain knew it.

He looked at her for a long moment, but the obsidian gleam that made her toes curl was absent from his eyes. His gaze was assessing her. Apparently satisfied with what he saw, Joshua cocked one jet brow and said, "Ben Hurly, Maddie. I sent Oliver to find the sailor who said Nat had departed on the *Sailfish.*"

"Why? Didn't you believe him?"

"Let's just say I become wary when things I want come too easily." He smiled, and this time when he looked at her, Madeline had to press her slippered feet to the hard wood deck to keep her toes flat.

"What *were* you thinking about?"

"When?"

"Back on the *Chesapeake,* when I came on deck. You had such an intense look on your face, as if you were thinking very hard about something—or someone."

The captain took Madeline out of the path of a hand-pulled cart filled with fruit. They were walking north on King Street and had almost reached the center of town, where it crossed Queen Street. It was Sunday, market day, and the parade grounds were teeming with natives and slaves alike, hawking their goods. The air was filled with the smells of fish and flowers, bananas and sweat.

It wasn't until they had turned the corner onto East Street that he responded, and in the form of a question. "Would it please you if I said it had been you?"

Madeline had stopped to brush the dust off her skirt, but her hand hung motionless just above the dark blue silk when she heard his words. "That you were thinking of?" Madeline wasn't sure she understood. Was he teasing her?

The captain nodded.

Madeline slapped at her gown, sending a myriad of dust motes adance in the bright beams of sunshine. "It would please me to be told the truth."

He cocked his head to the side. "In that case, it was Nathaniel."

"Your brother?" He *had* been teasing. Madeline was only glad she hadn't done something foolish like cooing, Oh, were you really thinking of me?

"Aye." She took the arm he offered as they entered a building.

Joshua motioned toward the steps at the back of a long wainscoted hall before he continued. "I can't understand why he didn't contact Henry before he left Jamaica."

Madeline stopped and turned toward her husband. He was following her up the steps but had stopped when she had. Now, two risers above him, Madeline could face the captain on eye level. She liked it.

"Perhaps he hadn't the time."

"Oh, there was plenty of that, considering when the *Sailfish* docked and when she left Kingston. I checked."

"Well, why do you think he didn't?" Maybe she should carry a small ladder about so that all their conversations could be held eye to eye. Of course, she did somewhat enjoy having him tower over her.

"If I knew, I wouldn't be thinking so damned hard about it, now would I?"

He turned her shoulders in a way that effectively halted their conversation, and then amazed them both by giving her behind an intimate pat.

"Ah, my boy. I was wondering who was debating on my steps. Come in, come in." Bracketed by an open doorway, Henry Smythe beamed down at them.

Madeline, hoping her face had lost some of the color the captain's pat on her bottom had brought forth, entered Henry Smythe's parlor. Sunlight shone through windows framed by brocaded draperies, highlighting the

204

creamy hue of the walls and the large russet and gold flowers woven into the needlework carpet. This was the kind of room Madeline had often seen during her visit to Williamsburg, and it suited the man who was shaking hands with the captain.

"I hope you don't mind our coming by on a Sunday." Joshua began, but he was cut short by the vigorous shaking of Henry's wigged head.

"Nonsense, my boy. I always enjoy a visit from you." The solicitor's shrewd eyes flicked to Madeline.

"I'm aftaid this isn't entirely a social call."

"Ah, but that implies it's not entirely business either." Joshua laughed. "Astute as always." He walked to the window and glanced down at the street below, purposely postponing the moment he knew Henry awaited. The moment when he introduced the woman standing in the center of Henry's parlor. Joshua knew he was being rude; he also knew that he was allowing Henry time to conjure up a number of theories as to who she was. Of course, none of them would be close to the truth.

"Madeline"—Joshua walked back to her side—"may I present Henry Smythe, Esquire?" He paused just a moment. "Henry, my wife, Madeline."

"Well, this is a surprise, Joshua. Why didn't you tell me you had come to Jamaica to take a bride?"

The captain's broad shoulders rose and then fell in a slight shrug, and he walked back to the window as Madeline and Henry Smythe exchanged pleasantries.

The solicitor had seemed somewhat amazed by the introduction, though he had covered his surprise much better than Oliver had. Joshua guessed that years of dealing with the courts and people had put Henry in good stead. Of course, the honorable Mr. Smythe had yet to find out that the woman Joshua had married owned the plantation the solicitor suspected of selling contraband.

Joshua hesitated only a moment before joining his wife and friend. "I have a favor to ask of you, Henry. Actually, I suppose it's my wife who has the request."

Since Joshua had tried to make it clear that he had no intention of wresting control of Hopewell from his reluctant bride, he decided he might as well let her do the talking.

To his surprise she did so without demurring. "I need an overseer, Mr. Smythe. One who's capable and willing to work, and I need him immediately."

A short, sharp laugh escaped the solicitor's thin lips. "My dear, that is a lot—"

"I realize I may be asking a great deal, but the captain said you know everyone, and if anyone can help me, 'tis you."

"He did, did he?" Henry smiled at Joshua, who returned the gesture. If the solicitor noticed anything unusual in the formal manner with which the young woman referred to her husband, he gave no indication. "Well, I may know of someone with the requirements you mentioned. His name is Andrew Burns. He's a young fellow himself, but his father has been manager of the Bennet plantation for nigh twenty years. Andrew grew up there, helping out, taking over when his father broke his leg."

Madeline wasn't sure she wanted someone who sounded so inexperienced. "I don't know—"

"The plantation is in a sad state of disrepair. There's been near a year of mismanagement," Joshua put in.

Madeline listened as he reviewed Hopewell's ills, from unplanted fields to damaged dock.

"Did I miss anything?" he finally asked, looking straight at her.

"No, I don't think so. Except the slaves. They seem to be quite discontent."

Joshua nodded. "She's right about that." He accepted the glass of Madeira Henry offered. "Well, do you think your Mr. Burns can handle the job?"

Henry Smythe laced his fingers across his ample girth. "'Tis not a pleasant picture you two paint."

"No," Joshua agreed. "But it is an accurate one."

206

The solicitor watched stray beams of sunlight splinter into rosy highlights in his goblet before he took a sip of the wine. "Andrew Burns can do the job."

Madeline's gaze drifted from the solicitor to the captain. He returned her stare, but said nothing. The decision would be hers.

"How soon can he begin?"

"Within a sennight, I imagine. Where is this plantation?"

Madeline smiled. She was feeling much better now that the matter of an overseer was settled. "On the Hope River."

Joshua watched Henry's eyes turn to him questioningly. He answered the silent inquiry. "It's Hopewell."

"You're Patrick O'Neil's daughter?"

"Why was your Mr. Smythe so surprised to learn I was from Hopewell and was an O'Neil?"

"Was he?"

Madeline stopped and grabbed the captain's arm, turning him toward her. They had been walking along the quay, and the milling crowd of tars, vendors, and whores paid them little mind.

"You know damned well he was." Madeline glared up into her husband's face. The sun was high and bright. They had spent most of the morning with Henry Smythe.

Joshua grinned. "I would have thought you'd have cleaned up your language a bit now that you're a respectable, good wife."

Madeline stamped one moroccan slippered foot. "Don't you dare try to change the subject. Henry Smythe took all that we told him in stride, though I've no doubt he was surprised by the fact that you were married to me, until you mentioned Hopewell. Now, I want to know why."

Joshua looked down at his wife, pondering exactly what to tell her. She was right. Henry Smythe had seemed a trifle nonplussed when Hopewell was mentioned. Joshua had hoped his wife wouldn't notice the break of Henry's composure, but obviously she had. Now she wanted to know why. Should he tell her all he knew about her plantation? And even if he did, would she believe him?

"Well?" If Madeline had doubted her perception of Smythe's reaction, her husband's lack of a response convinced her she'd judged his behavior correctly.

"Henry Smythe suggested I go to Hopewell. I suppose that's why he considered it a little odd when I showed up married to Hopewell's owner." Joshua took her elbow and began weaving her through the crowd.

"But why did he send you to Hopewell?"

"I told you I was looking for Nathaniel." Joshua waited for his wife's nod before he went on. "Well, Nat was supposed to contact Henry, but he didn't."

"Yes, yes, you told me that before. It still doesn't explain why Mr. Smythe sent you to Hopewell."

"Henry thought Nat might have gone there."

"Because your father knew Papa?" They had reached the *Chesapeake* and started across the gangplank.

"Henry didn't know we knew your father. At least, he didn't know we'd had more than a business relationship with him and that had ended years ago."

"Then why?"

Joshua took a deep breath and plunged forward. "Because he knew that Nat had come here to find out who was pirating Whitlock vessels and taking their cargoes—mostly flour—and he had heard that Hopewell was selling large quantities of flour."

"What?" Madeline's outburst attracted the attention of more than one crew member, prompting Joshua to suggest they continue this conversation in the privacy of his cabin.

She quickly made her way below. No sooner had the door closed than she turned on him. "Just what do you mean by saying we stole your flour?"

Had he really thought she might take this calmly? "I didn't say you stole it."

"You insinuated we did."

"Oh, for God's sake, Maddie." Joshua combed his fingers through raven locks. "I did not. Henry had heard a rumor; that's all it was. I went to investigate."

"And found?"

"Obviously not Nathaniel." Joshua slumped into the chair behind his desk and began examining his log.

Madeline grasped the edge of the oaken desk with both hands and leaned toward him. She'd be damned if she'd let him drop the subject. "I know you didn't find your brother. Did you find stolen flour?"

Joshua stared into emerald eyes. They were flashing with anger, and they were close to him. So was she, at least that part of her bent aggressively over the desk. Her breasts molded sensually against the blue satin of her gown with each angry breath she took. Joshua could smell the fresh scent of roses that clung to the skin rising above her bodice, and he realized, with very little effort on his part, he could lean forward and kiss that petulant expression off her lips.

Was his intention so obvious? Joshua figured it was, because suddenly she straightened, effectively increasing the space between them.

Madeline moved back a step, then another, until the backs of her knees knocked against a chair. The gleam in the depths of the captain's black eyes had been positively wicked. And though it had set her stomach aflutter, it had also frightened her more than a little. The look had been intense, and had seemed to demand the same degree of feeling from her.

She watched as the captain rose and walked around the desk. She found it an effort not to shrink back into her chair as he stood in front of her.

"I found no stolen flour, Maddie." His voice was calm and matter-of-fact, as was his countenance.

Relieved, both by his words and his tone, Madeline

looked up at him. She could almost believe that his earlier expression had been imagined, that he hadn't really looked as if he were on the verge of yanking her to him and ripping off her clothes.

"Any other questions?" Joshua folded his arms across his chest and leaned one hip against the desk. He hoped by appearing ready, even eager, to answer any queries, there would be no more. He hadn't told her about Sau or what he had found in the caves, and though he wasn't certain why, he didn't intend to do so.

"Just one." Madeline faced the captain, remembering the other reason she had been annoyed when they had left the solicitor's residence. "Why did you ask Henry Smythe to be Hopewell's attorney?"

Joshua shrugged. "I didn't think you'd mind. He superintends several properties for absentee landlords."

"But I'm not an absentee landlord."

"Well, you will be until we return."

"You mean we're still leaving Jamaica?"

"Hell, yes, we're still leaving. Why would you think otherwise?"

Madeline watched the square line of his jaw tilt at a stubborn angle. So much for that. She could be obstinate, too. "I thought you were looking for your brother. Didn't you yourself say he was headed back toward Maryland?"

"So?"

"So, you've found him. Now I can go home."

The captain abandoned his nonchalant pose and advanced on Madeline. "I'll have found my brother when I see him with these two eyes." His no-nonsense declaration brooked no argument, but she gave him one.

"You're just being stubborn."

"The hell I am. I told you that story about Nat going back on the *Sailfish* didn't quite make sense to me."

Madeline put her hands on her hips. "Do you think that sailor lied?" When the captain didn't answer, she went on. "Of course not, because there is absolutely no reason for him to do so."

The captain said nothing. He only stared at her from beneath black scowling brows.

Madeline threw up her hands in despair. "Oh, for heaven's sake, you act as if some sort of conspiracy is being carried on."

"We're going." That was all he said in response to her argument in favor of staying.

Madeline's jaw dropped in astonishment at his arrogance. "Well, I'm staying here."

His glare became more ominous.

"There's no reason why I can't." She hurriedly added, "Andrew Burns will be at Hopewell within the week, and I have Henry Smythe to keep an eye on things. With all that help I'll have Hopewell running smoothly by the time you return."

Madeline glanced up at him, and the hopeful expression left her face.

"You're coming with me to Baltimore Town."

"Why?" she asked, frustrated now. It wasn't as if the captain enjoyed her company. He had spent most of their brief married life avoiding her. And when they were together, it was more likely they'd be having a tussle of some sort. Madeline had ruled out his craving physical intimacy when he had not come to her bed the past night. She stopped speculating when she heard his angry voice.

"Why? You wish to know why I insist upon taking you along on a month's journey? Perhaps I have grown accustomed to your sweet disposition, or maybe I have learned to enjoy having my every behest questioned." The words were propelled at her with the force of a broadside. "You are my wife, dammit, whether I desire it or not. I have vowed to protect you, and I'll be damned if that's not exactly what I intend to do—or had you forgotten about Bompar?"

Madeline had forgotten, but she would not give him

211

the satisfaction of knowing that. "What if I don't want to be protected!"

The captain lowered his head until his nose all but touched hers. "That's just too damned bad."

"Oh!" Madeline was so angry that she could not immediately think of a response. Before she managed a retort, the captain turned on his heel and stalked toward the door.

"Where are you going?" It infuriated her that he was walking off in the middle of an argument.

"I'm going into town to celebrate my last night in port. We sail on the morning tide." The captain slammed the door behind him.

If Madeline had had the cutlery or even the mug she had thrown at him before, she'd have done the same and found some outlet for her anger. But when she glanced around the cabin, she could find nothing to hurl. Besides, he was already gone, so she'd just end up with a mess to clean up.

He is such an infuriating man, she thought as she sank down onto the bed. So he had vowed to protect her, eh? Well he had vowed other things too—like to love and cherish—and for damned sure he wasn't abiding by them. And what about the faithful part? Madeline suddenly realized she remembered more of her wedding ceremony than she had thought. He *had* sworn to be faithful to her! Well she had no doubt that vow would be broken by morning for he was "celebrating" tonight. He would probably visit every bawdy house in Kingston before dawn.

For some reason that thought caused a band to tighten around her heart. She lay down and clutched the goose-down pillow to her breast, but the tightness would not go away. She then tried to blot all thought of him from her mind, but couldn't. Even with her eyes squeezed shut, she could see her husband's long powerful form intimately draped over faceless female bodies. A single tear slipped through her lashes, then another. Madeline's breath caught on a sob. She hated herself for crying over such a despicable man, but was unable to stop. If only she didn't have to be near him . . . if only she could go home . . . "Oh, Papa, why?"

Celebrate? Was that what he had told Madeline he was going to do? Joshua stared down into his mug of grog. His eyes stung from the dense smoke in the grog shop, his sixth or seventh of the evening. In each one he had nursed a drink and asked the same question. Had anyone seen a young man by the name of Nathaniel Whitlock? No? Then how about a sailor named Ben Hurly? His drinking companions were friendly enough, but their answers were always the same. No one had seen or heard of either man.

Joshua pinched the bridge of his nose between thumb and forefinger. It did little to relieve the pounding in his head. He stood and made his way through the crowded room. The tangy salt air felt good on his face, in his lungs, after the stale, stifling atmosphere of the grog shops. He looked up the street. What little light there was came from lanterns hung near the entrances to the shops and bawdy houses. There were a few more places he hadn't been, but somehow he knew the answers to his questions would be the same.

Joshua started toward the quay, glad to leave the boisterous laughter and drunken sounds behind him. He had toyed with the idea of stopping off at a bawdy house he had frequented years ago. The Lord knew he could use some release from the pent-up desire that raged through him. Maybe such a visit would help him stop thinking of that night on the beach every time he looked at his wife. It wasn't as if she hadn't made her feelings on the matter quite clear. He knew what she thought of him and of the situation in which she found herself.

Well, it was not easy for him either, especially when he couldn't stop thinking of how it had felt to be buried deep inside her. He groaned at that memory and almost turned back toward town. But it wasn't some whore smelling of sweat and other men that he wanted.

With labored step, Joshua made his way to the *Chesapeake*.

Chapter 16

Where does he sleep?

Madeline lay abed the next morning contemplating this question. She had spent a great deal of the night tossing and turning, dozing fitfully, only to awaken at the slightest sound. It had taken awhile before she'd realized why. She'd been listening for the captain's return. It had never come. Madeline had tried telling herself she was glad. If he didn't come to the cabin then there was no way he could force his unwanted attentions on her.

Still, she wondered. From what she knew of bawdy houses—and admittedly that was very little—one didn't spend the night in them. Maybe he had a mistress in Kingston. That seemed to make more sense. He knew many of the people here. He had been in Jamaica often. A man could spend the night with a mistress, and, after all, there were two nights to account for—two nights that he'd spent away from his cabin.

Madeline stared at the ceiling as she tried to accustom herself to the idea that her husband had a lover. Madeline didn't even want to contemplate what this woman's body would be like, although she decided it was probably a lot fuller in certain areas than her own.

She glanced down at the sheet molding her form. Even with her nightrail on, she looked small.

215

Theirs was certainly no love match. Still, it hurt to think of the captain sleeping with another woman. Of course, after today he couldn't go to his mistress. So where would he sleep then? Madeline sat up and dangled her feet over the edge of the bunk as she mulled over this new question.

It was then that she noticed the motion. They were no longer at anchor.

She jumped up, cursing herself for the time she'd lain idle. If only she had risen and dressed when she had awakened, she would be on deck.

A knock sounded at the door, followed by a voice that could belong only to Oliver Chappel. "Miz Madeline."

"Yes, what is it, Oliver? No! Don't come in." Madeline had shed her nightrail and was hurriedly lacing the eyelets of her stays when she noticed the door begin to open. It slammed shut in a hurry.

"I'm real sorry, ma'am. I thought ya was tellin' me to come in," the first mate called out from the other side of the oaken panel, sounding embarrassed.

"It's all right," she replied, her voice muffled by the layers of cotton she was slipping down over her head. "Just don't come in right now." She tied her underpetticoats around her slender waist and reached for the cream-colored silk gown she had unpacked the night before. "What did you want?" she called through the door.

"Huh?"

Madeline plucked at the ruffles of her shift, freeing them from the confines of her sleeve so they spilled down over her elbows. "When you knocked at the door, what did you want?"

"Oh, that. The cap'n sent me ta fetch ya. Says you might want to see the *Chesapeake* sail outta the harbor."

"Oh, I do." She slid her feet into the moroccan slippers and tied her finger-combed hair with a wide blue ribbon.

"Ready." Madeline flung open the door to greet a surprised first mate.

"Ya want some breakfast 'fore you go up?" he blurted out.

"No." Madeline headed down the companionway. "I can eat later. How long have we been under sail?"

"Ain't been long. Why you in such a all-fired hurry?"

Madeline looked back to see a puffing Oliver trying to keep pace with her. She barely suppressed a giggle as she slowed her pace. "I'm sorry. I didn't realize how fast I was going."

"Criminy, what got inta ya, girl? Ain't ya ever been on a seagoin' ship before?"

"Of course I have." Madeline glanced back over her shoulder as she climbed onto the main deck. She expected to see a mocking expression on the older man's face, but there was none. Still, Oliver knew she'd been on a ship before. He was the one who had led her down this very passageway to the captain's cabin. Certainly he remembered.

"Well, what's all the hurry 'bout then?"

"I don't want to miss a moment of it."

"You'll get a bellyfull o' sea an' sky an' sails 'fore this journey's o'er."

Madeline just smiled over her shoulder. The first mate's whiskered face split into an answering grin that deepened the ravages time and weather had etched into his nut-brown skin. He was probably right, but for now she wanted nothing more than to feel the salt air on her face. She'd experienced this affinity with the sea the first time the sails of the *Deliverance* had filled with wind. She had known then why men went to sea.

Bright sunshine and painfully blue sky greeted Madeline as she emerged from below. She immediately regretted the haste that had kept her from seeking a shade hat for her head.

"Cap'n's up yonder." Oliver hitched his thumb toward

217

the quarterdeck.

"Oh?" Madeline had noticed where he was the moment she'd come on deck, but upon seeing him standing tall and proud, a flood of memories had washed over her. She tried not to think of where he had spent the night, tried instead to focus on the bustling activity around her. And there was definitely plenty of that.

At first, Madeline thought the crew to be in a state of confusion. But as she stood against the rail, in a spot of relative calm, and watched, she realized there was an organized beauty to the motions of the tars. Everyone appeared to have a job to do, and did it with an economy of movement. The boatswain shrilled his pipes, and the sailors moved smartly.

The anchor had already been weighed, but a few men were still busy catting it, passing a rope through the carved cathead and then through the anchor ring. With this done, the massive wood and iron anchor could be secured to a timber head.

Using her hand as a shade against the blinding sun, Madeline watched the nimble privateers climb the ratlines toward the still-furled shrouds. She held her breath, expecting at any moment to see a seaman hurtle to the deck, but none did. Always careful to grab hold of a new rope before letting go of the old, they moved about the rigging seeming as carefree as if they were ambling down Queen Street in Kingston.

"You'd be less likely ta be trampled underfoot up yonder." Again Oliver motioned toward the elevated deck at the *Chesapeake*'s stern.

In her preoccupation with the crew's activity, Madeline had almost forgotten the grizzled sailor who had brought her above. Much as she disliked the idea of being around her husband while his escapades of the previous night were fresh in her mind—and his— Madeline had to admit Oliver had a point. More than one busy seaman, while executing his duties, had jostled her.

Oh, to be sure, they had been apologetic and extremely polite, had touched their tar-covered hats in a sort of salute before moving on, but Madeline knew she was in the way.

Still . . . "The captain looks awfully busy." It hadn't been hard, even amid the noisy confusion surrounding her, for Madeline to pick out his deep baritone as he went about issuing orders.

"Reckon he is, but there ain't as many men up there, and the view is a helluva lot better, beggin' your pardon, Miz Whitlock. Besides, he did ask me to fetch you."

"In that case . . ." Madeline fell into step behind Oliver, who was making his way toward the quarterdeck, apparently considering the matter settled.

"Well, I see you've brought her." The captain's booming voice greeted her as she climbed the ladder onto the ship's command deck.

"'Twasn't easy." Oliver countered. "Had to pull her away from the main deck. Watchin' everything. Thought sure she was gonna start climbin' them ratlines."

Madeline's laughter echoed Oliver's and her husband's. "I was going to do no such thing. I was merely curious as to how they can move so effortlessly with naught but a few ropes below them."

"Sure you weren't tryin' to figure it out so's you could try it yourself?" the older man teased.

"Certainly not." Madeline countered, laughter lurking in the depths of her emerald eyes. "I prefer good old terra firma or, at the very least, a sturdy deck below my feet."

Oliver chuckled at that, then turned toward Joshua. "I better get below, Cap'n. The lads need me to get this tub under sail without no problems." He glanced at Madeline. "Think I better send someone to get a hat for the missus?"

After Joshua nodded his approval, Oliver winked at Madeline and disappeared down the ladder.

219

"It would appear you have another conquest." The captain had turned to survey his vessel. Madeline couldn't see his face, and from his tone she couldn't tell whether he was teasing her or not.

"I like him, though I certainly didn't think I would at first."

The captain looked down at her, and she read genuine affection for the older man in his eyes. "Oliver's a bit gruff at times, but don't let that bother you. Underneath, he's all mush."

"Mush?" Madeline laughed.

"If you tell him I said that I'll deny it with my dying breath," he responded with mock severity. "Tell you something else about him. If you give him half a chance, he'll mother you to death."

Through her dark lashes, Madeline slanted a look at him. "Does he do that with you?" She couldn't imagine anyone trying to mother this strong giant of a man, least of all his short, sinewy first mate.

But the captain's attention had been drawn by something down on the main deck. He was leaning over the rail and barking orders faster than Madeline could follow them. Maybe it was just that she didn't understand most of the words. *Deadeye, fiddle block, shiv.* However, they sounded enticing, though foreign, and she vowed to uncover their mysterious meanings before this voyage ended. Since she was being forced to leave her home and traipse after the captain on some wild-goose chase, she might as well get something out of it.

"Miss Madeline, I've fetched your bonnet."

Madeline smiled into the sky-blue eyes of Whitey. She had first met this shy youth, whose hair clearly bespoke the reason for his name, when along with Oliver he had brought dinner to the cabin the past evening. The first mate had explained that, likely as not, Whitey would be bringing her meals from now on. He had gone on to expound on the varied reasons for this, apparently not

220

wishing her to think he was abandoning her. But Madeline had already felt abandoned by the captain, so she had given his explanation little heed. She cared not who brought her meals and saw to the straightening of the cabin. If Whitey usually did it for the captain, that was fine with her.

Whitey had stood by during Oliver's discourse, nervously clutching his knit cap and not uttering a word. As a matter of fact, until this moment Madeline had not been sure the boy—she guessed him to be thirteen or fourteen years old—could speak.

Madeline took the proffered hat and thanked the cabin boy. She wondered if her face had ever been as red as Whitey's was at this moment. She hoped not. He mumbled something and then fled from the quarterdeck as fast as his gangly legs would carry him.

Another admirer, Madeline thought the captain might comment as she followed the boy's retreat, but he didn't. In fact, he seemed to have missed the entire encounter. His attention was still on the activity below.

Madeline stuck the silk-covered straw hat on her head, and tied the ribbons beneath her chin. Relieved of much of the sun's glare, she let her eyes drift toward the captain. His back was toward her so she couldn't see his face. But then, he couldn't see her looking at him either. And besides, she thought as her gaze slipped down from his broad shoulders, there was not a thing wrong with observing his back side. It came close to being as good to look at as the front of him. Madeline had long since given up denying that she found the captain very handsome. Of course, she thought as she watched knotted muscles move beneath the white linen of his shirt, not many women would deny that he was very attractive.

His mistress probably thought so. As Madeline played around with that disturbing thought, she noticed that the hair curling around his neck shone almost blue-black in the sunlight. He wore his hair shorter than most men,

221

and she thought that was a good thing in view of his habit of raking his fingers through it. Seeming to read her mind, the captain raised his arm and finger-combed his wind-blown locks before shouting at a seaman in the rigging.

He appeared to have forgotten her presence, so Madeline continued to look her fill. Did all men have such broad shoulders? she wondered. She didn't think she had ever seen any quite so broad before, especially any that narrowed down into such a trim waist. And his midsection was hard, lean, and, as she remembered, sunbaked,

Her gaze meandered lower until it snagged, then lingered, on the firm swell of his taut—

"Maddie?"

"What?" The word was a breathy croak, but Madeline managed to raise her head and meet his gaze.

"Are you all right?" Joshua had looked around to see a strange expression on his wife's face.

"Y-yes." Madeline tried to still the quiver in her voice. Had he noticed where she had been staring?

"You're certain?" He sounded genuinely concerned.

"Yes, I am," she snapped, wishing he would stop questioning her. What did he want her to say: I was looking at your rear and wondering if it was as muscled and hard as the rest of you, and I got caught? Well, he'd never hear such words from her lips.

"You don't have to get so upset; I was just asking."

Madeline glared at him. Didn't he know calm, logical Madeline O'Neil had been in upheaval ever since she had first laid eyes on him?

"Oh, never mind. Come here." Joshua motioned for her to join him on the stern end of the quarterdeck. "I want to show you something."

Before she did, Madeline cast a glance below. She was amazed by the change. While she had been ogling the captain, the crew had managed to get the *Chesapeake* under sail. The fore-and-aft rigs snapped smartly in the brisk sea breeze, their rakish canvas sending the *Chesapeake* skimming out of the harbor.

Joshua looked around and noticed the awe with which his wife was observing his vessel, and he was filled with pride for his ship. He moved to join her.

"She's a prime sailor," he said as he lovingly rubbed his palm over the polished wood of the *Chesapeake*'s rail. "There's no finer Bermuda sloop sailing the seas."

Madeline peered up at him. "You wouldn't be a wee bit prejudiced now, would you, Captain?"

"Me?" he asked in mock surprise. "Nay. If I praise the *Chesapeake* 'tis because I know her." Joshua's black eyes narrowed at taking in Madeline's expression of sadness. "What's wrong?"

"Oh, nothing." She gave her head a shake as if to clear it. "It was just that for a moment there you . . . well, you sounded just like my father."

"When he spoke of his ship?"

Madeline nodded. "He talked of the *Providence* as if she were a beautiful woman who had stolen his heart. I'm sorry." She gave him a wan smile. "I didn't mean to become maudlin. Please tell me more about the *Chesapeake*."

"There's not a person who would fault you for being mournful right now." She looked so tiny and sad he could almost forgive the lie.

"I know." Madeline swallowed back the lump in her throat. "But Papa wouldn't like it. He'd tell me to remember the good times and go on with my life." She stopped abruptly and looked up at the captain. Going on with her life required knowing what was to come of it, and at this moment she had no idea what the future might hold.

Joshua clasped his hands behind his back and stared at her. He didn't know whether she was going to cry or not, though the trembling of her bottom lip gave every

223

indication that she might.

And what then? Was he to comfort her as any good husband would, or refrain from touching her as she had demanded he do on more than one occasion? His preference leaned more toward playing the good husband. Even now he ached to take her in his arms and offer up his strength for her comfort.

A patch of green caught his eye, and he saw in it a momentary reprieve from making that decision. He would take her mind off her father, at least temporarily, and the tears would pass.

"Look!" He reached for her hand and led her across the deck. Madeline shaded her eyes, which even the wide brim of her hat failed to shield from the glare of the morning sun, and looked in the direction he'd indicated. There, in the distance, gleaming emerald-bright against the turquoise-blue of sky and sea, was a narrow strip of land, its eight miles forming a natural breakwater for Kingston Harbor.

"The Palisadoes," she murmured, enthralled by the natural beauty that she surveyed.

"Aye," Joshua breathed, resting his forearms on the rail. "Do you know why it's called that?"

"No."

"'Tis the tops of the coconut palms. 'Twas thought they looked like the spikes of a palisaded fence."

Madeline studied the area with a new perspective. "Oh, yes," she finally said. "I see it. Look!"

Joshua ignored the finger that she thrust toward the natural barrier and gazed instead at her animated face.

"I suppose"—the corners of his mouth curved to a grin—"someone with a very vivid imagination could conjure up a facsimile of a fence."

Madeline watched the tropical shoreline a moment longer. Then the magnetic pull of his gaze drew her eyes around and she saw his grin. "You're making fun of me," she scolded jestingly.

224

ACCEPT YOUR FREE GIFT AND EXPERIENCE MORE OF THE PASSION AND ADVENTURE YOU LIKE IN A HISTORICAL ROMANCE

Zebra Romances are the finest novels of their kind and are written with the adult woman in mind. All of our books are written by authors who really know how to weave tales of romantic adventure in the historical settings you love.

Because our readers tell us these books sell out very fast in the stores, Zebra has made arrangements for you to receive at home the four newest titles published each month. You'll never miss a title and home delivery is so convenient. With your first shipment we'll even send you a FREE Zebra Historical Romance as our gift just for trying our home subscription service. No obligation.

BIG SAVINGS AND **FREE** HOME DELIVERY

Each month, the Zebra Home Subscription Service will send you the four newest titles as soon as they are published. (We ship these books to our subscribers even before we send them to the stores.) You may preview them *Free* for 10 days. If you like them as much as we think you will, you'll pay just $3.50 each and *save $1.80 each month* off the cover price. *AND you'll also get FREE HOME DELIVERY*. There is never a charge for shipping, handling or postage and there is no minimum you must buy. If you decide not to keep any shipment, simply return it within 10 days, no questions asked, and owe nothing.

Get a Free
Zebra
Historical
Romance

*a $3.95
value*

"No, no, I swear it." Joshua threw up his hands in surrender. "'Twas not my intent. I've always admired people with vivid imaginations."

"And I suppose you do not have one."

"Precious little. Perhaps I could hire you to do my imagining for me," he quipped. He had meant the words to be a continuation of their good-natured banter, but the moment he uttered them he knew they were wrong. One didn't hire someone to do his imagining for him as he might hire a sailmaker or tailor. Visions and fantasies were integral parts of a person's mind, too intimate to be sold; they could only be shared freely. And even then, only with someone who could be trusted with one's private thoughts—an intimate.

Joshua stared into the emerald-green eyes that gazed up at him and wondered what imaginings lurked behind their sparkling glow. He wished he had the right to ask.

"Damn!" He had torn his attention away from her to look out over the stern when the expletive escaped his lips.

"What is it?" Madeline had been slowly drifting back down from the heights to which his sensual stare had carried her, when the captain's outburst hit her. It had the effect of jerking her back to reality.

"You almost missed it." Lord, I'm going to have to stop gazing into her eyes like that, Joshua thought. He was acting more like Whitey than an experienced gentleman of thirty.

"Missed what?" Madeline frantically looked about, trying to discover what it was she was supposed to be seeing. Damn the man anyway. If he'd wanted her to notice something other than the way sunlight intensified the ebony depths of his eyes, then he shouldn't have been looking at her as he had.

"There, I think you can still see it." Joshua pointed toward a promontory northeast of Port Royal at the harbor entrance. "Can you see that copse of mangrove?"

Madeline squinted. "Yes, I see it."

"It's Gallow's Point."

"*That's* Gallow's Point?" Madeline looked up at the captain in surprise, then back at the receding, high point of land.

"Aye. You've heard of it?"

"Certainly I've heard of it. It's where they used to hang pirates," she stated haughtily. "I just thought it would be more—"

"More what, Maddie? Surely you didn't expect to see blood-slickened nooses hanging from a crossbeam."

"Of course not," she snapped. "I guess I expected something more ominous."

"I'm sure it seemed plenty ominous to the men who died there."

"They were pirates, after all, deserving of whatever fate was dealt them."

"Perhaps," Joshua shrugged. "But they were men, too."

Madeline turned her back toward the sea and stared up at him. "Do I detect a soft spot for the breed?"

Joshua threw back his head and laughed. "Nay, but you no doubt think that because you suspect me of being one myself."

Madeline lowered her eyes self-consciously. She had believed him to be a pirate when first she'd met him, and even now, knowing him to be a privateer, she questioned the fundamental differences between the two pursuits.

Joshua placed a lean finger under her chin, raising her face until she was forced to peer into black eyes filled with amusement. "Admit it, Maddie, you think you're married to a pirate."

"I think no such thing." Her response was too quick and emphatic to be believable.

Madeline wondered if the entire crew could hear his booming laugh. She almost wished for the courage to leap over the side and swim through the clear soothing waters of the Caribbean to shore.

How was she ever to endure confinement on this small vessel with a man who, in turn, taunted and tantalized her?

Joshua rubbed the sleeve of his jacket across eyes made damp by laughter. "Poor little Maddie." He shook his head from side to side in response to her scowl. "I'm not, you know—a pirate, I mean."

"You plunder ships."

"Enemy ships!"

"Do you really take the time to identify a vessel's port of call before you attack, I wonder?"

His expression of pain told her she had gone too far. She had hurt him. Madeline knew it the moment the captain turned on his heel after making a curt explanation that he must see to things on the main deck.

Madeline didn't really believe the captain, for all his blatant masculinity, was the type of man to wreak havoc on innocent women and children. And she certainly couldn't see Whitey, or even Oliver, engaged in such an activity.

Maybe she should seek him out and apologize. She could explain that she was merely angered by his laughing at her expense. But then he might think she cared how he felt about her, and, of course, she didn't. Besides, what if he rejected her apology, or worse, ignored it? No, searching for the captain among his crew was a bad idea.

A head with hair as black as a raven's wing stood out above the rest below. All right, so she wouldn't have to search for him. She still wasn't going to run after him. If she happened to bump into him, then she'd apologize, but she would keep it simple. There would be no elaborate explanation about how she thought him far too honorable a man to commit such crimes. Just I'm sorry if I hurt your feelings; that was never my intent. Yes, that was what she would say.

Satisfied that she had solved at least one of her problems, Madeline turned back to bid a quickly fading Jamaica a fond farewell. It was like a gaudy jewel flashing in the late morning sun, her island home. Was there any place in the world that could boast bluer blues or greener greens? Anywhere that the sun kissed with as much daring or the breezes caressed as lovingly? Madeline watched until she could no longer make out the patches of sugar cane or the tropical forests of palm and bamboo, until the towering Blue Mountains with their halo of fleecy white clouds became but a dot on the horizon. Then she went below.

Her first day at sea passed quickly. After returning to the cabin, she unpacked and placed in the small commode beside the bed those personal articles she would need throughout the coming days. Finally finished with that, she pushed her sea chest into the far corner of the cabin.

Much larger than her quarters on the *Primrose*, this cabin seemed to her to be the ultimate in shipboard accommodations. She had noticed before that it was painfully neat, and now saw nothing to dissuade her from that earlier assessment. Even the maps and charts that dominated the sturdy oak desk were arranged in an orderly fashion. Madeline spent some time perusing them, but decided she would definitely need guidance to be able to decipher the web of crisscrossing lines. The captain understood them. Perhaps if she asked nicely, he would . . . Of course that would have to be after she apologized for her remark about his plundering ships.

Because of her experience on the *Primrose*, Madeline was reluctant to wander about above by herself. But when boredom finally sent her on deck, she found that no one denied her right to be there. The captain certainly didn't. Of course, she didn't see him. She purposely avoided the quarterdeck. Now that the *Chesapeake* was sail borne, the activity on the main deck had decreased considerably. Nonetheless, Madeline's presence seemed

228

to cause the men of the afternoon watch no problem. To a man, they treated her with the respect due the captain's wife.

A seaman named Lester, a short, skinny fellow with a long rattail of a queue wrapped in eelskin, even explained to Madeline the process of determining the *Chesapeake*'s speed.

She had been walking near the stern on the lee side when she had noticed him holding an hourglass. Before she could ask what he was doing, another seaman, who was holding the end of a rope that dangled overboard, yelled, "Turn." Lester inverted the glass and answered, "Done." Less than a minute later, when the sand had all trickled through the narrow opening, he yelled, "Stop," and the man with the rope hauled it on board.

Madeline had hesitated to ask the men what they were doing while they'd been engaged in their labors. But when the sailor with the rope—she now saw it was attached to a triangular wooden slab—walked away, she'd questioned the man who remained.

He turned to her with a friendly smile, introduced himself as Lester, and told her that they had been "heaving the log." The rope, he explained, was knotted every fifty feet, eight inches. By counting the number of knots let out in a half-minute, they could calculate how fast the *Chesapeake* was going.

It was hunger that finally drove her below to the captain's cabin. The delicately flavored crab and fresh fruit that Whitey served her was delicious, but the youth was quick to point out that in a day or two the fresh fruit would be gone, and any meat she received would, by necessity, be preserved in brine.

The captain didn't join her for dinner. Naturally, Madeline told herself she was glad about that. Maybe the entire voyage would be accomplished without having to see or talk to him. Hadn't she managed to entertain herself very well today on her own?

She was very close to convincing herself that the captain's presence was neither required nor desired by her when the man himself opened the door and sauntered into his cabin.

"Surprised to see me?"

"No," Madeline lied. "This is your cabin."

"It is, isn't it?" He looked about as if seeing the room for the first time. With long, lazy strides, he walked to the chair behind his desk and settled in. For countless minutes, the only sound in the small confines of his quarters was the scratching of his quill on the parchment of one of the charts.

"Did you enjoy your dinner?" He motioned with the feather tip toward the dishes still littering the small table beside Madeline.

"Yes, it was quite delicious. I had no idea your cook was so accomplished."

The captain grinned. "You will probably wonder how you could ever have thought such a thing before this trip is over."

Madeline smiled, his grin was so infectious. "Whitey indicated as much."

"Watching him eat, I would never have suspected the quality of the food bothered him."

She laughed softly and then quickly looked down at her clasped hands. It was pleasant sitting here with him, listening to his deep voice. She could readily imagine their sharing quiet times like this before they retired.

Joshua finished transcribing the log entry he should have written at noon, and would have, if his anger hadn't been so fresh and he hadn't known that she was in the cabin. Then, with a force that rang through the quiet of the room and sent the tiny flame of the desk-top candle aflutter, he shut the log.

"Where are you going?" Madeline bit her bottom lip, but the words had already escaped.

Joshua stopped on his way to the door and turned to

face the woman who sat demurely in the sturdy wooden chair. Her eyes were fixed upon hands clasped with white-knuckled intensity. "I was going to check the night watch."

"Oh," Madeline breathed out. Slowly, she raised her eyes. He stood in the center of the cabin, watching her. She hoped he didn't think she wanted him to stay.

He turned toward the door.

"Captain."

"Aye?"

She swallowed. "I'm sorry about what I said." She watched him slowly turn back till he faced her, an expression of surprise reflected in the ebony depths of his eyes. "I don't really think you are a pirate, and . . . and it was cruel of me to imply that I did." There, she had said it.

"Thank you for that." Joshua reached behind him for the door handle, wondering why his hand was shaking and why he was leaving. There was no need to check the night watch. He'd done that before coming below.

She had risen during her apology and was advancing on him. The hair he had admired earlier as it sparkled in the sun now gleamed golden in the subtle glow of candlelight. She looked soft, and innocent, and more alluring than any woman he had ever seen.

Madeline told herself she should stop. The cabin was small, intimate; and she knew she had moved much too close to him. But she seemed unable to control her own body. She could smell the sea air that clung to his clothes, could almost taste the salty tang of his skin. She resisted the urge to wet her too-dry lips with the tip of her tongue.

But it really wasn't necessary. For in the next moment the captain's warm, moist mouth was pressed against hers.

Joshua wasn't certain exactly when he'd decided to stay. He wasn't even sure it had been a conscious decision on his part. One minute his hand was clutching the doorknob, and he was silently cursing his own stubbornness, and the next his arms were wrapped around the small feminine form of his wife. And she was his wife. There was no reason, no reason at all, for him to be sleeping anyplace but right here.

It was happening to her again. That tingling and tightening of her body in response to his touch. Madeline clung to her husband's broad shoulders, kissing him back as thoroughly as he kissed her. She loved the way his mouth felt on hers. The way it moved, slowly at first, then with a hungry intensity that left her weak.

Joshua's hands moved up her corseted ribs, skimming the sides of her breasts, then tangling in her long silken curls. On a sigh, he pulled himself away, holding her head gently when she would have followed his lips with her own. Her lashes fluttered, opening slighty to shadow eyes languid with desire. Joshua pressed her forehead to his chin, breathing in the sweet scent of roses and whispered, his voice thick with desire, "Come to bed with me. I want to be with you as a man should be with his wife."

The long, slender fingers that had dropped to her shoulders were stiff and tense. With sudden insight, Madeline realized he was nervous about her answer, almost as nervous as she was. She studied the tight weave of his shirt, conscious of the rise and fall of the fabric against his broad chest. What was she to say to him? And why had he asked?

Her mind wandered back to the time they had made love by the bay. She hadn't wanted to stop him then, and she wouldn't have stopped him now. Certainly he knew that. But he wasn't going to allow her to be swept away by passion. Even now he'd stepped back, putting space between their bodies, making her long to press against his hard length.

Madeline raised her eyes, searching his, hoping to find the answer there. He'd offered no vows of love or everlasting tomorrows, but then she knew better than to expect that. After all, theirs was a marriage of convenience. But did it have to be a marriage of loneliness and longing?

She touched his cheek, trailing her fingers along the curve of his strong jaw. "Come to bed, Captain. It has been a long day."

The cot was small, barely large enough for one, let alone two people. Madeline had wondered last night as she'd lain between the wooden sides how the captain ever fit into it comfortably. Now she snuggled lower under the coarse sheet trying to imagine how they would both manage to sleep in its narrow confines. But then, sleep wasn't exactly what the captain had in mind.

Madeline fingered the cotton lace around the neck of her nightrail, worrying again if she should have put it on.

As soon as she had issued her invitation for the captain to join her in bed, he had pulled her to him, hugging her so tightly she could hardly breath, but making her glad she'd decided to accept him. He'd kissed her, his tongue plunging deep into the soft recesses of her mouth, and it had taken her a moment to notice the knocking. Madeline had been certain at first that the noise was the thumping of her wildly beating heart. But when the captain had torn his mouth away and mumbled a frustrated, "Damn," she'd known it was someone at the door.

When Whitey had said the captain was needed above, he'd gone—reluctantly. But before he'd left, he had touched the end of her nose and grinned. "I'll be back," he'd promised.

When? Madeline squirmed onto her side. The room was dark—extinguishing the lantern was the only other thing she'd done besides donning her nightrail—so she had no idea how long he'd been gone, but she estimated it was almost three-quarters of an hour. She sighed. Certainly she wasn't anxious for his return. But the instant she heard his footfalls in the companionway, the blood started rushing through her body, and she knew she'd only been fooling herself.

"Maddie?"

She could see his large frame outlined against the golden glow of the passageway as he opened the door. "I'm here," she whispered.

Joshua entered the room, and felt his way to a chair, sinking into it and prying off his boots. He glanced toward the bed, barely able to make out his wife's form in the darkness. He thought about asking her if he could light a candle, but decided it was no accident that the lantern had been blown out. Stepping out of his breeches, he wondered if she were as naked under that sheet as he was. He shook his head, thinking of the darkness. Probably not.

"Are you cold?" Joshua climbed onto the cot, noticing the sheet she clutched to her neck.

Madeline bit her lower lip. The bed's size allowed no room for privacy. The captain was practically on top of her. "No, not really. It is a bit chill—"

Before she could finish her ramblings his warm mouth cut them short and made her forget what she'd been going to say. Certainly, any thought of cold was forced from her mind. A wild heat rushed through her, and she doubted she'd ever be cool again. His lips traveled to her throat and white hot sparks seemed to flow across her flesh.

Madeline arched her neck, dropping the sheet, choosing instead to clutch his broad back. Her hand roamed across the hard ridges of muscle that bunched beneath the velvet texture of his skin. Oh, she reveled in the feel of him pressed so intimately against her: the powerful chest that caressed her breasts; his strong, muscular thighs; and that hard, swollen part of him that throbbed and teased her through the thickness of her nightrail and the sheet.

"I don't believe we need this."

The captain inched the offending fabric down her

234

body, and Madeline thought she'd never agreed with him more. The sheet became tangled around her legs, and she gave a kick that opened her thighs, allowing him to slip more comfortably into the cradle of her body. Her nightrail followed the sheet, and then there was nothing but heated flesh against flesh.

A small gasp escaped Madeline as he slid down her body, trailing his lips along her skin till he reached the rosy pink crest of her breast. With infinite care he drew the aching tip into the warm, moist recesses of his mouth, swirling his tongue across the hard nipple until Madeline could stand the delicious torment no longer.

Just when she thought she would surely scream from the pleasure he evoked, he shifted, the slight abrasion of his night-beard forging a path across the valley between her breasts. And then the wonder started anew.

Joshua was ready to explode. Why he deliberately prolonged this pain, he had no idea—except that it felt so damned good. It had been like this the other time, too. Merely being close to her, touching the gentle swells of her body, was enough to make him lose control, to make him wish it could last forever.

The other time . . . It would have been better if he hadn't thought of that. He certainly hadn't wanted it to last after he'd discovered her lie. He'd wanted to get away from her as fast as he could. But he hadn't been able to. He'd married her. And now he was going to get what he deserved from this marriage. After all, he was just satisfying his needs with her body. Wasn't he?

Joshua gave in to desire and plunged deep into her being. He heard her small, breathless moans, muffled against his bare shoulder, felt the hot, sheath of her womanhood mold around him; and he thought no more.

Madeline wrapped her legs around his waist, lifting herself to welcome each mesmerizing movement of his manhood. Her hands dug into the firm curve of his buttocks, conscious of his trembling as he slowly pulled

235

himself from her only to thrust deeper, harder into her softness. Then suddenly he drove so far into her that she thought he'd truly reached her soul. Bright, colored lights pierced the darkness and she wondered how she could be floating so high among exploding stars.

"Are you all right?"

The question filtered through Madeline's consciousness as she drifted back to earth. It was a moment before she trusted herself to answer. "I'm fine." She smiled and even in the darkness she could see the flashing whiteness of his answering grin.

It took some twisting and turning before they reached anything close to comfort within the restrictive boundaries of the cot. Madeline was on her side, bundled in the curve of the captain's arm, her own thrown across his hair-roughened chest.

"Damn, this bunk is small."

The captain's words, muttered in what could only be called disgust, offended Madeline who had just decided the bed was rather cozy. "I suppose it's nothing like what you've been used to the last two nights." Madeline could have bitten her tongue. Why had she brought up the nights he'd been away from the cabin?

She felt his body grow tense. "What do you know about where I slept?" Madeline squirmed and his arm tightened around her. "Maddie?"

There was no denying that he wanted an answer. Well, she'd give him one. She'd let him know just how nonchalant she could be about his other woman—no matter how much it hurt her. "I assume your mistress has a larger bed?" Certainly the woman would go out of her way to please a man like the captain, and he obviously didn't like small beds.

"My what?" He turned on his side to face Madeline, and the forest of curling, black hair on his chest swirled against her breasts.

She tried to ignore the sensation. "Your mistress," she repeated, annoyed that he wouldn't let the matter drop.

236

"You needn't worry. I realize it's perfectly normal— What is so funny?"

The captain had rolled on to his back, taking her with him, and she now lay sprawled upon his chest listening to his deep rumbling laughter. He ran a hand across his face, then settled it on the back of Madeline's neck. "I'll tell you what's so funny. You are. What made you think? . . . Never mind." He tugged Madeline's head down and touched her lips with the tip of his tongue. "I have no mistress, Maddie."

"You don't?" Her breath mingled with his.

"No. And I'll tell you something else. I spent the last two nights on deck curled up with a length of rope."

"Oh." Madeline didn't have a chance to say anything else because his mouth had closed over hers. But she couldn't help feeling relieved now that she knew where he'd slept.

Chapter 17

Rat-tat-tat!
The loud rattling noise was the first sound Madeline heard upon awakening. The next was a loud thump, followed by a searing assortment of swear words.

She opened her eyes, but could make out very little in the grainy, predawn darkness that enveloped the cabin. One thing was certain, she was alone in the bunk. "Captain, is that you?"

"Yes."

She exhaled slowly, realizing she'd been holding her breath. Even in her confusion at being awakened by the bloodcurdling sound, it was comforting to know the captain was near. "What are you doing?" Madeline sat up on the bed, wrapping the sheet around her and trying to distinguish the movements of the shadow she assumed to be her husband.

There was silence for a moment and then another mumbled curse. "I'm putting on my breeches."

"Oh." Madeline stopped trying to make out his form. "What was that loud thump? Did you hurt yourself?"

"No!" The rest of his answer was a series of expletive-laced mumbles as he forced his feet into his boots.

"What did you say?"

"Dammit, Maddie, I don't have time for this. I said, I fell out of the cot."

Madeline couldn't stop the giggle that bubbled from her throat but luckily the loud, rattling noise pierced the darkness again, hiding her amusement. "What is that?" She could hear the captain moving across the room.

"Call to quarters."

"But, what—"

"Battle stations, Maddie. It's a call for all hands to go to battle stations."

"Oh, my God!"

The captain had paused in the doorway. Silhouetted against the brighter light of the companionway, he'd provided this last piece of information. Madeline jumped out of bed, dragging the sheet behind her, and started to join him.

"Not you, Maddie. Stay put!" With that he was gone.

Stay put. Madeline wrung her hands and tried to slow the pace of her breathing. Only moments had passed since that horrible noise had awakened her, but they seemed hours. Now that it had stopped again, Madeline could hear much activity overhead—stomping boots, commands given and acknowledged, and something heavy being dragged from one place to another.

Againt the backdrop of all that organized exertion on deck, her own inactivity seemed ludicrous. If there was an enemy to meet, she most certainly would not confront him wrapped in a sheet. Even the minor task of getting dressed helped calm her.

Madeline groped around on the desk until she found the candle in its brass holder. Without even considering that she was disobeying the captain, she stole into the companionway and lit the wick from the flame of the lantern hanging there.

Being able to see was comforting. Hurriedly, she pulled on her cotton stockings and tied the garters above her knees. Then she flung off the sheet and covered herself with a white linen shift. She'd just finished lacing up the stays when the door burst open.

"Oh!" Madeline whirled around, ready to repel any

intruder, though, even in her panic, she wondered how she'd accomplish that. She slumped back against the desk when she recognized the captain.

"Sorry, it was not my intention to startle you."

"It's all right." Madeline stood up. "I suppose I'm a little on edge." That is certainly an understatement, she thought as she watched the captain check through some charts on his desk.

"Quite understandable, under the circumstances." He was now bent over, pulling a long box from the cabinet beneath the bunk.

"What *are* the circumstances?"

Joshua paused for a moment and looked up at her. It was then Madeline remembered her own state of dress— or more correctly, undress. Her shift hung only to midcalf, exposing a goodly amount of leg and ankle. And though she had not laced her stays tightly, they pushed the fullness of her breasts against the sheer fabric of her shift.

She resisted the urge to cross her arms over her chest, then realized the captain was looking at her face and seemed not to have noticed her attire.

"During the night we sailed alarmingly close to a French schooner."

"French." Madeline breathed the word. "Do you think it's part of Bompar's fleet?"

The captain resumed pulling the wooden box from beneath the bunk. "I wouldn't be at all surprised."

He removed the lid and extracted a cutlass and two pistols.

Madeline remembered searching for weapons to use against him the first time she'd been in his cabin. She hadn't thought to look under the bed. Now, she was glad for that oversight. She hated to think what she might have done if there had been a pistol at her disposal.

Apparently there was to be one now.

"Do you know how to use this?" Joshua stood,

240

extending one of the two matching pistols toward her. Its brass-trimmed grip shone in the candlelight.

"No—well, I mean yes, but I don't want to."

The captain shrugged. "Chances are excellent that you won't have to. It's merely a precaution. I'll prime it for you before I go above."

Madeline looked at the gun he'd placed on the desk, and then back at him. He was hurriedly getting dressed. His state of dishevelment was nearly as revealing as her own. When he had gone running off to answer the call to stations, he had pulled on a shirt, but just barely. It had been left open down the front and not tucked into his breeches. He set about remedying that now.

"Do you think there will be a battle?" she forced herself to look away as the captain unfastened his breeches to tuck in his shirttail.

"Possibly." Madeline glanced back at him as he spoke, and decided there was not anything too improper about watching him fasten his shirt. "We're trying to outrun her now, but she appears to have a good sharp hull." He shrugged. "I don't know if we can."

He donned his dark blue jacket, and it occurred to Madeline as he strapped on the cutlass and jammed the pistol into the waistband of his breeches, that he was definitely dressing for battle.

"What if you can't outrun her?" Madeline knew her voice was quivering, but she couldn't seem to help it. The thoughts of the captain, her husband, standing on deck, shooting that pistol, being shot at by someone on the other ship, was too distressing.

"Then we'll have to fight her." He spoke those words in such a matter-of-fact way that Madeline's response, a soft cry of anguish, sounded completely out of place.

Joshua stopped ramming the ball into the pistol's chamber and looked up. Poor little Maddie. She was obviously distraught and feared for her safety. How insensitive could he be? She wasn't used to battles, did

241

not feel the thrill of outrunning an enemy as he did. She was probably scared out of her wits. "Listen, Maddie, don't be frightened." He looked down at the gun to avoid seeing just how upset she was. "I probably shouldn't even leave this for you." Joshua turned the pistol over in his large hands and checked the flint. "If the worst should happen and the *Chesapeake* is captured, you'll be safe enough. Tell them I forced you to leave your home and come with me—not too far from the truth anyway, right?"

He looked up and grinned, but averted his eyes when he saw that his wife had failed to grasp the humor of his words. "They shouldn't have any trouble believing it once they see you. The French have always had a penchant for beautiful women, and they'll, no doubt, understand why I—"

"You think I'm beautiful?"

Joshua looked up, amazed by the disbelief in her voice. She stood before him like a vision from one of his more recent dreams. Her hair waved wantonly around the delicate oval of her face, then looped its way across her narrow shoulders and down her back. He remembered weaving his fingers through her tawny mane, inhaling the fresh scent of roses, kissing those sensual lips.

His gaze lowered and his mouth went dry as he noticed the alluring way her stays had pushed her breasts up until they came close to overflowing the sheer fabric of her shift. She was perfect, from those thick-lashed, green eyes to that small fragile body.

Joshua rose, pushing the chair back with more force than necessary as he realized just *how* perfect he thought her to be. His voice was gruff with emotion as he answered the question that still lingered in the depths of her emerald eyes. "Aye, I think you're beautiful. Didn't you know that?"

"No." The single word was said without coyness.

"Well, you know it now." Joshua slapped the pistol on

the desk and strode toward the door. He was almost anxious for the confrontation with the French schooner. Sea battles he understood: the emotions this woman evoked in him, he didn't.

"Captain?"

"What?" Joshua knew she had moved close to him even before he turned because he could smell those damned roses. The fragrance saturated the air around him.

Madeline didn't know what made her so bold. Maybe it was the fact that he thought her beautiful, and that made her feel beautiful. Or maybe it was because there was the possibility of a battle, and she was consumed with the same generosity of spirit that had been felt by generations of women as they'd sent their men to war. Or maybe, maybe, the thought of his dying, of her never seeing—touching—him again was so dreadful she could barely stand it. Madeline placed a hand on his arm, then gripped it. "Please be careful."

Joshua looked first at the small hand that clutched the blue fabric of his sleeve and then at his wife's face. He willed himself to say something glib. After all, he knew many appropriate retorts. He'd used a devil-may-care attitude to great advantage with women from Boston to Charleston. Every time he put out to sea, he faced danger. And those he left behind knew it.

But he couldn't make light of the fear he saw in her eyes—fear for him.

With more force than he intended, Joshua grabbed her to him. His lips easily found hers. They slanted, twisted, sought purchase and held, hungrily.

Madeline offered no shy, maidenly kiss. Her response was as passionate and desperate as the circumstances demanded. Her arms wrapped about his neck, her open mouth pressed to his. She gave all and took more. The clean, salt-air smell of his body, the taste of his tongue, the feel of his firm strength crushing her near—these would be hers long after duty called him away.

"Maddie." He wrenched his lips from hers to whisper her name into the cloud of hair around her ear. Was there ever a sound so sweet or so sorrowful?

Madeline's head dropped forward, its crown resting against his chest. She could hear his heart's steady beat, feel him begin to pull away. Yet still she clung, her arms unwilling to respond to the voice of reason and release their hold.

Slowly Joshua's hands followed the curve of her arms, around his shoulders and behind his neck. With gentle force he released her hands and brought them to his lips. Then he left.

For long moments Madeline could only stare at the closed portal. Gradually she became aware of her surroundings. There was still a lot of noise vibrating through the deck above her. If she listened carefully, she could distinguish some of the different sounds. She could well imagine the privateers moving about, getting ready for battle. Maybe there would be no battle. Hadn't the captain said they would try to outrun the enemy vessel first? Perhaps they were, even now, skimming across the waves out of harm's—

Madeline wasn't certain what the noise was, though she could guess. Only when she heard the answering salvo from the *Chesapeake,* felt the sloop recoil in the water, did she know there would be no escaping this confrontation.

She dressed quickly, then sat on the chair to listen. She made out another volley of cannon fire punctuating the lesser booming of musketry. What was going on? Madeline cursed her sex for it forced her to stay below in ignorance.

Her glance fell to the desk top, to the pistol, primed and waiting. Could she use it if need be? She traced the dull surface of the barrel with her finger. Zeb Turner had taught her to shoot years ago when he was Hopewell's overseer. Madeline ws pretty sure she remembered, but she doubted she'd be effective at any but point-blank range. Besides, if she sauntered on deck, brandishing a pistol, the captain would surely be in a temper, and with good reason. He had enough to worry about without having to protect her. As a sudden roll of the *Chesapeake* made Madeline clutch the edge of the desk, she hoped he was paying heed to his own safety.

She rose and began to pace the cabin. There must be something she could do.

The last broadside from the French schooner had hurled Joshua against the splintered deck rail. Air, forced from his lungs by the impact, hissed through his teeth as his body acknowledged the pain in his upper arm.

"Damn." He looked down to see a jagged line of crimson widening on the sleeve of his sweat-stained shirt. He glanced about, seeking something to stem the flow of blood, but found nothing. His coat and neckpiece had long since been abandoned in favor of shirtsleeves. With a jerky, one-handed motion, Joshua pulled the tail of his shirt from his breeches and tore off a piece of it. He held one end of the makeshift bandage in his teeth and wrapped the other around his upper arm. The final yank he gave the knot made him wince in pain, but at least the blood no longer flowed unrestrained.

A quick survey of the *Chesapeake* assured Joshua that she was basically still in one piece, though he wondered how much longer that would hold true. The French vessel was agile and swift, and Joshua had to admire the cunning of her captain. For every maneuver Joshua had initiated, the Frenchman had a countermove.

And the ugly truth was that even without the smart maneuvers of the French captain, the *Chesapeake* would have been in trouble. Less than five minutes into the battle, it had been painfully obvious that she was

245

sadly outgunned.

Joshua swiped at the acrid smoke around his face, then peered at the enemy vessel through his spyglass. She had tacked about to stern and was now closing in on the *Chesapeake*.

"Cap'n!" Oliver's grimy, sweat-smeared face appeared at the top of the quarterdeck steps. "They're aimin' to board us!"

"We'll see about that." The corners of Joshua's mouth twitched in delight. Just maybe he hadn't shown the French captain everything he had in his bag of tricks. But to be on the safe side, he snapped the order, "Prepare to repel boarders."

He kept a sharp eye on the schooner that was closing in fast as his men broke out the boarding pikes. The French captain was getting cocky. No doubt, he thought the smaller sloop was almost his.

"Oliver!" With his good hand, Joshua kept the wheel steady as he yelled for his first mate. "Oliver!" The noise of battle had died down considerably. The French schooner was following so close in the *Chesapeake*'s wake that the privateer's guns were useless.

"Aye, Cap'n." The wiry man bounded up the steps. "The men are ready."

"Good. Now send the topmen aloft. On my signal they're to spill the wind from the canvas."

Oliver's bearded face wrinkled into a grin—a grin that Joshua answered.

"Ain't licked yet, is we, Cap'n?"

Joshua motioned toward the steps with his head. "Get the men into the rigging, Oliver. And tell them there's an extra ration of grog tonight if they do it quickly."

"Aye, aye, sir."

Joshua shook his head and smiled at Oliver's interpretation of a quarterdeck salute as the first mate hurried to carry out the order. Joshua had the feeling Oliver knew what he was going to try and did not question whether the maneuver would be successful. Joshua wasn't as certain. Trying to ignore the pain in his arm, he glanced up at the *Chesapeake*'s colors and then back at the French schooner that rode her stern. The wind was holding steady; the flag of Great Britain snapped proudly overhead. If the breeze stayed steady as the enemy ship inched forward to the *Chesapeake*'s leeward side, maybe they would have a chance.

The topmen were in position. Of course, he had never doubted their ability to perform. The mention of extra grog had been more of a promise than a bribe. It was a promise he prayed he'd be in a position to fulfill by day's end.

Musket fire had resumed now that the French ship was again in range. The smell of saltpeter and brimstone was thick in the air. Joshua's nose and throat burned, and his eyes watered; but still he gripped the wheel and watched the enemy. They were so close he could make out the sweating bodies of the French sailors, could count the grappling hooks they held ready.

He waited. Seconds stretched into minutes as the wind carried the schooner abreast of the *Chesapeake*.

There it was—what he had been looking for. The French foremast was alongside the *Chesapeake*'s stern.

"Now!" He bellowed the command to Oliver, who immediately conveyed it to the men in the sails. At the same instant the topmen pivoted the sails into the wind, Joshua abruptly turned the helm hard alee. It took both hands and all his strength to change the course of the proud sloop, and once he had done it, Joshua leaned over the wheel, using his body to hold her on course.

Caught unawares by the privateer's quick turn in front of her, the French schooner soon found her bowsprit trapped in the *Chesapeake*'s main shrouds.

"Fire at will!" Joshua's command set off a barrage of cannon fire that raked the snagged schooner.

The French vessel's topsails were blown to shreds, and

247

Joshua noted there were no longer any men above attempting to repair the damage.

"She's struck her colors, Cap'n."

"Thank God," Joshua breathed. He was uncomfortable with the havoc the *Chesapeake* was wreaking on the enemy ship, but he was determined to avoid hand-to-hand fighting with Madeline on board.

The ungodly noise of cannon fire had ceased. And the last few sailors brought down to the makeshift surgery in the afterhold had indicated that the French ship had surrendered. With the sleeve of her dress, Madeline wiped perspiration from her forehead, and offered up a prayer of thanksgiving. Then, with the same efficiency she had displayed throughout most of that dreadful morning, she turned the screw on the tourniquet she had placed on a sailor's wounded leg.

"Am I gonna lose it?"

Her heart went out to the tar whose blue eyes looked up at her imploringly from a sweat-stained face. He was so young and so scared.

"I don't know," she answered honestly. She dipped her sponge in a bucket of relatively clear water and began cleaning the skin around the gaping wound. "It doesn't look too bad."

"It pains somethin' fierce."

"I know." Madeline wiped her hand on the front of the blood-encrusted apron pinned over her dress and then touched the sailor's cheek.

Her eyes sought out the cook, who was now acting as the chief surgeon. He was using a tenaculum on an unconscious man. With the hooklike instrument, he pierced and drew out a bleeding artery. He then tied it off and sopped up the blood with a sponge. A quick survey of the wounded man confirmed Madeline's earlier opinion that the cook would be busy with him for some time. This seaman was bleeding profusely from several other injuries. As Madeline gave her own patient some grog, she wondered what could have caused so many wounds.

"Thanks." Her patient let his head fall back onto the flat bedding and closed his eyes.

Nearby, a seaman swabbed the area and tossed the dirty rags into a bucket. Madeline closed her eyes and drew in a deep breath. It didn't help. The smell of vinegar and blood still enveloped her.

Resolutely she knelt beside a man she had treated earlier. He had been the first of the wounded she had seen to after coming below and offering to help. Madeline had been afraid they would spurn her assistance, or worse, seek out the captain and ask his permission. But they hadn't. Instead, the cook and the other men assigned to assist him appeared grateful for her efforts.

Madeline had worked hard and had given succor to a large number of the wounded. Tired as she was, she could not help feeling good about what she had done. And of course, the nature of her activities allowed her to keep track of her husband. No matter how busy she was, she had looked up every time a new man had walked or been carried into the hold. Each time she'd let out a sigh of relief that it wasn't the captain.

And if a sailor wasn't too badly hurt and wished to talk, Madeline had further appeased her worried mind. "How's the captain doing?" she had asked with as much detachment as possible.

"Oh, the cap'n's standin' up on that quarterdeck yellin' orders left 'n right," one man had answered. Once she'd been really lucky, and had been told what kind of orders the captain was bellowing and how he'd looked while doing that. That was how she'd found out he'd outmaneuvered the French captain and won the battle. She suspected the young sailor who'd told her that story had a bad case of hero worship. One would have thought he was describing Lord Admiral Howard's defeat of the

Spanish armada instead of Captain Whitlock's besting of one French vessel. Of course after she had heard the story a few more times from several different sources, Madeline began to wonder if her husband didn't possess certain heroic qualities.

"What ya smilin' 'bout?"

Madeline had been carefully packing lint into a wound, and hadn't even noticed that she was smiling until the sailor asked about it. She started to wrap a dressing over his arm while she tried to decide how to answer this man who looked as though he'd seen his fair share of battles.

She gave him an honest answer. "I was just thinking about your captain."

"Ain't no better man to sail for. Ya done good when ya married up with him."

It was in her mind to agree. She had even started to form the words, but she never had a chance to voice them.

"What the hell are you doing here?"

Madeline sensed she was the only conscious person in the afterhold who didn't turn to stare at the man who had bellowed the question. But of course, she knew exactly who he was and to whom he was talking—or more precisely, yelling.

From the moment she had remembered Oliver telling her about the place where wounded were treated during a battle, she had known this confrontation was inevitable. But that prior knowledge did nothing to diminish the anger she felt at the high-handed manner in which the captain had addressed her, not to mention the fact that he had chosen to yell at her in front of all these men whose respect she had just earned. Couldn't the big clod at least have waited until they were alone?

Slowly Madeline rose, keeping her back to the man who had so rudely intruded upon the surgery. Her anger fueled itself as she meticulously shook out the wrinkles from her ruined gown. She would tell him exactly what she thought of his arrogance, and if it bothered him to be reamed out by a woman, his wife no less, in front of his men, then that was too bad. After all, he was the one who had chosen this arena. She turned, ready to unleash a blistering salvo.

But the fire in her eyes melted to concern, and the knees that had sustained her throughout the long morning threatened to give way. "My God, you're hurt." It was all she could say. His left arm, from near his shoulder to the tips of his fingers, was covered in blood that varied in shade from dried brown to fresh bright red. The captain's face was pale beneath his tan, and etched with unmistakable signs of suffering. His usual proud bearing was weighed down by fatigue or pain, or both.

"Come, lie down over here, Cap'n. Let me have a look at that arm."

"No!" The cook's words had spurred Madeline to action. She didn't want the captain lying here with only thin ticking to protect him from the hard deck. "Take him to his cabin." She gave the order as if she expected it to be obeyed, and surprisingly enough, it was. Oliver had assisted his captain to the surgery. Now, without even looking at the younger man for consent, he turned and helped him out of the hold.

Madeline busied herself gathering up the materials she might need. "I'll send these back as soon as I'm finished," she informed the cook, then hurried after her husband.

"I can manage myself, dammit."

Oliver had opened the door to the cabin and was trying to help his captain inside. "Aw, come on, Cap'n. Anyone can see you're as weak as a new babe."

Joshua tried to straighten up—without much success. "The hell you say."

Neither heard Madeline come up behind them until

she spoke. "Stop arguing with the man, Captain, and let him help you into bed. You're too damned big for me to move around."

Joshua used precious energy to glare over his shoulder at his wife, but he kept his mouth shut and did what she said.

"Be careful with him." Madeline treated her husband as if he were made of glass as she helped Oliver lower him onto the bed.

"For heaven's sake, Maddie. It's only a scratch." But even as he said it, and watched while she ignored his words, Joshua knew the wound was more serious.

"Help me get his boots off."

She was giving orders so fast it was making his head spin, or maybe he was just dizzy. Joshua stopped trying to pay attention to what Madeline and Oliver were doing to him and closed his eyes.

"Ya reckon he's passed out?"

"No, I think he's just resting." As she had with the young sailor, Madeline touched the captain's cheek, but this time her hand lingered. The stubble of his unshaven beard abraded her palm pleasantly.

"I'll need some water." Madeline straightened. There was work to be done.

"Yeah, I'll get it for ya."

She followed Oliver outside and quietly closed the door. "How did it happen?" She kept her voice low even though the panel that separated her from the captain was sturdy oak.

"Ain't sure." The first mate rubbed his beard. "I didn't see it."

Madeline nodded. "I'd better get back inside. I'm glad you weren't hurt, Oliver."

"Aw, ain't no Frenchie gonna hurt me."

Madeline touched his arm, then turned toward the door.

"Miz Whitlock."

"Yes." She was impatient to get back to her husband, but tried not to show it.

"'Bout down there in the hold, when the cap'n yelled at ya." He hesitated. "I hope ya ain't mad."

The first mate seemed so upset that Madeline took pity on him. "No, I'm not angry. He was wounded and obviously in a lot of pain."

"'Twasn't that. Oh, I know he was hurtin', but he'd been hurtin' for hours. It was when he came here, to this cabin, and found ya missin' that he really got worried. I think he was scared you'd got hurt."

Had the captain actually been as concerned about her safety as she had been about his? More likely he was just angry because she had disobeyed his order to stay put.

"I'd better see to him."

"Sure, I didn't mean to keep ya none. Just . . . well, I don't think the cap'n meant to yell like he done." Oliver stuffed the hat he had been twisting in his hands back on his head and hurried down the passageway.

"You and Oliver out there planning a mutiny?"

The captain greeted Madeline with these words as she walked back into the room. Obviously the wound hadn't drained him of his sense of humor. She tried to match him in kind—it was preferable to thinking about the tear in his flesh.

"This would be an ideal time to try one, don't you agree?"

Joshua started to laugh, then stopped and grimaced in pain. "Just like a woman. Get a man flat on his back, then try to take advantage of him."

Madeline found the scissors in her sewing basket and began to snip away at the blood-soaked shirt. "Has that been your experience with women?" She carefully pulled away the hardened fabric of his shirtsleeve.

"Sometimes." His teeth were locked shut, and Madeline noticed that the tendons in his neck stood out in rigid cords.

253

Some of the linen had become imbedded in the wound. She retrieved her scissors and cut away as much as she could.

"Who put this bandage on you, anyway?" She certainly would have noticed if he had come below to get the wound dressed. Even if she hadn't, Madeline knew no one in the afterhold would have done such an incompetent job.

"No one."

"Well, someone must have because here I am trying to pull it out of the cut."

"And doing a damn fine job, too, Maddie." Even though his comment was filtered through gritted teeth, Madeline recognized the sarcasm in it. "I put it on myself."

"Yourself!" Madeline resisted the urge to yank free the remaining fragment of fabric. The darned fool. All that time she had been worrying about him—yet thinking him safe because he hadn't come below for treatment—and he had been wounded! He'd been treating himself, and almost bleeding to death. Oh, he was such a foolish man!

She sat on the edge of the bunk, staring down at him, until he noticed her inactivity and asked. "Well, aren't you going to clean it up or something?"

"Why should I?"

"What?" Joshua raised up on his good elbow.

"You heard me? Why should I bother to fix it for you?"

"Because it hurts like hell!"

"Oh, really?" Despite her words, Madeline lit several candles she'd found in a wooden box and then placed them on the bedside commode. Satisfied with the amount of light they afforded, she carefully spread the edges of the cut and began removing splinters of wood from it. "By the look of things, this has been hurting you for a long time; Oliver said hours. Is that true?"

Joshua noted the look of concentration on her face. When she stopped her gentle probing and looked over at him, he answered. "I suppose it's been hours. Yes."

"I see."

"What the hell does that mean? *'I see.'*" he mimicked.

"It means, why didn't you come below and have someone attend to this arm?" Madeline knew she wasn't actually acting the sweet angel of mercy, but his arm was full of splinters. Every time she touched one, he winced in pain. She thought maybe, if she concentrated on how angry she was with him for the way he'd treated himself, she wouldn't start crying.

Doesn't she know how to treat people in pain? Joshua wondered. He'd have gotten kinder words from that old salt, the cook, than he was getting from her. Here she was scolding him because he hadn't come below to have his arm patched up. Could she have forgotten what was going on? "I was fighting a battle up on deck, you know."

"So was everybody else, but the others managed to take care of themselves when they got hurt."

"Oh, they did, did they?" She was making him so mad he could hardly feel her gentle probing of his wound.

"Yes, they did. Every one of those men in the after-hold came, or was brought down, as soon as he was hurt."

"Well, how many of those men were responsible for this ship and everybody aboard her?"

The knock on the door saved Madeline from the need to answer. "Come in!" She yelled at the unknown intruder, but softened her tone when Oliver hesitantly entered the cabin. "Oh, thank you," she said.

He had a bucket of water in one hand, a dusty bottle in the other. "How's he doin'?"

Oliver deposited the wooden-staved barrel on the deck with a minimum of spillage and set the bottle on the commode.

Madeline's "I think he'll be all right" was all but drowned out by her husband's "I'm just fine!"

255

She shot the captain a look designed to quell him, but he was looking past her toward his first mate. "How's the rigging? Are the men getting it repaired?"

"Aye. They's almost done." Oliver tilted his bald head toward the small bedside cabinet. "Brought ya some brandy from the hold."

Joshua ignored the last remark. "How about the cracked spars?"

"Been fixed, Cap'n. They're all lashed up tight with them old oars."

"Good, I want to crowd as much canvas as possible into the sky and get the hell out of here." He hesitated. This was always the moment in the battle's aftermath he hated most. "The men?"

Madeline's annoyance with the captain had not diminished. She'd sat on the edge of the bunk listening to his questions about the repairs, knowing they prolonged the moment when she could finish seeing to his arm. Still, she couldn't help sensing his genuine concern as he asked the last question. It made her remember his words about responsibility.

"I talked to Cook," Oliver replied. "He asked 'bout ya, but I said ya was in good hands." Madeline returned Oliver's shy smile. "Ain't no mortal wounds, but Cunningham lost a leg."

"Damn." The captain's eyes closed as he breathed out the curse.

"We was lucky, Cap'n. If it wouldna' been for that fancy bit o' sailin' ya done—"

"That doesn't help Cunningham, does it?" Joshua's eyes remained shut as if the effort necessary to open them would be too great.

"And this conversation isn't helping *you* any." Madeline had finally lost her patience. "I'm sorry, Oliver, but if there's nothing else pressing . . ." She let her words trail away as she motioned toward the door.

"Oh, yeah." Oliver backed away from the bunk. "I

256

better get back on deck."

Madeline watched the first mate leave before turning to examine the captain's arm. "There don't seem to be any more wood splinters in your arm—or pieces of makeshift bandage, either."

The captain's eyes were open now. Madeline, feeling guilty for her harsh words, busied herself with dampening a swab of clean linen rather than meet his gaze.

After she had washed away the blood and dirt from around the wound, she retrieved a sturdy needle and some thread from the sewing basket.

"What are you doing?" Joshua eyed her suspiciously.

She squinted as she threaded a fine white strand through the eye of the needle. "I'm going to sew up your arm." She moved to the desk, grabbed a pewter mug, and poured a healthy swig of brandy into it. Then she poured some over the needle. "Maybe you should drink this first."

Joshua raised himself as best he could and swallowed the fiery liquid. He felt its warmth all the way to his stomach. "Have you ever done this before?" Madeline had removed the cup from his lips and taken a sip herself.

"Of course." She tried but couldn't stop her body from shuddering. Brushing away the tears that the brandy brought to her eyes, she picked up the needle. "Who do you think takes care of the people at Hopewell?"

Joshua sucked in his breath as she began stitching. "You?" Sweat broke out on his upper lip.

"Of course." Madeline gnawed at her bottom lip.

"Is that why you went down to the afterhold?"

She paused for just a moment before bending her head back over her work. "I suppose so. I wanted to be of some help."

"I didn't know where you were."

"I'm sorry. I didn't think you'd worry."

"I did."

257

"There." Madeline tied the thread in a knot and snipped off the excess. "Would you like some more brandy?"

Joshua shook his head. "I think I'd just like to rest a little. Don't let me sleep long. . . ." His words faded away as he drifted off.

Madeline wrapped a clean bandage around his arm, then gathered up her supplies. When she had finished, she pulled the blanket over the captain, being careful not to disturb his arm. He looked so spent lying there. Tentatively, she leaned over him until her lips touched his cheek. "Rest well, my captain," she whispered before settling into the chair by the desk to begin her vigil.

Chapter 18

"What do you think you're doing?" Madeline kicked the door of the cabin shut while balancing the heavily laden wooden tray in her hands.

Joshua paused long enough to glance up at her before resuming the difficult chore of forcing his foot into a boot. "What does it look like I'm doing?"

His arm felt as though someone had lit a fire in it, and the rest of his body didn't feel much better. The last thing he needed was grief from this woman.

Madeline watched as he bent over his task. Her own hunger, and the knowledge that the captain would need nourishment when he awakened, had driven her from the cabin less than a quarter-hour ago. Some of the crew had relit the fire in the galley, which had been extinguished prior to the battle, and she had been able to get some warm food and hot water for tea. The captain had been resting so soundly, with only an occasional moan punctuating the soft sounds he made in his sleep, that she had thought it safe to leave him.

Obviously, it hadn't been. His left arm hung limply at his side, and Madeline could almost see its painful throbbing from across the cabin. Still, he struggled with the boot.

"Here, let me help you." She set the tray on the desk and hurried over to him. She certainly didn't think he

259

should be up; however, if he insisted on this lunacy—and his scowl told her he did—the least she could do was assist him.

"I don't need your help." The words might have been a growl, had he been able to put more force behind them.

Madeline ignored them. "Nonsense. It's quite clear you need assistance from someone, and I happen to be the only person available." She bent over to grasp the top of his boot, and her hand accidentally touched his leg.

"Why, you're burning up!" Even through the nankeen of his breeches she could feel the heat. Her hand went to his cheek, his forehead, to confirm her diagnosis.

The captain tried to pull away from the contact, but he was sitting on the bed, and the only direction in which he could move was back. Madeline had no qualms about following him across the bed.

"You are! You're with fever." Madeline had been worried that this might happen, but she hadn't realized it would come on him so fast—or so strong. "Lie down this instant."

"I'm going on deck," he insisted, but his body wanted to obey her.

"You are not! Everything is fine on deck anyway." Madeline pushed him down onto the ticking, secretly sorry he seemed unable to put up more of a fight.

"How do you know everything is fine?" Inwardly Joshua sighed with relief. It felt so much better to be lying down, though he'd never admit it to Madeline.

"I checked. Before going to the galley I went on deck and found Oliver. He said to tell you we've left the 'damn Frenchies behind, and we're on course.'"

Joshua laughed at her imitation of the crusty colonial's accent.

"He also told me you are a terrible patient." Madeline pulled off the boot the captain had managed to put on.

"Me?"

Madeline's expression, when she straightened to face him, was sardonic. "Yes, you." She pulled the woolen blanket up over his hips. "I believe he compared you to a bear who's been awakened in the middle of winter."

She ignored the captain's "Humph" as she poured some steaming tea into a mug.

"Drink this." Madeline slipped an arm under his head to lift him up. "More," she ordered curtly when he stopped sipping. He glared at her but managed to finish most of the tea.

"Now," Madeline began as she dipped a linen cloth into the tepid water in the basin, "I'm going to try to cool you down by washing off your body—uh, some of it—I mean your face and arms and . . . chest." Madeline's face turned scarlet as she held the damp rag and stumbled through her explanation.

Despite his discomfort, Joshua couldn't help noticing hers. He gazed at her through heavy-lidded eyes that sparkled with fever and just a hint of mischief. "You don't think there are other parts of my body that might need cooling off?"

"No!" Madeline was trying hard to regain her composure, and his teasing wasn't helping. She would just try to pretend he was like any of the men she had ministered to this morning, or the countless slaves she had helped at Hopewell. But, of course, she couldn't.

When Madeline wiped the cool linen across his forehead, the captain's eyes closed and his languorous, black gaze no longer met her own. That didn't help. A lock of raven hair fell across his brow and, more leisurely than circumstances warranted, Madeline brushed it aside. His hair was as pleasant to the touch as she remembered. Had it only been last night when she had run her fingers through the silken curls that grew at the nape of his neck? She could almost smell his heady maleness, feel his weight atop her.

Madeline jerked her hand away. What was wrong with her? The man was wounded and feverish, and she was thinking of lovemaking. Wouldn't the captain think her a silly besotted female if he knew?

261

With crisp, precise motions she dipped the washcloth into the basin and wrung it out, wiping it across his lower face. The linen snagged on the thick, black bristles on his unshaven cheek.

"In a few days you'll be as bearded as Oliver." Madeline watched his wide, sensual mouth broaden into a smile at her words. She dragged the cloth down along his strong jaw. The heavy, dark shadow of whiskers made him appear deliciously wicked, almost like a pirate. She cocked her head to one side, studying him as she redampened the linen. She liked the earthy, unrefined look of him with coarse, black whiskers shading his face. Then again, she liked him clean-shaven, too. As the cool cloth trailed down his neck, Madeline admitted that she just liked the way he looked—period.

His collarbone was sturdy and broad, and she traced it toward his shoulder, careful to avoid his wounded arm as she leaned across his body. The linen curved along his biceps. Even as his arm lay relaxed on the mattress, the muscles bulged with strength. Thickly dusted with black hair, his forearms seemed equally strong. And his hands . . . Their long, lean fingers lay limp now, but Madeline remembered how they'd felt on her back, tangling in her hair.

She wet the cloth again, then swallowed. She had noticed the captain's chest the very first time she'd seen him. When she'd come to his cabin his shirt had been open down the front, exposing the breadth of his upper body. Though part of her had been shocked to see a man in such a state of undress, she had been drawn to him even then. Now she touched him. Through the cloth she could feel the springy texture of the dark hair that wove across his chest, then arrowed toward the blanket draped across his waist.

Madeline fought to keep her breathing steady, but when the linen skimmed across one of his hard, flat nipples and he moaned, her breath caught in her throat. "Did I hurt you?" To her amazement her voice was a husky whisper.

"No, that feels good." His voice, too, was husky.

"It's cooling you off then?"

For the first time since she'd started his bath, the thick-lashed lids of his eyes opened. As his obsidian stare burned into her, Madeline wondered how it happened that *she* now was with fever.

Joshua closed his eyes. Cool? Did she think she was cooling him off? He did feel a little better though. When he'd tried to get up earlier, the resulting aches and pains had convinced him his body would never be the same. Now he'd discovered that at least one part of him was working only too well. He wondered if Madeline noticed the way the blanket tented below his waist.

She did. A fresh wave of heat spread through her and seemed to settle at the apex of her thighs.

She all but jumped off the edge of the bed.

"Ow! Where are you going?" Her movement had jarred his arm.

"To get some . . ." Madeline's heart was so tight her voice cracked. She was forced to start again, but only after she'd taken a few deep breaths. "I thought I might ask Cook for the medicine chest. There might be something in it to bring your fever down."

"I liked your method better."

Madeline plopped the cloth into the basin, splashing tiny droplets of water onto the commode top.

"It wasn't working." She retreated toward the door, anxious to make her escape, but remembered she had left him partially uncovered. Even though the day was warm, a person with a fever should not risk a chill. Quickly, she retraced her steps and pulled the blanket up around his shoulders. The telltale bulge ws still there.

Joshua waited until he figured she'd had time to clear the aft passage. The way she'd run from the cabin, that wouldn't take long. She was so skittish. It wasn't as if she didn't know what went on between a man and a woman, especially after last night.

He levered his long frame out of the bunk. He was not going to let her boss him around, nor was he going to stay abed. He'd been hurt plenty of times—worse than this. And he'd always been back on deck before the day was spent. Well, he would be this time, too.

A knock sounded at the door, and before he realized what he was doing, Joshua almost got back into the bunk. "Damn," he muttered as he caught himself. Why was he feeling guilty about getting up? Besides, it probably wasn't Madeline. She wouldn't knock—at least she hadn't the other time when she'd caught him leaving his bed.

"Who is it?" he growled, wondering why the boat was lurching so that he couldn't get a steady footing.

"It's me, Cap'n." Oliver stuck his head through the door first before the rest of him entered. "Ya think ya should be gettin' up—with the fever on ya and all?"

"*She* sent you down here, didn't she?" Joshua gripped the edge of the desk for support, and winced as pain shot up his wounded arm.

"Well now, Cap'n," Oliver answered sheepishly, "I did run into your wife, assumin' that's who you're referrin' ta, and bein' she's the only 'she' on board, I guess 'tis."

"Stop the drivel, Oliver. She sent you to spy on me." Damn the woman! She was turning his own men against him.

"Miz Whitlock did mention ya was awfully anxious to be up and about, but she thought ya needed a mite more rest."

"Well, I don't."

"Seems ta me as if the lady has a point now, Cap'n. If it's the *Chesapeake* you're worried 'bout, I can tell ya how she's doin' in one word—fine."

Joshua held onto the desk for a minute, trying to decide what to do. The rational part of his mind, if he were to admit it, agreed with Madeline and Oliver, especially since he didn't think he could take a step or even let go without falling flat on his face. He decided he'd lost a lot more blood than he'd realized. Still, he didn't like giving in to her like this. "Oh, hell, help me back into the bed, will you, Oliver?"

The mate's grizzled beard separated into a broad grin as he moved to assist the younger man. "That's a good boy, Cap'n. Ya ain't got nothin' to worry 'bout. I'll take care of the *Chesapeake,* and Miz Whitlock can take care o' you."

"Humph."

"Aw, Cap'n. It ain't that bad. I mean, well, a man could do a lot worse 'n havin' his missus watchin' out for 'im."

Joshua pulled the blanket up over himself with his good arm, Oliver's words still sounding in his ears. Hadn't he been thinking the same thing earlier when she'd insisted upon bringing his fever down? It had been nice, having her take care of him like that.

Joshua didn't recall any other woman ever doing it. He supposed his mother had, but he really didn't remember the woman who'd died giving birth to Nathaniel. There had been those through the years who'd have been willing, but he'd never felt the urge to stay around and give them the chance, until now.

"Ya know, Cap'n . . ."

Joshua had been so deep in his own thoughts, he'd forgotten Oliver was still in the room. Now he looked up to see his first mate planted firmly in the sturdy wooden chair beside the desk. It appeared Madeline had convinced him to stay. Of course, with Oliver's mothering instincts, that wouldn't have taken much doing.

". . . I've gotta tell ya," Oliver continued, "I was real surprised when ya brought that little lady on board." He chuckled. "I mean, not that I ain't seen ya sweet-talk your way 'round lots of gals, but marryin' up with 'er in three days. . . ." Oliver rubbed his beard, his eyes sparkling with mischief. "Three days," he repeated, more to himself than for Joshua's benefit. "She must o' really knocked ya over, Cap'n, for ya to have worked so fast."

She knocked me over all right, Joshua thought. From the first moment he'd recognized her as the girl from his cabin—a fact that obviously had eluded Oliver—he'd been slipping and sliding toward his eventual fall.

"And ya didn't know her before?" Oliver was shaking his head, chuckling away.

"Never been introduced," Joshua agreed. There was no reason to disillusion the old man.

"Well she sure is a pretty little thing, Cap'n."

Joshua smiled his thanks. He really didn't want to get started on just how pleasing he did find his wife's looks. Oliver wouldn't want to hear that he thought her hair the color of warm honey, or how soft and sweet-smelling it was. Nor would his mate want to know about the way certain tendrils escaped any restrictions she tried to put on them and curled around her face.

Her face . . . Joshua never knew anyone could have eyes quite that shade of green or a nose quite that pert, or a mouth quite that sensual and inviting.

". . . ya gonna do with her?"

"What?" Joshua guiltily turned toward Oliver. Had he actually missed his first mate's words because he'd been mooning over his wife's looks? No, actually he had only been thinking of her face and hair. He hadn't even started thinking about the graceful way her neck blended into her shoulders, or the way she looked when dressed only in her shift and stays, with her breasts . . .

"I said, what ya gonna do with her? She done real good with the wounded this morning, but a privateer ain't no place for a lady."

"Hell, I know that." What did Oliver take him for, a fool? It was bad enough that Madeline was on the *Chesapeake* now. He certainly wouldn't take her along again. This morning had been hell when he'd thought he might lose the ship. For all his brash words to his wife about the French not hurting her, he hadn't been sure

266

they wouldn't. If they had touched her—

"Ya ain't thinkin' of givin' up privateering, is ya?" Oliver seemed shocked that he'd even had to voice the question.

But hadn't Joshua been thinking of doing just that when he'd been back at Hopewell? Yet, he hadn't meant to do it now. Sometime in the future. Surely, not now.

"No, I'm not giving up privateering." So what was he going to do with a wife? "I thought she could stay in Baltimore Town for a while—with Nathaniel." He'd take her back to Hopewell, eventually. After all, he had promised. But not the way things were now. They'd been lucky to escape from one of Bompar's squadron this morning.

Oliver nodded his head. "Aye, Baltimore'd be good. Ya can even visit her sometimes when we get to port."

Why did the thought of seeing Madeline only a handful of times a year seem totally depressing? Of course, that would be more than he'd see her once he took her back to Hopewell.

His wife chose that moment to enter the cabin. "Oliver?" was the first thing she said.

"You needn't feign surprise at seeing him here. I know you sent him to see that I heeded your advice."

For an instant those sea green eyes rested on him, then she turned to Oliver. "I wasn't surprised to see him, just pleased." The smile she gave the first mate made Oliver blush to the top of his bald pate.

Madeline noticed the contents of the pottery bowl. "I see you've gotten down some of the broth. Are you feeling any better?" She didn't even wait for a reply before continuing. "I've brought some sallow bark and gentian root. I think it will help bring your fever down." She moved toward the bunk, stopping long enough to deposit a small, dark brown bottle on the desk before standing before him. "You look better."

For a moment Joshua thought she was going to touch him. He could almost feel her soft, cool hand caressing

267

his cheek, but she glanced over to where Oliver sat watching, and let her hand drop.

"I told you your other method was working," Joshua whispered suggestively. He was rewarded by the blossoming of color on her cheeks.

Oh it was working all right, Madeline silently agreed. For me as well as you. But that type of close contact wasn't bringing either of their temperatures down.

She slanted him a look. "As I recall, you didn't say it was working, you simply said. 'you preferred it.'" Madeline poured some hot water into a pewter mug and measured a generous amount of the foul-smelling powder from the bottle into the liquid.

Joshua eyed the contents of the dented mug suspiciously. "What is that stuff?"

"I told you, sallow bark and gentian root."

"Are you sure it's safe to drink?" He hadn't moved the cup any closer to his lips.

"I'm fairly certain it is." Madeline tried to keep her face expressionless as she delivered those words.

Not so the captain. His eyes flew open, and he stared at the brown liquid as if it had suddenly become reptilian. "Fairly certain," he parroted moments before Madeline and Oliver burst into laughter.

The first mate slapped his thigh. "I told ya, didn't I? He just ain't a good patient."

"You did warn me." Madeline tried to regain her composure before leveling her gaze on the captain. "Of course it's safe, I was only teasing. Do you imagine I would give you anything that wasn't?" She ignored the blatantly skeptical look he gave her. "I use it all the time at Hopewell."

The captain grimaced, but raised the rim to his lips. "My God, it tastes awful!"

"It's supposed to."

Joshua drank the bitter brew. What choice did he have with Oliver and Madeline standing over him, watching to make sure he imbibed every drop.

"Am I allowed a bit of brandy to wash away the taste?" His wife was looking entirely too smug, and he began planning for the day when she'd have a fever, nothing serious of course, but just enough to need a dose of this "tea." He would be only too glad to watch her drink it. But then he realized that if she ever did become ill, he wouldn't be with her. She'd be in Baltimore and later in Jamaica, and he'd be at sea.

"I don't imagine a spot of brandy would counteract the medicinal effects of the herbs. What do you think, Oliver?"

"I ain't never known brandy to hurt nothin'," the older man replied with a twinkle in his eye.

"Very well then."

Joshua noticed the graceful way Madeline moved as she went to the desk and poured brandy from the bottle Oliver had brought up earlier. He also saw the broad wink his first mate gave his wife. They were acting like fellow conspirators—and at his expense.

He drank the brandy—she had given him a hearty measure—in one gulp. Its smooth heat burned away the last remnants of the bitter potion that clung to his mouth and throat.

"Captain," Madeline said quietly.

Joshua's eyes had drifted shut, and he opened them to see that she was leaning over him.

"I have to look at your arm again." She sounded apologetic.

Carefully Madeline sat on the edge of the bunk and began to unwind the linen bandage. "Is it hurting you very much?" She smiled down at him. The medicine, or perhaps the brandy, had begun to work, and she could tell he was having a difficult time staying awake.

"No." Joshua basked in her smile and, without thinking, reached up to touch her cheek.

Madeline could have stayed there all night, exploring the depths of his ebony eyes with her own, reveling in the contact his caress made against her skin. She possibly

269

would have, if Oliver hadn't cleared his throat, making her start self-consciously.

"I best be checkin' the second dogwatch," he mumbled as he rose and ambled to the door.

"Oliver."

"Aye, Miz Whitlock?"

"I was thinking. The captain's arm still looks pretty sore, and, well . . . I wouldn't want to bump it accidentally. I mean . . . in my sleep." Madeline hoped her flush was hidden by the cabin's dim light. She shouldn't be embarrassed by the fact that she and the captain slept together; after all, they were married. But it was all so new to her.

Madeline glanced at the first mate, who was watching her expectantly. "Do you know of someplace else I can sleep tonight?"

"Ya can have my cabin," Oliver offered. "I'll just swing a hammock on the berth deck."

"Oh, no. I couldn't ask you to give up your quarters. Besides, the captain may need me during the night." Madeline watched Oliver nod in agreement. "Is there any way a hamock can be hung in here?" she asked.

"Now wait a minute." Joshua had been close to dozing off, but his wife's conversation with Oliver was reviving him. "There is no reason to go to all that trouble. The bunk will do just fine—for both of us."

Madeline swung around toward her husband. He certainly was stubborn. She had no doubt he'd argue with the devil himself. "You know as well as I do that the bed is too small for two people."

Joshua glared at her, then glanced over at Oliver. This wasn't the type of argument he liked having in front of the older man. And by the glint in Madeline's eye, he wouldn't be at all surprised if she'd mentioned that he'd fallen out of bed that morning. "Oh, go ahead. She probably won't be able to get into it anyway."

Madeline ignored that mumbled slur, and tried to remember that he was in pain. It certainly wasn't as if she

270

didn't want to sleep with him. Last night had been wonderful. But there would be plenty of other nights after his arm healed—at least until they reached Baltimore. And then the captain would be taking her back to Hopewell. . . .

Joshua watched Oliver retrieve the stretch of unbleached canvas from his sea chest and sling it between two hooks in the cabin.

"There ya be," the first mate announced when he'd finished. "Ya just holler now if'n ya need me."

"Thank you, Oliver, but I don't think I shall. You take care of the *Chesapeake;* I'll see to your captain."

After Madeline had seen the older man out of the cabin, she returned to the bunk and the job of changing the dressing on the captain's arm. His eyes were closed, and she hoped he'd fallen asleep. But as soon as she settled onto the mattress, she knew that thought had been too optimistic.

"Why did you do that?"

"What?" Madeline kept her eyes on her task, unwinding the linen bandage.

"Dammit, Maddie, you know what I mean. Why'd you have Oliver hang that." He pointed at the offending hammock swinging from the rafters.

Madeline shrugged. "I needed a place to sleep."

"What's wrong with sleeping with me?" Joshua knew he was acting foolish, but he'd just gotten her into his bed, or rather gotten back into bed with her, and now this had happened.

Madeline sighed. She'd hoped the argument had ended when Oliver had left. "Nothing is wrong with sleeping with you." She felt color pool in her cheeks. "You need rest, and your arm shouldn't be disturbed." Despite her embarrassment, Madeline looked at her husband. "It is only for one night, two at most."

Joshua returned her stare. How could he be angry with her? She was doing it for him, wasn't she? But what if she'd decided that she didn't want him to touch her after all? This could be a convenient way to stop the physical aspect of their relationship. "It's bloody uncomfortable."

Madeline rewrapped his arm, glad that it was looking better. "I'll manage."

He fell silent. She was probably right. She would manage. She'd get herself up into that hammock and sleep through the night and fare very well. Confound the independent wench.

He shifted in the bunk, trying to get comfortable. His arm felt much better, but there was still a dull ache in it.

"Do you need anything before I snuff out the candles?" Madeline's smile was tentative, and when Joshua saw it he was ashamed of his thoughts—and actions.

"No," he answered. "I'm all right." He smiled back at her.

"Then good night."

She extinguished the candles and lantern, shrouding the cabin in darkness. Against his will, Joshua found his imagination running wild.

Unable to see through the heavy black mantle of night, he found his other senses surging to the forefront. The air was filled with the hot, thick odor of smoldering tallow. It floated above and around him, saved from unpleasantness by the faint scent of roses it carried. His nostrils flared as he breathed in the fragrance that would have announced her presence even without the further proof offered his ears. The sounds were unmistakable. She was undressing.

Joshua turned his head toward the sound and strained his eyes, but to no avail. Resignedly, he lay back and gave his ears and mind free rein.

With whispers of fabric against flesh, Madeline freed her body from the bodice of her gown, first one arm, then the other. The murmur of silk skimming over cotton heralded the loss of her skirt. The soles of her slippers tapped against the floor as she stepped out of the gown.

272

Next, her petticoats floated to the deck, and Joshua knew she was dressed the way he'd seen her that morning. Even allowing for all the provocative outfits he'd encountered on fancy women, he'd never seen anything as enticing as Madeline in stays and shift. Listening as her capable fingers loosened the laces, Joshua realized he still had not seen Madeline in less. His loins tightened as he remembered how the flesh that lay beneath the whalebone and cotton had felt, and tried to imagine how it looked.

She sighed as the corset came free of her body, and Joshua hoped the sound had covered the involuntary moan of desire that escaped his lips.

It hadn't.

"Captain, are you all right?" Her voice was sweet and innocent. She obviously had no idea of the havoc she was wreaking on his senses.

Joshua swallowed and tried to force normalcy into his tone. "Yes." To him the monosyllable sounded husky with longing as he waited for the sensual sound of a linen shift sliding over her head. It never came. Apparently, Madeline would be wearing more than she had during the past night. Oh, well, he'd make sure she slept naked on the next one—he closed his eyes as his arm began to hurt again—or maybe the one after that.

Joshua heard Madeline climb into the hammock. The hemp ropes strained as she struggled to find a comfortable position. She'd had a hard day, too. He thought of her caring for him, of the way she'd doctored his men. "Maddie?"

"Yes."

"I apologize for yelling at you earlier. I should never have done that. It was very kind of you to help with the wounded, and I thank you for it." Though it had scared the hell out of him when he'd come down below and found her missing, he had to admit that she was one special woman for doing what she had.

Madeline smiled in the darkness. "Thank you."

273

"Oh, and Maddie?"

"Hmmm?"

"May I get out of bed tomorrow? I really think my fever is gone."

Madeline laughed aloud. "What is this? After fighting me at every turn all day, you suddenly ask my permission to do something. Why?"

"Maybe I've realized how right you were."

"Even about the hammock?" Madeline couldn't help teasing.

"Especially about the hammock. Comfortable?"

"Very." Her answer was a little too swift to be believed. Besides, Joshua could still hear the heavy canvas groan as she twisted about. He had bunked in the crew's quarters for enough years to recognize the sound.

"What about tomorrow? May I get up?"

"I seriously doubt I could stop you, but if you don't quiet down and get some sleep, you'll be so tired I won't even have to try."

"I can take a hint. Good night, Maddie."

"Good night, Captain."

Joshua snuggled into the soft down of the pillow, letting the effects of the medicine and the brandy overtake his body while his mind remained alert. His memories of the preceding night were too vivid—the way Maddie had felt, all warm and loving wrapped around him, her just kissed lips begging for more. Yet, in his imaginings, it was not Captain that she had called him, but Joshua.

Sunshine, filtering through the heavily leaded panes of the porthole awakened Madeline the following morning. Without looking, she knew the captain was not in the cabin. Hadn't he said as much last night? she thought as she raised her head to look at the bunk? The bed was neatly made, and she wondered how he'd accomplished that with his wounded arm.

274

The hammock swung precariously as she tried to get out. It was even worse than climbing in. Thankful that he was gone and could not have watched her awkward descent, she dressed quickly, anxious to see the sun after a day of being confined.

She found the captain on the quarterdeck, staring out to sea. He was so intent he didn't notice her standing at the top of the stairs, and she had time to study him. If she hadn't known about his arm, hadn't noticed that he favored it ever so slightly, she would never have guessed he had been wounded just yesterday.

"I see you've decided you're well enough to be up and about." Madeline approached until she was leaning on the rail beside him.

"You said that I could."

Madeline laughed at the flirtatious sparkle in his black eyes. "As if it mattered what I said."

He feigned surprise. "I listened yesterday."

"You were too weak to resist."

Joshua grinned. "I'm much better today."

She returned his smile, then looked out to sea. The ocean was a clear turquoise blue, and nearly as smooth as glass. Such calm was irreconcilable with the violence that had taken place the previous day.

"How is Cunningham?" Thoughts of the battle had reminded her of the privateer who had lost his leg. She watched as the captain's jaw tightened.

"As good as can be expected."

"Is there anything I can do?" Madeline touched his sleeve.

"No. His wound is healing well enough. It's worry about what will happen to his family now that he can't take care of them that troubles him."

"He has a wife?" Madeline was surprised, and couldn't hide it.

"Aye, and children. Four when we left New York, maybe five by now. May was heavy with child when we sailed."

275

"I didn't think many of your men had families."

"They don't. You saw what happened yesterday. That's only one of the risks the men on this ship take. It's not a good idea for any of them to have families depending on them." Joshua unconsciously rubbed his sore arm.

"Does that include the captain?" Madeline held her breath as the full force of his gaze was turned upon her.

Joshua had thought of little else since he'd visited Cunningham early that morning. What had happened to the sailor could just as easily have happened to him. And then where would Madeline be? But she was married to a privateer. The sooner she realized that, the better. "Especially the captain, Maddie."

Chapter 19

At least she wasn't carrying his child.

Madeline sat in the chair by the desk, supposedly sewing a button on the captain's waistcoat. But she was deep in thought and paid very little heed to the job of pulling the needle through the heavy silk.

It had been days since she'd realized her earlier fears were unfounded. There would be no child. The idea of having the captain's baby hadn't really bothered her since they were wed . . . until the morning after the battle, when he'd made it clear how he felt about children and families. They weren't something a privateer needed—or wanted. That morning, over a sennight ago, Madeline had realized how silly she'd been to think their marriage could be anything like she'd pictured it.

The captain must have realized it, too. He hadn't come back to her bed. Madeline glanced at the wooden-sided bunk, remembering how cold and lonely it had been last night and the night before . . . wondering how many more endless nights it would take before she forgot the way his body felt, warm and hard, next to hers.

She sighed, then forced her attention back to her mending. The captain was right. She'd seen it in the tight set of his jaw when he'd talked of Cunningham. A privateer had no right to a wife and child. Well, there wasn't much the captain could do about the wife part now. She existed, though by the way he'd ignored her, Madeline didn't think it would be long before he decided to return her to Hopewell. But a baby . . . Making sure he didn't add that burden—another millstone around his neck—was a good idea.

She should tell him so. Madeline stabbed the needle into the cloth. And he had a right to know there would be no additional responsibility, no child. When he came down to dinner—*if* he came down to dinner—she'd tell him.

A knock at the door interrupted her musings.

"Oliver." Madeline jumped up and cleared a spot on the desk for the heavy tray the older man carried. "You didn't have to bring this down. I could have come to get it. Where's Whitey?"

"Busy." Oliver set the tray down and slipped the wool hat from his head. "Him and the cap'n, too. Cap'n said to tell ya to go on and eat. He ain't gonna be able ta join ya."

"I see." Madeline tried not to sound upset. This message was delivered to her more often than not anymore, though it was usually the cabin boy who brought it. She tried to console herself by acknowledging that it really didn't matter if the captain were here or not. They never talked of anything important. Cunningham or his family was never mentioned. Their discussion and the ensuing silence on the morning after the battle never came up. The fact that he left the cabin right after eating, not to return for the rest of the night was never even alluded to.

"They's waterin' down the sails again."

Madeline looked up at Oliver. "Still no sign of a breeze?" The captain had explained that maneuver to her when they had first encountered failing wind about a week ago. Wetting down the sails made them heavier and more apt to pick up the slightest breeze.

Oliver rubbed his whiskered chin. "Nary a whisper."

"Whitey was so certain that sticking his pocket knife into the mast would muster up a good blow." Madeline

278

bit her bottom lip to keep from laughing at the boy's superstition.

"I never know'd that ta work." Oliver paused, and Madeline was glad the first mate was above such nonsense. "Whistlin's what does it."

"Whistling?" Madeline wasn't certain she'd heard correctly.

"Sure. Ya gotta get all the hands whistlin' together. That'll bring up some sailin' weather, sure."

"I see." So Oliver nourished his share of superstitions. Madeline busied herself in removing the food from the tray. "Well, I shall certainly practice up on my whistling."

"Not you, Miz Whitlock." Oliver looked stricken. "Beggin' your pardon, ma'am, but ya ain't one of the crew. You start whistlin', we're likely ta have a gale."

"I wouldn't want to be the cause of that," she agreed. "Rest assured, Oliver, my lips will not pucker."

The old man looked relieved.

"Can you stay a moment and join me for dinner?" Madeline didn't know whether she was making a serious breach of shipboard etiquette, but she was becoming increasingly tired of her own company.

"Uh, well, I really should be gettin' back."

"It's lobscouse," Madeline cajoled, lifting the pewter lid to allow the aroma of the dried potato and salt-beef mush to work its persuasive magic. The captain had described her the unlikely combination sitting before her, saying that when they were far enough out of port for fresh food to be but a lingering memory, this dish was the crew's favorite. She had even developed quite a taste for it.

"Well . . ." Oliver was obviously weakening.

"Look at the amount Cook sent me. Altogether too much for me to eat by myself. And you said the captain couldn't join me. . . ."

"Oh, all right. Guess it couldn't hurt none. But I gotta be quick. Cap'n might need me."

Madeline began spooning the lobscous onto one of the heavy pewter trenchers. "I don't mind if you eat quickly. It's just nice to have some company."

"Cap'n's awful busy."

Madeline could swear she saw understanding and even sympathy in the first mate's eyes. "Yes," she responded, then hurriedly fixed herself a plate.

"It ain't easy bossin' a ship like the *Chesapeake*. Cap'n has gotta know everything 'bout it." Oliver paused to take a bite. "And with this calm, well, he just don't have no extra time."

"I know that." Madeline was sorry she'd let her loneliness show. She hoped Oliver wouldn't go straight to the captain with the story. "I really didn't mean to complain. There's plenty to keep me occupied."

"That's good." He took another bite, not bothering to swallow it before he continued. "What ya need is a passel of young'uns to keep ya busy while the cap'n's at sea."

Madeline chewed a piece of sea biscuit. Obviously Oliver didn't know his captain's thoughts concerning privateers and families. But she nodded in agreement. "Like Mrs. Cunningham."

Why did the idea of having the captain's baby suddenly seem so appealing? Madeline silently admitted it wasn't sudden at all. She'd wanted to have his baby. Maybe that was why she'd put off telling him she wasn't going to. Or was it because if the captain thought she was already pregnant he'd have nothing to lose by returning to her bed.

"Huh?" Oliver washed down a mouthful of food with a swallow of grog and used the back of his hand as a napkin.

"Mrs. Cunningham," Madeline explained. "The captain said she has four children, maybe five by now. They probably keep her very busy."

"Yeah, I guess so."

"I'm sure she'll be anxious to see her husband, and, hopefully, it will lift Cunningham's spirits to be home again." Madeline had tried to talk to the seaman, but he was most despondent and had resisted all her attempts to cheer him. "Does he live in Baltimore Town?"

"Cunningham? No, he lives where most of us do when we ain't on the *Chesapeake,* in New York."

"New York?" Madeline laid her spoon on the table. "But how is Cunningham going to get back there?"

Oliver looked up. "Why I s'pect the cap'n'll take him after he drops ya off in Baltimore."

"Drops me off?" Madeline was beginning to feel like the parrot Hattie had kept. She seemed able only to repeat words tossed her way.

"Aye." Oliver pushed his chair back, obviously finished with his meal and the conversation.

But Madeline wasn't.

"What makes you think the captain plans to leave me in Baltimore?" She didn't remember that being part of their agreement.

Amazement appeared on the first mate's face, and he stared at her as if seeing her for the first time. "He . . . he said so."

If Madeline hadn't been so angry she would have laughed at seeing the grizzled man stuttering with fear.

"Told me we'd check on Nat, drop ya off and get back ta privateering."

"And that means sailing to New York?" Madeline demanded.

"Aye. that's our port o' call."

"I see!" It was all she could do to resist storming up to the captain and demanding to know what was going on. She had agreed, reluctantly, to accompany him to Baltimore Town to find his brother, but then, he'd said, he'd take her back to Hopewell. Well, he could hardly do that if he was to be privateering off the coast of New York.

"Miz Whitlock?"

"What?" No longer content to sit quietly on the chair, Madeline had been pacing, but when Oliver spoke her name she turned to him.

281

"I better be gettin' up on deck, ma'am." He twisted his cap.

"Of course." Oliver's obvious discomfort made her aware of her display of temper. It wasn't his fault that his captain was a lying, no-good rogue. "Thank you, Oliver, for your company at dinner."

"Sure, Miz Whitlock, anytime," he said, though his demeanor clearly indicated "anytime" would not be sometime soon.

After he left, taking with him the remnants of their meal, Madeline sat down and tried to think things through. It was difficult. Anger at the captain kept disrupting her thoughts. To think she had judged him to be a man of his word!

There was the possibility that Oliver was mistaken, yet Madeline thought not. He'd appeared genuinely surprised that she wasn't aware of the plans. No, it wasn't the first mate who had the facts wrong.

Damn the captain, anyway.

Madeline rose and began pacing about the cabin. It wasn't as if the problem were insurmountable. Luckily, she had thought ahead enough to secret some gold in one of her trunks. She could secure passage on a vessel bound for Jamaica as soon as the captain left her in Baltimore. She would have wasted a lot of time sailing back and forth between the Colonies and the sugar isles, but once she got back to Hopewell, she could pick up the threads of her life and move forward.

Not that things would be the same. Papa was dead—Madeline had to keep reminding herself that he wasn't at Hopewell awaiting her return—and the plantation was in a deplorable state, though Henry Smyth and the new overseer might have improved conditions there. And—she bit her bottom lip in an attempt to suppress the next thought, but it was no use—the captain would no longer be in her life. That shouldn't bother her, yet it did. Even after all he'd done to her.

Madeline's stubborn chin angled upward. Whether it

mattered or not, she'd be boiled in oil before she'd let him find out. A smile softened the determined lines of her face as she remembered the last time she'd insisted boiling in oil was a preferable alternative. Well, that had been different. She'd had no choice but to marry the captain. After all, *she* kept her promises.

"My God, Oliver, it's about time you got back here. What the hell were you doing down there?" As soon as Joshua flung these heated words at the first mate, he regretted the anger they conveyed, but some perverse need prevented him from revoking them. He really did want to know why it had taken the older man so long to deliver a simple message. At three bells into the first dogwatch, Joshua had sent Oliver to tell Madeline that he was too busy to have dinner with her. The bell had just struck six times in the second dogwatch. An hour and a half!

If the first mate was surprised by the captain's angry words, he gave no indication of it. Joshua thought he was probably getting used to his captain's foul mood.

"I had supper with her."

"You mean my wife?" For some reason this annoyed Joshua. If anyone was going to eat with Madeline, he felt it should be he. Never mind that he'd said he couldn't. Come to think of it, he'd sent his regrets, through Whitey, for almost a week now. But damn, that was about as long as they'd been stuck with no wind.

"'Course I mean your wife."

"Why?" A reasonable question, Joshua told himself.

"'Cause she asked me to."

Joshua had been afraid of that. Of course she'd asked Oliver to have dinner with her. She liked *him*. She was always sweet to *him*. But let Joshua come within ten feet of her, and she closed up like a clam.

Ever since that morning on deck when he'd tried to let her know what life as a privateer's wife would be like, she'd drawn away from him. Obviously she didn't care enough to risk standing by him if he had a leg blown off, or worse.

Maybe he shouldn't have told her what to expect, but she had asked, and besides, she'd been the one to stitch up his arm. She knew his situation. Still, they had been getting along so well before that. Oh, they'd had their little squabbles, but Joshua didn't mind them. In truth, he rather enjoyed matching wits with her.

"I think she misses your company, Cap'n."

Joshua looked at his first mate, and wondered how a grown man could be so naïve. "No, she probably just wanted to talk to you. She lost her father recently, and I think she was used to spending a lot of time with him. Come on. Let's help keep this canvas watered down." Joshua motioned toward the line of men he had left when he'd spotted Oliver climbing through the hatch.

Like them, Joshua was stripped to the waist. Muscles bulged beneath the sun-baked skin of his back, and his arms rippled smoothly as he joined the line of sailors passing buckets of seawater. The jagged welt where he'd been wounded was discolored and puckered, but it didn't bother him much anymore.

"How long ya think this'll last, Cap'n?"

Joshua wiped the sweat from his brow with a forearm. The droplets glistened like diamonds on its curly, black hair. "I don't know." He grabbed the heavy bucket passed his way and gave it to the man beside him. "I hope it doesn't last much longer."

"Aye, Cap'n. I ain't fond of bein' a sittin' duck."

"Well, there's one thing positive about this. No one else is going any place in this calm. If need be, we'll break out the oars."

Joshua laughed at the grunt of disdain this suggestion brought. No self-respecting sailor appreciated manning oars on anything larger than a longboat.

"We better have a blow soon, Cap'n."

"You keep your eye on the dog vane, Oliver, and let me

know when it comes." Joshua chuckled.

The first mate shaded his eyes and looked into the rigging. The chicken feathers moored in their cork dishes barely moved in the feeble breeze.

They passed the next few buckets in silence before Oliver asked, "What ya think young Nat's gonna have to say for himself; leadin' us a merry chase like he done?"

"I'm not sure," Joshua began, a look of mock severity wrinkling his brown. "But after forcing me to be a part of this bucket brigade, he'd better have a good excuse for sending us on a wasted trip."

"Ya ain't forgettin' the missus, are ya?"

"What?"

"Miz Whitlock. If it hadna been for chasin' Nat to Jamaica, ya might never o' married up with her," Oliver explained.

"Ah, yes, my wife. I'll be certain to thank Nathaniel when I see him." More than likely he'd sock his younger brother in the mouth, or, worse yet, foist Madeline off on him. That would teach Nat to go off chasing after pirates.

Who was he fooling? Nathaniel would be happy to have Madeline's company. She was witty and charming, not to mention pretty and sensual. Why, Nathaniel would probably fall madly in love with her within a fortnight. The train of Joshua's thoughts came as a shock, and he spilled briny water from the bucket he was passing all over his breeches.

Nathaniel had better not try anything with Madeline.

Joshua let his breath out through his teeth. What was he thinking? Nathaniel—his brother—would never do such a thing, no matter how tempting Madeline might be.

But would she? He envisioned her wrapped in Philip Spencer's arms. Of course she hadn't been his wife at the time, but damned near. The very thought made Joshua see red. She'd lied to him about that first night they'd spent together, had flaunted Spencer before him, and now she'd let him know that she didn't care enough to put up with the uncertainties of being a privateer's wife—still he wanted her.

"Somethin' wrong, Cap'n?"

Oliver's words, along with a less than gentle nudge in the ribs, brought Joshua's attention back to what he was doing. He shoved the bucket he'd apparently been holding for some time into the next seaman's hands. The startled sailor grasped the rope handle. He, along with three or four of the others nearby, including Oliver, stared at Joshua as if he'd suddenly grown another head.

Joshua muttered an oath. The damned woman was filling his mind, and there was no room in it for anything else, not even the simple task of passing buckets of seawater. All he could think about was how soft and sweet she'd felt lying under him. Well, maybe she didn't like the idea of being married to a privateer, but she was. He'd let her alone for over a week because he'd thought that was what she wanted, however, the strain of abstinence was becoming more than he wished to bear.

"I'm going below." Joshua didn't even wait for the boatswain's pipes to signal the end of the watch. He had a strong desire for his wife, and felt there was no time like the present to indulge it.

Madeline had been waiting for him. Still, his entrance, which interrupted her pacing, came as a jolt. It wasn't that he was noisy about it. On the contrary, in her angry, agitated state, Madeline hardly noticed the metallic rasp of the latch or the creak of the hinges. But at one moment the cabin seemed so empty, and in the next it was filled to overflowing with his presence.

It wasn't possible that a man, even a large man, could take up all the air in such a spacious cabin. Madeline knew that. But, as she stared at the captain, she had to struggle for every breath.

Outrage, she decided. Since Oliver had divulged the

captain's plans to her, she had been wallowing in the emotion. It stood to reason that once the object of her ire appeared, she'd be too angry to breathe. The only problem with that explanation was that she was also experiencing a tightening in the pit of her stomach—and lower—that had nothing to do with anger. How could he do this to her just by walking into the cabin, especially looking as disreputable as he did? He was sweaty and dirty and, for heaven's sake, barely dressed. His raven hair glistened and formed dark, damp curls on his head and across the wide breadth of his naked chest. With the exception of his boots, the only item of clothing he wore was his breeches. And they were soaked. The nankeen fabric clung to his powerful thighs and to his . . .

Madeline struggled to draw in another breath. For some time, whenever she'd been alone with the captain, she'd found her gaze flowing over him. And often, though she tried to prevent that, it drifted to a spot between his waist and legs. The fall-front flap on the breeches he usually wore couldn't disguise the bulge she noticed there. But never in all her past observations had that protuberance been as obvious as it was now. It was hard. Madeline could tell that by looking. Though she had never seen it like this, she had felt it—against her thigh, against her stomach, inside her. . . . My God, what was she doing?

Madeline closed her eyes because she simply couldn't stop eying him any other way. Unfortunately, there was no way to ignore his musky, male scent, but without the sight of him to contend with, she was able to regain a portion of her earlier indignation. This man had forced her from her home, he planned to take her to a strange place, and worse, much worse, he had made her feel as if she didn't care.

Madeline had been on the verge of believing that anywhere in the world would suit her as long as her captain was with her. She had suspected he didn't share the feeling, though she had never thought, until today, that he cared so little for her he would just dump her and leave. He had promised to take her back to Hopewell. Was she such a "burden" that he wasn't even going to keep his word?

When Madeline opened her eyes, anger and hurt had formed a bulwark against any desires that sight of him might evoke. "What do you want?"

Her words were icy hard, and Joshua felt their chill through the warm air of the cabin. Had he mistaken the passion he had read in her eyes moments ago? It certainly wasn't there now. Emerald fire had crystallized into shards of green glass. Maybe viewing her as he had, with his own burning need, he'd thought he'd seen something that wasn't there.

Still, he was surprised by her words. He had prepared to meet the reserved withdrawal he had been experiencing for a week, but not this blatant anger. She made him feel like an unwanted piece of refuse.

He looked down at himself. He guessed he must look pretty bad to her. He was sweaty and dirty. That hadn't bothered him when he'd decided the strain of their relationship had become unbearable. But, naturally, it would matter to her. She was a lady and his wife. He wouldn't even present himself to a tavern wench dressed like this.

"I need to wash up." Offering this excuse for being in the cabin seemed preferable to announcing that he had come to make love to her.

"Oh." Madeline certainly wasn't going to argue with him while he did *that*. "I'll wait on deck."

"You needn't leave."

She swallowed. "As you wish." Let him wash. She'd show him that it didn't bother her in the least. After all, his plans for her were what she was concerned about, not the way his sweat-slick skin glistened in the lantern light. Determinedly, she took up the waistcoat she'd been mending earlier and plopped into a chair. Never had she studied a needle and thread so intently as she now did.

288

"There's still barely a breeze." The captain's words startled Madeline. Her concentration not withstanding, she let the silvery point of the needle stab her finger rather than the fabric.

"What's the matter?" Joshua looked around when he heard a muffled "Ouch."

"Nothing."

"Did you prick yourself?"

"No. I often sit and suck my finger," Madeline retorted sarcastically. Some of her venom was lost, however, since the words were garbled by the finger in her mouth.

Damn, she's touchy, Joshua thought as he poured water into the basin. She didn't have to snap at him like that. It wasn't as if *he* had jammed the needle into her. Well, maybe she was in pain. Joshua knew he certainly wasn't lovable when he was injured. He dipped the linen wash rag into the clear water.

"What are you doing?" Madeline tried hard to inject an icy aloofness into the question. But even she knew, with the touch of his hand on hers, that so much heat was bound to cause a thaw. The captain had crossed the small cabin and was now kneeling in front of her, gently pulling her finger from between her lips.

"I thought I'd wash your hurt for you, Maddie."

"It doesn't need—" She tried to jerk her hand from his grasp.

"Don't be stubborn." He refuted her attempts to free her hand with frustrating ease. "You took care of me when I was wounded. It's only fair that I return the favor."

"I'm not wounded."

"Now, Maddie." He uncurled the fist she had made and, with painstaking thoroughness, examined the finger that had been in her mouth. As he looked at it, a tiny pinpoint of crimson blossomed on its smooth pad.

At first Madeline thought he meant to kiss her hurt finger, and she stiffened to absorb the shock waves she

289

knew such contact would cause. But when, instead, he drew the wounded finger, still wet from her mouth, into his own, her body melted, and she was lost. Her lashes drifted down and her senses were filled with him. He smelled of manly sweat and sea air, and she longed to run the tip of her tongue along his flesh, to taste his salty essence the way he was tasting hers. But more than that, she wanted to rest her head on top of his and say, Why don't you want me? I have lost so much—my father, my home. Please don't take away someone who has become all-important to me. Please, don't leave me.

But she became aware that her body was shifting off the chair toward him. That movement, along with the captain's release of her pricked finger, had allowed her to regain some sanity, and she was now astonished by her own thoughts. She would never beg him to stay with her—never. Besides, she had already decided that as soon as he left her in Baltimore Town, she would find passage back to Hopewell. Then she'd forget him. Dammit, she would! She'd forget she ever knew him.

"Better?" The word was husky and sensual, as if he knew exactly what his touch had done to her and that, given half the chance, he could do a lot more.

Madeline couldn't decide whether to slap his smug face or to ignore him altogether. For once, she took the less impetuous route. Her unemotional "It's quite fine now. You really should volunteer your services to Cook during the next battle" seemed to deflate him.

Joshua rose and turned away quickly, cursing her for being a cold woman. He had gotten harder than a cannon ball just from having her finger in his mouth, and it hadn't affected her at all. Angrily he splashed water over his face and chest, heedless of the waste of fresh water and of what the droplets might dampen. He then grabbed a linen towel off the commode and vigorously rubbed it over his skin. Whether she had been watching him all along or had just chosen that moment to look up would remain a mystery to him, but her expression, full of disdain, was easy enough to decipher.

He dropped the towel. "Is there a problem I don't know about?"

"What makes you think that?" Now that the moment to confront him was at hand, Madeline was strangely reluctant to do so.

But apparently he didn't feel like avoiding the issue, for he simply glared at her through narrowed black eyes.

She straightened her back. "There's a problem all right, but you know about it. I was the one who didn't."

Joshua folded his arms across his bare chest and waited. When it was clear that she didn't intend to go on, he said, "You're talking in riddles, Maddie, and frankly, I haven't the time or the patience to muddle through your words." He'd been on deck since morning watch, He was tired and hungry, and if she wanted to fight, he just wished she'd come right out and tell him what they were arguing about.

"Oh!" He didn't have the time, did he? She had put up with his not having the time for her for about a sennight now, and *she* was losing patience with that. Well, it was just too bad if he was busy and found her an unwanted burden. He was going to have to take the time to hear her out. "I'm referring to the fact that you have no intention of taking me back to Hopewell!" Her indignation demanded she rise, and Madeline stood glaring at Joshua, her hands balled into tiny fists.

Well, there it was, Hopewell again. She just couldn't wait to get away from him—back to her sugar plantation. "What makes you think that?" He certainly hadn't said he wouldn't take her back, though he'd hoped she'd want to stay with him for a while first.

"Then you deny that you told your first mate you were planning to drop me off in Baltimore Town and go on to New York."

Hell, he couldn't remember telling Oliver that. He probably had, because that had been his plan. "No, I don't deny it."

"Aha."

Joshua watched her strike a belligerent pose. The sudden movement of her head caused her hair to flare out angrily.

He mimicked her stance. "What is that supposed to mean—'aha'?"

"It means I thought so. You lied to me."

"You had best be certain of your facts before you call a man a liar, Maddie." His voice was tense from tightly controlled anger.

"Oh, really." Madeline mocked his severe tone. "And just what do you intend to do, run me through with your cutlass?"

"And sully a fine-tempered steel blade?" The captain took a menacing step forward. "Not likely. Besides, I can think of several less messy ways to punish a wasp-tongued wife."

"You don't frighten me." Madeline hoped she had convinced him because she certainly hadn't convinced herself. Staring at his towering form, it was all she could do to keep her knees from knocking.

"Really?" He didn't sound convinced. "Well, you should be. It would take no effort for me to turn you over my knee and let my hand, on your soft, round bottom, teach you the consequences of jumping to conclusions and questioning my word. Besides, *you* hardly seem the one to be complaining about being lied to."

"What do you mean?" Madeline stepped back when she saw the anger in his eyes.

"I mean, my dear Maddie, that you are the master of lying, or did you think I didn't know." Joshua hadn't meant to bring up her deceit, but because she'd doubted his word, the remarks had just come out.

It occurred to Madeline that somehow he had discovered she wasn't with child and blamed her for not telling him sooner. She knew she should have told him and began to say so. "I was going to let you know—"

"It would be interesting to know when? Did you

292

honestly think you could hide it from me? But then you didn't plan on my getting close enough to you to find out, did you?"

"Close enough?" Madeline couldn't imagine what he meant.

"What happened that night on the beach, Maddie? Did things get out of hand? When you demurred at first, I had no idea you were trying to hide your virginity."

"My virginity!" Madeline felt heat pool in her cheeks. "You stole my virginity that night in your cabin. On this very bunk." She thrust her finger toward the offending piece of furniture.

Joshua shook his head. His eyes narrowed and watched her speculatively. She still had the nerve to deny it. "Did you take me for such a callow youth that I wouldn't recognize a virgin when I took one? You were a maiden till we made love at Hopewell."

Madeline stared into the jet black fire of his eyes, and gasped. Was he saying she'd been a virgin until the night they'd made love. Memory of piercing pain shot through her—a memory of when he'd entered her. No, it couldn't have been then that she'd lost her maidenhead. But she knew it was. She'd accused him of ravishing her, and he hadn't. Well, maybe she had jumped to a hasty conclusion about what had happened that first time in his cabin, but it wasn't as if she hadn't had reason to do so.

"Captain," she began. "I don't believe you understand."

Madeline was interrupted by a short bark of laughter. Abruptly, he moved toward her. "I admit, *my dear wife,* that I was slow to understand." It made him furious that she didn't admit to her deception. He also realized how angry he'd been ever since the night her father had died—angry at her and angry at himself, for wanting her regardless of her lies. Even now he couldn't look at her without feeling an unwelcome pang of lust. That knowledge made him lash out. "Tell me, Maddie, I'd like to hear it from your own lips. What was your motive for making me believe I raped you?"

"Why, you can't honestly believe—"

"That you plotted the whole thing?" The captain was sitting in a chair now, but there was nothing relaxed about his posture. He was like a watch spring, wound and eager to let loose.

"Plotted!" Madeline could hardly believe what she was hearing.

"Oh, I'll grant you that our first meeting was accidental and so was my arrival at Hopewell, but after that you used every feminine wile to get what you wanted."

"And that was?"

"To marry me."

"Ha!" Madeline could hardly believe her ears. "You think I wanted that? You conceited bastard."

"Rest assured, conceit has nothing to do with it. I am not such a fool as to think you desired *me*."

"You think I married you just for your name?" Madeline retorted.

He was out of the seat now, and she was surprised the chair had contained him as long as it had. "Any name, Maddie, any name."

"Oh, I was so anxious for marriage that anyone would do? If I was so desperate, then why did you desire me?"

"I didn't say you weren't coveted as a bed partner, but you do have certain characteristics that make you a less than desirable wife."

Madeline's mouth flew open, but he continued before she could demand to know what he meant.

"You are too independent by half, you will not listen, and you have one of the sharpest tongues I've ever encountered in a female." In his anger, Joshua forgot that these very traits had attracted him to her in the first place.

His words hit Madeline like physical blows. So that was how he viewed her? "Then why did you go ahead with the wedding? You said you knew the night my father died

294

that you hadn't ravished me."

"Why?" He seemed surprised by the question. "Whether on my ship or on the beach, I had taken your virtue, so there was a good chance you were carrying my child. *And* you had your father ask me."

"I did no such thing."

The cold look he gave her clearly indicated he didn't believe her denial. She truly doubted, in his present state of mind, he'd believe anything she told him. But that didn't stop her from going on.

"I neither coveted nor sought marriage with you. And as for my being desperate for a man, if you'll remember, I had another proposal."

"How could I forget that milksop Philip?" The captain's mouth twisted into a sneer of contempt.

"Milksop!" Though it might be true that Philip was less bold than the man who stood before her, he was hardly a milksop. And furthermore, Madeline resented the captain's insinuation that no one but a poor imitation of a man would want her. "There's more to Philip Spencer than you know."

"Really." He was goading her.

"Yes, and in truth, I can't imagine why I didn't ignore my father's request and marry him."

"Nor can I."

"I wish I had."

"So do I."

After their raised voices had resounded throughout the cabin, the sudden silence that followed their final words was deafening.

Madeline stared at him, yearning to take back her angry statement. She hadn't meant it, not really. How had they ever gotten to this point anyway? If only he had let her explain, but then he didn't really want to hear the truth. He was content to think she had lied to him.

She watched as he turned on his heel and stalked out of the cabin. Then she sank into the chair and buried her face in the palms of her hands.

Thank goodness she had some money with her. She rose and crossed to her sea chest. Lifting its brass-edged lid, she rummaged through rufles and silks until she found the leather pouch filled with gold. Her hand closed around it protectively. Let the captain abandon her in Baltimore. She'd make her way back to Jamaica, Admiral Bompar or no Admiral Bompar. She didn't need the captain, nor did she want him. But even as she secreted the pouch among her petticoats, Maddie knew she was not being honest with herself. She loved Joshua, brash, bold and unreasonable though he was. She'd tried not to, but even now, when she knew how he felt about her, she couldn't help herself.

"What do you have there?"

Madeline had been strolling idly along the forecastle—she'd avoided the quarterdeck like the plague since her argument with the captain ten days ago—when she'd noticed Oliver squatting against a pile of hemp. At her approach, he'd set aside what he'd been working on.

"Oh, it ain't nothin', Miz Whitlock."

Madeline smiled. No matter how often she had invited the crusty old seaman to address her as Madeline he still insisted on calling her Mrs. Whitlock. "Well, it must be something. May I see it?" She had caught a glimpse of a delicately carved powder horn before he'd stuffed it between himself and the hemp.

Slowly, Oliver extracted the horn from its hiding place and handed it to her. "It's just somethin' I mess around with in my spare time."

"Oh, this is lovely." Madeline examined the horn critically. Someone, she assumed it was Oliver, had scraped down the ox horn until it shone like warm ivory. Then intricate designs had been etched into it until they nearly covered the surface. "Did you do this, Oliver?"

"Well, yes'm, Miz Whitlock, but it ain't nothin' much."

"Nothing much." Madeline sounded incredulous. "Why, it's beautiful." With a fingernail she traced one of the etchings. "This is the *Chesapeake,* isn't it?"

Oliver beamed under her praise. "Aye, how were ya knowin' that?"

"It's obvious—the cut of her hull, her topsails. And this." Madeline turned the horn, delight lacing her voice as she discovered what he had been working on earlier. "It's a battle."

In tiny weblike lines Oliver had drawn the *Chesapeake* attacking another ship. Though the depiction of the battle was not quite finished, it was obvious which vessel was destined to be victorious.

"Aye, the one we had with that French schooner as we was leavin' Jamaica."

Madeline gingerly touched the outline of the French ship. "So that's what the enemy looked like. The captain wouldn't let me on deck to see it."

"He didn't want ya hurt." Oliver said it so vehemently that Madeline wondered if she had sounded critical.

"Tell me about the other pictures." She gathered her skirts and sat on a coil of hemp.

Oliver was an excellent teller of tales, and time flew by as he shared with her an illustrated history of the *Chesapeake.*

"And this one?" Madeline pointed to a grouping of three ships. The Bermuda sloop appeared to be sailing right between two, much larger vessels.

Oliver chuckled. "That there's the *Dolphin.*" He gestured to one of the ships. "She's a warship we ran into one day."

"You mean you actually fought a battle with her? But she looks so much bigger—and there are two of them." Madeline's eyes were wide with surprise.

Oliver rubbed his whiskered chin. "Cap'n figured she'd be slow to respond, and she was. Did her a lot o' damage, we did," Oliver stated with obvious pride. "But yer right, there was two of 'em. Passel more than two, really. I just didn't have room to put the others in the picture."

"Well, what happened?"

Oliver's eyes shone. "Cap'n had the idea to sail right betwixt 'em and hide in the fog. We was faster, and they was afraid to use their guns for fear o' shootin' each other." Oliver shook his head. "That sure was somethin'."

"Oliver, why were you fighting a warship in the first place. Did she attack you?"

"Naw, we attacked her."

"But why? I thought privateers only went after merchant ships. Certainly you didn't hope to gain anything when attacking a man-of-war." Madeline had refrained from using the term "steal" when she had asked her question, though she supposed that was what she'd really meant.

"We does, usually. But the Cap'n, he ain't just in it for the money, and he figured we could at least hurt her some."

"I see." Oliver's words couldn't help but revise Madeline's notions about privateers. She looked back at the horn. "Well, I suppose you're glad we haven't run into any merchant vessels this trip; you're almost out of room on the powder horn."

Oliver laughed. "I got others. Besides, I knew there weren't to be no privateering this trip. We've sailed away from a half-dozen merchant ships." He had taken back the horn and was scratching the finishing touches onto the French schooner with his marlinespike.

"Why?" Madeline watched his gnarled fingers, fascinated.

"Cap'n won't allow it. Said 'twas bad enough runnin' into this"—he motioned to the ship he was working on— "and he wasn't gonna invite no more trouble with ya on board. Scared him bad when that French ship 'bout had us beat. Never knowed him to worry 'bout someone like he does ya."

Madeline pressed her hands together and looked out over the sea. The slate blue waters of the Atlantic had replaced the turquoise Caribbean. She didn't want to think about the captain caring for her . . . before their argument.

"Where are we, Oliver?" The wind had started up almost miraculously the day the captain had stalked from their cabin, and since then they'd made good time.

"We ain't far from the thirty-seventh."

"The thirty-seventh?" Madeline asked, perplexed.

"Aye, parallel, the thirty-seventh parallel. That's 'bout even with Cape Henry."

"At the mouth of the bay?"

"Uh-huh." Oliver was rubbing lamp soot into the lines he had etched. It made the design stand out against the creamy background of the horn.

"Well then, we're almost there." Madeline didn't know whether to be happy or sad that her ordeal with the captain was soon to be over. Of course, she had rarely caught a glimpse of him since their fight. He never came to the cabin, never even sent an excuse now. And Madeline only left his quarters when she felt the four walls would suffocate her.

"I said, that depends," Oliver interjected.

Apparently Madeline had missed the first time he'd said it because as he repeated his words he looked at her strangely.

"Depends on what?"

"If'n we can catch an easterly wind. Ships been know'd to jog about for weeks waitin' for the wind to change. Ya got yer prevailin' westerlies there."

"Well, what do you think? Will we have to wait long?"

Oliver wiped his darkened hands on his breeches. "Don't know. We been lucky so far. 'Ceptin' for that calm we run into, we had smooth sailin' up the Gulf Stream. Didn't even have no rough weather off Hatteras."

"Oliver?"

"H'm?" He was examining his work critically.

"Does the captain know about your talent?"

"Ain't no talent, Miz Whitlock, just somethin' I does in my spare time."

"All right." Apparently Oliver didn't realize how good he was. "But does he know about it?"

"Sure, done some things for him in the past."

"Oh, really?" Madeline smiled as she played with the unraveled end of the rope she sat upon. "What?"

Oliver shrugged. "Couple things. His razor handle for one, a pipe, stuff like that."

Madeline's teeth caught her bottom lip as she thought about the razor she had used to attack the captain. Had its handle been etched? She tried to remember, but Oliver's next words wiped that concern from her mind.

"He ain't happy, ya know."

"Who?" Madeline winced at her own cowardice; she knew exactly who he meant.

Oliver's expression told her he knew of the game she played with herself. "The cap'n. It ain't like him to stay down this long. Even when he was worried 'bout Nat he weren't like this."

Madeline looked away from his accusing stare. "I'm sorry, but there's nothing I can do about it."

"Ain't there?"

"No!" Madeline quickly rose from the hemp and grabbed at the railing. She clutched it until her knuckles turned white and the pristine sky and sea were blurred by her tears. "I don't know what the Captain's told you but—"

"He ain't tole me nothin', but I got eyes."

"Yes, well, this whole thing has been a mistake. When we get to Baltimore, I'll book passage home and he'll go back to being a privateer. Then we'll all be happy." Madeline sniffled and hastily wiped at her eyes.

"Ya ain't believin' that any more than me."

Madeline turned toward him, her eyes beseeching. "But I have to; there's no other way."

"Ain't there?"

"Would you stop that?" She threw her hands up in the air. "Of course there's no other way. If there were, don't you think I'd do something about it?"

He didn't even have to goad her with words this time. Just the questioning look on his grizzled face was enough.

"We had a fight," Madeline explained as calmly as she could. "Your captain thinks I lied to him, and he wants nothing more to do with me." There, that should satisfy the nosy old man.

"Did ya?"

Madeline sighed in exasperation. "Did I what?"

"Lie to him."

"No! Well, not on purpose. I told you, it was a mistake." Madeline thought about how she had failed to tell Joshua there would be no baby. "I may not always have told him everything."

"Tell him now," Oliver said sagely.

"He won't listen," she replied, and stared back toward the sea.

"It ain't none of my concern—"

"You're right; it isn't."

"But I think yer both actin' like a couple of young'ns."

Madeline sniffled again and said nothing.

Oliver rose and stretched. "Like I said, it ain't none of my concern."

Madeline sucked in her breath and swallowed. She was trying not to break into tears. She hoped he would leave.

"Miz Whitlock?"

"What?"

"I got somethin' in my gear. Come by a piece of ivory once and scratched the *Chesapeake* on it. Ain't very good, but I'd like ya to have it."

Madeline hazarded a glance over her shoulder. The first mate was standing nearby, twisting his knit hat in his hands. His powder horn was slung over his back by its leather strap.

"I couldn't take that from you."

301

"I wants ya to have it. Kinda like somethin' to remember us by."

Madeline heard him shuffle down the deck.

Something to remember them by, he had said, as if she'd ever be able to forget.

A fish sprang free of the waves, and Madeline watched the play of sunlight upon its iridescent body as it curved in a graceful arc. Too soon it was gone from view, swallowed up by the sea, its beauty lost to her forever. Was that how it was to be with the captain? For all of her life was she to have only the memory of their brief time together? And what of his memories? Would they ever mellow? Would there come a day when he'd regret that she had been like the fish, only a fleeting vision in the sea of his life?

Madeline stared at the heavy oak door and admonished herself for the hundredth time to be brave. This had to be done, and she was going to do it.

Raucous laughter sounded from within, and Madeline grabbed the latch to stop herself from running away.

She had barely known this room, aft of the officers' quarters, existed until thirty minutes ago. She could still picture the smug expression on Oliver's face when she'd sought him out and asked if he knew the captain's whereabouts. Oh, she would have much preferred not to have been forced to seek out the first mate, but once she had decided it was time she and the captain had a talk, the man was nowhere to be found.

"The wardroom," Oliver had said. "That's where he's spending his evenings, wrapped around a mug of grog and lookin' like he ain't got a friend in the world."

So here she was, clutching the latch and ready to barge into the room where the ship's officers spent their evenings.

Another rumble of laughter sounded inside, and Madeline thrust the door open before she could convince

302

herself that there probably was a better time to do this.

No one seemed to notice her at first, but when the boatswain—Jamieson, she thought his name was—saw her his gasp focused a half-dozen pairs of eyes on her—including those of the captain.

"I'd like"—Madeline's voice failed her and she cleared her throat and started again—"I'd like to talk to you for a moment, if I may." Her eyes were on the captain, and no one seemed to think she meant anyone but him.

Madeline waited while he put his mug down with a slow deliberate motion. Oliver had been right. He looked awful. Well, that was probably an exaggeration. The captain could never look awful, but he did look tired. His eyes were bloodshot, and he seemed to have lost some weight. Madeline knew she hadn't been sleeping or eating well, but it had never occurred to her that he might be suffering as well.

Finally, when she could stand his silent stare no longer, she asked, "Would you step into the passageway, please?"

"I'm quite comfortable where I am."

Madeline took a deep breath and tried to control her temper. Oliver was right, he was acting like a baby. Thank goodness she had given up such childish actions.

"Fine." She settled herself on the bench across from her husband. "I'll say what needs to be said right here."

He wasn't going to back down. She could see it in his eyes, but thank goodness his men weren't as stubborn as their captain. With a flurry of scraping chairs and mumbled excuses, the spectators left the arena to the two combatants.

Now that they were alone, Joshua at least seemed willing to speak. "Say what you have to, and then leave." He took a hefty swallow of grog, and Madeline thought how delightful it would be to pour the contents of his mug over his raven locks.

"I shall. First of all"—Madeline drew in a breath and then let the words flow—"I was not always totally honest with you." She noted that this admission didn't seem to surprise him. "I had known for over a week that I wasn't carrying your child, and I didn't tell you."

"A week?" His tone indicated he thought she had underestimated the time by a good month.

"Yes, a week." Madeline stiffened her back and stared at him. "I also should not have accused you of"—she tried not to stumble over the word—"molesting me when I didn't know for certain that you had. However, you never denied it."

"I couldn't remember!" Joshua knocked the bench over as he stood up and slammed his palms against the rough-hewn table. The nerve of the woman, blaming him for not denying something he couldn't recall.

"Well, I couldn't either!" Madeline jumped to her feet, and though her motion wasn't accompanied by banging furniture about, it was dramatic.

"What are you talking about?" His face was calmer now, and he watched her through narrowed eyes.

"I'm talking about the fact that I had been adrift on the sea for three days. I got sick and passed out in your cabin, and when I woke you were lying across me, naked. I thought you had, but obviously you hadn't; and that's all I have to say, except I'm sorry." She started toward the door.

"Maddie."

She swiped a strand of hair away from her face. "What?"

"How'd you say all that without breathing?"

"Oh!" Madeline stomped her foot in frustration and then lunged for the door, but the captain was quicker. Before she could open it, he had grabbed her arm.

"I'm sorry for making light of it. What I meant to ask is, why did you come in here and tell me this?"

"Because it's the truth, and I thought you should know." Madeline jerked her arm free and left the room before he could stop her, if indeed, he wanted to.

*   *   *

A seaman passed Madeline as she stood on the deck, and she averted her eyes. She was sure that by now every man on the ship knew about that disgraceful scene in the wardroom. Not that she would have cared, had it done any good. But it hadn't. The captain hadn't followed her, and in the hour since her public display he had made no effort to talk to her. She hadn't even seen him. But then she hadn't been looking anyplace but out across the blue Atlantic. She had soaked up a great deal of the late afternoon sunshine before the clouds had rolled in and the wind had picked up, and that was good because she didn't think she could face coming out of her cabin again until they docked in Baltimore.

"It looks as if we're in for a bit of a storm."

Madeline spun around at hearing those unexpected words, and gazed up into the midnight black eyes of the captain. He looked at her a moment, his expression unreadable; then he turned to stare out to sea. Her heart raced as she studied his handsome profile silhouetted against the gray sky. He seemed in no hurry to say anything else, so she tried to fill the silence. "You may be right about the storm, but the wind feels so good. I can still remember all those days with nary a breeze, and how I longed for just—"

"Maddie." His single word broke the flow of her ramblings.

"Yes."

He was looking at her again, but this time his expression made her feel as if all breath had been knocked from her body. "We need to talk, but for now I think you'd better get below."

Why didn't he just say whatever it was that needed saying? She sucked in a breath. Was he going to tell her he'd made a mistake by marrying her? If that was it, Madeline wanted to hear it now. "But why can't you—"

"Look there, on the horizon." He motioned with a long arm, and the wind tore at the linen fabric of his sleeve. "That's a squall."

Madeline watched the turbulent weather approach

305

from the south. It was obvious that the murk she'd noticed earlier on the horizon was windswept rain.

"Is it going to overtake us?" Already the wind had become less friendly.

"I think so. But you needn't concern yourself. I took the necessary precautions before I came looking for you. You'll be safe enough."

"I never doubted I'd be safe with you." As soon as she said the words, Madeline wished she could retract them. He was going to tell her their marriage was over, and she was telling him how safe she felt with him. He must think her a foolish female. His eyes narrowed, and Madeline swiped the wind-blown hair from her face.

Suddenly she could stand his appraisal no longer. She began to turn as the wind whipped at her skirts. "You're right, I'd better go be—"

Before she could take a single step, her shoulders were grasped, and his large hands jerked her around and drew her against the hard length of his body.

Madeline's gasp of surprise was lost as his lips found hers. Somewhere in the recesses of her mind, she realized he hadn't mentioned their argument or her apology. But she didn't want to think of that right now. She didn't want to think of anything but how right it felt to be in his embrace.

The angry wind stormed about them like a jealous lover trying to pull them apart, to insinuate itself between them, but to no avail. Madeline clung to him as if he were her lifeline. And when zig-zag streaks of lightning raced across the sky, they illuminated but one entwined silhouette on the deck.

No longer shy about the need that raged inside of her, Madeline put her heart into the kiss. When his mouth opened, so did hers; when his bold tongue thrust out, it found hers willing, nay eager, to join in the foray.

She did not try to understand the reasons for her responses. Her desire had become as untamed and tempestuous as the storm that surrounded them.

The captain's hot, moist lips raced across her cheek, down the curve of her jaw, and lower, heedless of the streams of tawny curls the wind lashed about. Madeline moaned and arched her body to aid him in his ravishment of her flesh, yet her fingers never left the tangles of his tempest-tossed hair. They wove through crisp curls of midnight black, and when he brought his mouth back to hers, they tightened. The kiss was not gentle, but neither was the tossing of the ship or the whipping of the wind. And she did not wish it to be. Gentle was for quiet moments and holding hands. Madeline's hunger was as fundamental and savage as the raging sea, the stormy sky.

"No." The groan of denial swept through her as she became conscious that her body was no longer pressed against his. He had pushed her away. Deprived of his embrace, she became aware of the fat, wet drops beating mercilessly against her. It had begun to rain, and she hadn't even noticed.

"Go below, Maddie!" he shouted.

How could he do this to her? "But—"

"There are things I must see to!" His voice was as harsh as the weather. "Go below!"

Madeline swiped the streaming hair from her face, then rushed toward the ladder. Frantically she grabbed the rain-slickened bannister and began to climb down from the quarterdeck. She jerked away from the captain's hands when he tried to aid her slip-sliding progress down the steps. He yelled something to her, but she had no wish to hear; and even if she had, the wind would not let her.

She scrambled through the hatch and heard a dull thud as it closed behind her. How could she have thrown herself at him like that? Even when he had tried to stop her, when he'd sent her away, she had begged for more. "Oh." Madeline groaned at the memory.

Thankful that no sailors were in the companionway, she lifted up her sodden skirts and ran toward her cabin. Once inside, she paused only long enough to light a

307

candle from the lantern flame before tearing at the fastening of her wet dress.

Rain streamed from her hair and blended with her tears as she stepped out of the soaked gown and petticoats, and flung them into a soggy pile in the corner of the cabin. Oh, she could never face him again after the wanton way she had kissed him. The captain must certainly know how much she wanted him.

Madeline reached for the laces of her stays, but before she could loosen the knotted ribbon, the cabin door flew open, and she turned to look, wide-eyed, into the tempestuous gaze of the captain.

Chapter 20

"Is it your design, Maddie, to deny me by doing away with yourself?" In his tone was a gilt-thin veneer of control, but that was not so in his eyes. Their agate black depths raked Madeline's near-naked form with uncurbed lust.

"No." Her whispered denial was lost as he kicked the door shut, but he could not misinterpret the negative shake of her head.

"Then take more heed of your actions, for my sake, if not your own. Running full speed along a wet, tossing deck is a good way to end up in the sea." Joshua advanced on her slowly.

Oh, how she wanted to save him the effort, to rush into his embrace; but her recent embarrassment was too fresh in her mind. Madeline tilted her chin defiantly, not realizing that the gesture exposed more of her long glistening neck to his hungry eyes. "I should think picturing a giant wave swallowing me up would have great appeal to you."

"Is that what you believe, that I want the sea to savor your delicacies? Oh no, Maddie." He moved closer, till his breath fanned against her cheek. "That sweet repast belongs to me."

She thought he would kiss her then, but he appeared in

no mood to be rushed. His stare left the trembling temptation of her lips to travel leisurely down the delicate stem of her neck and then linger on the lush fullness her stays pushed into prominence. The linen of her shift had been made nearly transparent by the dampness that had seeped through her gown.

Joshua's finger followed the path of his eyes. Rosy nipples, already hard and puckered from the rain, strained against the gossamer fabric as he traced the swell of her breasts. Madeline's soft sigh of pleasure drew his glance back to her face.

"You are so lovely. Often in my dreams you are garbed like this. Though usually you are dry." He grinned. "In my imaginings I didn't know what I was missing."

His voice and his words were hypnotic, and Madeline reached for him as if he were her only link to reality.

Her touch seemed to shatter the controlled tempo of his lovemaking. The hand that had earlier played a slow, sensual melody against her flesh now seized her and drew her to him in a passionate embrace. He kissed her, and as she had each previous time, Madeline could do naught but welcome the onslaught.

Still she tried to resist. "The storm," she breathed out, as the heat of his mouth rained fiery kisses along the side of her throat.

"'Tis upon us, Maddie."

The words, almost fierce growls, pulsed against her nèck and freed her to accept him. He was right. They were caught in a wild, untamed whirlwind. Like the storm that raged around their tiny vessel, the turbulence inside of them, so long denied, could not be controlled.

Viewing the dusky pink crowns of her breasts through the veil of cloth was no longer enough, and with a flick of his hand Joshua released their creamy soft fullnesses and turgid tips to the demands of his mouth and tongue.

Liquid fire rushed through Madeline as his lips posssessed her straining peaks. He suckled as his impudent tongue swirled to the primitive rhythms of her rapidly beating pulse.

Her hands, which until now had been molded to the masculine contours of his chest, clutched at the solid muscles of his shoulders as her knees crumbled.

Large hands cupped the curves of her buttocks to keep her from falling, and instead of the hard deck her body had anticipated, she was drawn up against the equally hard, but infinitely more pleasurable, length of his body.

Her arms twined around his neck, and she found her own tongue eagerly tracing the curve of his ear, drinking in the diamondlike raindrops that clung lovingly to the rugged slant of his jaw.

Madeline could feel the delicious vibrations of his voice against her flesh, but his words were muffled in the valley of her breasts.

"I didn't . . . Oh," she moaned as his mouth returned to her nipple, his teeth grazing the sensitive peak, drawing it even more erect.

"Didn't what, Maddie?" He raised his head and trailed hot, fleeting kisses along her temple and cheek.

"Hear you." Madeline gasped. "I didn't hear what you said."

"I asked if you could take this off." His onyx black gaze lowered to indicate the stays that impeded his complete examination of her body.

"Yes."

The Captain lowered her feet to the floor, yet kept a firm grip on her behind. Madeline fumbled with the laces, but with the blatant proof of his need pressed rock-hard against her stomach and the melting sensation she felt between her own legs, the routine task of untying them became nearly impossible. It was much easier to give in to her body's longings and writhe sensually against him.

"Later," he moaned like a man possessesd.

"What?"

"Take it off later," the captain breathed out as he lowered her onto the bunk.

Madeline's wet hair felt cold against the fevered skin of her back, but her mind barely had time to register the sensation before another overshadowed it. The captain had followed her onto the pallet, his hands swiping away the expanse of shift that concealed from his hungry eyes and mouth what he desired.

He lowered his head and his whisker-roughened face, abrading the smooth, flat flesh of her belly, sent quivers of want spreading through Madeline. She pressed her legs together to assuage the aching need she felt, but it did not help. Only when she felt his long fingers tangle in the thatch of tight curls above her thighs, then skip through to the core of her passion, did she know any relief.

With a ragged cry of joy she opened herself to him. Her fingers twined in his damp hair, but she felt her hold loosening as his head and swirling tongue moved lower along the plains of her body.

"Noooo," Madeline moaned, not sure whether she was protesting the cessation of the stroking pleasure of his finger or what she knew would take its place. She struggled to twist away, but his strong hands made that impossible, and the moment the shocking heat of his tongue touched her, she no longer tried. He offered no quarter as he plundered her quivering flesh unmercifully. And Madeline could ask for none, for wanton waves of pleasure washed through her.

Long before the aftershock, the tremors, had subsided, she felt the pressure of his long body sliding up from between her thighs. The muscles of his chest and arms bulged sensually beneath his clinging shirt as he supported his weight while he fumbled with the buttons of his trousers.

Having experienced the joys of their passion, but wanting still more, Madeline's own hands reached between them to tear away the barrier of their union. The captain's sharp intake of breath when she touched the hard, hot length of his staff gave her a thrill of pride, she could give as well as receive.

Joshua tried to restrain himself. He had wanted to apologize for believing she'd lied to him. He had envisioned love words and soft embraces, whispered sighs, but that was beyond him now. From the moment he had touched her on deck, he'd been lost. And now . . . He moaned again as her hand skimmed his length, circled the tip, and retreated down the other side.

She was ready, and the motion of her eager body begged him to do what he desired most. Boldly he thrust forward. She was small, tight, and the pleasurable friction of her body opening constricting around him was almost more than he could bear. Joshua held himself still and looked down into her face. Her eyes were open, two luminous emerald pools in a face alive with wonder. He probed deeper and watched her lips part, the tip of her pink tongue peek through. He touched it with his own. "Do you like that, Maddie?"

"Yes, oh yes." Her words were a breathless whisper, but she knew he heard them by the smile that warmed his face.

"Good, because I like it too." He withdrew, then slowly began to slide back into the hot slippery core of her. But this time Madeline arched her hips.

"Oh God," she heard him moan as his pace quickened. In and out he drove—deeper, faster. And she met each thrust with an upward movement—a hungry movement. It was as if her body was trying to devour all of him. Madeline's hands clutched at his wet shirt, then descended to his smoothly muscled buttocks.

His mouth locked on hers, and the wild, pulsing motion of his tongue matched the driving power of his hard plunging flesh.

Madeline knew a split second of panic. Had the storm increased in fury so that the ship was tumbling wildly

313

through the heavens? Then she knew it wasn't the tempest outside, but the one within that had sent her soaring. She let herself go, flying toward the stars. They exploded, erupting into a maelstom of vibrant colors that inundated her senses.

"Are you all right?"

His voice rasped in her ear, echoing her own breathlessness.

Madeline answered with a slow, sensual smile, and after a moment, his mirrored it. Joshua rolled onto his side, one arm thrown possessively across her waist, his face nestled against the side of her neck. Madeline lay on the bunk, savoring his nearness, but it didn't take her long to notice that not all of the storm-tossed feelings she'd had had been in her imagination. The *Chesapeake* was lurching back and forth, buffeted by the wind and sea.

Joshua realized it, too. "Damn." He expelled the word against the softness of her skin, and the resulting vibrations sent delicious chills down her spine.

Joshua pulled himself up. He didn't want to leave but knew he had to. He touched the curve of her cheek, the blush of her just-kissed lips. "I'm needed on deck. The storm," he explained needlessly. "Stay here, Maddie." He hesitated, remembering the last time he'd given that order and the result. "Please," he added. "I told you earlier I don't want you washed away on a wave, and I meant it. When I get back we'll talk."

When I get back we'll talk. The words still rang in Madeline's head the next afternoon as she sat in the cabin—waiting. The storm had raged through the night and into the next day. There had been times when the *Chesapeake* had plunged into the trough of a wave, nearly overturning in the process, and she had wondered if the sea would ever become calm. But it had, and the gentle roll of the deck under her feet made the tempest seem like a bad dream.

Several times during the long night and day, the captain had sent someone to check on her, but he had never come. And though she'd always been assured that he was fine, Madeline wanted to see for herself.

The door opened and she got her wish. The captain stood before her, dressed in the same clothes he'd worn to fight the storm. Lines of fatigue were evident when he made a feeble attempt to smile.

Madeline jumped up. "Are you all right?" She tried to keep panic from her voice, but he looked so weary.

"Just tired." Joshua's eyes strayed longingly toward the bunk. "You don't mind if I . . ."

"Of course not."

He sank onto the soft ticking and yanked off one boot.

"I'm not the least tired. I stayed in bed, remember?" Madeline's cheeks blossomed with rosy color after her inadvertent reference to their lovemaking.

"I remember."

Joshua ceased unfastening his shirt and looked at her with such undeniable desire that Madeline stepped toward him. Only when she again noticed how exhausted he looked did she stop herself. He needed to be in bed—alone. Madeline told him as much, and then hurried out of the cabin before he could argue.

The storm had done some damage to the *Chesaspeake*, but no one was injured, and most of the crew seemed pleased to see the sun again. Madeline stayed on deck till that glowing orange sphere disappeared below the surface of the sea.

When she went below, she opened the door as quietly as she could and tiptoed into the cabin. But she needn't have worried about disturbing the captain's slumber. He sat at his desk, shaved and freshly garbed. He turned, but didn't rise when she entered.

"What are you doing up?" He didn't look tired

anymore, but she hadn't been gone that long.

"I was waiting for you." He grinned. "I told you we needed to talk."

"About what?" Madeline bit her lower lip and sank into the chair opposite his. She had almost hoped that after last night they didn't need to discuss anything.

"About the wardroom for one thing."

He was still smiling, but Madeline wasn't sure how he felt about her invading that all-male domain.

"It was a pretty stupid thing to do."

"Oh, it wasn't so bad. I can think of a lot more idiotic things to do."

"Like what?" Madeline glanced up. The captain appeared to be giving her query serious thought.

"Oh, like a man accusing his wife of tricking him into marriage."

Madeline's heart began to beat faster. "That is a rather half-witted thing to do. Still, I'm certain the man had his reasons for believing as he did."

"Perhaps," Joshua conceded. "But any man with an ounce of sense would have listened to his wife's explanation instead of jumping to all the wrong conclusions."

"Well, his wife was probably so angry she was slow to explain—"

"For heaven's sake, Maddie." Joshua ran his fingers through his hair, tossing the curls he had taken such pains to brush down. "Would you stop making excuses for me?"

"Oh!" She feigned surprise as she slanted him a look from below her lashes. "Were we speaking of you?"

Joshua scowled. "How many other half-witted husbands do you know?"

"At the moment, none."

Joshua seemed to accept this with good grace. "Can you forgive me, Maddie?"

Madeline wondered if the captain could hear her heart

pounding against her ribs. "Do you truly want to be forgiven?"

"Hell, yes! I was wrong, and besides, I've been miserable without you." At that moment, slumped down in the chair, his long legs spread out before him, he certainly appeared forlorn. But he didn't look as hopeless as Madeline had been without him. She rose and approached him, not stopping until the crisp, light silk of her gown brushed against the V of his powerful thighs. "There's nothing to forgive. We've both made mistakes. I . . ." Madeline searched her mind for words to express how she felt at this moment, but she had forgotten that the captain was a man of action. Before she could think of anything else to say he had hauled her onto his lap and was *showing* her exactly how he felt.

She opened her mouth under the pressure of his lips, and decided his way was definitely preferable to talking.

It was happening again. The sweet, fiery pleasure that his touch aroused was flowing through her like warm honey. She molded herself against him and reveled in his moan of need.

His hands moved over her, caressing the silken threads of her hair, the straight line of her back, supporting the weight of her breasts. "Oh, Lord, I missed you." He tore his mouth away from hers and, with it, blazed a trail to the base of her neck, where her pulse vibrated. "I missed the roses, the freckles. . . ." His aggressive lips forged lower.

The imp in Madeline couldn't help but wonder if he had missed all of her. He had professed to dislike several things about her, and the memory of that criticism lingered even as he made her body sing with want. Impulsively, she asked, "And what of my sharp tongue? Did you miss that?" For emphasis she stuck the pink tip out between her lips.

Joshua lifted his head, ceasing his pleasurable exploration of her breasts. He remembered his remark and regretted it. "Ah, the sharp tongue." He tilted his head to better examine it. "I think perhaps I missed that most of all."

Madeline gasped as he touched the tip of his tongue to hers, then slowly, sensually, drew it into his mouth. Now it was her moan of need that vibrated between them as their kiss deepened to dizzying proportions.

Ruffled yards of petticoats and skirts proved no barrier to his persistent fingers and hands, and Madeline lay back across his arm, the ends of her tawny hair nearly touching the floor, as he found the very center of her desires.

"Who is it?"

Madeline first noticed the rapping on the door when the captain growled the question against the sensitive skin of her neck.

"It's me, Cap'n. Oliver."

She felt the captain's muscled arm contract as he drew her to a sitting position. He took a ragged breath. "What do you want?"

"I've got somethin' for Miz Whitlock. Told her she could have an etchin' I did of the *Chesapeake*," Oliver called out.

Joshua's black eyes fixed on Madeline, and she offered him a sweet smile before insinuating her small hand between their bodies and caressing the throbbing staff of his sex.

"Vixen." The word was husked into her ear on a breathy whisper, but Joshua forced his voice to be firmer when he addressed his first mate. "Bring it to her tomorrow, would you, Oliver? Mrs. Whitlock is in bed."

Joshua and Madeline held their breath while they listened to Oliver's retreating steps; then, as one, they broke into laughter.

Joshua dug his fingers into her thick curls, and drew Madeline's face to his. "What are you trying to do to me, lady?" He chuckled, as the warmth of his breath spread across her cheek.

"Me?" Madeline's expression was as innocent as a babe's, yet her hand continued its fondling. "But, Captain, I think I've caught you in a tiny fib."

"A fib?" Joshua nuzzled into her hair and found the tender lobe of her ear.

"Yes." Madeline drew back until she could look him in the eye. "You told Oliver I was in bed, and any fool can see, I am not."

"An oversight on my part that I intend to remedy as soon as possible." Joshua's grin was long and lascivious, a promise of what was to come.

Chapter 21

"Ouch!"

Madeline raised her head and peered through the filmy web of her hair at the captain. "Is . . . something wrong?"

"I hit my arm against the damned headboard."

"Oh." She sighed and wriggled back down. "Either the bed is too small . . . or you are too . . . big."

"Too big am I?" Joshua raised his hips and watched in delight as she arched against him. "Is that what you think?"

"No . . ." Madeline's answer was a breathy gasp as his large hand covered her buttocks and pressed her down more firmly against his hard length.

They had made slow, sensual love during the night and finally had fallen asleep, replete and contented, in each other's arms. Lying beside him, nestled in the curve of his shoulder, her hand draped intimately across his broad chest, Madeline had slept better than she had in months. And so, when he'd awakened her at first light with the suggestion that he was becoming uncomfortable lying they were, she was perplexed and a little hurt. Was their new-found closeness to come to an end?

She soon found her worries to be unfounded. With an ease that bespoke his strength, the captain had lifted her body atop his. His discomfort, he had admitted, was caused by the longing ache in his groin, and the only cure, he assured her, was to be buried deep inside her moist heat.

That had been almost twenty minutes ago. Since then he had alternately brought them to the brink of euphoria and allowed their desires to cool to simple ecstasy by the skilled use of his mouth and hands.

"Mmm." Madeline moaned. "I . . . never thought . . . it could be like this."

Joshua slid his fingers between their bodies and began to stroke. "What? With you on top?"

"No." Madeline laughed and tugged on a clump of chest hair. Joshua winced, but more from the pleasurable sensation her laughter caused than from any pain caused by her playful pulling. "So wonderful. I never knew it could be so . . . wonderful."

As if to prove the truth of her words, Joshua's hips began twisting and thrusting in continuous rhythmic waves. His hands skimmed up her torso to tease the tips of her breasts, then strayed down again to tangle in the thatch of tight curls where their bodies melded into one.

Madeline braced her hands on his chest, over his hard nipples, and met his every upward thrust with a plunge of her own. Her motions became frenzied, the tantalizing torment almost unbearable. Then it was there, the sweet simultaneous release that sent them soaring. Madeline clutched at his shoulders as fiery spasms charged through her body.

The last shiver of his sizzling release was a fading vibration when Madeline collapsed on his sweat-slick chest. For a moment he was content for her to lie there, covering him with the warm blanket of her body. But then the intensity of his emotions became too great. Slowly, he drew her up, savoring the sensual glide of flesh against flesh. With infinite gentleness, he brushed aside dampened curls and gazed into her face. Her green eyes were still luminous from the impact of her climax,

321

and her lips were slightly parted and moist. He brushed his mouth against hers, then returned to drink more deeply of her. His breath ragged, Joshua tore his lips away and clutched her small body to his.

"My God, Maddie," he rasped into the fragrance of her hair. "What have you done to me?"

"Thank you." Madeline looked at the disk of etched ivory she held in her hands and then back at its creator. When she had encountered the first mate on deck as she was taking her morning stroll, he had given her the present he'd promised her. "Oh, Oliver, it's so lovely. I shall treasure it always."

At her words a rosy pink glow swept over the first mate, to the crown of his bald head. "It really ain't much."

"Nonsense." Madeline ran her finger around the edge of the palm-sized oval. "You've captured the *Chesapeake* perfectly. When I look at this, it won't matter where I am or what I'm doing, I'll be able to hear the breeze singing in the sails. And I'll see the endless blue of sea and sky, smell the tangy salt air." *Feel the strong, muscular arms of my captain holding me close.*

Madeline swallowed back the tears that threatened at that thought. "Oliver, you have given me more than you can imagine." She leaned forward and kissed the first mate's grizzly cheek, the gesture bringing forth a fresh and much brighter surge of color in him.

"What's this?" a deep voice sang out in mock outrage. "I leave my wife to her own devices for half a morning, and I find her busy enticing my men."

Madeline, her eyes shaded by her hand, tilted her head to gaze into the laughing eyes of her husband.

"Aw, Cap'n, I wouldn't be too hard on her. Ya know none of the ladies can resist me." Oliver's snaggled teeth flashed in a smile. "'Sides, I likes ya too much, Cap'n, to be stealin' your woman from ya."

"Well, that's a relief." Joshua gave his first mate a playful slap on the back.

He felt in fine form. The sparkling rays of the sun had transformed the sea into a glittering bed of sapphires; the glorious wind that filled the *Chesapeake*'s sails had a definite easterly bent to it; and, of course, there was last night. Even the nagging fear that the woman standing at his side had cast a bewitching spell on him could not dampen his spirits. If what had happened to him in their cabin was any evidence of her magic, he'd be a willing subject.

Never had he known a desire so great or a fulfillment so complete. "Wonderful" she had called it. Joshua glanced down at his wife. Had she any idea that it was she who'd made it so?

"Oliver gave me this likeness of the *Chesapeake*," Madeline said, conscious of the spell his eyes were casting upon her and unwilling to succumb to it in full view of the crew of privateers.

"Oh, is this what you brought by last evening, Oliver?" Joshua examined the piece of ivory Madeline held up to him.

"Yeah, when Miz Whitlock was in bed."

"Asleep." Madeline blurted out the word without thinking. Her memory of what she had done in bed with the captain had been so strong, she was certain the first mate could read her mind. Suddenly and with startling clarity, she realized her outburst had only served to make her position worse. Both men were staring at her with amused twinkles in their eyes, and she was sure her face was as red as a hibiscus blossom. "I was asleep," she mumbled again, as if repeating it often enough would convince them.

"She was very tired." Madeline couldn't tell whether the captain meant to substantiate her claim or to tease her. In either case, what he said next helped to alleviate her embarrassment by taking the focus of attention from her. "May I see the likeness, Maddie?"

She didn't even look his way as he took the oval from her, but that didn't keep a razor-fine prickle of desire from traveling down her spine at the touch of his hand.

"Excellent workmanship, Oliver. All your etchings are superb. Yet I think this might be your best."

The captain's words, as well as Oliver's, seemed to fade until they became no more than a blending of murmurs as Madeline stared out to sea and pretended she'd disappeared.

"He's gone." The warmth of the captain's hand on her shoulder brought her back from self-imposed exile.

She looked around to see that they were indeed alone. "Oh, I wanted to thank him again for his present."

"He knows how much you like it. Besides, it's not as if you won't see him again."

As the truth of this hit her, Madeline felt the heat of another blush warm her cheeks. Joshua's low chuckle only made them brighter.

"Don't be embarrassed, Maddie. Most married people often do what we did last night."

"Well, we didn't."

"You're right." His large hands squeezed her shoulders and pulled her back against the solid wall of his chest. "More fools we."

His words, spoken softly into her ear, rang through Madeline's head. Had they been fools to waste so much of the time they had together? Or was she now playing the fool? Nothing had really changed between them. Oh, physically it had. She now knew he desired her. The hands that caressed her arms from shoulder to elbow were proof enough of that. But there had been no words of love or commitment, no indication that he was beset by even half the need that consumed her.

When he left her in Baltimore, for he'd never said he wouldn't, he would probably miss the warmth of her in his bed, but what of his heart? Would it ache, nay break, as hers did even now at the very thought of their separation? Might it not have been better never to have known the wonder of his touch than to have it linger forever only as a memory?

"Maddie."

"Mmm." The pressure of his hands was stronger now, and she found her pulse pounding in counterpoint to the rhythm of his fingers.

"You forgot your bonnet."

"I did?" She reached up as if to check, her fingers touching her husband's chin which was resting on the top of her head.

Joshua brushed a kiss across her finger, biting it gently before releasing it.

"Perhaps we should go to the cabin and get you one before the sun burns you to a crisp."

How could he accuse the sun of burning her when it was his very presence that set her blood aboil? How was she to fight it? "Now? But—"

"Come with me, Maddie." When he turned her toward him, she knew what his slow, sensual words had only implied. The lustful gleam in his eye was unmistakable. It was also impossible for her to resist. Knowing in her heart that it was just going to make the inevitable that much harder to face, yet unable to help herself, Madeline slipped her hand into his and followed him below.

Much later she stood on the quarterdeck, her woven-straw sun bonnet held firmly in place by a wide turquoise blue ribbon.

"Isn't it better with the hat on?"

Madeline looked across the deck to where her husband stood, his large hands resting casually on the wheel. "A lot you care."

"Why, Maddie, your remark cuts me to the quick." He grinned at her, and she smiled back at him as she leaned against the bulwark. "Wasn't it I who insisted we go below so you could get it?"

"My hat?"

His grin broadened. "What else?"

"What else, indeed. If I hadn't remembered it moments before we left the cabin, I'd be up here bareheaded again."

"Well, I may have been momentarily distracted from my goal by"—he hesitated and let his decidedly wicked gaze rake over her—"other things."

Madeline laughed and turned toward the stern, as much to protect herself from her thoughts as to let the breeze cool her heated cheeks. It was so easy to laugh with him. Almost as easy as allowing him to distract her from getting her hat. Of course they both knew he had done that long before he'd lifted her and pressed her against the inside of the cabin door. Making no pretext of finding her bonnet, he had yanked up her skirts and had wrapped her legs around his hips. And she had not thought about her bonnet as she'd fumbled with the buttons of his breeches, allowing his manhood to spill forth, then slide inside her.

Their coupling had been natural, heated, and exquisitely passionate. Madeline's arms had twined about his neck and her lips had rained breathless little kisses over his throat and face and finally had come to rest on the moist heat of his mouth.

It was amazing to Madeline that such wild, uncontrollable excitement could be ignited so quickly. The way his hands had clutched and kneaded the sensitive flesh of her buttocks, moving her rhythmically over and around his straining staff brought her rapidly to the brink of ecstasy, though it had been mere hours since they had made love in the dim light of early morning.

The captain must have wondered at this quick reawakening of desire, too, for when he'd brought her back above, he'd positioned her on the far side of the deck from his post. Then he had run his finger down the curve of her jaw and had whispered in a low, husky voice. "I enjoy the pleasure of your company, little Maddie, but please come no closer to the wheel than you are, else I shall get nothing accomplished today except dragging you to our cabin."

She had blushed and promised to stay put, and he had laughed at her solemn manner and tweaked the end of her nose before taking over the helm from the coxswain.

Madeline tried to gather her errant thoughts. Since the night of the storm, it seemed she had spent the majority of her hours either making love with the captain or thinking about it. It was time she set her mind on something else.

"Captain?"

He turned and smiled at her, and she felt her newfound resolve weaken. Deliberately, she set her gaze on a spot of sail above his head.

"Oliver told me you have refused to attack any French merchant ships since we left Jamaica."

"He did, did he?" Joshua turned the wheel a tad to starboard. "I suppose he also told you why."

"Well, yes, as a matter of fact, he said it was because of me." Madeline broke her promise by moving closer to him.

He said nothing and stared straight ahead, yet he was fully aware that she was moving up behind him. He was not the least surprised when she stepped around the wheel and faced him.

"Is it true?"

"It's true," Joshua admitted. "Though to be honest, very few have crossed our bow."

"And you've steered clear of those that have?"

"I've gone out of my way to avoid any confrontation, if that's what you're asking."

"How do the men feel about this . . . this policy of yours?"

It was clear he didn't like anyone questioning his orders. "The *Chesapeake* is my vessel, and I'm her captain. Any and all decisions made concerning her are mine alone to make."

"I see." When she started to turn away, Joshua reached out with one hand to grasp her arm. He really hadn't meant to sound that highhanded.

"Why should it matter to you?"

"It wasn't of myself I was thinking." Madeline stood still and he released her arm. "I was merely concerned about your crew. If there is to be no plundering, how will they earn their hire?" It had been about three weeks so far and promised to be at least another before they made Baltimore. And that still didn't take them to the fertile shipping lanes of the North Atlantic.

"They get paid."

"But how?"

"Dammit, Maddie, you ask more questions than anyone I ever knew, except maybe Oliver. No wonder you two get along so well."

She glared at him. So much for his being unable to resist her charm.

"I shall pay them from my share of our last trip. Are you satisfied?"

Even though Madeline had suspected that was the case, she couldn't suppress her surprise at actually hearing it. "But how can you do that? It must be costing you a fortune. I truly don't mind if you attack a few merchant ships along the way."

"How magnanimous of you, Maddie. But you see, I do mind. Exposing you to danger is not something I relish. Besides, this little venture is not depleting my funds." His voice softened, and a smile tugged at the corners of his generous mouth. "Did you think you had married a poor man?"

"I didn't know."

"Rest assured, you did not."

In reality, Madeline had not thought him a pauper, but his last words implied more wealth than she had ever credited him with having.

"My mother was very rich in her own right. Her family was from England and, though they didn't live in the Colonies, owned several large tobacco plantations. She was visiting, on a tour of the families holdings actually, when she met my father. They married, much against her parents' wishes, and she stayed in Baltimore."

"It sounds like my father and mother," Madeline interjected.

"A bit," Joshua conceded. "But my father was a bitter man. Oh, I think he loved my mother, in his way. However, long before she died, I'm certain she regretted her decision to stay in Maryland. She might have left him and returned to England, had her parents not died. There was no one else."

"But what of you and your brother?"

"My mother didn't have much patience with us. Besides, I was at sea from the time I was old enough to sign on one of my father's vessels."

Madeline's heart went out to the young boy raised without a mother's or father's loving hand. Some of her sympathy must have shown in her eyes because he shook his head.

"Please don't feel sorry for me. That was certainly not my intent when I began this little family history."

"For the most part I had a very happy childhood. Being at sea was my wish as well as my father's. Captain Greenhow of the *Mary Patricia*—that's the schooner I was on—was a kind and scholarly man who probably taught me more than I would have learned from tutors. Of course, Oliver took me under his wing, so to speak. And don't forget, I *was* the owner's son."

"But what about a home?"

"Oh, I had that. The *Mary Patricia* was not a large schooner, just over twenty tons, so we normally confined our business to the bay and coastwise trade. I was often at home." He paused, and Madeline guessed that his time in Baltimore was far less pleasant than that spent at sea. "Nat and I were . . . very close."

Madeline wanted to reach out to him, to comfort him in some way; yet she hesitated. Since last night she had been secretly wishing they would never reach Baltimore. Now she saw how selfish that had been. It was obvious he missed his brother terribly.

Joshua shook his head as if clearing it of memories that had dogged him. His smile was self-effacing. "I seem to have gotten off the track. What I meant to explain to you was about the money. My mother must have cared for Nat and me—or perhaps she just did it to spite my father. But for whatever reason, when she died, her will called for her property and wealth to be split evenly between Nathaniel and me. Nat was younger and, against my advice, gave most of his inheritance to my father."

"But you did not."

"Nay. He wanted me to. But by that time I was a grown man, I had no desire to settle in Baltimore—another of his demands. I kept the money, had the *Chesapeake* built, and invested the rest."

"So, that's why you have money?" Madeline had listened to his story with great interest, but somehow she felt there was more to it than she was hearing. She thought of the tale her father had told her about the captain's aunt, and wondered if he knew.

He grinned that rakish smile of his. "That, and the fact that privateering can be a very lucrative business."

"But dangerous?"

"At times." He shrugged his broad shoulders.

Soon after their conversation, one of the able-bodied seamen came to relieve her husband at the helm. The captain offered to take her with him as he performed his other duties, but Madeline pleaded fatigue and retired to the cabin. She had become accustomed to doing such chores as straightening the room and mending the captain's clothes.

And things had been happening so quickly between them that she needed time alone to think. The captain's story had fascinated her. His life had been so different from hers, so full of adventures that Madeline could barely imagine it. Yet in some ways, their experiences had been similar. Both had borne many responsibilities for a long time—she at Hopewell, he on the high seas.

What kind of father would force a boy to go to sea? Oh,

330

the captain had said it had been his choice, too, but was that a decision a child could make? And her husband had said his father had been bitter. Madeline thought of the tale her father had told her of the three partners. Were Justin's sister's death and Matthew Burke's deception to blame?

Madeline looked down at the petticoat in her hands and realized she'd been holding it for some time. With a shake of her head, she finished folding the soft linen material and stowed it in her sea chest. Ruminating about the captain's past was not going to do one thing to change her future. If anything, it tended to make it bleaker.

The captain obviously loved the sea. It had been a major part of his life since his boyhood. He had refused to give it up for his father, and it seemed unlikely he'd give it up for a woman he'd married only to fulfill a promise to a dying man. No matter how often and how ardently he desired her, Madeline didn't think lust a strong enough emotion to bind him to her.

Would she be able to live, loving him as she did, with the doled-out portions of time and affection he would allot her? Or would she be better off returning to Hopewell and living completely without him?

Madeline could not decide, and by dinnertime, tired of thinking about it, she was overwhelmingly glad to see her husband. He brought their repast himself and delighted her by playing cabin boy and serving the food.

"After all," he said, "I've had plenty of experience."

"And is this part of your experience, too?" Madeline laughingly pushed against his chest after he'd demanded and received an extremely sensual kiss as payment for dishing out her portion of sea pie.

He admitted, with a sparkle in his eye, that it really wasn't standard procedure, but declared that maybe, with a little more practice, he could make it so.

"To your chair, boy," she ordered in her best imitation of a captain's voice, but she softened the command by adding that with his expertise, kissing was not something he needed to practice.

"Just trying to sweeten the salt beef for you, madam," he explained with a roguish wink.

"As if anything could." Madeline answered his wink with a scowl. But she was forced to admit that whether it was the kiss or the company, the generous dish of meat, vegetables and pastry crust had never tasted better.

"And now for dessert." Joshua laughed as he pulled her onto his lap.

Madeline curled her arms around his neck and gave herself up to the pleasurable sensations he inspired.

"Mmm." He released her mouth and smacked his lips. "Better than Shrewsbury cake any day."

Lacing her fingers behind his neck and pulling back so she could look into his jovial face, she quipped, "You'd better not let Cook hear you say that. He thinks his cake the best thing around."

"Well, I did too," Joshua assured her, "before."

There was no need to ask before what, for he was already nudging her curls aside and nibbling the side of her neck. "Ah, Maddie." As he reached the apex of her shoulder, he let out a sigh. "You smell like roses and taste sweeter than any cake."

Madeline giggled. "Such praise. You shall surely turn my head."

"What!" He lowered his raven brows and burrowed his face between the gently rounded mounds of her breasts, tickling her until she convulsed with laughter. "Not content to be compared with Shrewsbury cake? Then shall I compare you to a sunset?"

With astonishing grace for someone his size, he stood up, letting her slide slowly down his body. After one more resounding kiss, he draped his arm around her shoulders and started to guide her above.

"We'll be heading through the capes soon," he explained as they made their way down the companionway toward the main hatch.

"Then we're almost to the bay?" Madeline tried not to

sound as defeated as she felt. But his own excitement was such that she needn't have worried that he'd notice any despondency in her.

"We are. Before I came below, I caught the scent of pine trees. One more week should find us walking along Charles Street in Baltimore."

"Is that where your brother lives?" She tried to be happy for him, but all she could think about was that he would soon leave her.

"Yes, in a fine brick house close to the harbor. You'll like it there, Maddie, and you'll like Nat, too." They were on deck now, watching the fading sun streak the sky with vivid colors.

"I'm certain I will." Would she like his brother? Would she even stay long enough to find out? There were times—like now, with his strong body pressed against her back and his fingers massaging her neck and shoulders—when Madeline felt she must stay. Seeing him only occasionally would be better than not seeing him at all, she'd tell herself.

But there were the dark moments when she thought of not knowing whether he was safe or not, of waiting months, even years, for some word from him. Then she thought the only solution was to make a clean break.

"You're very pensive." Joshua turned around and stared down at her.

"Am I? I'm sorry. I didn't mean to be." Madeline made her smile as cheerful as she could.

"Good. For now is no time to be glum. My noon sighting showed we shall strike the coast at the thirty-seventh parallel, and we have a good stiff easterly to carry us home. But just to make sure, we're going to check the sounding."

Madeline followed the captain forward to where a group of privateers had gathered.

"It's lookin' good, Cap'n. Should make landfall soon." Jamieson's remark greeted them as they joined the men.

333

"What was your last reading?"

"Ain't found bottom yet, but I reckon it will be soon. Take a gander at that sea."

Madeline didn't imagine the comment had been meant for her, but she looked out over the rail anyway. The ocean had changed. The deep-blue hue of the past weeks had mellowed into an off-shore green. While she watched, a branch, probably separated from its mother tree during a recent storm, floated by.

The captain, too, watched the changing face of the sea as if he were reading a book. "Let's take another sounding."

Madeline watched as Jamieson secured to the main chain a line which was marked at intervals by bits of leather and colored cloth. Then, swinging the cylindrical lead weight over his head, pendulum style, four times, he let go with a mighty heave. The lead flew out well ahead of the bow, and the attached line was taut by the time the *Chesapeake*'s aft sailed past it.

"We've found bottom." A cheer rang out among the tars at Jamieson's words.

"Well, haul her up, man, and let's see the nature of that bottom." Madeline noted that the captain was just as excited as his men. He reached over the side and dragged in the heavy lead. Carefully, he scraped from it bits of debris that had stuck to its tallow-primed base.

"Mud, sand, and oyster shells," he announced after a careful examination of the particles in his hand.

"We've hit her then, Cap'n."

"Aye, we have, lad. Fasten this lead to the mizzen-mast." The captain turned to Madeline. "He'll inscribe the fathom reading under it in chalk. If this wind holds we should be sighting Cape Henry by late tomorrow."

True to his word, it was late the following afternoon, just as the setting sun painted the sky with streaks of brilliant mauve and bright orange, that shouts of "Land, land" rang out. Madeline was on deck and found herself peering in the direction of all the pointing fingers with more enthusiasm than she felt.

"Won't be long now, eh, Madeline?" Joshua had come up behind her, and he gave her shoulders an affectionate squeeze. She had been thinking the same thing. Not long until he left her. Not long until she was compelled to make her decision. She forced a smile and turned about, intending to agree with him, but he had moved on down the deck.

"Hollings!" she heard him yell to the seaman who had first sighted the tiny spot of terra firma on the southern horizon. "Stop by my cabin after your watch, and I'll have a little something for you."

"Aye, aye, Cap'n," Hollings replied. "I ain't never one to disobey one of your orders."

This response brought an assortment of hoots and hollers from the crew on the deck, and by the look of it, just about every seaman who wasn't needed eslewhere was there.

"He'll be gettin' whiskey."

Madeline had watched the precedings with a combination of amusement and confusion. She hadn't noticed Oliver move up beside her, but she acknowledged his explanation with a grateful smile. "I was wondering."

"Yeah, thought ya might be. It's kinda a tradition, givin' the first person to sight the cape a bottle of whiskey."

After that, the sighting of land became commonplace. With more haste than Madeline wanted, the *Chesapeake* made her way up the great bay for which she was named.

With his ever-present Hoxton Chart in his hands, the captain pointed out landmarks to her as they skimmed by. They sailed past Hampton Roads, where the James met the bay, and the wide, lazy mouth of the York, Mobjack Bay.

"There's Windmill Point," he said later as they stood on deck. The long point of land at the mouth of the Rappahannock was dressed in all her spring finery, though there was a chill in the air. The winds of

Chesapeake Bay, whose most predictable characteristic was variability, had turned during the night. Now blowing from the northwest, they brought with them the tangy taste of life beyond the tropics. Last night, snuggled in her husband's arm, Madeline had barely noticed the chill, but today . . . She wrapped her knitted shawl more firmly about her shoulders.

"Cold?" Joshua had noticed the gesture, and he pulled her closer to the warmth of his body. "This won't last. We're too far into May for the breezes to make you shiver for long."

By the time they passed Tangier Island, opposite and just above the mouth of the Potomac, the wind had changed. Although it filled their sails, it had become a gentle reminder that summer would soon be upon the land.

They had left Virginia behind them. The virgin forests and rose brick plantation houses they now passed were in Maryland. Every hour, took them closer to their destination. Madeline tried to be happy for the captain, tried to pretend that her life would return to normal as soon as he left and she returned to Jamaica; but she knew it wasn't true.

Often, as she'd lain awake at night listening to his even, sonorous breathing, she had considered asking him to stay with her. Certainly, they could have a good life in Baltimore or even back at Hopewell, she reasoned. She seemed to make him happy; at least she tried. And even if he didn't love her as she loved him, she felt certain he cared for her.

But then, she would remember the reason he had married her. He had made it clear from the beginning that he had no real desire for a wife. He would enjoy her while she was handy, then return to the life he loved—a life at sea.

As much as she wanted to, Madeline couldn't find it in her heart to blame him for that. Her father had forced her on him. His agreement might have been spurred by a

336

guilty conscience, but they now knew even that was baseless.

She would try to view this time with him as he did. She'd relish it and let tomorrow take care of itself, she decided.

And she tried. But as the water lilies and waving cattails at the marshy mouth of the Patuxent River appeared off the bow, Madeline could no longer hide the distress she felt.

She had been watching an eagle circling, hanging almost motionless in the sky, over a swampy field of wild rice when she heard the captain approach. Sunlight reflected off the glistening white head and tail feather of the huge bird.

"You've hardly said two words all day."

Madeline closed her eyes, leaned back against the temporary comfort his long body offered, and said nothing.

"Is something wrong?" He bent down and with his chin, nudged some errant curls that had escaped her braid.

"No." She knew she should leave it at that, knew she'd regret saying more, but that didn't stop her. "I'm a little nervous about what will happen when we get to Baltimore."

"Why?"

"I don't know." She bit her lower lip, sorry now that she had opened up this topic to discussion. "Things will be different."

"How?"

Was he trying to play dumb? How could they be anything but different? They'd be apart? But she wouldn't tell him that.

"How long has it been since you've seen your brother?" Madeline hoped that would change the subject.

"Four years. Is that what you're worried about, my brother?"

"I'm not worried." Her tone was too defiant for her to be believed.

"Well, you certainly act as if you are. You've been like this for days, and the closer we get to Baltimore, the worse it gets."

"Well, maybe I don't act as excited as you do, but that doesn't mean I'm concerned about anything." His elation had been growing steadily as the Bermuda sloop sailed up the bay, and now Madeline was beginning to wonder at the reason for it. After all, if he had let four years go by without seeing his brother, why was he so anxious to see him now?

The warmth the captain had generated dissipated as he moved away from her, and Madeline silently chastised herself for her brittle words. Forearms resting on the rail, he studied the eagle as it swooped down toward its nest in a tall pine.

"Are you still angry about leaving Hopewell?" Joshua had hoped she'd come to realize the necessity for that move, but maybe he'd been wrong. Time away from Eli Creely and the threat of Bompar might have diminished their importance in her mind. He had never told her about finding the flour bags in the caves or about what Sau had told him. It didn't seem to matter, since he felt sure that would be taken care of by the time they returned. Why spoil her innocent memories of her home?

Madeline studied his strong profile. It surprised her that he seemed concerned because she might be upset about it . . . because she no longer was.

"No, I realize you had your reasons." A sudden inspiration came to her. Maybe after he visited with his brother, he would take her back to Hopewell. She realized the *Chesapeake* was a privateer, but just this once perhaps it could carry cargo to the islands so the trip would generate some revenue. Madeline felt certain that given more time she could make him love her. Then he might decide to stay with her in Jamaica. And if not? She sighed. At least she'd have another month with him.

"Captain?"

"Hmmm?" Joshua took a deep breath of the fragrant spring air and turned toward his wife. He had been glad to know it wasn't leaving Hopewell that had her upset.

"I was thinking. After you spend some time with your brother, do you suppose you could take me back?"

His back straightened, the momentary aura of contentment shattered. "You want me to take you back to Hopewell?"

"Yes." Madeline's voice broke on the words. Why was he so angry? Perhaps she should explain. "You see, I thought we could load a shipment of flour and—"

"Forget it!"

"What?" He really was angry. His bellowing had frightened a covey of ducks floating at the water's edge, and had turned the heads of several seamen.

"You heard me, I said forget it."

"But you told me you'd take me home." Did he care for her so little that he was going to break his word?

"And I will, when it's safe." Dammit, it *was* Hopewell. She just couldn't wait to get back there—and away from him.

"How do you know it isn't safe now?"

"Have you forgotten Bompar's fleet?"

"No, of course not." Oh, she hated it when he was patronizing. "But we made it through before."

"At what cost?"

How could she have forgotten? She thought of Cunningham's leg, and her eyes—moments ago they had sparkled with anger—slowly closed.

"You see, Maddie, there's more to be considered here than your all-fired determination to be reunited with Hopewell."

"You're right, of course."

Joshua almost put his arms around her then; she looked so shaken. The fresh spattering of freckles that the sun had coaxed out on her nose appeared more

339

prominent as color left her face. But he could not forget her request. She wanted to go *home*. How could he have been so stupid as to believe that, just because she was in his bed, she wished to stay in his life? He'd even told Oliver they were going to stay in Baltimore for a while to have the *Chesapeake* careened and refitted at the same West River shipyard where she'd been built.

Hell, he'd even considered staying here permanently. He had thought he could help Nat get the family shipping business back on its feet, and later they'd go back to Jamaica and make Hopewell a sugar plantation of which she could be proud.

The challenge had excited him, but not as much as the thought of being with his wife. What a fool he'd been to confuse her natural human desires for love. Feeling it himself, he decided, was no guarantee he could recognize it in someone else.

That evening he sent word to her that he was taking the night watch. He was being an ass, he told himself over and over as he walked the quarterdeck. It wasn't as if she had lied or changed her feelings. She had never pretended that theirs was anything but a marriage of convenience, so why was he so angry? Was it her fault that he had changed—that he had fallen in love with her?

"An ass," he mumbled to himself, but he stayed for the midwatch, too.

The following night, when he entered the cabin Madeline tried to control her excitement. The night before had been awful. She had lain awake counting the bells, wishing he'd come, knowing he wouldn't.

This is the way it will be when he's gone, she had told herself—a lonely bed, a lonely life. Arguing that she would forget him didn't help.

When he hadn't come below for dinner earlier, she'd thought he meant to stay away for good. Oliver had told her that they'd make Baltimore Town sometime late tomorrow. But here he was, standing before her, handsome and splendid and achingly close.

Madeline started to speak, then stopped herself. Somehow her words often came out wrong when she was around him. They came out all jumbled and mixed up. When she'd wanted to say "I love you. Please stay with me," it had come out "Take me back to Hopewell."

She moved toward him. *No words tonight*. Rising on tiptoe, Madeline stretched her arms around his neck. *No words*. She tugged gently till he lowered his lips to hers. *No words*.

Chapter 22

Baltimore Town, on the fall line of the Patapsco River, was only thirty years old that June when the *Chesapeake* docked in her harbor. Despite her tender age, the burg was fast becoming a leading center of trade, exporting large quantities of the flour ground at nearby Jones's Falls from the wheat grown in Maryland's upcountry and Pennsylvania. Little remained of the town perimeter in the early 1750s. Several hard winters had hastened the logs disappearance; local residents apparently deeming heat more important than keeping the animals within or the Indians without Baltimore's limits.

But Madeline could see little evidence of any of these things as she walked down Water Street, clutching her shawl against the unseasonable chill in the night air.

"I don't understand why we just didn't wait till morning." She whispered her words, unwilling to disturb the late-night silence any more than necessary, but she was annoyed. She had hoped for one more night with the captain aboard the *Chesapeake* before she lost her husband to his brother.

"It can come as no surprise to you that I'm anxious to be home."

"No." Madeline gave a little skip in order to catch up with his long strides. He must have noticed the attempt, for he slowed his pace and offered her his right arm. But they continued walking through the ever-advancing puddle of light spilling from the lantern he held in his left hand.

They were finally here, and she had been right. Madeline was not the least surprised by his haste. Ever since they'd headed up the Patapsco, he had made no attempt to hide his pleasure that the voyage was nearing its end.

They had sailed into the harbor that night, guided only by the light of the moon and the captain's uncanny abilities. Now, instead of waiting for a presentable time to go calling, they were trudging down a deserted street lined with wooden shops and dark houses. A hoot owl's plaintive cry drove Madeline to clutch the captain's strong arm.

" 'Tis not much further," he reassured her.

Angry that the owl had frightened her, and that he had noticed, Madeline forced herself to pull away. As his good humor had increased, hers had dwindled even more. Oh, she had kept her feelings carefully hidden—this time—and had made every attempt to be pleasant company, but it had been a strain.

Many times she had wanted to grab him and cry out "Please don't leave me" or "Take me with you. I don't care if you are a privateer—just let me be able to know that you're save." But of course, she hadn't. Instead, she had laughed at his quips or had responded with witty remarks when she could, and she'd made love with all the passion her pent-up emotion and his lusty nature brought forth.

"He's probably asleep, you know."

"No doubt." As if to prove his words, the captain ushered her to the right along a wide brick walkway and then stopped before a house whose windows were devoid of even the faintest hint of candle glow. "Here we are," he stated.

Aided by the lantern he held aloft, Madeline peered through the darkness for her first glimpse of her husband's home. It appeared to be made of mortar and brick and, if the doorway was any indication, was constructed along the Georgian lines. The clouds that had been gathering since they'd landed momentarily broke to allow the moonlight to aid Madeline in her inspection. The house was large—she could tell that now—with a double row of windows that gleamed as darkly as the captain's eyes. As she looked at this dwelling, gilded by silvery light, a chill that had naught to do with the damp air or the rising wind ran through Madeline.

"Are you going to awaken Nathaniel?" She had been guided up the four steps to the front stoop by her husband and was now watching him reach into his frock-coat pocket.

"Good Lord, no." Joshua chuckled as he extracted a key and fitted it into the lock. "My brother is a bear if awakened after he's taken to his bed."

The door creaked open, and Madeline pulled her shawl more tightly around her. The light from the lantern splashed inside, revealing a cavernous central hall.

"If you didn't plan to wake your brother, why did we come?" She tried not to conceal the apprehension that was settling over her. Maybe it was the late hour or the wind that brushed limbs against the windows or the echo of her own voice, but the house seemed so empty. Madeline almost wished she'd been left behind on the *Chesapeake*.

Joshua lit the candle he found on the gateleg table in the hall and then beckoned her to follow him up the broad staircase. He had a wide grin on his face, and appeared oblivious to Madeline's discomfort. She glanced around the entranceway again, then chastised herself for her silliness. It was just a dark house with all its inhabitants asleep, nothing more.

"Come on. There's something I want you to see."

When Madeline joined him on the steps he draped an arm around her shoulders, letting his thumb skim idly

344

back and forth across the crest of her breast, and her feeling that things were not quite right deserted her.

"I'll show you why we came tonight." The words were whispered against her brow as he touched his lips to her forehead.

Their footfalls were muffled by a long, Turkish runner as they passed several closed doors.

"That's Nat's room." Joshua gestured to a door across the hall before opening another. "And this is mine."

Damp, musty air assaulted their nostrils as the door to Joshua's room swung open. "They weren't expecting me, so I suppose no one has aired it out for a while."

That was an understatement. Even in the dim light afforded by the candle the captain held, it was obvious that the room had been deprived of more than an airing, and for quite a long time. Cobwebs laced the shadows and an accumulation of dust blanketed the floor, the bureau, and the curved posts of the large, tester bed.

"Well, what do you think?" Joshua set the brass candlestick on the bedside table, then smiled down at her in anticipation.

Madeline glanced around the room again. There was no denying, even in its present state, that it was extremely handsome. Heavy brocaded curtains that matched the bed hangings bracketed each window. The walls were painted in what appeared to be a light gold shade, and were wainscoted beneath a sturdy chair rail. The furnishings seemed well made and, from what she could tell, were imported from the mother country. "Your room is very nice." Madeline realized the statement sounded inane, but she really didn't know what else to say.

His amused chuckle ruffled her hair as he came up behind her. Cradling her shoulders with his warm hands, he bent and whispered in her ear. "'Twas not the room I was referring to, little Maddie, but the bed."

Tingles of anticipation ran down her spine.

"I thought perhaps you would enjoy . . . ah . . . sleeping in something other than a tiny bunk with wooden sides."

"Sleeping?" Madeline turned into his arms and nuzzled her cheek against the satin of his waistcoat. "Is that what you had in mind?"

Madeline could hear the low rumble of laughter deep in his wide chest. "Eventually" was all he said before his lips melded with hers.

Her heart sang. For tonight, at least, he was hers. He had brought her here with the idea of loving, not leaving, her—tonight.

Her hands stole up around his neck, burrowing into the silky curls there. Tonight, Madeline vowed to herself, she'd show him what he would forfeit when he left her. But even as she felt his strong arms lift her up against the hard length of his body, she knew she would be showing herself as well.

"Your dress," he husked against the tender flesh of her neck. "Does it open down the front or the back?"

"The back." No sooner had she breathed the words than his nimble fingers were working their way down a row of buttons. With her feet, if not her fancies, back on the ground, Madeline watched him slip the rose silk down over her shoulders. Soon it landed on the dusty floor beside her forgotten shawl.

Her shift was sheer and lacy. Madeline had worn it in the hope of seeing exactly the expression it brought to the captain's handsome face.

His black eyes, bright with desire, sought her face and then roved down the stem of her neck before leisurely perusing the soft mounds her stays had pushed into prominence. The heat of his gaze caused her dusky pink nipples to pout and thrust forward against the gossamer material of the shift.

"So pretty," he murmured as he let a lone, lazy finger follow the path his eyes had blazed.

It was exquisite—excruciating—watching his sun-darkened digit skim slowly across the pale trembling of her breast. But when the tip of his finger grazed the achingly hard crown, she lost the ability to follow his progress.

Her head fell back, her long ropelike plait of hair bouncing sensually against her buttocks, and a low moan vibrated from deep within her. As if to capture the sound, his lips caressed her exposed neck, while his finger continued to work its magic. "You like that, Maddie." There was no question in his voice.

"Mmmm." Denying it was impossible with the blatant proof of her body's response displayed before him. But his words brought some focus to the hazy recesses of her mind.

She'd never questioned what he could do to her with a touch, a glance. Now she needed to remind him of what she could do to him, for him.

Madeline stepped back and let her hands drift suggestively down his body. Joshua seemed a little surprised, but she gave him a smile she hoped was flirtatious and reached for her braid. The captain liked her hair—he'd told her so often enough—and tonight he was going to get everything he liked. Slowly she released the silken curls, finger-combing the tangles, watching him from beneath her thick lashes.

Joshua shifted restlessly. He didn't know exactly why she had set him away, but her movements were driving him insane. In shift and stays, he found Madeline almost as appealing as when she was nude. And her fingers slid so sensually through her hair. . . .

He moved to close the space between them, but before he could get a good handhold on her tawny curls, her small hands captured the edges of his jacket and, standing on tiptoe, she began to ease it down over his shoulders.

"Isn't it awfully warm for a jacket, Captain?"

Warm? He was burning, but Joshua didn't think the temperature of the room to blame.

When the blue, lozenge silk jacket lay amid a swirl of

dust motes, beside the rose silk gown and shawl, she began unfastening the silver buttons of his waistcoat. Joshua's breath caught in his throat as her slender fingers inched toward the protruding ridge that was poorly disguised by the fall-front placket of his breeches. Finally the last button was undone, and Joshua felt his hard member pulsate as her hands teased the bottom points of his waistcoat before slipping that, too, off his shoulders.

She was undressing him! With slow seductive movements, she was returning the favor he had bestowed upon her countless times over the course of their voyage.

"Oh, Maddie," he moaned when, as she removed his shirt, she trailed her short, rounded nails up through the springy curls of his chest hair and across the nubby granite of his nipples.

Madeline let the snowy white linen drift from her fingertips, while her gaze caressed the naked splendor of his upper body. Though the idea of undressing him had, at first, made her quail, she now knew her boldness had been well taken. And his masculine beauty was breathtaking. A fine sheen of perspiration gilded the mountains and plains of his powerful arms and shoulders, while, hanging at his sides, the captain's hands clenched spasmodically, contracting his muscles and making the glistening bronzed skin of his chest ripple. Madeline's eyes lowered to follow the gradually narrowing band of hair that arrowed toward his pants. There was more of him to uncover.

Brazen fingers reached out to pluck at his breeches, but apparently the captain had reached the limit of his endurance. He grabbed a tentative hand and pressed it against his hard staff. Madeline glanced at his face and, in the passionate heat of his gaze, read his desire. Instinctively, she curved her palm around his throbbing warmth and rubbed. Her pulse was pounding in her ears and something—could it be the stays?—was preventing her from taking a deep breath.

348

His fevered moan registered in her brain moments before he propelled them both back across the bed.

"Ah-choo!" Madeline turned her head away from the counterpane as swirls of dust, freed by their bodies bouncing onto the mattress, danced about them.

"Oh . . . no." She sneezed again, more violently this time, and struggled to extract her hands from between their bodies.

"Are you all right?" Joshua rose and unceremoniously pulled her to her feet.

Madeline nodded vigorously while wiping her streaming eyes with the back of her hand. "It's just that dust sometimes makes me ah—ah—"

"Sneeze." Joshua said as she aptly demonstrated her distress.

"Yes." Madeline didn't know whether tears were pouring from her eyes because of the dust or her embarrassment. She had wanted this night to be so perfect.

"Maybe we should go back to the *Chesapeake*," Joshua offered.

"No." She muffled her next sneeze in the handkerchief he had found in the pocket of his coat. "It doesn't usually last long. See?" She wiped her nose and tentatively looked up into his concerned face.

It was true; her sneezing had subsided.

"But, Maddie, if you can't lie on the bed without sneezing, where are we going to . . . sleep? Mrs. Jenkins, the housekeeper, is old, and I doubt any of the other rooms, except Nat's, are much cleaner than this."

Madeline looked down at the bed. Except for the gold brocade counterpane, it looked so inviting, and she longed to cuddle into its soft depths with the captain. An idea, borne of desperation, sparked in her brain. "'Tis only the covering that's dusty."

The captain must have been arriving at the same conclusion because, without further explanation, he bundled her to the far corner of the room. Facing her

349

toward the wall as if she were a recalcitrant child, he admonished her to stay put. "And Maddie"—he peeked around her hair and brushed his lips across the soft curve of her cheek—"try not to breath."

Hardly an easy order to follow, Madeline decided as she listened while he hurriedly crossed the room. She balled up the handkerchief and used the fine linen to filter her air.

The captain's touch on her arm gave her a start, and she realized she'd become quite intoxicated by the musky smell of him that permeated his handkerchief.

"I think this should work." He sounded quite pleased with his handiwork.

Madeline hazarded a glance over her shoulder. He had removed the heavy-brocaded bed covering, and the offending material, balled into an ignominious heap, lay in the opposite corner of the room. The sheets were folded back enticingly, and upon seeing them, Madeline experienced a strong desire to rumple their pristine smoothness.

Tentatively, she lowered the handkerchief and approached the bed.

"The blanket is comparatively clean," Joshua explained. "I found it in the clothespress."

Madeline eased herself onto the mattress and bounced ever so slightly. No dust, no sneezing. She bounced a little harder, remembering the vigorous way the captain made love. Still nothing. When she looked up at him in satisfaction, it was to find his eyes dancing merrily.

"Shall we give it a try?"

Much later, as they lay entwined and replete on the great feather mattress, Joshua nuzzled the side of her neck. "How do you feel?"

Madeline's body arched, and she ran a hand over the tightly muscled rises of his buttocks. "Mmmm, wonderful."

Joshua raised up on an elbow, a devilish twinkle gleaming in his eyes. "I meant, have you recovered from

350

your bout of sneezing?"

An embarrassed flush swept through her, but she tried to ignore it and, in her haughtiest voice, forced out a lie. "That was what I meant. I'm quite recovered, Captain."

"Are you now?" He grinned down at her, and lifting a lock of her hair, brushed the curling ends across the rosy bloom of her breasts. They responded prettily.

"Maddie?"

"Hmmm?" The light feathering strokes were now traveling across her stomach.

"Why do you call me that?" His voice had lost much of its seductive timbre, though he still played over her body with silken strands of her hair.

"What? Captain?"

Madeline watched as his head, cradled in the palm of his hand, nodded agreement. "Well, I don't really know. It's what everybody calls you." She was well aware that this wasn't the reason. She had begun thinking of him as the captain when she'd hated him. It had been a way of expressing her contempt, and even though that had long since been replaced by a deep and abiding love, the name had stuck.

"I wish you'd use my given name."

"All right." Her hair, which reached only to her waist, had been replaced by his fingers as he ventured to explore lower, and Madeline was feeling very agreeable.

"Say it." His fingers raked through the tight curls at the apex of her thighs, then slid fleetingly across the core of her femininity.

"Joshua."

The word escaped on a pent-up breath of air, and he felt its whisper-soft caress as he bent closer to her mouth.

"Again." His fingers stroked.

"Joshua . . . Joshua . . . Josh—"

Madeline woke, as she often did these days, to the

351

sound of her husband's tuneless whistling. "Joshua?" She brushed hair out of her face and sat up.

"Good morning." He stopped buttoning his pants to give his wife an admiring grin. Fresh from the arms of Morpheus, her hair tangling wildly about her face, the sheet caught precariously on the swell of her breasts, she made an adorable sight. "I didn't mean to wake you."

"You didn't. I think it was the sunshine. I'd forgotten what it was like to have real windows." Madeline thought her husband probably felt the same, for evidently he had opened the curtains wide upon rising.

"I'm going to talk to Nat and see about getting some water. I imagine you wouldn't be opposed to a bath."

"A bath?" Madeline cooed in her best imitation of her cousin Abigail's flirtatious drawl. "Why, sir, are you trying to turn my head?"

Joshua chuckled. "Perhaps." He plucked his shirt off the floor and shook out the dust. "I'll send someone to fetch our trunks. Till they arrive, can you make do with yesterday's dress?"

Madeline glanced at the pink satin heap on the floor, but her mind was on his words. He had said "our trunks." Maybe he wasn't going to leave Baltimore Town immediately.

Joshua tucked his shirttail into his breeches and finger-combed his unruly locks. "Damn, I'm anxious to see that brother of mine."

"Well, run along then." The thought that he might be staying, for a while at least, coupled with memories of the past night had greatly buoyed Madeline's spirits.

After a kiss that Madeline guessed had lasted a little longer than her husband had originally intended, Joshua left the room. A faint musty odor assailed her nostrils as she nestled back into the sheets. It reminded her of the condition of the room. It really was in need of a thorough cleaning. Even the windows were grimy. She had just decided that Nathaniel could use a wife to assume some of the housekeeping duties when the bedroom door burst open.

"He's not here!"

Joshua was almost frantic, and it took a moment before the reason for his upset sank into Madeline's mind. "Maybe he's gone for the day . . . visiting or—"

"No, dammit. He's not here. He hasn't been here since I left for Jamaica."

"Well, Joshua, I'm sure he's . . ." Madeline let the words fade off. She really had no idea why his wayward brother wasn't here, but at the moment she certainly wished he were. She'd love to shake some sense into Nat for causing the captain—Joshua—so much anguish. Right now her husband was buttoning up the waistcoat he had opted not to don earlier. His movements were so hurried that Madeline was surprised any of the buttons remained attached to the fabric.

He also seemed to have forgotten she was in the room.

"Where are you going?" She was starting to feel a little frantic herself as he grabbed up his coat and headed for the door. Dressed as she was, in nothing, Madeline was averse to jumping from the bed to follow him, but for a moment she thought that was her only alternative. Fortunately, her modesty was preserved when, with one hand on the doorknob, the captain appeared to remember her presence and glanced over his shoulder. "I'm going down to the harbor to see what I can discover there." He turned the knob. "Oh, Mrs. Jenkins is bringing some water. I'm afraid not enough for a bath." Joshua paused and sighed. "She's old," he offered by way of explanation. "But I'll send someone back with your trunk."

Your trunk? Within ten minutes "our trunks" had become "your trunk." Madeline forgot modesty. In desperation, she threw back the sheets and leaped from the bed. The morning air was chill, and the floor her bare feet touched, was downright cold; but she didn't notice as she threw herself at the captain. "You are coming back?"

What was meant as a command came out a question,

and Madeline grabbed handfuls of silk jacket, willing him to answer in the affirmative.

Surprised by her behavior, Joshua slowly wrapped his arms around her. When he did, he realized she was trembling. "You're cold. Get back under the covers."

"No." Madeline burrowed further into his warmth.

"Maddie." The word was drawn out and his tone hinted at exasperation, but his arms enfolded her against him. "I have to go, honey, and I don't think it would be a good idea for me to drag you along like this—though I'm certain most of the men down at the harbor would disagree."

Despite herself, Madeline started to laugh at picturing the ridiculous sight they would present. He, clothed to perfection in his best silk jacket, his matching breeches thrust into gleaming black boots, and she wrapped only in him.

He was laughing, too. Madeline could feel vibrations rumbling through his chest, and she pressed her cheek to them.

"Now are you going to let me go alone, or must I drag you naked through the streets?"

Her response to this was to press closer.

"Maddie. I'm only going down to the harbor. I'll be back soon." If she didn't let go of him, and soon, Joshua knew it would be quite a while before he made it out of this room. Even now, his resolve to take some kind of immediate action concerning Nathaniel was wavering because of the woman molded intimately against him.

"You are coming back then?"

She moved away, and Joshua breathed a premature sigh of relief. Now he could see her, and the dusky pink nipples peeking through tangles of honey-colored hair were arousing.

"Yes, I'm coming back. Did you think I was just going to sail off into the sunset? That would be rather difficult to do at this time of day."

Realizing he was teasing her, Madeline forced a smile.

"No, I didn't think that." But of course, she had. Why else would she be standing about in the nude, clutching her husband's coat? She let go of it.

After he left, Madeline just had time to straighten the clothes she had discarded the night before and climb back between the sheets before Mrs. Jenkins brought the water. As she washed and dressed, she examined her surroundings and decided that regardless of the length of time she and the captain might spend in them, the place needed a thorough cleaning.

She found Mrs. Jenkins in the kitchen, pouring wate. into a china teapot. One look at the way the housekeeper struggled to lift the iron kettle confirmed Madeline's earlier assessment that this woman would be very little help on the project she had in mind.

"I thought you'd be liking some tea, mum," Mrs. Jenkins said as her gray head bobbed, jiggling her mobcap.

"Thank you." Madeline glanced around the room she'd just entered and found it in need of a scrubbing. "Do you live here alone, Mrs. Jenkins?"

"Since the old gentleman died and Mister Nat left, yes, mum."

"And how long has that been?" Madeline took a sip of her tea. Since she had seen the frantic expression on Joshua's face that morning, she had been wondering about this.

"'Bout three months now, I suppose."

Three months. Madeline took another sip of tea. That didn't seem an overly long time for someone to be on a voyage. Certainly not long enough to merit the kind of intensive search Joshua seemed bent on conducting. Oh, she knew Nathaniel had left a letter implying he'd gone off in search of pirates, but wasn't it possible that he was simply on an adventure and would return home when he had satisfied his wanderlust? Perhaps when Joshua came back she would mention this possibility. After all, her husband hadn't seen his brother in four years—a long

355

time. And people do change. . . .

"More tea, mum?"

The housekeeper's words made Madeline aware that she had been staring out the window while holding an empty teacup. "No, thank you." Madeline set the cup down.

"Do you know any women in town who might be willing to do some work for me?" Madeline watched Mrs. Jenkin's wizened brow furrow, and she hastened to add, "The captain and I may be staying for a while, and I've a mind to tidy up the house a bit. We'll need you to supervise, of course."

"Well"—the housekeeper seemed relieved that she wasn't about to be dismissed—"I have some nieces who live down by the inn on Gay Street. They might be persuaded to help out."

"Excellent. Do you suppose you could send someone around to fetch them?"

"Now, mum?"

"Now."

It wasn't long before two middle-aged matrons who looked enough alike to be twins, though Madeline had been assured they were merely sisters, appeared at the door. Mrs. Jenkins introduced Hannah Wiggins and Sarah Deye. Their husbands worked at the shipyard, and though times were good because of the war, both women were anxious to earn some extra coin. What's more, when Mrs. Jenkins and her nieces got together, they seemed to know exactly what needed to be done.

Madeline had spent the hour before their arrival exploring the house and trying to decide what to do first. Upon realizing the enormity of the job, she had almost been tempted to give up before she'd started.

Besides the central hall and the kitchen, the downstairs boasted a library, a dining room, a parlor—complete with harpsichord—and a study. Upstairs were four bedrooms, all equal in size to the one she and Joshua had occupied, and a fifth room, narrower and much cleaner than the rest, that had obviously been inhabited by the housekeeper.

The furnishings and window hangings all appeared to be of high quality, though Madeline doubted any of the unholstery would ever be fully restored, even after the layers of dust were removed.

But remove them they would. Mrs. Jenkins's nieces had brought with them brooms and buckets, rags, and soft, gooey lye soap; they soon had the sleeves of their cotton dresses rolled up and the mops were flying. Even Mrs. Jenkins—Madeline guessed she had lived the better part of seven decades—bent to the task.

The three women appeared a little dubious, however, when Madeline mentioned her problem with dust. She made it clear that she wanted to help, but after a dozen more sneezes on her part, they assigned her the job of scrubbing the kitchen walls. The chore was not exactly to her liking. The pungent odor of soap made her eyes water, and the strong suds reddened her hands, but at least she had no uncontrollable bouts of sneezing.

Madeline wiped her hands on the front of the apron she'd pinned over her dress, and examined the section of wall she had just cleaned. It looked much better. With something akin to pride, she stuck her brush back into the murky liquid and began to scrub again.

Joshua found her moments later, a cloth tied protectively about her tawny curls, rivulets of dirty water streaming down her raised arms to soak into the fabric of her sleeves.

"You're back." A flutter of movement had caught her eye, and Madeline had turned to see him watching her, an unreadable expression upon his handsome face. Suddenly conscious of her appearance, she pulled the kerchief from her head. "I didn't expect you till much later. What do you think?" She motioned toward the dripping wall behind her.

"How well do you know Philip Spencer?"

"What?" The question had been so totally unexpected

that she could hardly believe she had heard him correctly.

"I said—how well do you know him?"

Though his tone was hushed, Madeline sensed there was nothing tranquil about his mood. And his question . . . what possible reason could he have for asking it?

"Why do you—"

"Answer me, dammit. What is the man to you?"

Gone was any facade of composure. The force of his words drove her back until she bumped her leg against the bucket, sending soapy water sloshing over the edge. Too stunned to even notice the spreading puddle at her feet, Madeline stared at her husband's angry countenance as she wondered why he should care about Philip Spencer. She could understand if he'd been upset about his brother, but Philip . . . "He was my friend."

"Friend!" He nearly spat the word at her. "You forget I saw the two of you together—more than once."

Together? The way he said it the word implied much more than there had ever been between her and Philip. Her husband seemed to be accusing her of having been intimate with the man.

Anger began to boil up through her shock. How dare he suggest that she and Philip had— He, of all people, should know how untrue that was.

Squaring her shoulders and stepping out of the pool of slippery water, Madeline faced Joshua. "I don't understand your question."

"And I had always thought you so clever. Of course, maybe I really never knew how clever you were—or how deceitful." His voice was lower now, but contempt laced his words. "You had me fooled, Madeline. Oh, how you had me fooled."

Madeline watched him run his long slender fingers through his already rumpled hair, and for an instant she thought she saw a flicker of pain in the obsidian depths of his eyes. But it was quickly masked by an angry scowl before he turned away.

Madeline had seen him like this once before. It had been a misunderstanding then, and she was certain that was so now. If only he would tell her, what all this was about.

"Joshua." She moved over to him and touched the sleeve of his coat. He jerked away as if he'd been burned.

"Don't!" He turned on her. "The only thing I want from you is to be told where Nathaniel is."

"Nathaniel? I—"

"Captain Parks of the *Sailfish* told me about Ben Hurly working for Spencer, so you needn't bother to lie. No wonder you became nervous as a cat when we got close to Baltimore. You knew Nat wasn't going to be here. Of course, you had no way of foreseeing that the *Sailfish* would be blown off course by a storm and would still be in the harbor. I imagine you thought yourself fairly safe."

What he was saying to her made no sense, but Madeline was wary of questioning him, and in a moment it wasn't necessary.

"I knew Creely wasn't smart enough. I knew it!" He ruefully shook his head before fixing her with a penetrating black stare. "But I looked into those damned green eyes of yours and thought I saw innocence."

"I am innocent, damn you! I have no idea what you're prattling on about."

Joshua stared at her for a long while, then he forced himself to look instead at the spot of creamy clean wall behind her. Surrounded by the dark smoky residue of countless meals, it reminded him of a halo of purity. He shook his head again to dispel the thought. Even with all he knew, with all that linked her to his brother's disappearance, Joshua wanted to believe her blameless. He wanted to—but couldn't.

"I know all about it, Madeline."

Why did it hurt so much to call her by that name? She used to hate it when he shortened it to Maddie. Now it hurt when he didn't.

"Sau told me how the contraband is brought into Hopewell, how it is secreted in the caves."

"That's not true."

His bark of laughter held no mirth. "Very convincing, but I saw proof." Joshua clenched his fist. This was proving even more difficult than *he* had expected. Since his interview with the *Sailfish*'s captain, what he'd learned had been rattling around in his head. He had wanted to confront her, to hear her beg for forgiveness. If she had told him that Spencer had made her do it, he'd have believed her. He had even pictured her throwing herself at him, swearing she loved him. But no, she had done none of that. She'd done nothing but deny the undeniable.

"As much as I want to know what has happened to Nathaniel, I don't seem to have it in me to torture the information out of you, and you don't seem inclined to tell me voluntarily." He turned away from her.

The movement brought Madeline back from her deliberations on what he had said. "Where are you going?" She almost lunged at him.

"To Jamaica, Madeline—back to Jamaica. And I don't believe I will be as chivalrous with Spencer."

"But I don't know . . . anything." Madeline's words faded out as she realized she was talking to empty space. He had strode out of the kitchen, and seemingly out of her life, without a backward glance.

She stood in the middle of the room, her wet skirts clinging to her legs. From somewhere at the front of the house came the sound of laughter. She couldn't tell which of the nieces had found something amusing, and she didn't know why she cared. But trying to remember which of the ladies had a high-pitched laugh was easier than trying to make sense out of the last ten minutes.

If she'd understood the captain correctly, and Madeline was in no way certain that she had, he somehow blamed Philip for Ben Hurly's lie about Nathaniel being in Baltimore. Why this had led him to believe that she knew where his brother was, she couldn't imagine, except that Joshua seemed to believe she and Philip were much closer than they had ever been. And there were his remarks about Hopewell. . . .

Madeline thought back. Several times her husband had suggested that all was not right at the sugar plantation. She hadn't believed him, and she wasn't sure she believed him now. But even if Creely was in some way connected with hiding stolen cargo, that didn't mean she was involved. As for Philip Spencer, Madeline couldn't think of a less likely thief. It was all so ridiculous, and the more she thought of it, the more she became convinced that Joshua would arrive at that same conclusion.

She wouldn't go to him now but would give him a day or two to come to his senses. Nathaniel's absence must be bothering him more than she had imagined. She'd try to bear that in mind when he came back, begging her forgiveness. That knowledge would make it easier to bury her anger and to forgive him for doubting her.

When he came back . . . He would come back. He had to.

Without realizing what she was about, Madeline lifted the brush out of the soapy water and began to widen the circle of lye-cleaned wall.

Chapter 23

He did not come back.

For the remainder of that day Madeline waited for her husband to come to his senses. By late afternoon the clean spot on the wall had expanded to include the entire room, and she fell into a sturdy kitchen chair, exhausted, too tired even to look up when Mrs. Jenkins came to fix the evening meal.

"You done a fine job, mum," the older lady said for the second time that day. She had first said it when she'd come to the kitchen with her nieces to say that the younger women were leaving. Madeline had been scrubbing the whitewashed wall surrounding the huge fireplace then.

"They'll be back tomorrow, bright and early," Mrs. Jenkins had said after commenting, with a touch of surprise in her voice, on the cleanliness of the walls.

Hannah and Sarah had bid Madeline good day and had hustled off, presumably to prepare evening meals for their own families. Both women had several children still at home, as well as a few who were married.

That had been a good hour ago, Madeline imagined, and by the looks of Mrs. Jenkins, the housekeeper had spent the time since they'd left freshening up. She now wore a well-worn but clean, blue linen dress and a crisp, white apron.

It occurred to Madeline that she could also do with a thorough sprucing up. Her gown was ruined. Silk was not meant to be worn by washerwomen, she thought as she shook her head.

"I haven't anything fancy to fix for supper," Mrs. Jenkins announced. "Tomorrow I'll go to the market, but for tonight we'll have to make do with what's in the larder."

Madeline looked up to find the housekeeper examining her, an odd expression on her face. She wondered if Mrs. Jenkins had heard her confrontation with Joshua. With a sigh, Madeline came to the conclusion that the woman probably had. For one thing, Mrs. Jenkins had assumed it would just be the two of them for dinner.

"I'm really not very hungry. Anything you fix will be fine with me, Mrs. Jenkins." Madeline's words seemed to appease the older woman because she turned and went about putting slabs of bacon into a large iron skillet. The fire she had started earlier was now sending waves of unneeded heat into the room.

"Are there any leaks in that tub?" Madeline asked, pointing to the hip bath in the far corner of the kitchen.

Mrs. Jenkins looked up from the sizzling meat. "I think it's sound."

After hearing that, Madeline spent the remainder of the time before dinner carrying water in from the outside well.

The meal was composed of simple fare—bacon, day-old Sally Lunn bread, and tea—but Madeline barely knew what she was eating. Her spirits revived a little when she settled into the tub of warm water; however, any small pleasure she derived from her bath was offset by remembering that she had nothing clean to wear.

No one had brought her trunk around, and she began to wonder if she would have to go down to the dock herself to retrieve it. Luckily, Mrs. Jenkins had anticipated the problem and had brought Madeline one of her own unfitted short gowns. The garment was not of the

363

quality to which Madeline was accustomed, but the block-printed cotton was clean. Worn over her petticoats, it would be presentable until her sea chest arrived on the morrow. Having bathed and eaten, Madeline felt more optimistic. She was sure Joshua would come back the next day.

She bid Mrs. Jenkins a good night, deciding that she truly liked the old housekeeper, and then climbed the stairs. Even with only the flickering light of the candle she held, Madeline could tell that a lot had been done toward cleaning the house. Indeed, the sheets she slipped between were clean and the bedding had been aired. No musty odor assailed her as she nestled into the goose down. Yet she would readily have traded the fresh, early summer smells that clung to the bed linens for the warmth of her husband's long body.

She began to wonder whether Joshua was as lonely for her as she was for him, but exhaustion overcame her, and she fell asleep. Fatigue had had its way.

Once during the night, she thought the captain had come to her, but upon awakening she realized it had only been a dream. And in the wee hours of the morning, as she lay abed, Madeline decided that waiting for Joshua to come to her was a waste of time. She would go to him— tomorrow—and make him see reason. Then maybe, just maybe, she'd forgive him for this awful day.

Sunlight slanting across her pillow told Madeline she had overslept, the chance lifting of her arm told her the reason. All of her muscles ached from the unaccustomed labor she'd put in the day before, but her arms and neck were especially sore.

"Damn you, Joshua Whitlock," Madeline murmured as she slipped from beneath the sheets. It wasn't bad enough that she had worked hard on a task he hadn't even noticed or appreciated, now she had to suffer alone.

"Oh." She pulled on the shift that she had washed out last evening, trying to ignore the burning sensation in her arms when she moved them.

With each piece of clothing she donned, Madeline became more angry at her husband. Had she asked him to bring her to Baltimore? No! Had she ever wanted to marry the oaf? No! By the time she stepped into her pink, brocade slippers and felt lingering dampness seep between her toes, she was livid.

How dare he be angry with her? Ever since she had met the arrogant captain, he had done nothing but wreak havoc with her life. She didn't need that, and she didn't need him! Oh, maybe in a moment of weakness brought on by the lonely blackness of night, she had thought a reconciliation would be worth the price her pride would pay, but no more.

She'd return to Hopewell. That had been her plan before, and that was what she would do now. Once she was there, she'd prove that what the captain had said about her plantation was untrue. There was no smuggling at Hopewell.

Madeline stuck her arms into the short gown Mrs. Jenkins had lent her. The cotton enveloped her tiny frame. She must get her own clothes.

As if her thoughts could conjure up action, Mrs. Jenkins chose that moment to tap on the door and give her the message that someone had brought her sea chest. As much as she tried, Madeline couldn't stop the fluttering of her heart at the thought that the captain himself might have brought her trunk. She exerted all of her will power to keep herself from running down the stairs; however, in the end it mattered naught. It wasn't the captain below but his first mate.

"I've brought your sea chest and things," Oliver said when he saw her, and Madeline wondered if he could tell how crestfallen she was that the captain hadn't come.

"Thank you." She finished descending the wide staircase with its hand-carved spindles, then added, "I'm greatly in need of a gown." She plucked at the loose-fitting garment she wore; it would have covered two of her.

365

"Aye, 'tis obvious that dress ain't yours."

Madeline ran her palm down the sides of the cotton frock.

"He ain't with me."

The surprised "Who?" died on her lips as she looked up into the kind, wrinkled face of the man who had become her friend. Madeline had hoped he'd missed her surreptitious glance behind him, but apparently he hadn't. Or maybe Oliver just knew what was in her heart.

Rejecting any pretense of misunderstanding, she sank onto the bottom riser. "I see," she said. Disappointment flooded the empty shell of her body like hot candle wax fills a mold.

"He's real busy, trying to get provisions on board for another crossin' . . ."

"Don't pretend with me, Oliver. We both know the good captain's absence has naught to do with his frenzied activity—though I don't doubt for one moment there is plenty of that."

Air whistled through the gap between Oliver's teeth as he plopped onto the dark green sea chest. Resting one elbow on his knee he looked Madeline straight in the eye. "The boy thinks ya deceived him."

Madeline would have laughed at Oliver's referring to her husband as a boy—hardly the description memory conjured up for her—if the rest of what he'd said hadn't been so sobering. "I didn't."

"Now did ya hear me askin'?"

A trace of a smile tugged at the corners of Madeline's mouth, but she kept her gaze firmly on the tightly laced fingers of her clenched hands. "No."

"Good, 'cause I weren't. Knew ya hadn't. Told him so, too."

"So did I."

"Wouldn't listen to me none."

"Me neither." Madeline sighed.

They sat that way in companionable silence for a time.

Then, somewhere in the recesses of the house, Madeline thought she heard Mrs. Jenkins talking to her nieces. She didn't know when the two women had arrived, but she supposed she should have guessed they'd be here, it being so late. It momentarily crossed her mind that maybe she should stop them from cleaning Joshua's house. He might consider this project meddling in his affairs.

"We're sailin' tomorrow."

Oliver's words wiped from her mind any concern over the advisability of tidying up. "So soon?" Madeline forced her voice not to reveal how upset she was by the news. What good would it do for him to come to his senses if he were on the high seas? It wasn't as though he would turn back.

"Aye, Cap'n says 'nough time's been wasted."

"Oh." Was it the time spent with her he considered wasted? she wondered.

"He's hurtin' inside, ya know."

He's hurting. "Yes, I imagine he is."

"Ya shoulda seen 'im when he got that letter saying his pa was dyin'. Never had much good for the old man myself—didn't think the cap'n did neither—but I guess blood pulls are strong."

Madeline thought of her reaction to the post she had received while in Williamsburg. It had only hinted at the possibility of something being amiss, and she had rushed to Jamaica. She nodded her head.

Oliver didn't appear to notice the motion. It was as if he were looking through her into the past. "Cap'n, he sailed for home on the next tide, but it weren't fast enough. His pa was dead when he got here." The first mate's eyes seemed to focus. "Guilt." He shook his head. "Terrible thing—guilt."

Madeline wiped her damp hands against the cotton of her petticoats. At some time during Oliver's speech she had begun to cry, and the tears that had drifted down her face to quiver on her chin, now plopped onto the hands folded in her lap. Madeline didn't know whether her sadness was for her husband who'd arrived home too late, or for the pain she would have felt if she had missed those last precious days with her own father. Somehow, she imagined it was a little of each. She looked up at Oliver. "Did the captain feel much of it—guilt, I mean?"

"Did and does, I reckon. Shouldn't." The word was fraught with emotion. "I told him, ain't none of it his doin', but"—Oliver shook his head, and Madeline saw in that hopeless gesture just how much he loved the younger man—"didn't do no good."

Madeline leaned over and touched the homespun linen of his sleeve. "It may take time, but he will get over this."

"Not until he makes sure Nat's okay, he won't. Blames hisself for the lad goin' off like he done."

"But why?"

Oliver shrugged his shoulders. "They was always close, them two. Different. They's as different as night and day. And o' course, the cap'n, he's a sight older than Nat. I think each brother secretly wanted what the other one had. The cap'n, he'd o' liked to o' been coddled a little more, and Nat"—Oliver chuckled—"he'd o' liked some adventure."

"Don't you think that may be what Nat is about? I mean, couldn't all Joshua's worry be over nothing more than a young man's desire to take a voyage, to be adventurous?"

"I don't know. It's possible, I guess, though it ain't like Nat at all." He paused. "But I know damned sure the cap'n don't think so."

Madeline sighed. "I don't believe I'm going to stay in Baltimore."

"Goin' back to Jamaica?" Seeing Madeline's nod he continued. "Thought ya might, though I think you're makin' a mistake. He'll come back for ya. Of that I'm certain."

"I won't be here," Madeline whispered.

Oliver cleared his throat. "Well."

He stood, and Madeline did, too. Together they walked to the wide, paneled door.

"There's somethin' I've been meanin' to give ya." The first mate reached into his pocket and extracted several gold coins.

She looked at the money he offered her in surprise. "What is that for?"

"Cap'n sent me lookin' for ya after that first time ya was on board the *Chesapeake*. Wanted me to give ya these."

"You knew?" Madeline was aghast. All this time she could have sworn the first mate had no idea she was the woman that had been plucked from the sea—the woman the cap'n had taken for a whore.

"Not at first. But after I got to know ya better I had my suspicions. Asked the cap'n 'bout it once, and he came near to takin' my head off." Oliver chuckled at the memory.

"Why are you giving these to me now?"

Oliver closed her fingers around the coins he had laid in her palm. "'Cause I wanted ya to know that even way back then, when he thought ya somethin' ya weren't, the cap'n cared about ya. Remember that."

Remember that. Madeline stood clutching the body-warmed gold long after the grizzled first mate had bid her farewell. It wasn't till Mrs. Jenkins bustled into the hall, announcing she was going to do the marketing, that Madeline realized the length of time she had spent reviewing Oliver's words.

She wished she could believe what he had said, or at least implied. Did the captain really care about her? Would he come back because of her? If only it were true . . . But Madeline couldn't help remembering the way Joshua had looked at her the day before. It hadn't been love she had seen glowing in the depths of his eyes.

369

The memory of those midnight black orbs glaring angrily made her shiver even though the day was becoming uncomfortably warm. She felt she couldn't bear to have him look at her like that again.

Still, Madeline couldn't resist rising early the next day. She walked to the quay in the rosy light of dawn to watch the *Chesapeake*'s departure from Baltimore harbor. The breeze off the river was crisp and clean, carrying with it the salty tang of the Patapsco's tidewater. Madeline lifted her chin and breathed deeply of its essence as she watched the wind zing through the canvas of the rakish Bermuda sloop. She could almost hear the hum of ratlines strummed taut by billowing sails, the busy chatter of the tars as they catted the anchor, the commanding voice of the captain. . . .

She should go back to the house. People were beginning to fill the dock area—fishermen heading out for their day's catch, workers unloading the cones of sugar. They probably wondered about the young woman who stood biting her bottom lip, her arms wrapped around her waist as she stared into the rising sun. But Madeline didn't turn to walk up Water Street till the *Chesapeake* disappeared from view, heading toward the great inland bay whose name it bore.

Was she going insane?

The ugly thought invaded Madeline's mind for probably the hundredth time in the fortnight since the *Chesapeake* had sailed. It grabbed her now and, like a hungry dog with a bone, refused to let go.

It was long after sane people had sought their beds. Mrs. Jenkins had retired hours ago. And still Madeline sat, curled in a cushioned wing chair, trying to make a decision—trying to force rational thought into her head.

370

Should she return to Hopewell or stay? The argument was always the same. It was her resolution that changed—from day to day, from moment to moment.

As the sun rose on any particular day she might decide to book passage on the next vessel bound for Jamaica. But by the time she dragged herself from bed, memories of the captain had permeated her thoughts and convinced her there was naught to do but await his return.

The vacillation was beginning to wear on her as much as the problem. Madeline had never had the slightest difficulty making up her mind. If sugar stalks needed cutting, she had them cut; if a servant needed discipline, she saw to it. But all that had changed when Joshua Whitlock had exploded into her life.

It was because she loved him. That was the one thing Madeline knew for certain. She had strongly suspected it before, had fought it as long as she could, but there was no denying it now. "Damn," she muttered to herself. Why did the one thing she was sure of have to be a fact that made her so unhappy?

"Enough." Madeline stood, angrier still now because she was talking to herself. She would go to bed. At least lying under the wide tester, her body—if not her mind—could rest!

She looked around the small study. She had been spending much of her time in this room, probably because it reminded her of Papa's library. Sometimes, when she sat in the high-back chair, Madeline could almost feel her father's presence. Once she had even tried to solicit his help with her dilemma, but no startling revelation had come to her so she had decided just to enjoy the aura of love which surrounded her.

Madeline lifted the brass candle holder and headed for the door, but the moment she stood up she knew sleep would not come easily.

A book. She walked beside the open shelves, trailing her finger along the worn leather spines of the volumes.

371

Voltaire, Shakespeare, all the classics were here, but none appealed to her in the slightest. She was about to give up and coax slumber in another way when the candlelight fell upon a book that looked unfamiliar to her. It was a journal written by Justin Whitlock. Curious, Madeline opened the binding and touched the crinkled yellow parchment that smelled faintly of old ink, attics, and days long past. She sat back down in the wing chair.

The first entry was dated May 9, 1722. In bold, dark print, Joshua's father had described the events of that day. Madeline skimmed through the pages, pausing now and then to scan an interesting anecdote. It seemed strange reading about Justin Whitlock as a young man, and she wondered if Joshua had ever perused this diary or even knew of its existence.

Somewhere around the middle of June, Madeline's head began to nod and her eyelids drifted shut. One more page, she told herself, as if looking at one more page would assure her of slumber. Well, she was wrong. By the end of the next page, she was more wide awake than ever.

The June seventeenth entry described in detail Justin's meeting with her father. "Patrick O'Neil appears an amiable sort." Madeline smiled as she read the description. Apparently a rapport had been struck between the men because the next few pages were peppered with her father's name.

There was another name also—Matthew Burke. It looked almost benign scrawled on the page, but Madeline knew better. An ominous gloom seemed to permeate the room as she remembered what her father had told her about the man—and she wondered what he had refused to tell her.

Was the entire story in this book? Madeline's heart pumped furiously; she could hear its rhythmic beating. Her hand trembled as she turned a page, then another, until she had followed the three young men through summer's heat into fall. It was all there, just as her father had described. They had bought the schooner. With Patrick as her captain, the *Providence* had completed several successful ventures in coastwise trade.

Justin Whitlock had a flair for writing. The accounts of his life, and his descriptions of those people with whom he came in contact were witty and interesting—until the November twenty-eighth entry. Madeline sucked in her breath at the raw emotion in his stark words. "I'll kill that bastard Burke!"

It was a moment before she could continue. When her father had told her the tale, she couldn't wait to hear more—was disappointed when he hadn't. But this . . . Justin Whitlock was not going to temper the facts out of love for her. And, Madeline thought as her fingers toyed with the page's corner, the journal's contents were so personal. She almost felt as if she were delving into the recesses of a dead man's mind.

"You silly woman," Madeline chided herself, shaking her head and trying to laugh away her reaction. But her laughter sounded oddly forced, even to her own ears. Nonetheless, she decided her best course was to plunge ahead.

. She turned the page and stared. The new entry was dated almost a fortnight hence and contained no mention of Matthew Burke or a duel. She turned back to assure herself that no pages had stuck together, then examined the centerfold to make certain nothing had been torn out.

Nothing. Justin Whitlock had simply waited two weeks and then had started writing again as if nothing had happened.

Madeline ran her finger along the lines as she reread the page. "It's not the same," she whispered. She read it again. The tone of the words was different. Justin Whitlock was different. Gone was the carefree young man Madeline had wished Joshua could have known, and in his place she sensed the beginnings of the hard man her husband had known.

It took the reading of almost twenty pages before Madeline found any reference to the reason for this change. Nestled among household accounts was a short paragraph.

> We're sending Catherine to live with a family near Concord till the baby is born. She doesn't want to go, and I hate that she must, after all she's been through. . . . But Mother thinks it best.

A baby. Madeline had suspected as much that night in her father's bedroom.

She read on. The entries were short now—devoid of emotion. Her father's name was still mentioned occasionally but not with the same warmth as in the earlier part of the journal. Madeline almost thought there had been a breach of some sort between them until she came to the page dated April fifth, almost a year after the first entry.

> Patrick's leaving, too. Can't blame him. I haven't been much company of late. He's to captain a brig headed for the Indies. I've known for some time that plying the coast from Boston to Charleston was less than he wanted. He deserves the best. I'll never forget how he stood by me, his offer to wed Catherine. He lost more than I when M——stole the *Providence*. Good luck, dear friend.

So her father had been willing to marry Justin's sister and his offer had been declined. Madeline smiled. "Don't worry, Papa; Elizabeth Bennett is waiting for you in Jamaica," she said aloud.

Her eyes ached, and her limbs were heavy with fatigue, yet even though pale ribbons of dawn were streaming through the window, she couldn't stop reading. She did allow herself the luxury of skipping ahead, however. If the baby were conceived in November it would be born in—Madeline counted the months on her fingers—August. August seventeenth to be exact.

> The baby's a boy. I can barely look at the child without remembering M——, but Catherine seems to like him. Giving him up will be hard for her.

Catherine was going to abandon her child? Madeline read on. Less than thirty pages later she had her answer.

> Catherine won't come home. I've tried everything. Even pleaded loneliness since Mother died. She laughed and told me to take a bride. How can she stay and marry that yokel? The Spencers were supposed to take the baby, but their son is taking my Catherine.

Chills raced across the tiny ridges of Madeline's spine, but she didn't know why. She was happy for Catherine, although Justin's pain was real. However, something was disturbing her. She read the passage again—unable to find a reason, yet unable to shake the sensation.

> November twenty-eighth. My need to see Catherine was too great to resist. Today, of all days, I should have tried harder. Why can't I accept her apparent happiness? But Catherine in homespun is not my Catherine. It's all because of M——. Does he know I still search for him, I wonder?
>
> She dotes on the boy. How can she love a child born of rape? But in her eyes Philip can do no wrong.

Madeline stood up so quickly that the journal crashed to the floor. "No," she whispered. "No, Catherine's baby can't be Philip Spencer." But she knew he was.

Frantically she picked up the abused volume and set it

on the library table. She found the page she had just read and leafed forward, mindless of the old parchment.

"January thirteenth. Leaving Boston. Can not stay after what happened!" caught her eye.

"My God, what happened?" Madeline turned back, examining each page carefully.

> December twenty-seventh. Dead. I know it was M—— who killed her, though constable not sure— worthless fellow. Husband dead. Baby gone.

Madeline felt as if she had run a race and tried to slow the cadence of her breathing. So this was the awful thing to which her father had alluded. Could Matthew Burke have done it? There were other possibilities—Indians for one. Madeline had read that they occasionally stole young children. But she knew Philip Spencer, and he didn't appear to have been raised by savages.

The letter must have been jogged loose when she dropped the book, for when she turned the page it nearly fell into her hands. The brittle quality of the paper dated it, though no day or year was noted on the correspondence. There were only two sentences on the page, but they were enough to strike fear in Madeline's heart:

"Justin, you have dared to steal my son. For that, yours shall die. Matthew."

Yours shall die. "Oh, Joshua."

"Sure you don't want me to go along, Cap'n?" Oliver Chappel said as he followed the younger man down off the quarterdeck.

Joshua paused, took a deep breath, and tried to hide his exasperation as he answered the same question for at least the tenth time. "No, Oliver. I need you here."

"But, Cap'n—"

"Here, Oliver!" Joshua combed his hands through a windblown tangle of his hair. He had lost his temper again. God, when would he ever learn?

It had been his temper, along with a lack of rational thought, that had sent him raging to confront his wife in Baltimore. He could still see the stricken look on her face when he had accused her of knowing where Nathaniel was. What a fool he had been. Madeline was a lot of things—most of them good—but she wasn't deceitful. Oliver had tried to tell him. He hadn't listened.

It had taken almost a sennight at sea, with naught to do in the evenings but think and remember, before Joshua had realized exactly what he had done. By then, it was too late to turn back. He could only go forward and hope that she was still in Baltimore to receive his letter of apology. Joshua had written it while the *Chesapeake* was still at sea, and his first act upon landing in Kingston harbor had been to find a vessel ready to depart for the Colonies that would deliver the letter.

Now that he had done that, Joshua was ready to go to Hopewell.

Joshua looked over to where Oliver leaned against the rail. "Sorry," he said, "but this is something I have to do alone." He clapped his friend on his shoulder.

"Could be dangerous."

Joshua grinned and straightened his tall frame. "Do I look like someone who can't take care of myself?"

"I'm serious, Cap'n."

"So am I." Joshua's countenance sobered. "Listen, I'm just going to Hopewell to see if I can find out where Creely is. With any luck, he'll have left word where to reach him when he left the plantation. Through him, I think I can find Philip Spencer. I should be back in a day or two.

"In the meantime, I want you to get the men started on graving the hull. We made damn poor time getting here, and I want those barnacles scraped off."

Well, he had managed to placate Oliver, Joshua

thought as he galloped up the familiar tree-lined drive toward the great house. For the past half-hour he'd been riding on Hopewell land, and to his amazement, he'd noticed no improvement in the fields since his last time there. It was difficult to believe that someone Henry Smyth had recommended wasn't doing a better job. Of course, it had only been about two months, less if you really considered that Andrew Burns hadn't started as soon as they'd left. Maybe it was just going to take a lot longer than Joshua had anticipated to rectify the damange of almost a year of mismanagement.

Still . . .

Joshua slowed his stallion to a walk, then reined him in as he entered the curved drive in front of the house. The high-strung horse crushed shells beneath his hooves as Joshua stood in the saddle to get a better view. *Shouldn't there be some people about?* Thinking back, he realized he hadn't noticed anyone since he'd left the Kingston Road cutoff. Joshua sank back into the saddle and touched his heels to the horse's flanks.

When he dismounted, no one came to take his horse, so he began walking him toward the stable. Then the closing of the great house's front door caught his attention, and Joshua turned to call a greeting. But the words were never spoken. Instead, Joshua dropped the horse's reins and advanced on the man who stood near the veranda.

"What the hell are you doing here?"

Eli Creely began to back away, obviously wary of the hostile glint in the captain's eyes.

"Answer me, dammit!" Joshua grabbed the front of the overseer's stained shirt and lifted him off the ground.

"If you put him down, Captain Whitlock, perhaps I can answer your question for you."

Joshua had been so angry to find Creely still at Hopewell, he had momentarily forgotten that the overseer's presence eliminated the problem of locating him. And in his rage he hadn't noticed that another man had come out of the great house—until he heard the cultured voice.

Joshua's elation at seeing Philip Spencer evaporated the instant he glanced toward the veranda and saw the pistol aimed at him. Of course Joshua had a pistol also—packed in his saddlebag.

Creely still dangled inches off the ground, his hands clutching impotently at Joshua's, his nervous sweat fouling the air. Before it occurred to Joshua to use the overseer as a shield, Spencer forestalled that move.

"Don't be foolish enough to assume, Captain Whitlock, that positioning Mr. Creely between us will prevent me from pulling this trigger. Just put him down so we can conduct our little conversation in a civilized manner. I am certain you have some questions you'd like answered. We'll start with your inquiry as to why Mr. Creely is still at Hopewell."

The muscles of Joshua's arms burned from holding Creely aloft. Would Spencer shoot through the overseer to get to him? One look at Creely's face, with its narrow, worried eyes, assured Joshua that contemptible man thought so. In disgust Joshua tossed him aside. Creely landed on the pink shell drive with a thud. He kept his eyes fastened on Joshua as he skittered out of his reach.

"Much better, Captain Whitlock. Now, shall we assuage your curiosity in the house?"

At the moment, Joshua didn't think he had much of a choice. The pistol, primed and ready, was still leveled at his chest. Slowly, he climbed the few steps to the veranda and led the way across the gray and white tiles into the great house.

It was strange, but upon entering the pleasant coolness of the hallway, Joshua almost felt he was coming home, although of course, one didn't usually receive this kind of welcome upon returning.

"The library, if you please, Captain."

Joshua glanced behind him to see Spencer motion toward the room to the right. He briefly considered

379

trying to wrest the gun from him. If he moved quickly enough, and he thought he could; Spencer wouldn't know what hit him. But if Joshua risked a confrontation now, Spencer could be hurt, and as appealing as the possibility was, what he needed were answers. He decided to let loose his animosity after he had learned what Spencer knew about Nathaniel.

Spencer motioned for him to sit in the tent-stitched, wing chair, then settled himself into the leather chair that had been Patrick O'Neil's favorite.

Joshua noticed with distaste that his adversary was, as usual, impeccably dressed. From the large silver buckles on his shoes to his curled and powdered hair, Philip Spencer was every inch the wealthy dandy—except for the pistol. That didn't go with the image he presented.

"I've been expecting you, Captain, though I must admit you arrived a little sooner than I expected, hence Mr. Creely's surprise."

"Speaking of Creely"—Joshua was glad his voice didn't betray the anxiety he felt—"why is the man still at Hopewell? I sent someone to replace him."

"Andrew Burns?" Philip asked pleasantly.

When Joshua said nothing, Spencer continued. "Oh, he arrived. His letter of introduction from a Mr. Henry Smythe was very impressive. Unfortunately, the young man didn't wish to accept my word that the arrangements had been changed. He insisted upon making a nuisance of himself."

"Where is he now?"

"He met with an unfortunate accident."

"I want to see him." Joshua clutched the arms of his chair to keep from launching himself at Spencer.

A smirk stretched the corners of Philip's mouth. "Perhaps I didn't make myself clear. It was a fatal accident."

"You bastard . . ." Joshua instinctively moved forward, but he had enough presence of mind to notice Spencer's finger tighten against the trigger. Getting

380

himself killed would do poor Andrew Burns no good. And now that he knew exactly what Spencer was capable of, his fears for Nathaniel were heightened. Joshua forced himself to ease back into the chair.

Spencer acknowledged Joshua's action by loosening his grip on the gun. "Wise move. But then, I took you for a clever man the first time I saw you. After all, you managed to ingratiate yourself with the old man and to win Madeline and Hopewell right out from under my nose. They were supposed to be mine, you know."

"Really?" Joshua crossed his booted feet. It occurred to him that Philip Spencer might be insane. If he was, or even if he wasn't, keeping him talking seemed to be the best tack to take at the moment. Joshua hoped that eventually Spencer would get around to telling him about Nathaniel.

"Yes. It was a stroke of good fortune when she went to Williamsburg. At first, I thought I'd abhor my duty— keeping her occupied there—but I soon found myself warming to the task—and her. I even toyed with the idea of suggesting to my father that I marry her and keep her around for a while—till I tired of her at least."

"Your father?" Joshua's prompting was ignored. Spencer seemed intent on revealing only as much as he wanted him to know.

"When she departed for Jamaica without warning. I was even a little worried for her safety. Creely had orders to allow no one to interfere with the operation."

"The operation?" Joshua steepled his fingers under his chin. "That would be stealing, smuggling, and the subsequent selling of flour?"

"You *are* clever," Spencer said with a trace of admiration.

"Obviously not clever enough, because I haven't a clue as to why you're doing this—outside of the profits in it, that is. And I can't believe the yield on flour is that large."

"That's because you're thinking in terms of monetary

381

gain. Other things can be equally important."

"To a thief? I *am* surprised." Joshua was afraid he had gone too far when he saw Spencer lean forward and raise the pistol from his knee.

But the man quickly gained control of himself, for he chuckled softly as his finger played over the mellow brass that trimmed the gun's handle. "Do you suppose you can bait me into becoming careless, Captain? It will not work. We've waited too long for this. My father will have his revenge, cousin, and I shall have mine. Madeline will make a lovely widow, and I shall be only too happy to console her. And though I'll probably end up killing her, in the meantime she can offer me hours of pleasant diversion and, of course, Hopewell."

What was the man talking about? He had called him cousin and had referred again to his father. But Joshua had no cousin named Philip Spencer. The part about Madeline becoming a widow he understood. And he knew that even if he were to die, he didn't want this bastard around her. "You've done all this for Hopewell?" Joshua was hard pressed to believe the sugar plantation was worthy of such an intricate plot.

"Hopewell?" Spencer paused. "Yes. And Whitlock Trading. We've taken that away from your family, too. But mostly we did it for revenge. To right an old wrong, if you will."

"I don't understand."

Spencer seemed to be losing patience. "Then please allow me to explain. Your father and Patrick O'Neil once conspired to keep me from my rightful father, and now we have taken their children from them."

"What have you done with Nathaniel?" Joshua stared at Spencer through angry, narrowed eyes. He still didn't completely understand what the man was talking about, but he knew it was somehow related to his brother's disappearance.

"I wondered when you would ask about him. He has proven to be a bit of a problem. His attempts to escape have made him very unpopular. I'm afraid some rather stringent actions have had to be taken."

"What have you done to him?" The words were hissed through clenched teeth. Joshua gripped the chair arms, but that did little good. This was not the time to act, he tried to tell the coiled muscle of his body. *Wait.* But the waiting was over. Spencer lifted the pistol, and as Joshua lunged forward, his finger tightened around the trigger. Joshua was afraid it was too late for Nathaniel, but he hoped to save himself and Maddie. Maddie. How could he have believed her a part of this madman's scheme?

He saw the tiny spark, smelled the gunpowder, a heartbeat before the ball burned through his body. His forward motion carried him toward Spencer, and he grabbed at the man who had murdered Nat and who had threatened to hurt Maddie.

Air. He clutched only air, and felt himself falling. When he struck the floor, he felt only a small jolt. His body was already beginning to go numb. Like his mind. Numb. Black.

Maddie, forgive me. The letter. Read my letter. Know I love you. Black.

Philip Spencer looked up as Creely and two other men burst into the room.

"I heard a shot. Ya all right?"

"Yes, of course." Spencer placed the pistol on a side table and rose. "But our friend, the captain, appears to have gotten himself shot."

"He dead?" Creely gave the prostrate figure a kick.

"Certainly close enough. Get him out of here. He's bleeding all over the carpet."

"What you want we should do with him?" Creely motioned for the other two men to grab hold of the captain's arms.

"Toss him in the river. This game is beginning to bore me."

*   *   *

Dora hadn't heard Captain Whitlock arrive. She hadn't heard anything out of the ordinary till the pistol blast rang through the house. She quit gathering Master Spencer's dirty linens and crept to the top of the wide staircase. Peering down through the spindles into the hall below, she gasped at what she saw.

Turning, she then ran back through the upstairs corridor and down the servants' steps. She ignored her friend Tilly, who asked where she was off to and almost ran smack into the stable boy. But that didn't stop her either. With a singleness of purpose, Dora lifted her homespun skirt and raced toward the east cane piece.

Chapter 24

The brilliant colors of sunset reflected off the sea, tinting the normally turquois waters a vivid magenta. At moments such as these, when the world seemed so alive and beautiful, Madeline could almost believe she had overreacted to Justin Whitlock's journal. There couldn't really be people who would plot to destroy her husband because of something that had happened before he was born. Yet, hard as it was to understand, she knew there were.

As soon as she had read Joshua's father's account of those long-ago happenings, her indecision had left her. Within a sennight, she had closed up the house and boarded a packet bound for Jamaica. She had but one goal in mind—to find and warn Joshua. He had suspected a plot involving his brother, but he had no idea of its magnitude—or that he was also its target. That was why she stood on the deck of the *Mary Rose,* marking the spectacular close of another day that brought her closer to Joshua.

"I'm certain you're anxious to see your husband again, Mrs. Whitlock. Will he be meeting you in Kingston on the morrow?"

Captain Bellamy had come up beside her, catching Madeline unaware. Because his comment was so close to what she had been feeling, it took Madeline a while to focus on his words—and to remember her lie.

The *Mary Rose* was captained by a friend of Joshua's, and her master had been reluctant to offer his wife passage during such violent times. However, Madeline had convinced him that her husband deemed it necessary for her to meet him in Jamaica at once. It had been easy enough to keep up the pretense during the voyage, but they would make Kingston harbor by morning and, unless the Fates were unusually kind, there would be no eager husband to greet her.

Madeline looked up at Captain Bellamy, a man of nearly the same age as her husband, but lacking Joshua's stature and rugged handsomeness. "I'm to meet him at our sugar plantation," Madeline said, hoping the man beside her wouldn't insist an armed escort accompany her.

His next words proved that wasn't unlikely. "Your husband intends that you should travel overland alone?"

Captain Bellamy sounded so incensed that Madeline really was afraid he would insist on accompanying her himself. "No . . . I mean . . . I intend to travel with our solicitor."

She sighed with relief as Captain Bellamy's countenance relaxed. Even though she longed to tell him exactly how well she could, and had, taken care of herself, Madeline didn't think this was the time or place for such a discussion. So, after exchanging a few banal pleasantries, she excused herself and went to her cabin. Though not nearly as large or accommodating as the quarters she had shared with Joshua on the *Chesapeake*, it was ample for her needs.

Madeline changed into her nightrail and laid out the clothes she would need in the morning. Then, as had become her habit, she took out Justin Whitlock's journal and reread the portion about Philip Spencer. Did he harbor the same hatred for the Whitlocks as his father had? Madeline remembered that it had been one of

Philip's men who had lied about Nathaniel Whitlock, and she decided again that Philip probably did. But then, why had he not said or done anything to Joshua when they were both at Hopewell? Oh, it had been obvious that Philip hadn't liked the captain, but there had been nothing to indicate the degree of animosity that inspires killing. And what had happened to his father? Was Matthew Burke alive or had he, like Joshua's father and her own, died?

As usual, mulling over the strange situation created more questions than answers. At least, tomorrow she'd be in Jamaica. When she found Joshua and showed him the journal, maybe they could figure it out together.

In the morning, after the *Mary Rose* docked, Madeline wasted little time disembarking. After promising to convey Captain Bellamy's regards to Joshua, she followed her sea chest down the gangplank.

As she walked across the quay, Madeline took a deep breath. The air was alive with the scents of flowers, spices, the deep, peaty earth, and, of course, the sea. Its essence added a tang to the sweet smells of this lush tropical paradise. Its eternal rhythm provided the cadence of the island's song. The slow drawling speech of its people, the whisper of its breezes—all sounded to the pulsing beat of the sea.

It was good to be home. Madeline felt more optimistic than she had since she'd found the diary.

Her first stop was to be Henry Smythe's. If anyone in Kingston knew where her husband was, it would be he. Madeline took a room at Rafferty's Ordinary, then walked across the street to call on the solicitor. His offices on the ground floor were empty, so she climbed the stairs and knocked on his door.

"Enter," Henry Smythe's cheery voice called from within.

Slowly, Madeline opened the door that led to the solicitor's parlor.

"Ah, Mrs. Whitlock, this is a pleasant surprise. Do forgive me for not standing, but I fear the gout has me down."

"I should say it has," Madeline agreed as she surveyed Henry Smythe. He was ensconced on a love seat, his right foot propped up with pillows.

"Does it hurt badly?" Even through his stockings, Madeline could tell his toes were swollen.

"No, no, dear lady. That is, not as long as I keep my foot elevated. But do come in, and sit down. I thought you and Joshua had gone to the Colonies for a time. When did you get back?"

Any hope Madeline had cherished that Henry Smythe would know something of her husband's whereabouts faded, but she asked, "You haven't seen Joshua, then? I just arrived in Kingston today, but he's probably been here about a fortnight. I felt certain he'd come to see you."

"A fortnight you say? No, he's not been here. And since I've been laid up longer than that, he couldn't have called and found me out."

"Well, it probably means nothing." Madeline tried to keep the panic out of her voice. There was no need to upset Henry Smythe, especially when he could do naught but worry in his present state. "I imagine he was anxious to be at Hopewell."

"Are you going there?" Henry grimaced as he tried to adjust the pillows under his foot.

Madeline noticed the gesture and rearranged his affected limb more comfortably. She made the decision quickly. "Yes."

"Tell Andrew he owes me a report. I've written to him several times but have yet to receive a reply."

"He hasn't answered your letters?"

"No, but I'm certain he's been busy. Just remind him

to send me a report as soon as possible."

Madeline tried not to appear impatient as she bid the solicitor farewell, but it had occurred to her that she hadn't looked over the harbor for the *Chesapeake*.

She forced herself not to hurry as she headed for the quay. But when she saw the bold, clean lines of her husband's sloop she gave up any pretense of demure behavior. With a small cry of joy she clutched up her apple-green skirt and ran.

In her haste to reach the vessel, she ran headlong into a sailor who had just walked down the gangplank. The man grabbed Madeline's waist to steady her as she looked up.

"Oliver!" she cried, and threw her arms around the grizzled first mate's neck.

"Miz Whitlock, is that you? What you doin' here?"

Madeline gave Oliver an extra squeeze before letting go. "I had to come. I found something—a journal. It explains everything . . . well, almost everything. I need to show it to Joshua. Where is he?" During her breathless speech, Madeline had been leading the way up the gangplank and onto the deck. Now she turned toward the first mate, her eyes expectant.

"That's just it, Miz Whitlock. I ain't sure."

She took a step closer. "What do you mean you aren't sure?"

Oliver fidgeted from one foot to the other, and Madeline felt as if the blood were beginning to drain from her body.

"He went to Hopewell—"

"Alone?"

"You know the cap'n. He wouldn't let none o' us go with 'im. Said we was to stay here. Said he'd only be gone a couple days."

"How long ago was that?"

"Ten days."

"Ten days!" Madeline went to the rail and gripped it

389

till her knuckles turned white. She looked back over her shoulder. "Did someone go after him? Anything could have happened to him in that amount of time."

"Went myself." Oliver shook his head. "He weren't there—never got there. Leastwise, that's what that dandy fella said."

"Dandy?" The word sounded strange as she sucked in her breath.

"Aye, he was that. Though I probably shouldn't be sayin' it, seein' how he's a friend o' yours. Philip Spencer, he said his name was."

The blood had left Madeline's body, and in its place flowed water from the coldest mountain stream. She shivered. "Philip Spencer is at Hopewell?"

"Aye, and he said the cap'n never got there. So I backtracked, but couldn't find no trace of 'im. Thought maybe I'd get some more o' the men together and go lookin'. That's why I come back."

Madeline barely listened to Oliver's plan. She was too busy devising one of her own. If what she had concluded in Baltimore was correct, Philip Spencer was continuing the vendetta his father had started. There was evidence, however slim, to link him to Nathaniel's disappearance, and now Joshua was missing. And Philip had been in evidence.

"Oliver," Madeline interrupted his naming of the men he planned to take with him. "I don't want you to go back to Hopewell."

"But—"

"At least not by land. There is a small cove along the coast. It's secluded and fairly close to the great house. To the west is a spit of land that separates it from the bay. I want you to sail there. You can lay at anchor behind that piece of land and no one in the cove can see you. Can you do that?"

The first mate looked at her as if she'd asked him to leap overboard. "The cap'n went by land, and he might o'" gotten hurt somewhere along the road."

"He didn't. I'm convinced he's at Hopewell someplace and that Philip Spencer knows where. I just need to persuade him to tell me."

Oliver's eyes narrowed. "What you talkin' 'bout?"

Madeline sighed. "It's a long story, but I think this man you talked to at Hopewell is involved with Nathaniel and Joshua's disappearance."

"Why?"

She was losing patience. Having decided what needed to be done, she was anxious to get on with it before doubts undermined her resolve. "Listen Oliver, if what I think is true, all this was caused by something that happened long ago—before the captain was even born. I don't have time to tell you about it now."

But Madeline found that she had to make time because Oliver would have no part in her plan unless she explained everything. And once she had, he was reluctant to let her go on alone. Before she had convinced him she'd be perfectly safe, she'd told more untruths than she cared to consider. But she didn't think for one minute that Philip would tell her anything if she showed up at Hopewell with a dozen of Joshua's men in tow. Perhaps he wouldn't tell her anything, anyway. But she felt her only hope was to appear vulnerable, and to do that she had to be vulnerable.

The next day her carriage stopped in front of the house that had always been her home—her safe refuge. Judging outward appearances, it still was. No obvious evil lurked among the wide, white columns of the veranda. And the sturdy front door still beckoned, promising cool respite from the glaring tropical sun. The house was the same. It was those who dwelled within that had changed.

Tears sprang to Madeline's eyes as it struck her that her father would not be sitting in the library. There

391

would be no loving questions about her trip. She resolutely blinked. Now was no time to be weepy. On the contrary, if ever she'd had to keep her wits, it was now.

Madeline still wasn't certain she could carry out her plan. As a child with few playmates, she'd enriched her leisure hours by inventing imaginary characters. Indeed, she had often acted out little scenes for her father, and he had said they were quite interesting diversions.

But this was no child's play. Madeline had to convince Philip Spencer that she had returned to Hopewell—and him—that she had abandoned a husband she'd been forced to marry to come back to her true love. Just how far would she—could she—go to convince Philip this was true? She didn't know. If Joshua was still alive, and Madeline clung to the belief that he was, his life might depend on her acting ability. And if he wasn't? She bit her bottom lip. Nothing really mattered then anyway.

As the driver opened the coach's door and lowered the steps, Madeline pasted what she hoped was a flirtatious smile on her face. Smoothing the brocaded flowers of her skirt, she then left the concealing shadows of the coach.

At first, as she entered the cool interior of the great house, Madeline thought all her preparations had been in vain. There didn't seem to be anyone here to appreciate the extra time she had taken with her toilet, the elaborate way in which she'd fashioned her hair, the gown that clung alluringly to her fragile figure. The heels of her slippers rang against the floorboards as she traversed the hallway, looking in first one door, then another.

"Madeline?"

No matter how prepared she'd thought herself, at the sound of the cultured voice she had learned to despise, icy fingers danced along her spine. He'd come up behind her, and she had to turn and face him—she had to.

"Phillip?" she said in mock surprise. Then again, "Philip." Her voice had a breathy quality, and she hoped, in his vanity, Philip would mistake it for an emotion other than fear.

"What are you doing here, Madeline?"

What am I doing here? Madeline had to bite her tongue to stop the caustic question from being voiced. Remember Joshua, she reminded herself, and feigned a swoon, aiming herself toward Philip. "I've come back," she said, and was pleased that he caught and held her to him. "Oh, Philip, I was such a fool to leave Hopewell—and you."

Madeline felt his body tense, and feared he wouldn't believe her; but then he relaxed, and his hands began to caress her back. She wrapped her arms around his waist, tried to ignore the cloying smell of his perfume, and prayed for the courage to keep up her facade.

"Madeline dear." He had drawn her into the parlor and now sat facing her on the love seat. "How were you able to get here? After you sailed, I thought I'd never see you again."

"I left him. No, that's not exactly true." Madeline stared at his clasped hands. "I suppose in actuality the captain left me. He abandoned me in Baltimore Town."

"Baltimore?"

"Yes." Madeline sniffed. "As soon as he left I found a vessel bound for Jamaica. Oh, Philip, you were so right! I should have refused to marry that brute." Madeline chanced a surreptitious glance at his face. Although she'd feared her performance too sickening to be believed, Philip appeared convinced.

"My poor darling, it must have been terrible for you."

"Awful," Madeline agreed. "But, Philip, you haven't told me why you are here. Have you been at Hopewell since I left?"

"No, darling. I was in Kingston, preparing to leave Jamaica, but I wanted to return to Hopewell once more, in case you had come back. I hope you don't mind."

So you can lie, too. "Of course not." Madeline smiled into his hazel eyes. "I can only be thankful you did." She knew he was going to kiss her, and steeled herself against

393

the unpleasant sensation of his touch. It was all she could do not to turn her head as his lips approached hers. She had tolerated his kisses before, and, if the truth be known, had almost enjoyed the caress he had given her in Williamsburg when he had asked to marry her. But now she felt only revulsion.

"Oh, Philip." Madeline drew away from him, pretending to be frustrated. "I can't. If only I hadn't married that beastly man. Is he always to come between us?"

Philip's frustration appeared to be genuine as he rose from the settee and stalked to the window. "You must forget Captain Whitlock ever existed."

"I want to." She leaned toward him, conscious of the effect of the décolletage of her gown. "But I can't. I took vows." Madeline willed tears to appear in her eyes, but none did.

"The hell with your vows!"

She gasped at the unexpected vehemence of his outburst. It was her first unplanned gesture since she'd arrived at Hopewell.

"I'm sorry, Madeline dear. It was not my intent to shock you. It's just that the man doesn't deserve any consideration from you. He abandoned you."

"I know." She walked to the window and took his hands in hers. They were cool and smooth. "If only I knew where he was."

He pulled his hands away, and Madeline cringed. She hadn't meant to say that.

"Why do you care where he is?" Philip asked, and a furrow marred his brow.

"I don't . . . I mean"—Madeline tried to think quickly—"if I knew he'd never come back to haunt me, then I'd feel free to express my feelings for you." She held her breath. She really wasn't very good at this. She tried to imagine how quickly she could make it to the cove and the sloop that awaited her there. Probably not before Philip could catch her. But there was no need to run. Philip was smiling at her and reaching for her hands.

"You're fatigued from your trip. Why don't you go to your room and rest? We can talk about this later."

"Philip," Madeline cooed, "I'd almost forgotten how wonderful you were."

"I'll see to it you shan't be tempted to do so again."

As Madeline climbed the spiral staircase, she couldn't shake the feeling that Philip's last statement had sounded almost like a threat. Was he suspicious? She couldn't tell. He'd seemed enamored of her, but he hadn't told her anything.

Rest. That was the last thing she wanted. Madeline entered her room and looked about. Everything was exactly as she'd left it. She went to the mirror and viewed her reflection. Large, green eyes shone forth from a pale face. Had Philip noticed her lack of color?

Too restless to remain in any place for long, she opened the French doors leading on to her balcony and walked outside. She could see the garden, its splash of red and pink flowers brilliant against the emerald green grass. Beyond it, the sea spread out forever. Its eternal rhythm vibrated through the moist tropical air, through her body—gently pounding, constant. The surf seemed to echo a name, as if it, too, searched for the one she had lost. Glistening tears ran unchecked down her cheeks as her whisper joined nature's. "Oh, Joshua, where are you?"

A fine blue mist wreathed the towering peak, shrouding the nearly impenetrable foliage. Viewed from the edge of the rocky precipice, it was a primeval wealth of mahogany, breadfruit, mango, and almond. But there was no man in sight.

"Sau'll come," the wizened old woman said.

Joshua Whitlock looked around at her and nodded. "I know. I'm just restless . . . I suppose."

The old woman chortled, and her face creased with the myriad lines time had etched into her dark skin. "Too restless."

"It's healed." Joshua slipped easily into the debate he and the old woman had been having for the past few days. "You've made me as good as new." For emphasis he lifted the rough, homespun shirt Sau had brought him. The puckered scar in his side was red but no longer angry and raw.

"Humph." She waved a gnarled hand. "Too soon."

Joshua grinned at her antics, then turned back to scan the forest. "It was today that he said he'd come, wasn't it?"

When Joshua received no answer, he glanced behind him. She was gone. As used to her comings and goings as he had become, her ability to move without being heard still amazed him. The first time he'd noticed it—the day the fever had left him—Joshua had thought maybe she practiced some sort of magic that allowed her to disappear at will. He rubbed his hand over near two weeks' growth of whiskers, and chuckled at his own foolishness.

Not that he didn't have reason to think the old woman magical, or a witch doctor, for that matter. From what Sau had told Joshua the last time he'd visited the old woman's highland hut, Joshua had been more dead than alive when he'd been brought to her. He had been able to remember nothing after hearing the deafening bang of Philip Spencer's pistol, but Sau had pieced together the subsequent events for him. He'd described how Dora had run up to him in the cane field, panting and breathless, yelling something about the big white man being shot. He'd told of following the cart with Joshua in it, and watching Spencer's men dump the unconscious body

396

into the river. As soon as the others had gone, Sau had heaved Joshua out of the water. According to the big black man, it had been easy to sneak off the plantation and bring Joshua to the mountain because no one really kept track of the slaves anymore.

But even after Joshua knew the particulars of his arrival here, how the old woman had saved his life remained a mystery. The powder of the tamarind tree for fever, balsam for curing the wound, she had told him when he'd asked. Still, Joshua preferred to believe she was just a witch doctor. Besides, she looked the part. With her sparse white hair and hunched-over form, one could easily picture her stirring a boiling cauldron of lizard parts.

Laughter at the image he'd conjured up made Joshua flinch, then grab his side. Quickly he looked around to assure himself that the old woman hadn't returned. The wound still caused him some pain; but she didn't know about that, and he wanted it to stay that way. There was no reason to give more fuel to her argument that he wasn't completely healed. He was anxious to return with Sau today.

Joshua noticed a slight movement in the underbrush; then Sau emerged from between two coco palms.

"Ya lookin' better." The large black man smiled as he approached.

"I'm feeling better." Joshua flexed his muscles to demonstrate this, carefully so as not to strain his side too much.

"It too soon for him to go," the old woman said, stealing up behind Joshua on silent feet.

Sau laughed. "Ancient one, da man is cured. Ya just hate ta give up his comp'ny."

"Humph." The old woman disappeared inside the hut.

Joshua turned to Sau, a wide grin on his face. "Who is she anyway? I owe her—and you—my life."

"Nobody knows." Sau shrugged. "But she has da gift

ta make folk better. Ya ready ta go?"

"Yes, let me say good-bye to her first." Joshua wondered if the old woman might be willing to share some of her secrets when he brought his wife home to Hopewell. Madeline seemed to be pretty good at healing people too, though he was certain she didn't know all the ancient cures the old woman did.

Thoughts of Maddie again made him thankful that she was safe in Baltimore Town. When he had taken care of Spencer, he'd get her and bring her home, but for now, it was much too dangerous for her here.

After he had said farewell and expressed his thanks to the old woman, Joshua followed Sau into the forest. Except for his boots, he was dressed the same as Sau, in a rough, homespun shirt and loose-fitting trousers. His own clothes, stiff with blood, had been cut off him by the old woman.

As they descended the slopes, they left the coolness of the mountains behind. Deep in the tropical forest it was hot and humid, the air thick with the shrieks of parrots and macaws. A harmless yellow snake slithered by, unnoticed by the two men.

"How many men does Spencer have?" Joshua was trailing Sau, who used a bill, the broad, curved knife used to cut sugar cane, to hack away at the foliage that impeded their progress.

Sau stopped and wiped his sweaty brow with the back of his hand. "Sometimes many. Sometimes, not so many."

Joshua, glad for the short break, squatted down on the cushiony forest floor. The odor of rotting vegetation assailed him. "How about now? Are there many men with him?"

Sau shrugged. "Don't know."

Joshua hoped they'd get to the plantation in time for him to scout it out a bit before the onset of darkness, yet he wanted to be damned sure no one saw him. Spencer thought him dead, and Joshua wanted to keep it that way for a while.

After talking the situation over with Sau, Joshua had decided the best course of action was to get to Kingston and alert the governor of Spencer's activities. He then planned to bring some of his crew back and take care of the man who had shot him—after wringing Nathaniel's whereabouts out of him.

He knew Oliver was worried. He had told him he'd be gone only a few days, and it had been close to a fortnight. Well, with any luck, he'd be able to relieve the first mate's mind by morning.

Tonight he was planning to "liberate" a horse from Hopewell's stables and ride to Kingston. It galled Joshua to leave without attending to Spencer, but he had learned his lesson. It wasn't a good idea to underestimate the man. No matter how he might dress and speak, Philip Spencer was no dandified fop.

"Sure you okay?"

Joshua looked up into the scrutiny of Sau's black eyes.

"Fit as they come," he lied as he bounded to his feet. Maybe he should have waited another day to attempt the trip, he thought as the pain in his side increased. No, there were too many people depending on him. He had to take care of matters quickly. Joshua took the bill from Sau and began hacking through the dense foliage.

Madeline had spent the last half-hour pacing her room. She had hoped to be able to talk to Hattie, had looked around upstairs for her, but she'd been unable to find the servant. And much as she wanted to ask about her, she had decided it wouldn't do to appear too curious.

But this waiting was driving her crazy. She would go riding. That should appear innocent enough. She opened the lid of the sea chest a slave had brought up and yanked out a riding habit. Her fingers trembled as she unfastened her gown and pulled the scarlet dress over her head. Madeline knew Hopewell better than anyone. There wasn't a cove or cave or slave's hut that had escaped her notice. If there was any clue to Joshua's whereabouts on the plantation, she'd find it. And tonight, after everyone went to sleep, she'd search the house.

Madeline was feeling more optimistic as she crept down the stairs—until she heard Philip's voice. He was approaching from the rear of the house, talking with someone. At first, she was tempted to duck into the parlor, but there was no guarantee that he wasn't headed for that very room. In the end, she decided it would look less suspicious if she just continued on as though nothing were amiss. She had no idea how much of her story Philip had believed or how much he'd be willing to tell her about Joshua.

She'd almost made it to the door when Philip's question stopped her.

"Madeline dear, are you going someplace?"

The question seemed innocuous, but his tone of voice sent waves of fear rippling through her. I will not let him know how frightened I am, Madeline thought, and she pasted a smile on her face as she turned to him.

Her smile froze. Beside Philip, stood Eli Creely, his brown hair lanky, his pale eyes evil. Philip had been talking to *him?* And why was Creely still here? What had happened to Andrew Burns? Madeline's gaze darted from the overseer to Philip. Then she took a deep breath and willed her voice to be steady. "I thought I'd take a ride. It's been such a long time since I've had the opportunity."

"Excellent idea."

Madeline tried to conceal her joy. She had realized upon seeing Creely that she had taken on more than she could handle, and had decided that as soon as she and her horse, Medusa, were out of sight of the house, she'd head straight for the cove and Oliver. But she hadn't planned on Philip's astuteness.

"It will only take me a moment to change, and then I'll join you."

Madeline knew how a soap bubble felt when it burst. "I . . . I wouldn't want to inconvenience you. I really don't mind riding alone. As a matter of fact, I ofttimes prefer it."

"Ah, but, Madeline dear, I insist that you allow me to accompany you. One never knows what dangers might be lurking about."

"Of course, Philip, since you put it that way."

She sank onto one of the side chairs that lined the hallway and watched him ascend the stairs.

"Nice to have you back, Miz Madeline."

Except for her initial observation of him, Madeline had pointedly ignored Eli Creely. Now, after his comment to her, she turned her haughtiest look on him, determined not to allow this disgusting little man to intimidate her.

"Don't you have some duties that require your attention, Mr. Creely?"

"Oh, I reckon I can stay a little longer." The overseer smirked.

"Mr. Creely, I—"

"Remember what Mr. Spencer said 'bout dangers?" Creely interrupted. "I'll just stay and make sure none befall you till he gets back."

Trapped. She was trapped, and there seemed to be no way out. Even Creely wouldn't be so insolent unless he was certain he had the upper hand. Apparently, either Creely or Philip were going to be with her at all times. Madeline wondered how long Oliver would wait before coming to look for her.

She nervously bit her bottom lip, noticed that Creely was observing her, and forced herself to stop.

Fear was her worst enemy. Spencer and Creely might be watching her every step, but she didn't think they would harm her—at least not now. Philip, for all his evil ways, seemed to desire her. Marriage to Joshua had shown her it was possible for a man to want her, and she hoped to use Philip's lust to her advantage. It didn't seem likely he'd tell her anything about Joshua, but maybe his craving would cause him to spare her life till she could escape. However, she wondered what she would have to do to guarantee her own safety.

"You haven't changed your mind about a ride, have you, my dear?"

Madeline looked up as Philip reached the bottom step. He had changed into a scarlet frock coat with the skirts caught back on each side. And he now sported a pair of leather riding boots.

"Of coures not." Madeline gave him her most dazzling smile as she rose and gracefully approached him. "I'm looking forward to our ride."

"Damn, I hate sneaking around—and on my own plantation." Joshua ran his fingers through his hair in frustration.

Sau simply shrugged and sat back against the dark brown bark of an ebony tree.

Joshua and Sau were hidden from view by the dense grove of trees that bordered the road leading from the sugar works to the great house. Since arriving at the plantation a few hours ago, they had scouted around the caves and main house, but had found nothing amiss. Now they were resting, waiting for night's cover to take a horse from the stable.

But Joshua was sick of inactivity. His wound was bothering him, and he was anxious to repay Spencer for the discomfort. Besides, as he had told Sau, it irked him to steal around on Hopewell. It belonged to him, at least it belonged to his wife, and there was no logical reason that he should have to hide among the trees. *No reason except that you have no weapon, are one against many, and*

402

experience has shown you what facing Spencer unprepared can mean.

Thoughts of Spencer brought him back to the question that had plagued him for months. Why was Philip Spencer doing this? What possible reason could the man have for lying about Nathaniel? And not just Nathaniel. What motive could Spencer have for wanting him dead? Joshua was certain Philip believed that the gunshot had proven fatal. Joshua couldn't wait to show him otherwise.

"Horses!"

Sau's excited whisper caused Joshua to roll up to a sitting position. In another lithe movement he turned onto his stomach and wriggled closer to the edge of the road. Carefully, he pushed aside one of the round leaves of a sena shrub. It occurred to him that the horses, whose hooves he now could clearly hear, might belong to anyone—friend or foe. Oliver or Henry Smythe might be coming to check on him, in which case Joshua couldn't let either man ride, unsuspecting, into Hopewell.

The horses were closer now. Joshua sensed the big, black man had crawled up beside him. Across the way a macaw rose toward the sky, its bright blue and orange feathers glistening in the sunlight.

There were two riders. Two riders. Joshua watched as they cantered toward him. It was difficult to see from his vantage point. The road was dry, and the horses hooves kicked up a veil of dust.

The rider closest to him was Spencer. The moment Joshua realized it, he had an uncontrollable urge to burst from the foliage and yank the bastard from his horse. His muscles tensed in preparation to leap, and then he heard it. The laugh. It was soft and sweet and achingly familiar.

Joshua's gaze flew to the other rider, and his breath caught in his throat. Perched atop Medusa, her head tilted alluringly toward Spencer, sat the woman he had seen most recently in his dreams.

They were by him in an instant. As he started to his feet, he felt the pressure of Sau's hands holding him down. Joshua gave his shoulders a shake, but the black man's hold remained.

"Let go of me." He hissed the words through clenched teeth.

"He'll kill you sure dis time."

"God damn it, Sau, that was my wife!"

Chapter 25

"What if I can't do it?" Madeline murmured to herself as she sat in her room staring into the dressing-table mirror. The reflection that greeted her showed the care with which she had prepared for the evening. Her hair was combed straight back, exposing the delicate contours of her forehead and temples. Though most of her tawny locks were bunched atop her head, she had allowed a few stray strands to curl over her bosom.

Pleased with the image she saw in the looking glass, Madeline sighed and bit her bottom lip. This was it. After spending the afternoon riding with Philip, she had returned from that excursion mentally exhausted, and she'd decided she would continue playing the part of the enamored female through dinner—but no longer. If subtle inquiries into Joshua's whereabouts produced no results, she would employ more direct means. When Philip came to her room—and he had made his intentions to do so abundantly clear during their ride—he would find much more than he'd bargained for.

Madeline opened the top drawer of her dressing table and touched the pistol nestled among the ribbons. The solid strength of its smooth, cool steel seemed to penetrate her body. When she looked back into the mirror, she saw a determined face.

Bringing the gun with her had been an impulse. She

had found herself alone in the captain's cabin while the *Chesapeake* was in Kingston harbor, and had immediately thought about the matched set of dueling pistols under the bunk. Joshua had given her one to use once so she'd decided to borrow a pistol. When she had opened the box, she had been pleased to find that one of the pair was missing. That meant Joshua was armed. And so was she.

Madeline stood and smoothed the overskirt of rose silk over her hoops. She took a deep breath and left the room. Philip wasn't waiting for her at the bottom of the steps or in the parlor. She was starting to sit on one of the hall chairs to wait when voices came from the library. Though she told herself she mustn't, Madeline glided silently down the corridor.

The door to the library stood ajar, and the voices filtered into the hall. The only deterrent to hearing the words clearly was the pounding of Madeline's heart.

Philip and Creely were speaking, Madeline realized as she forced herself to calm down and listen.

"You're sure it's tonight?"

"Yes, Mr. Creely, I'm certain. I received a message yesterday from Kingston. The *Sea Witch* has dropped him off there and was to sail directly here with its last shipment."

"Hate ta give this place up." Creely made a slurping sound, and Madeline assumed he was drinking.

"It is a pity. I had hoped to keep Hopewell, maybe even limit some of my other activities, but . . ."

"Well, why can't we?" Creely whined.

"Haven't I explained this to you more than once? There have been too many complications. Sooner or later that solicitor is going to send someone to check on the replacement overseer."

Creely chortled. "We'll take care of him, same as we done the other one."

In the hall, Madeline drew in a breath as she grasped the implication of Creely's words.

406

"We cannot continue killing people indiscrimi-
nately." Philip sounded exasperated. "Eventually someone in authority will come to investigate all these disap-
pearances."

"Never knowed you to be squeamish about killing
before."

Madeline jumped at the loud pounding noise that
followed Creely's statement. When her heart began to
beat again, she realized Philip had been hitting a table or
desk.

"The others deserved what they got, as does Nathaniel
Whitlock. He's on the *Sea Witch* by the way. So by
tomorrow morning we will have taken care of everything."

"Not quite everything."

From Creely's tone, Madeline could imagine the smirk
on his disgusting face.

"Meaning?"

"Talking about that little bit of baggage you got waiting
upstairs for you."

"Madeline needn't be any concern of yours."

"Maybe not mine, but I'm thinking he ain't gonna like
it none."

"You overstep your bounds, Creely." Philip was
annoyed. "Just call me when it's time to give the signal."

"I can do it." There was a pause, then Creely
continued. "All right, I'll call you. Where you gonna
be?"

"I shall be entertaining, my 'little bit of baggage,' as
you so eloquently called her, in her room." Madeline
heard the creaking of her father's leather chair. "I
wonder what is keeping her?"

How she made it back to the stairs she would never
know, but when Philip and Creely emerged from the
library she appeared to be descending the last step.

"Ah, there you are, my dear." Philip approached her
and took both of her hands in his. "I have never seen you

look lovelier."

Madeline smiled, for she was unable to trust her own voice. She hoped he couldn't hear the terrible racket her heart was making or, if he could, that he attributed it to his presence.

She led the way into the parlor, wishing she could be alone to think about all she had heard. But Philip didn't seem eager to do without her company.

"Is that a new gown?"

"Not really, I had it made in Williamsburg." *You killed Andrew Burns. Who else have you murdered? Please, not Joshua!*

"It's very becoming. The color compliments your complexion and the cut . . ." Philip ran his finger along the low décolletage. "Beautiful."

Madeline tried not to cringe. "Thank you." *How am I to save Joshua's brother from this madman? How am I to save myself?*

As Philip's cool lips traced the gentle curves of breasts above her bodice, Madeline threw back her head and closed her eyes. Please, please, she prayed silently, let me be able to do what needs to be done.

Madeline sat at the table she had shared with her father all her life and pushed the food around on her plate. She could eat nothing. If Philip noticed her lack of appetite, he did not comment on it. He didn't eat much either, but used most of his energy to devour Madeline with his eyes. She found this so unsettling that she almost welcomed his suggestion that they forgo desert and retire to her room. Almost.

He allowed her a moment alone, presumably to undress, but Madeline had no intention of using her time that way. The candle she held trembled when she used it to light others, chasing the shadows from her room. Once she had done that, there was only one other thing she must do. The pistol was heavy, but she welcomed its weight. After checking the charge, she deftly slipped the gun between the folds of her overskirt and rested it in the pocket she had earlier tied around her waist. Now all she had to do was wait. Her plan was simple. Confront Philip about Joshua, at gunpoint, then climb down the trellis and make her way to Oliver. Together they might be able to rescue Nathaniel from the *Sea Witch*.

She was going to have to shoot Philip, and amazingly enough—she had never purposely hurt anyone in her life—her main concern was the noise the shot would make and how that would affect her escape. She had seen Creely leave the great house before dinner, but she had no idea where he lurked.

She was looking out at the trellis and trying to calculate how long it would take her to reach the *Chesapeake* when there came a tapping at her bedroom door. Resolutely, Madeline turned from the magical world of twinkling stars to face reality.

"Come in." She gripped the pistol.

Philip entered and came toward her, moving as smoothly and silently as water on glass. He wore a brocaded silk banyan that touched his slippers as he walked. "As lovely as that gown is, I expected you to be out of it by now. Do you need assistance?"

"No."

"Then I suggest—"

"What have you done with my husband?"

Neither the question, nor Madeline's demanding tone appeared to have any affect on him. He simply stared at her with his cold, hazel eyes. "Why do you care?"

Her fingers tightened on the gun. "Suffice it to say, I do."

"I see."

Madeline thought she heard regret in his voice, but if it had been there it was quickly replaced by anger.

"You are a damned foolish woman, Madeline."

409

Philip's upper lip curled scornfully. "If you had pleased me tonight, and I had no doubts you would, I was prepared to take you with me. Now . . ." He let the words hang in the air as he advanced on her.

Madeline could feel sweat trickle down her back, could smell her own fear, but she forced herself to remain outwardly calm. Slowly she drew the pistol from her pocket and aimed it at the purple brocaded flower that covered Philip's stomach. He didn't appear quite so disdainfully aggressive now.

"My husband, Philip? I want to know where he is."

"We both know you're incapable of shooting me, Madeline, so why don't you just give me that pistol?"

Madeline ignored the hand he extended toward her. "Tell me where he is, Philip!"

"Dead." His pale eyebrows rose. "That's right; your beloved husband is dead. But fear not, Madeline. You shall join him soon. First however, I shall—"

"You're lying! Joshua's not dead! He's not!" Madeline's words were fierce, yet within her, she wept.

"I shot him myself, Madeline," Philip said, and a feral grin spread his lips. "Now give me that pistol." He took another step toward her.

"No." Madeline didn't know if she could ever accept Joshua's death, but she was not about to succumb to hysterics. If she let her guard down, she did not doubt that Philip would kill her. At the moment, she wasn't sure she cared; however, there was Nathaniel to consider. Finding his brother had been important to Joshua, so it was important to her.

"Give it here!"

Philip had come so close that Madeline could feel his hot fetid breath as he ground out the words. Her finger tightened on the trigger.

"Engaging in an early evening tryst, are you, Maddie?"

That voice. Had she completely lost her wits? Madeline

whirled around, unmindful of the gun in her hand, and Philip was on her in an instant, grabbing the weapon and wrapping his free arm around her waist.

Joshua immediately realized his mistake. He had climbed over the balcony rail moments earlier and had seen Maddie and Philip awash in soft candlelight. They had been so intent upon each other that they hadn't even heard him enter the room, and the jealousy that had been festering within him since he had seen his wife that afternoon had prompted his impulsive remark. If he had been in a position to see Maddie's expression or the weapon she held, he would have realized the foolishness of his outburst. Now the full brunt of his stupidity struck him as he took in the stunned horror on his wife's face and the gun Philip was aiming at him.

"Joshua." The relief Madeline felt at seeing him alive made her voice tremble. Despite the pain of Philip's hold—when she had uttered the name he had tightened his arm considerably—Madeline couldn't take her eyes off her husband. He was thinner than before and hairier. A thick, black beard covered much of his face. But despite his rough clothing, he looked as handsome as ever.

"So, Captain Whitlock, you didn't die after all. Would you care to elaborate on how you escaped the jaws of death?"

"Not particularly."

"Pity. I'm certain it's an entertaining tale, though I suppose it matters naught. You shan't escape this time."

Joshua shifted his weight onto the balls of his feet. If only Spencer weren't holding Madeline, he might be able to wrest the pistol from him.

"Why don't you let her go. This really has nothing to do with her."

"I hate to disagree with you, Captain, but it does. Besides, she was planning to shoot me. Weren't you, Madeline dear?"

Madeline said nothing, not wanting to provoke him further, but Philip jerked her slender frame against him, cruelly digging his fingers into her flesh.

"Weren't you, Madeline?"

"Yes! Yes, I planned to kill you. I'm just sorry I didn't succeed."

Philip's laugh was sinister. "Just one more disappointment for you. First you travel all this way to find your husband, and then when you do, it's just in time to watch him die."

Why didn't Joshua do something? He was just standing there and waiting for Philip to shoot him. Madeline's gaze met his, and in that instant when green melded with black, she knew. It was because of her. He wasn't going to initiate anything that could get her hurt. He didn't know that Philip planned to kill her anyway. But even if Spencer hadn't made his intentions toward her plain, Madeline was not going to let Joshua sacrifice himself for her.

With a movement so abrupt it surprised even her, Madeline twisted about and raked her nails down Philip's face.

That was all Joshua needed. He leaped at Spencer, knocking the pistol from his hand. He had anticipated that Madeline was going to do something, had known it by the look in her eyes. Spencer tried to free himself, but Joshua wrestled him to the floor.

The first contact of fist to face was gratifying; the second, more so. By the time he had landed half a dozen punches, Philip was lying between Joshua's legs and appeared to be knocked senseless. Blood oozed from his lip and gushed from his nose. Madeline cursed her welter of petticoats as she tried to crawl across the floor. She had seen the pistol fly out of Philip's hand, but in the ensuing scuffle had lost track of it. Now she searched frantically for her weapon.

"Maddie."

She barely heard her name, but when two strong hands clasped her shoulders she turned, then fell forward in relief, burying her face against the strong breadth of his chest.

Joshua sank onto his knees, and wrapped his arms around his wife's quaking body. "It's all right. He can't hurt you anymore," he crooned, stroking the golden curls now spilling down her back.

"He was going to kill you." Madeline had been resolutely calm, at least outwardly, during the preceding events. Now that it was over, she could not stop shaking.

"But he didn't. Look at me, Maddie." Joshua placed a hand under her chin and forced her gaze to meet his.

There it was. Madeline never had been able to resist his grin. Even now, surrounded by a growth of black whiskers, it warmed her heart.

She nearly tumbled Joshua backward as she propelled herself at him, her arms encircling his neck, her body pressed to his. Hungrily, her mouth sought his lips. Joshua's hands had instinctively gone to her waist, to steady her—himself. But when the moist heat of her kiss seared him, his arms tightened around her, drawing her closer. Thigh to thigh, breast to chest, they clung. She could feel him, smell him, taste him.

Madeline languorously opened her eyes to see him. A glint of flashing metal caught her eyes. "No . . . !" She barely managed to get out the word before Joshua shoved her out of the way.

Madeline screamed as she saw blood spurt from the knife wound in Joshua's shoulder an instant before he backhanded a revived Philip, and the two men fell to the floor in a jumble of arms and legs, Philip's knife gleaming.

She found the pistol. It had been lying beside her all the time, concealed by the spread of her skirt. It was useless. Joshua and Philip rolled around on the carpet, first one on top, then the other. There was no way to

413

shoot without risking Joshua's life.

He was atop Philip now, but lurched to the side when the knife slashed in an upward arc. He grasped Philip's wrist as Spencer struggled to gain the topmost position. Madeline saw the tendons in her husband's arm bulge as he fought to turn the deadly blade away from himself. She aimed the pistol, willing the men to separate. Philip raised himself up, seemingly trying to regain his feet, and Madeline's finger tightened on the trigger. But before she could fire, Joshua kicked Spencer's legs out from under him and he tumbled forward, falling on his own knife.

"Is he dead?" Madeline rushed to Joshua's side, helping him up.

Joshua tried to regain his breath. "I don't know." He reached over and held his hand under Spencer's nose. "It appears so." Damn, Joshua couldn't believe how careless he'd been. He'd had no business dallying with his wife while Spencer lay there unconscious. Even with the man dead, the place wasn't safe.

"Come on." He grabbed Madeline and began pulling her toward the balcony.

"What are you doing?" She tugged against his hand. "You need to stay still so I can bandage your shoulder." She had yanked a pillow out of its cover, and had been busy tearing the linen into strips when he'd seized her arm.

"Forget my shoulder. We have to get out of here."

Joshua had forced her across the room with amazing ease, probably not even noticing her token resistance. But when she was propelled past the door, she caught hold of the jamb and held on for dear life. That got his attention.

"What the hell is wrong with you?"

"We can't leave," Madeline implored, holding fast to the sturdy door frame.

"Listen, Maddie"—Joshua plunged his fingers through his hair in frustration—"I know what Hopewell means to you, and believe me, we'll come back, but we can't stay now!"

Did he honestly think she was refusing to leave because of a house, a piece of land? "You big oaf." Madeline's green eye flared as she glared at him. "Hopewell's not the reason we can't leave. It's Nathaniel."

"Nathaniel?" Joshua searched her face. "Nathaniel's here?"

He had let go of her arm, and she gingerly rubbed the spot he had held. "No." She hurried on before Joshua could speak. "But he'll be here tonight. He's on a ship called the *Sea Witch.* Have you ever heard of it?"

Joshua tried to search his memory, but all he could concentrate on was getting out of there. "I don't think so," he finally said.

"Well, it's coming *here,* tonight."

"All the more reason to get you away from this house. I'll think of a way to rescue Nat. Now come on."

"Will you stop!" Madeline was angry. It was all well and good for her husband to want to protect her, but after all, she had done a fairly decent job of taking care of herself. "Listen to me. The *Sea Witch* won't unload without the signal, and Philip was the one who was to give it."

Joshua glanced into the room at Spencer's lifeless figure. His signal-giving days were past. "How do you know all of this? Did Spencer tell you?" Joshua couldn't help but wonder about the nature of their relationship since Spencer had provided Madeline with so much information. Her next words should have relieved his mind, but didn't.

"Of course not. I listened outside the door while he was talking to Creely."

"My God, woman!" Joshua threw his hands into the air in exasperation. "Do you realize how dangerous that was? What if Spencer had discovered you? What do you

415

think he'd have done to you then."

"Well, he didn't."

Joshua turned away and took several deep breaths of cool night air. He found her utter disregard for her own welfare frustrating.

A new concern presented itself. He looked back at his wife. "What are you doing here anyway? I left you safely in Baltimore?"

Left me was right, Madeline thought. She intended to let him know how she felt about that later, but this was not the time. A plan had begun to develop in her mind. She sensed he wouldn't like it. Actually, judging from his overbearing attitude, she figured he'd probably hate it.

"Well?" Joshua had been waiting for her explanation, and none too patiently.

"I found your father's journal. It explains who Philip is—was." Madeline grimaced as she thought about the body in her bedroom.

Joshua's eyes narrowed, and he looked at her questioningly.

"It's not important now. I just wanted to warn you about Spencer." Madeline reached for Joshua's arm. "Listen, I don't know when Creely will come up here; we'd better hurry."

Finally! Joshua was thinking the only way he was going to get her off the balcony was to toss her over his shoulder and carry her from it. "Let's go."

"Go? Didn't you hear me?" Madeline put her hands on her hips. "Creely's going to come up here to get Philip. He's expecting him to signal the *Sea Witch*."

"Well, it's a little late for Spencer to do any signaling," Joshua commented wryly.

Madeline blew out her breath in irritation. "I know that. But when Creely comes up here and finds Philip, he won't signal the *Sea Witch*."

"He'll signal it because after I get you safely out of here, I'll come back and make him do it." She was just as

416

stubborn as he remembered. He'd given her a perfectly reasonable explanation, yet he could tell by her stance that she was going to argue with him.

"Creely won't do it."

"Oh, he'll do it all right."

The light was dim. Maybe that contributed to the aura of primitive power that emanated from him. Madeline thought he looked quite savage with his unruly black hair and dark determined eyes. This must be how he appeared at the helm of the *Chesapeake* during battle—undefeatable. Madeline had no doubts he could handle Creely and more, except . . .

"Joshua, if you force Creely to give the signal, he'll probably give the wrong one. You'd have no way of knowing if he sent a sign that warned of trouble." Madeline touched his arm and noticed with relief that the bleeding from his shoulder had slowed. "The men from the *Sea Witch* might come ashore heavily armed, or they might just leave, taking your brother with them."

"Hell, Maddie, you think I don't know that." Joshua covered her hand with his own. "I've no other choice."

"We could trick him."

"We?"

"Yes." Madeline had been thinking over her plan while they talked, and now she was convinced it could work. Of course, she knew some things that her husband didn't. For one thing, Joshua was unaware that Oliver and the *Chesapeake* were anchored near the cove.

Madeline was starting to tell him this when she noticed the negative shake of his head. "What do you mean, no? You haven't even heard what I propose."

"I know I don't want you involved. These are dangerous men, Maddie."

"Oh!" He was just as unyielding as she remembered. "I just helped save your life."

"And I'll be eternally grateful, but—"

"Then listen to my plan, dammit!" Madeline glared at

417

Joshua, daring him to deny her.

He glared back. Didn't she realize how much he wanted to hear any idea that would help him rescue Nat? It was just that he couldn't stand the thought of anything happening to her. But it seemed, no matter how hard he tried, he was unable to keep her out of harm's way. Maybe he should trust in her abilities more. She did seem to have an uncanny way of surviving the roughest ordeals. "All right, Maddie, what's your plan?"

Madeline smiled and began to outline her idea as she wrapped a makeshift bandage around his shoulder. When she got to the part where she faced Creely alone, Joshua started to protest.

"It's the only way. He expects to find him in my bed. I overheard Philip tell Creely he'd be in my room. From the way he said it, I don't think he planned to spend his time talking to me."

Joshua felt a surge of fury toward Spencer upon learning he'd planned to force himself on her; then he remembered the pistol. She'd had it aimed at Philip when Joshua had come into the room. Maybe Madeline *could* take care of herself. Still . . . "So how are you going to convince Creely to light the signal?"

"I'll say that Philip left word with me that he was to do it."

"And Spencer, what about him?" Joshua asked.

"Well obviously he's not going to contradict me." When Madeline saw her husband's grimace, she hurried on to explain. "Spencer will be in bed, asleep. At least, that's what Creely will think. Actually, you will be under the counterpane, with the candles snuffed, I don't think he'll be able to tell the difference." Madeline waited nervously for his reaction. It came quickly.

"It just might work." Joshua hated to expose Madeline to Creely, but he had to admit her idea was good. It would be up to him to rescue Nathaniel once the pirates came ashore. Sau would help him. And the black man had indicated there were a few others he could count on for assistance. Of course, if it came to a fight, the slaves would be unarmed or, at best, have their bills. The curved knives were great for cutting sugar cane; Joshua wasn't sure how effective they'd be against a cutlass. But he did have the pistol. Joshua took the gun from the waistband of his pants. He'd stuck it there when he'd pulled Madeline from her bedroom. The weapon looked awfully familiar. "Where'd you get this?"

"From your cabin on the *Chesapeake*. I went to the sloop while I was in Kingston. That's when I told Oliver to sail to Hopewell. He and your men should be anchored in a small inlet east of the cove by now."

"My men, here?" Joshua couldn't believe it. It was beginning to seem more and more as if he might be able to rescue Nat. He grabbed Madeline to him and gave her a quick kiss. "Have I ever told you what a ingenious woman I think you are?"

"No." Madeline giggled as his whiskers tickled her cheek.

"Well, Maddie Whitlock, consider yourself told."

One more kiss, and he let her go. Madeline watched in surprise as Joshua went on to the balcony and made some noises not unlike the sounds of a loud tree frog.

Within minutes Madeline could hear leaves rustling as someone climbed the foliage-covered trellis that led to her balcony. She recognized the large black man who climbed over the railing as Sau, one of her field hands.

Joshua clasped Sau's shoulders. "My wife says there's a boat landing tonight," Joshua stated without preamble. "I've found out my ship is nearby. Is there someone you can send there with a message from me? Someone Creely won't be likely to miss when he gathers you together to help unload the boats?"

Sau nodded and followed Joshua into the bedroom. Madeline went in also.

"Looks like you'z had some trouble." Sau motioned

419

toward Spencer's body which still lay sprawled on the floor.

"Aye, I did that. Spencer took exception to the fact that I'm still alive and tried to remedy the situation. Thanks to my wife, he failed."

Joshua sat at the small cabriole-legged writing desk in the corner of the room and began listing his instructions to Oliver on a piece of parchment. While he did so, he outlined for Sau what he hoped would happen. "It's going to be dangerous. There's no question about that. And I don't want you feeling obligated to help me. You've already saved my life once."

"Danger ain't a problem. I'z lived with dat a plenty."

Joshua looked up and returned the black man's grin. He'd hoped Sau would stand by him, and he silently vowed to do what he could do to improve the big man's existence and the lot of the other slaves when this was over. But now he had to worry about the *Sea Witch* and Nat.

Joshua sanded the paper and stood up. "Have your messenger give this to a man named Oliver. He'll know what to do then. I don't know when the ship is coming, but as soon as Madeline can talk Creely into signaling the vessel, I'll meet you at the cove. That's where Creely has the slaves wait, isn't it?"

Sau nodded and stuck the letter in the waistband of his pants.

"Good. There's one more thing you'll need before you go. Madeline?" Joshua turned toward his wife. "Do you have a key to the storage shed where the bills are kept?"

"The knives for cutting sugar cane?" Despite all that had happened, all that she owed Sau, Madeline couldn't disguise her surprise. Nor could she alter her opinion that giving weapons to slaves was foolish. She had lived her life as a member of the white upper class that was vastly outnumbered by blacks. Hopewell's slaves, until recently, had always been treated well and had never

420

shown a desire to rebel, but Madeline was not immune to the gruesome stories she'd heard about entire families being murdered in their sleep by armed blacks.

Joshua knew the history of the island, too, and he sensed his wife's concern when he saw her apprehension. He crossed to her and gently placed his hands on her shoulders. "I owe Sau my life. We've spent a great deal of time together, and I trust him completely. Besides, it would hardly be fair to ask him to fight heavily armed pirates with no weapon."

Despite Joshua's assurances, some doubts still nagged at her. However, she was certain her husband was right about one thing. Unarmed, neither Sau nor any of the others would stand a chance against Spencer's men. She went to her dressing table and took a large ring of jingling keys from the top drawer, then crossed the room to Sau. As tall and broad as her husband, the black man seemed even more formidable at close range. "This is the key you'll need." Madeline handed him the lot after indicating the correct one.

Sau took the keys and grinned. "Thank ya, Miz Madeline."

Madeline's answering smile was spontaneous. "No, Sau. 'Tis I should be thanking you."

Joshua came up behind his wife and, draping his arm around her shoulders, gave them a quick squeeze. He knew she'd been nervous about giving slaves access to weapons, and he admired the courage it had taken for her to do it. To Sau, he said, "I suppose that should do it then. I'll meet with the men from my ship as soon as I can, and we'll be hidden behind the rocks near the cove. Remember, don't do anything 'til you hear my signal."

Sau nodded, then looked across the room. "Ya wants me to take care of dat for ya?"

Joshua followed Sau's gaze to where Spencer lay. "I'm certain Mrs. Whitlock would appreciate it if you would. I'll help you get his body down the trellis."

421

While Joshua and Sau wrapped Spencer in a blanket, Madeline straightened the room. By the time Joshua returned from helping Sau with Spencer's body, she had done the best she could to eliminate any sign of a struggle.

"Do you suppose this will work?" She looked around when she sensed Joshua behind her, and before she had time to realize what he was doing, she found herself enveloped in his strong arms. His face nuzzled the hair away from her ear, and he playfully tugged at the lobe with his teeth.

"I love you, Maddie, I do." Joshua's voice was a low, husky whisper. "I know I've never told you before, but the feeling's been there for a long time." As he held her close, Joshua wasn't sure why he had told her now. This really was no time for outpourings of the heart. But when he'd seen Madeline bent over, trying to cover the bloodstain on the carpet with her sea chest, he'd been unable to restrain himself.

She hugged him tighter, wrapping her arms around his narrow waist, breathing in his manly scent. With her cheek pressed against the coarse fabric of his shirt, her words were muffled. "Oh Joshua, I love you, too. I've wanted to tell you for so long. I just couldn't. . . ."

"I know." Joshua trailed his fingers through her curls. "We've both been fools, especially me. How could I ever have accused you of betraying me?"

"Hush." Madeline looked into the depths of his eyes, and covered his lips with the tips of her fingers. "'Tis no matter now."

Joshua lowered his head and kissed her palm, her forehead, the tip of her nose. "By the time we'd reached the bay I knew how wrong I'd been." His breath fanned across Madeline's cheek. "I wrote you a letter begging your forgiveness."

Madeline tangled her fingers into the springy hair at the nape of his neck. "I never received it."

"No matter. You probably wouldn't have been able to decipher the post. 'Twas nothing but lovesick drivel."

She rose on tiptoe and brushed her lips across his. "*You* wrote lovesick drivel?"

Joshua's teeth flashed white against his whiskered face as he grinned. "Come to think of it, I'm certain it was more eloquent than that." He kissed her gently, knowing circumstances demanded their contact be brief.

A noise coming from downstairs plunged them back to reality.

"That could be Creely," Joshua said as he loosened his hold on Madeline.

"Will you untie my stays?" she asked, lowering the bodice of her gown and letting it drop around her slender frame.

"What are you doing?" Joshua gaped at her. Before his eyes she had stepped out of her dress and petticoats.

"Do you suppose I could have driven Philip to exhaustion dressed in that?" With the brocaded toe of her shoe, Madeline gave the growing pile of clothing a kick. She then began unfastening the stay ties herself.

"I don't like to think of you driving any man but me to exhaustion, and I sure as hell don't want Creely seeing you dressed like *that*."

"You're right," Madeline teased. "I'm wearing too much." Joshua's possessive reaction to her disrobing was helping to keep her mind off the impending encounter with her former overseer. Though she was putting up a brave front for Joshua, she was nervous about facing Creely.

"Too much, huh?" Joshua searched through the clothespress till he found a shawl. Draping it across her shoulders, he stopped her protest with a kiss. "There's a chill in the air," he whispered, before pulling down the coverlet and crawling into the bed, carefully so as not to hurt his wounded shoulder. He reached for the pistol on the bedside table and checked its charge. "If there's any

423

indication—and I mean the slightest sign—that Creely doubts your story, I want you to drop to the floor. As soon as you're out of the way, I'll blow that bastard straight to hell."

"He'll believe me," Madeline said, with more conviction than she felt. "You just be still." Carefully, she pulled the ruffled coverlet up around his shoulders. Oddly enough, his rugged dark looks appeared not the least bit out of place in her feminine bed.

Madeline had just snuffed the last candle, leaving the room lit only by silvery strands of starlight, when there was a knock on the door.

Joshua mumbled something she assumed to be a warning, but his words were lost in the muffling blankets. Madeline let the shawl fall over her shoulder as she opened the door. As light from the hall sconces spilled into the room, she shifted to block Creely's view of the bed.

"I need to be seeing Mr. Spencer."

Madeline momentarily overcame her fear and dislike of the man who stood before her. "Shhhh." She touched her finger to her lips. "Philip is asleep."

Creely looked past her into the room. "He told me to get him." His tone was as insolent as ever, but he had lowered his voice.

"Yes, I know, when the *Sea Witch* arrived." Madeline smiled at the shocked expression that spread across the overseer's narrow face. "Before he fell asleep, Philip asked me to relay a message to you."

"What is it?"

Madeline did her best to sound sincere. "You're to signal the *Sea Witch* that all is safe, and then supervise the unloading of her cargo."

"While he sleeps?" Creely again maneuvered to look past her.

"Yes. Those were his orders." Madeline moved aside, hoping Creely would take the gesture as proof she had nothing to hide. "You may wake Philip if you like, but I can't guarantee what his reaction will be. I was under the impression he expects his orders to be followed."

Madeline judged from his reaction to her last words that Creely had felt the effects of crossing Spencer before. He quickly assured her that there was no need to bother the boss and made a hasty departure.

She watched the scrawny manager until he started down the steps, then closed the door, leaning against it wearily. Now that the pressure of confronting Creely was over, the courage that had sustained her seemed to have seeped from her.

"You were wonderful, Maddie. I almost believed you myself." Joshua had climbed from the bed and was now gathering his trembling wife into the shelter of his arms.

Madeline took a deep breath. She regained her composure. "I'm all right," she whispered into her husband's shirt.

"Are you certain?" Joshua drew away, trying to see her face, but the room was so deeply shadowed he couldn't make out her expression.

"Yes, I'm fine." Madeline hated to have lost control. Maybe her part in their plan was over, but his was just beginning. He did not need the extra burden of worrying about her. "They'll be waiting for you." She started to back out of his arms, but he drew her to him again.

"God, I hate to leave you like this."

She reached up and touched his whiskered cheek. 'You must go. I'll be perfectly fine. 'Tis your safety that worries me."

Joshua reached behind her and locked the door. She was right. He had no choice but to leave, yet he didn't want her worrying unnecessarily. "You know me, Maddie. I've the devil's own luck in battle." He took her hand and they walked toward the balcony. "Stay here till I come back for you. The pistol's beside the bed. It's all primed and ready if you need it." Joshua had reached the rail now, and still he hesitated.

Madeline knew his reluctance to leave stemmed from concern for her, and though that touched her, she could not allow him to risk the success of their plan. "Go," she urged. "I want to meet this brother of yours."

Joshua laughed and gave her nose an affectionate tap before climbing over the side of the terrace.

After he'd gone, Madeline went back inside. Slowly, she pulled her dress back on and then sat by the window to wait and pray.

Chapter 26

"They's comin', Cap'n."

Joshua leaned against the rock's hard surface and waited. There was no reason to respond to Oliver's comment. The old sailor probably didn't even realize he'd voiced the observation that was on all their minds. Having grown increasingly louder, the swish of oars through water was now impossible to ignore.

A dozen crewmen had met Joshua, on the road leading to the cove, as he'd asked. That had been two hours ago. He had spent the intervening time outlining the details of the plan and worrying. Mostly worrying, he admitted to himself.

The plan itself was simple enough. Oliver, Jamieson, and the others had needed only a brief explanation. Wait for the pirates to reach shore, then, on Joshua's command, rush from their hiding place behind the rocks, and, with the help of the slaves, overpower the men on the longboat. Simple. And dangerous.

Joshua had no idea how many cutthroats they'd be facing. There was a good chance they'd be outnumbered, and considering that the slaves were armed only with bills, an even better chance they'd be outgunned. Joshua had had no choice but to leave some of the crew on board the *Chesapeake*. Even now, he knew the Bermuda sloop was lurking behind the spit of land to the west, ready to attack the vessel that lazed at anchor in the bay. He smiled. Surprise. That was their advantage. And he intended to exploit it.

Joshua shifted his position, then cursed under his breath as the movement reminded him of his wound. It had bothered him after climbing up and down the trellis, but then, as now, he'd forced himself to ignore the pain.

The longboats were almost ashore. Joshua could hear their wooden hulls scraping against the sandy bottom. He also heard Creely's voice, low and insistent, issuing last-minute orders to the slaves. Joshua took a bead on the sound. When the fighting started, Creely was going to be his first order of business. If things did not go Joshua's way this day, at least there'd be no bastard overseer to point an accusing finger toward Madeline.

Joshua peered over the top of the rock. The last time he had tried to survey the area, darkness had made it next to impossible to distinguish anything but the small group of slaves and he could see them only because of the torches they held. But now ribbons of pink dawn fanned across the slate gray sky, illuminating the *Sea Witch* lolling offshore and the men tugging four longboats onto the beach.

Joshua gripped the hilt of the cutlass Oliver had brought and tried to find the tall, sparse frame of Nathaniel among the men climbing from the boats. He spotted his brother and nudged the first mate. "Oliver."

"I see 'im, Cap'n. Don't worry none, I'll get the boy."

Joshua had dwelled upon the need to protect Nathaniel. Since not all of the *Chesapeake*'s crew knew his brother, he had been thorough in his description of him. But it was to his nimble first mate and friend that Joshua had given the task of freeing Nat.

The pirates were on the beach now. Joshua pulled the pistol, another boon from Oliver, from his waistband. Sweat, too extensive for the gentle trade winds to combat, rolled down his back as Joshua raised the gun above his head.

"Now!" he roared, as he exploded over the rock.

Certainly he hadn't meant for her to stay in her bedroom, Madeline thought as she made her way down the long spiral staircase. He'd meant that she should remain in the house. One room in the great house was as safe as another, and she could no longer stand the confinement of her bedroom.

She had been all right—or as well as she could be, considering the circumstances—until she'd heard the faint but unmistakable sounds of gunfire. Though hardly unexpected, they had startled and alarmed her. She'd experienced this same restless anxiety aboard the *Chesapeake,* when she'd had to stay below during the battle. At least then there'd been some relief for her nervous energy. Tending to the wounded had been a way for her to feel useful, and it had helped to take her mind off what was happening. Now there was nothing to distract her.

Madeline was drawn to the library. With practiced ease, she climbed onto the window seat and drew her knees up under her chin. The pistol knocked against her leg, so she set it in the space between the pillow and the casement. She seriously doubted she'd need it. With the exception of an occasional burst of gunfire, it seemed deceptively peaceful. Madeline turned her head toward the window and strained to see any sign of the battle. As she'd expected, the foliage was too thick and the struggle too far off for her to distinguish anything.

She pressed her forehead against the window's smooth surface and sighed.

"You would be Patrick's daughter."

Madeline's head spun around at the sound of the oddly familiar voice. Standing in the doorway was a man she had never seen before.

"Who are you, and how did you get in my house?" She swung her feet down and stood up to face the intruder. He was at least fifty years old, and had the look of a gentleman about him. His clothes were expensively tailored and fit his tall, lean frame well. But gentleman or not, he had no right to enter her home without being invited.

The stranger smiled. "I'm a friend of your father's, and as to how I came to be in your house, I simply walked through the open door."

"The door was open?" Madeline watched the man warily as she moved past him. When she glanced down the hall, a prickle of unease danced across her flesh. The front door was ajar. The light of dawn had erased some of the horror of the night, but the distant rumbling of ships' cannons reminded Madeline that danger still existed.

She turned and discovered that the man had moved up behind her. Involuntarily she took a step back. "My father has passed away, and I'm unable to receive guests now. If you could return at another time, Mr. . . ." Madeline let her voice drift off, assuming he would give her his name.

He didn't, nor did he appear inclined to grant her request and leave. Instead, he took one step, then another, till he had closed the gap between them. Madeline flinched when he reached for a strand of her hair.

"You are just as lovely as he said."

She swallowed and tried to back up, but her foot struck the wall. "Who, my father?" She wished she could place his voice. She had heard it before, she was sure . . . or one like it. But where?"

"No, my son." The response was cool.

The prickle of fear Madeline had felt now spread to every cell of her body. She looked up into light eyes and noticed what she had missed before. There was something not quite sane about the gleam in their depths.

430

Who was this person, and why was he bothering her? She didn't know, but she was sorry she'd left her pistol across the room. Passing him was now the only way to get to it.

She took a deep breath and tried to squeeze by him. "Tell me who your son is so I can thank him for the compliment, if ever I see him again."

Fingers tightened in her hair, stopping her retreat.

"But my son is here. I've come to see him."

"No . . . nobody's here." Madeline cringed. "You're hurting me."

The man ignored her last statement. "Don't lie to me. I know Philip's here."

Madeline tried to swallow again, but couldn't. "Philip! You're Philip's father?"

"I am. Where is he?"

As the clawlike hand twisted into her hair, Madeline bent her head to relieve some of the pain. "I don't know."

"You're not being truthful with me, girl."

"I am." Madeline thought about what this man had done to Justin's sister and tried to stay calm. She didn't think she stood a chance if she tried to fight him. "Philip was here, but he's gone."

"He wouldn't leave. Philip knew I was coming."

The man had pressed her up against the wall, but snatches of the conversation Madeline had overheard came flashing back to her. *He's coming.* She could remember Philip saying those very words to Creely, in a voice so like his father's. At the time she had been fearful of being discovered, and hadn't attached much significance to the statement. Actually, she'd all but forgotten it until this very minute. She chided herself for her foolishness. She had always assumed that Matthew Burke was dead, and she'd had absolutely no reason to think that.

"What is that noise?" Burke had been watching her intently, but now he cocked his head toward the window.

431

Madeline said nothing, only returned his stare.

The blow was so quick she didn't see it coming, couldn't have warded it off even if her arms had not been caught between their bodies. Black dots danced before her eyes as pain exploded in her head, then narrowed to the vicinity of her left cheek. She sucked air into her mouth on a sob. *I won't cry. I won't cry.* The words echoed in her mind, yet even as she told herself not to show Burke her fear, tears streamed down her face.

Madeline winced as his hand touched her throbing cheek. But when he let his fingers trail down the side of her neck and lower, her skin crawled in revulsion, and she thought she'd be sick.

Burke bent over her, and his hot, acrid breath wafted around her. "Shall I show you what happens to little girls who don't cooperate with me?"

"Damn." Joshua hissed the word under his breath as the tip of a cutlass sliced into his thigh. A sixth sense had made him whirl around moments after he'd stuck his own blade into the gut of a redheaded giant of a man. Without that movement, the wound would have been a lot worse.

Blood trickled down his leg to mix with sweat and grime, but Joshua had no time to think of it. The pirate who had cut his leg seemed bent on doing further damage. Joshua leaped to the side, his boots sinking into the wet sand, as his opponent's cutlass swiped at him and missed. That error was the pirate's last. With a powerful thrust, Joshua sank his weapon into his assailant's chest. His stocky adversary tumbled backward to sprawl over one of his dead comrades, and bright red blossomed on his tattered shirt as Joshua extracted the blade.

Nausea gripped Joshua, and his head pounded. He wished for nothing more than to sink onto the beach and sleep. But reason warred with fatigue and won.

A quick survey of the area confirmed what Joshua had suspected since the fighting had begun. Outnumbered as

432

they were, his men—his friends—had defeated the pirates who'd ventured on shore. He shaded his eyes and looked over the glistening waters. The boom of cannon fire had stilled, and even without a spyglass Joshua could see his privateers swarming over the *Sea Witch*.

Things had gone well. Now, he could seek out Nathaniel. He had lost sight of his younger brother shortly after the fighting had begun. As Oliver had jogged toward him, Joshua had been tempted to keep an eye on them. But battles had no place for observers, so Joshua had, instead, rushed after Creely. The cowardly overseer had started to run at the first sign of trouble, and when Joshua had tackled Creely from behind he'd thanked God he'd thought to make the elimination of the overseer his personal charge. During the frenzy of fighting, it would have been easy for the disgusting man to slink away. Joshua didn't want to think what might have befallen Madeline, alone in the great house, if Creely had happened upon her. But he couldn't stop such thoughts. So it was with more satisfaction than he cared to admit that Joshua knocked the pistol from Creely's hand and ended the overseer's life.

He now glanced about him as he crossed the beach. Creely hadn't been the only one to pay for his foul deeds this day. His men were checking through the carnage for survivors.

"Over here, Cap'n."

Joshua's face broke into a wide grin when he looked toward the person who'd called his name. It was Oliver, beaming like a lighthouse, and beside him stood Nat. A thinner, possibly tougher, Nat, but Nat just the same.

Joshua strode over to him, unmindful of the cut in his leg or his exhaustion. "So, we've found you at last," he said, clasping his younger brother about the shoulders. He'd been right; Nat was thinner, a fact even more apparent by touch than sight.

"You took your time about it, big brother," Nathaniel retorted with an answering grin.

433

Joshua laughed. He hadn't missed the newly acquired lines on his brother's face, or the guarded glint in the depths of Nat's eyes, but at least his brother hadn't lost his sense of humor. "You're right, Nat. I must be slowing down in my old age. Certainly had more trouble tracking you than I did Mr. Benville's cow."

"Ho, I'd almost forgotten about that." Nat laughed.

"Maybe it's being married that's slowin' ya up, Cap'n." Oliver injected.

"Married?" Nat looked incredulous. "You, brother?"

"Of course me." Joshua sounded as if that were the most natural thing in the world, and, in fact, to him it had become just that. "I'd better go up to the great house before Maddie decides to come investigate."

"You run along now, Cap'n. I'll see to finishin' up things here. Looks like we got quite a haul." Oliver motioned toward the longboats filled with kegs and crates. "Ain't sure what all that stuff is. What ya plannin' on doin' with it, Cap'n?"

"I guess you could say we all earned a share of whatever the *Sea Witch* is carrying this morning," Joshua told him with a wink. Then he turned back to Nat. "Why don't you come with me and meet your new sister? It's thanks to her that I knew you would be on yon ship." He looked out across the bay at the *Sea Witch*, now linked by grappling hooks to the *Chesapeake*.

Nat wrapped his arm around his brother's shoulder. "I guess you're going to have to share my thanks with your wife, then. I'd love to meet the woman who finally caught you, but aren't you going to clean up some first?"

Joshua looked down at himself. His clothes were torn and bloody; and dirt and grime covered him. He rubbed his fingers through his beard. Nat did have a point. Maybe he should wash off in the river first. He was about to agree when he thought of Madeline alone up at the house, not knowing what had happend. "No," he declared. "I'm going to go see Maddie. Believe it or not, she's seen me looking almost this bad before.

434

You coming?"

Nat shook his head. "I'll be along in a few minutes. Your wife may be used to seeing you like this, but I don't intend her to see me first as a filthy scarecrow."

"Suit yourself." Joshua turned and started toward the road. He had no desire to fight his way through the thick foliage between the shore and the house.

Tired though he was, his pace quickened as he got closer to the great house. He couldn't wait to tell Madeline the good news. Nathaniel was found, the *Sea Witch* had been captured, and few of those aiding him had suffered more than minor wounds.

A parrot fussed at him from a button tree as he started to jog along the drive. Joshua turned around and grinned at the bird. "Chide me for being happy, will you?" He bent down, scooped up a shell, and made as if he would throw it toward the unblinking bird. Laughing, he then tossed the shell back onto the drive and ran up the veranda steps.

"Who's that?" Matthew Burke tightened his grip on Madeline's hair and yanked her out of the chair.

"I . . . I don't know," she lied. She'd heard someone approaching the house and had felt it was Joshua even before he'd burst through the front door calling her name.

"He's calling you. I think you should answer him." Burke nudged her cheek with the pistol he had already pulled out of his coat pocket. "Call him!"

Joshua was upstairs now. Madeline could hear panic in his voice as he discovered that she was gone from the bedroom. Since Burke had grabbed her, she'd both prayed for and dreaded Joshua's return. She had told her tormentor some of what was going on. He knew there'd been a battle between the *Sea Witch* and another ship, but he didn't know his son was dead. And he didn't know Joshua was alive.

435

"You heard me, girl. Call him in here!"

Burke hissed the words into her ear as he trailed the gun barrel down her naked arm. Her gown was torn. Philip's father appeared to have a penchant for rending silk. She was thankful that age seemed to have dulled his proclivity for more active forms of harassment. He had bullied and threatened—and torn. But though his words and suggestions were vile, he'd done no real harm.

Madeline could hear the steps creak as Joshua came running downstairs. "Maddie," he yelled, and the anguish of that single word tore at her heart. He was coming down the hall. She couldn't let him walk into the room. "No, Joshua, he has a gun," she screamed.

That didn't stop him. Just as Madeline ducked and felt the butt of Burke's pistol strike her shoulder, she saw Joshua burst through the door.

He stopped abruptly. Fear, such as he'd never known before, washed over him as his mind processed what his eyes were seeing. Madeline was in the clutches of a madman. Her cheek was bruised and swollen, her gown in shreds; and as he'd come into the room, Joshua had seen her almost fall when the bastard had hit her with the pistol. That same pistol was now aimed at him.

Joshua took a deep breath and forced himself to remain rational. This was no time for futile attempts at heroics that would, likely as not, get them both killed. He looked into Madeline's eyes, trying to impart the need for calm and strength, and was pleased to find her sending the same wordless message to him.

Joshua shifted his focus to the man who held her, and that's where he encountered confusion and doubt.

"Who are you?" Burke demanded as he pulled Madeline more squarely in front of himself.

"Captain Joshua Whitlock at your service." Joshua bowed slightly, though he never took his eyes off the stranger. "And who may I ask, are you. More importantly"—Joshua could feel his hard-fought composure

436

slipping—"what in the hell do you think you're doing to my wife?"

Madeline felt Burke's body stiffen when Joshua gave his name. "Whitlock, eh? I was told you were dead."

"Sorry to disappoint you," Joshua retorted in a voice that sounded anything but apologetic.

"No matter." The slight readjustment of the gun Burke brandished clarified his intention. "Ah, but I'm being rude. You asked me several questions which I have failed to answer. I, sir, am Matthew Burke"—he inclined his head—"and your wife and I have been waiting for my son to return."

"Your son?" Joshua had been inching forward, but he stopped when Burke seemed to notice.

"Yes. Philip."

"Spencer?" Joshua recalled that Philip had said something about his father right before he'd shot Joshua.

"His name is Burke actually, but at times he felt it more convenient to use the name *they* gave him."

"They?" Joshua had noticed that the more Burke talked, the less alert he seemed to be. He had been able to move a step closer during the man's last speech.

"It was really Justin, though she wouldn't admit it. With her dying breath, she denied it. I had to kill her, you see."

Madeline could tell Joshua was confused. She wished there'd been time to tell him what she'd found in his father's journal. Hopefully she'd be able to show him later.

Madeline hadn't missed Joshua's movements, though it appeared Burke had. She'd also noticed that the longer Burke talked, the more irrational he sounded *and* the more relaxed his grip on her hair became.

"I would have taken her with me, even after I'd learned of her deception, but she said she didn't want to come. Laughed at me—*me!* I showed her. She stopped laughing."

Madeline tried to ignore the chill Burke's words evoked, and concentrated on Joshua. She could tell he was ready. His eyes were narrowed until only slits of jet black shone between the lids, and his body was coiled like a spring. She had to stop him. The gun was aimed point-blank at his chest. If he jumped Burke now, he'd be killed. She knew what she had to do. Upstairs, she'd been able to distract Philip long enough for Joshua to overpower him.

Madeline started to twist herself around, but what had worked so well before seemed destined to failure this time. At her movement, Burke tightened his fingers in her hair; then, before she could do him any harm, he hurled her away from him.

Tears sprang to Madeline's eyes as her hip struck the wall. Worse than the pain was the realization that she'd failed. A glance toward Burke showed her that he still held the gun trained on Joshua. She closed her eyes and turned her head away in despair. When she opened them, she noticed the beauty of the sunlight streaming through the window and berated herself. This was no time to notice such a thing. The window! Her heart beat faster, and she tried to stop her hand from trembling as she pulled herself up to the window seat.

Joshua had barely stopped himself from going after Burke when she'd been tossed aside. Only the thought of what Burke might do to her if he were shot had stopped him from making an impetuous move. Burke had never so much as glanced away when he'd thrown Madeline against the wall. Whereas, Joshua tried to keep his eyes on the man, but his gaze wandered to his wife. She was all right. He let out a breath he hadn't realized he'd been holding.

"That was very foolish of you, Madeline," Matthew Burke said, though he didn't face her. "But what can one expect from the get of Patrick O'Neil. He was always worrying about things that weren't his concern. Just like you, Justin."

Joshua noticed that Burke had called him by his father's name. Had it been a mere slip of the tongue, or did Burke actually believe him to be his father? "What did I do, Matthew?" Joshua tested the depth of Burke's insanity.

Burke laughed. "Don't pretend you don't know. You never thought me good enough for Catherine. Well, she's not the pure princess you think. I've seen to that. But you know. After all, it's the reason for this duel. *Your* honor. *Your* revenge. Because I soiled your sister. I'm not going to run away this time, Justin. No, this time things will happen the way they should. This time I'll kill you." His finger tightened on the trigger.

The report of a pistol echoed through the room. Joshua braced himself for the pain. It never came, and in the next instant he realized why. It hadn't been Burke who had fired. He lay sprawled, facedown, on the rug, a plume of scarlet spreading from the gaping hole in his chest. Beyond him stood Madeline. Veiled by wispy smoke, her face was stoic. Her arms were stretched in front of her, still clutching the pistol she'd just fired.

It wasn't till Joshua reached her side and gently pried the gun from her hands that she stopped staring at the empty space where Burke had been. "He was going to kill you." Madeline's eyes were calm as she looked up at her husband.

Joshua let out a sigh of relief when he saw her expression. He had been concerned that the violence had been too much for her. He should have known she was stronger than that. Joshua bent over and brushed a kiss across her bruised cheek. "Yes, he was. But you stopped him, sweetheart."

Madeline smiled and leaned against her husband. "I remembered the pistol. It had been heavy, and I'd put it behind the window-seat pillow while I was waiting for you."

439

Joshua folded his arms around her and rested his chin on her head. "You're a brave woman, Madeline Whitlock."

"This is unbelievable."

"I know." Madeline nestled herself more comfortably against her husband's bare chest. She looked at the journal propped across his stomach and commented, "It becomes even more incredible as you read on."

As Joshua turned a page, the faint, musky scent of the past escaped into the air. "So Spencer really was my cousin. He called me that once, before he shot me, but I didn't know what he meant." He leaned his head back against the frilly, white pillows on Madeline's bed. "I seem to recall my father mentioning he had a sister named Catherine, but I'd always assumed she'd died in infancy."

Madeline closed her eyes. He sounded sad. And why shouldn't he? The story was sad—even more so when you read the journal. In doing so, you almost seemed to be living it.

Madeline had been thankful the day before when Joshua hadn't asked to see the journal. She had told him most of the major details recorded in it, and had hoped that would satisfy his curiosity. Now she realized he hadn't asked to see it because there'd been no time. The day had been spent in treating the wounded, burying the dead. There'd been cargo to inspect and a letter to the governor to write. On top of all that, Joshua had seemed most unwilling to let either Nat or her out of his sight. Luckily, he'd made an exception at bedtime—with his brother, at least.

And during the past night, there'd been no time for reading. But the first thing this morning he'd asked for the journal, and she had had no choice but to retrieve it from her sea chest.

Now Madeline looked down to see the page that described Catherine's death. She didn't need to read it. Memory had etched the words into her mind.

Joshua seemed to have forgotten she lay on the bed beside him, and Madeline wondered if he might prefer to be alone when he read the personal family history. Without looking up, he released her when she slid away from him. He even ignored her when she sat up. But when Madeline swung her legs over the side of the high tester, his hand found her naked back.

"Where are you going?"

"I thought I'd get up," she answered without looking at him.

"Why?"

Madeline didn't want to explain how unsure she still was about her place in his life, to say that she didn't want to intrude on his privacy. Instead she made an excuse. "You're busy reading, and Hattie will be along at any minute." The return of her old nanny had been a real joy for Madeline. Hattie, along with some of the other house slaves, had escaped Hopewell when Spencer made life unbearable for them. They'd lived in the hills until the day before when Sau had brought them back. Joshua tugged on her honey-colored curls till Madeline looked around. "I've finished reading, and Hattie isn't coming."

He didn't seem sad now. As he closed the journal and set it on the bedside table, Madeline thought he acted most pleased with himself. "But she always comes in the morning. She's not ill, is she?" Madeline had talked to Hattie the day before, and she'd appeared fine. But she was old. . . .

"She's fit as they come." Joshua let loose of her hair and traced the curve of her shoulder. "I just offered her first choice of the calico I found on the *Sea Witch* if she'd make herself scarce this morning." Joshua didn't mention that he'd included every morning for the next sennight in his deal.

441

Madeline turned, and Joshua took advantage of her new position to explore the rosy pink tips of her breasts. "You bribed Hattie?"

"Aye." He used his free hand to pull her closer. "But I think I was had. Judging from her lascivious grin, I don't think she was planning on bothering us anyway."

Madeline laughed. "That sounds just like Hattie. She's a born matchmaker."

Joshua lifted Madeline on top of him after kicking away the sheets. "Did she match you up with me?"

"From the very beginning." Madeline looked down at his face. He'd shaved off the beard before coming to bed last night. "She thought you were 'purty.'"

"Pretty?" Joshua sounded indignant, but he couldn't hide the amusement in his voice. "Men aren't pretty."

Madeline ran a finger down the column of his neck, then tangled it in his thick chest hair. "That's what I told her. But you know Hattie. She insisted that was what you were."

"Wait till I get my hands on her," Joshua said. But it was his wife he was really interested in handling. Her back and buttocks were creamy smooth as he gently reacquainted himself with her skin's texture.

Warm and sweet. Madeline let the sensations flow through her. Last night they'd been tired and they'd been hungry for each other. It had been too long since their desires had been fulfilled to indulge in slow, languid lovemaking. This morning was different. Now there was time.

Slowly, Joshua moved his leg, letting its hair-coarsened texture caress the tender flesh of his wife's inner thigh. Rough against smooth. Hard against soft. Man against woman. He pressed higher, desire raging through him as his skin touched the moist heat of Madeline's arousal.

She watched him, as he did her, eyes that glowed like black coals burning into her soul. His breathing was unsteady, became ragged when she traced the narrow strip of hair down his flat stomach. She touched his throbbing manhood and gloried in the low groan that rumbled through his broad chest. Madeline loved him, wanted him; was loath to think of the time when he'd return to the sea.

"Maddie . . ." The breathless whisper sang through her body as she brushed her lips across the expanse of his shoulder blade. His sun-darkened skin was hot and damp, salty to the taste. The tip of her tongue skimmed lower, intoxicated by his essence, anxious to know all of him. All of him. Madeline knew eventually he must leave, but for now only all of him would satisfy her.

"My God, Maddie." Joshua hardly knew the primal moan had escaped him. He hardly knew anything at all. His hips arched and his shaft pulsed compulsively as the magic of her lips surrounded him. As his world spun out of control, he grabbed for Madeline—his anchor to reality. With one motion he turned her—them—and buried himself deep inside her.

Madeline opened to receive him—all of him. Without Joshua she was incomplete. Now she was whole. He plunged deeper and she arched in counterpoint. Together their bodies flowed, finding a rhythm as old as mankind, as fundamental as life. Stronger—faster—their movements became till with one final thrust they soared to a world of splintered rainbows and exploding stars.

Joshua collapsed atop her, replete and content. It wasn't till he felt her slight movement that he remembered his wife was not of a size to bear his weight for long. Gently he grinned and levered himself off her. "You have a way of making me lose track of place and time," he whispered, and pulled her into the bow of his arm.

Time. Madeline's mind snagged on the word and couldn't break free. How much time did they have? Joshua had professed to love her, but he'd never

443

mentioned staying. Don't think, just feel, she told herself. But it was useless. She raised up on one elbow. Her hair formed a curtain around them as she looked down at her husband.

"When are you leaving?" The question was asked before she lost her nerve. Though frightened of his answer she had to know.

"In a few days." His hand never stopped its lazy exploration of her body. "I'll make certain things are . . . What's the matter?"

"Nothing." Madeline had thought to have a few months, maybe weeks with him. Never had she imagined he planned to leave in a few days. She bit her lower lip and tried to control her plummeting emotions. Hadn't she told herself she'd be content with the lot of a seafaring man's wife?

"Well, something's wrong." Joshua had felt her stiffen. He could detect, even now, her tenseness.

Why does he always insist upon an explanation? "I just didn't think it would be that soon."

"I suppose I could put if off for a while." Joshua lifted his hand and touched her bruised cheek. "Is this bothering you? I meant to be gentle, but . . ."

His touch was so tender. "No. It's a little sore, but it will be fine."

"Does something else ache—your hip?" Joshua paused. "Burke didn't hurt you in any other way, did he?"

"No, no," Madeline assured him. "I would have told you if he had."

Joshua realized his wife was rolling away from him. He wrapped his arm more securely around her shoulder, and pulled her back to his side. "I don't understand why you want to prolong this departure. Is it Hopewell? I told you I'd try to get things settled—"

"Of course it isn't Hopewell!" So much for being able to control my emotions, Madeline thought as she raised

444

up and glared into her husband's startled face. "How can you think I care more for the plantation than I do for you? If you plan to leave—fine. There doesn't seem to be anything I can do about it. But don't blame my melancholy on Hopewell."

He didn't think she cared more for the plantation than for him—hadn't she said she loved him? Joshua grabbed her arm when Madeline started to get out of bed. "I thought I'd tamed that shrewish tongue of yours." At her look of outrage, he decided to amend this statement. "All right, maybe I never really thought *that,* but I did think we could have a rational conversation. Yet here you are yelling at me, and I haven't a clue as to why. You saw me write the governor yesterday afternoon. If you were so opposed to our going to Kingston to see him, I wish you had told me then."

It took a moment for what he'd said to sink through the haze of Madeline's anger. He wasn't speaking of leaving Jamaica. "*We're* going? To Kingston?"

"That's what I had planned, but if you'd rather stay here I can—"

"No. I'll go."

"Good." I'll never understand women, Joshua thought. Then he decided maybe it was just Madeline he'd never understand. A minute ago she'd been spitting flames, now she was cuddled into the crook of his arm, rekindling another type of fire.

Much as he wanted to give himself over to the pleasurable sensations she was evoking, Joshua knew there were matters that needed to be settled. Their recent argument, if it could be called that, had shown him how tenuous his position was. Did she want him to go? Did she want him to stay? His wife professed to love him, but now would she feel about his plans?

"Maddie, I'd like to talk with you about something. Actually, several things."

"All right," Madeline leaned back against the pillows

445

and pulled the sheet over her breasts. So this was it. He was going to tell her he planned to go to sea. She bit her bottom lip and prayed for the courage to accept him as he was—a son of the waves.

Now that the moment was at hand, Joshua was strangely reluctant to discuss staying at Hopewell. He decided to begin with an idea she was more likely to accept. "I'd like you to consider giving Sau and Dora letters of manumission."

"You want to free them?" This wasn't what she had expected.

"Yes, it's not unheard of, and they did save my life, not to mention helping to rid Hopewell—"

"You needn't list your reasons." Madeline looked over at her husband. He was now sitting, like her, with his back against the pillows. He looked darkly masculine against the frilly white bolsters. Though she knew it couldn't be true, he seemed almost wary of her reaction to his request. "If you wish to give them their freedom, I am more than willing. What's more, I agree they should have it."

"Excellent. We can discuss the particulars with Henry while we're in Kingston."

Madeline waited. He'd said there were several things he wanted to discuss. Was he reluctant to bring up his departure? Maybe he was wary of her reaction to the news. Finally, when she could bear the tension no longer, she asked, "Is there something else?"

Damn! This was a bad time to bring it up. She looked so serious. "We should decide about the *Sea Witch*. The way I see it, she's half yours."

"The *Sea Witch?*" Now he was talking of the pirate ship. Didn't he know the only thing she could think of was him? "I don't understand."

"Well, in a way she's a replacement for the *Providence*. Since you are Patrick's heir, his share belongs to you."

Madeline brushed hair out of her face. "And you wish

446

to know what I want to do with it?" When her husband nodded, she said, "I suppose you have a suggestion."

"I do. Investing in Whitlock Trading seems a sound idea."

"And is that what you're going to do with your share of the *Sea Witch*," Madeline queried.

"If you agree." Joshua grinned. "I thought it would be nice to keep it in the family."

"All right. I guess this makes us partners," she responded, but she was wondering if that might make him stay with her any longer.

"Oh, we've been partners for a long time, Maddie." Joshua ignored the hand she offered and leaned over and kissed her. His lips tugged gently at her bottom lip, then he said, "Now Nat will have two vessels."

"Two? Your brother told me all his ships had been lost."

"They had. I gave him the *Chesapeake*."

"But you said the *Chesapeake* wasn't a merchant ship; she was a privateer." Madeline's heart began to beat faster.

"No longer, Maddie. Oliver discovered while in Kingston that the Admiralty has passed a Privateer's Act. It seems some view privateering as a license to plunder any vessel—friend or foe. Now the Admiralty will no longer grant letters of marque to vessels with tonnages of less than one hundred. The *Chesapeake* carries eighty."

"But you love the *Chesapeake!* How can you give her up?" Madeline realized she was arguing against what she wanted most, for Joshua to stay with her. But the thought that he would be unhappy because he'd had to give up the sea was unbearable.

"It's all right, Maddie." He took her in his arms. "I could probably get a special license if I wanted it. The truth is, I don't."

"But—"

Joshua touched his fingers to his wife's lips. He had to

447

know if she'd accept his idea, accept him in her life. "I thought I might try my hand at growing sugar cane. Granted, I know very little about it, but since I have a partner who's been doing it for years and she seems to know—"

Madeline stopped his explanation by throwing her arms around his neck and pressing her lips to his. When she loosened her hold, Joshua's eyes were sparkling with laughter.

With a quick motion, he pulled her beneath him. His fingers tangled in her tresses as he sank into the cradle of her body. "Does this mean you want me to stay at Hopewell?"

"Oh . . . yes . . . yes." Quick, affectionate kisses punctuated her words of agreement.

"Good." Joshua's tongue traced her ear's shell-like curve. "Because nothing means more to me than our future—together."

Sensual island sounds floated through the open window, carried aloft by the trade winds. Soft and sweet, they filled the room with nature's music.

But Madeline heard none of them. Her husband's words filled her head—her heart. *Our future together*, he'd said. *Together*. As Madeline smiled up at Joshua, her joyful sigh joined the eternal symphony of life.